W9-BGN-924

DATE DUE

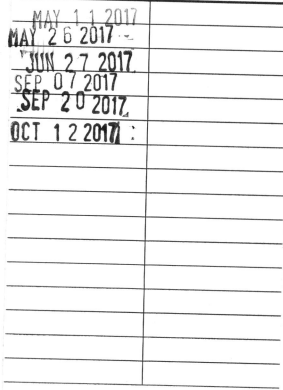

BRODART, CO.   Cat. No. 23-221

WHERE THE LOST GIRLS GO

Center Point
Large Print

**This Large Print Book carries the
Seal of Approval of N.A.V.H.**

WHERE THE LOST GIRLS GO

—A Laura Mori Mystery—

R. J. Noonan

CENTER POINT LARGE PRINT
THORNDIKE, MAINE

The text of this Large Print edition is unabridged.
In other aspects, this book may vary
from the original edition.
Printed in the United States of America
on permanent paper.
Set in 16-point Times New Roman type.

ISBN: 978-1-68324-336-6

Library of Congress Cataloging-in-Publication Data

Names: Noonan, Rosalind, author.
Title: Where the lost girls go : a Laura Mori mystery / R. J. Noonan.
Description: Center Point Large Print edition. | Thorndike, Maine :
Center Point Large Print, 2017.
Identifiers: LCCN 2016059550 | ISBN 9781683243366
    (hardcover : alk. paper)
Subjects: LCSH: Large type books. | GSAFD: Mystery fiction.
Classification: LCC PS3614.O665 W47 2017 | DDC 813/.6—dc23
LC record available at https://lccn.loc.gov/2016059550

For my friends and colleagues
from the magnificent mystery machine
that was Mega-Books of New York,
thanks for loading my toolbox with
red herrings, MacGuffins, and cliff—
h
a
n
g
e
r
s.

WHERE
THE LOST
GIRLS GO

—Prologue—

Blossom's chin lolled toward her sternum as she looked down to switch the little car into third gear. Ease on, ease off. Damn but her head was heavy. She forced herself to lift that bowling ball and look up at the road. The horizon teetered back and forth as the car was tossed through the water, listing and rolling on the stormy sea.

Sea? She squinted through the windshield as something rose up from her belly and lodged in her throat. Where was the ocean?

No. No water. Only trees, hundreds of trees surrounding her as she squeezed the steering wheel and tried to focus on the black road that seemed to shrink in front of her.

What was wrong with her? What the fuck? She'd had some close brushes before, and the adrenaline kick had always, always gotten her through. But tonight was different. Something cold and wobbly penetrated the zip of energy and fear; nausea and dizziness rippled through her with the speed of electricity. She hadn't felt this sick since she'd had the flu back in junior high. Like she needed the flu on top of everything else.

Oh, my God. She tried to say the words, but they came out garbled and distant, as if someone was talking to her from outside a fishbowl. A metal fishbowl with a skeleton steering wheel and round dials on the dashboard that didn't mean much of anything to her right now. But she knew this little bucket. She had learned to drive in this car, pumping the gear stick and coordinating her feet on the clutch and brake. Ease on, ease off. Weird that she remembered her driving lessons from so long ago when the details of this day were thin and elastic, like dough stretching until it snapped away into nothing.

A stand of fat trees reared up in front of the car, calling to her.

Come to us. Rest here. Close your eyes and just let go.

Alarm tingled down her spine as she jerked the wheel left and then right again to stay on the road. What the hell was wrong with her, thinking that trees were talking to her? It was like she was drunk or high or something, but she was totally sober. He had offered her a drink—men always wanted her to drink with them, as if it would forge a bond between them, but she always refused. Her life was effed up enough without that shit. The Prince always laughed when she said that, but it was true. So she had insisted on drinking Pepsi while he drank whiskey, and he had seemed okay with that.

She wanted to squeeze her eyes shut and stop the world from spinning around her, but how could she stay on the road if she couldn't see it?

Besides, she knew you couldn't will the twirling motion to stop when you were sick. The spinning bed knew no mercy. She'd learned that when she had been a kid, sick as a dog after she had swiped a bottle of screw-cap wine from Mama's stash and gulped the sweet liquid down in the dim clutter of the bedroom closet. In the three days it took her to recover, she had wished she could die—just go to sleep and end the nightmare visions and vomiting and spinning world.

The Prince's warning came back to her. "You're out of control. Totally."

"I'm always in control," she had insisted, assuring him that she could handle things. She could take care of herself. She knew what she was doing.

Only now . . . now she was afraid the Prince had been right.

I can do this! The voice inside her boomed. *I'm in control.*

The contents of her stomach surged up into her throat with a Pepsi burp. She coughed and swallowed hard to keep it all down. The sudden sickness had come out of the blue, slurring her words, jumbling her thoughts, and making her mind swim in confusion. Right now she knew she had to get away . . . get away fast . . . and then she could figure things out from a safe distance.

His smoky eyes appeared in the fogging windshield.

11

"You're so beautiful," he always said, and she had gotten used to hearing it, a firefly glimmer of approval.

Just as he'd said it tonight.

"You're so beautiful. Come here, you." She had gone to him. Easing her skirt up, teasing him, she had enjoyed the look on his face when he saw that she wasn't wearing underwear.

"Nice," he said. "Show me more?"

She teased the skirt up until he couldn't bear it anymore, and he pulled her onto his lap.

But something had gone wrong.

When? How?

It started when the woman walked in on them in the heat of the moment.

The woman who thought she owned him.

What had happened after that?

Angry words. Claws out, mud slung.

Blossom wasn't proud of herself, but it wasn't all her fault. Or was it? Already the details were getting soft and wobbly, and the car was going way too fast for this twisting, narrow road.

The brakes. Moving her foot to the pedal, she pressed down hard and the car slowed slightly.

Slow down, slow down! her mind screamed as she steered clear of a tree and pumped the brake pedal. Why couldn't she get the car to stop? Something was wrong with the brakes. Or maybe she wasn't pressing hard enough. Or maybe the old car was giving out. Panic stabbed at her brain, shrieking in alarm, *Wake up! Drive the damn car. You're a survivor, girl. Get your shit together.*

A wave of dizzy, sweaty sickness came over her as the car veered left and her head slid against the window. It was an effort to sit up; it was torture to collect her soggy thoughts and focus. *Focus!* She had to stay on the road, get away . . . as fast and as far as possible. Wasn't that what the woman had said as she'd pushed the keys toward Blossom?

"If I were you, I'd get the hell out of here."

Blossom saw the answer in her escape. He would come running after her—she knew he would. And that one, that other woman, well, she could just eat their dust.

The brakes worked well enough to keep the car from skidding as it sped out of Stafford Woods and shot through the intersection. Thank God there were no other cars, no lights, no deer. Just the little sports car carrying Blossom away, far away from here.

—1—

The fireball lit the night, its glow illuminating the skyline and summoning us like a beacon. My heart thrummed, persistent as a buzzing cell phone, but I forced myself to slow the patrol car as we approached the red light at Stafford Road.

Two vehicles bathed in blue waves of light from our unit stayed put as I crept through the intersection. Time: 19:53.

"Come on, Mori," Cranston muttered from the passenger seat. "Give it some gas. Christ almighty, you drive like a girl."

"I drive with caution." Seeing that the road ahead was clear, I hit the gas to pick up speed on the hill. "And we won't be able to help anyone at the scene if we don't get there in one piece." I was repeating the advice of one of my excellent training officers at the Oregon Police Academy. The academy teachers had taught me more in the first day of training than Cranston had covered in two months in the field.

"Yeah, but we need to get there today." He shook his head. "I can't believe they're turning you loose after this shift, but the higher-ups think you're ready. They don't know that you're a bundle of nerves."

"I'll be fine." *Once I shake* you *loose,* said the half of me that was pure American girl. It was always at odds with the polite, mannered Japanese girl people saw before them.

Although there were safety advantages to having two cops in one car, I was looking forward to shedding the mulish, old-school Cranston— my field training officer—and doing the job on my own. Cranston's constant ribbing had made it clear that he didn't like women on the job, and he felt particular disdain for quiet, laid-back women like me. "Wimpy chicks," I'd heard him complain to another cop when he thought I was out of hearing range in the station headquarters. "They're ruining the job."

While I realized that Cranston was a walking HR complaint, I had held my ground and forged ahead in the hopes that I would eventually win him over with my actions. He was not the first man to judge me based on appearance. My slight build, blue-black hair, and pale, serene face were more representative of an ad for my father's Japanese restaurant than a police department recruitment poster, but I was determined to make my mark as a cop with equal parts strength and compassion. A twenty-four-year-old wimpy chick with the sinewy strength of a willow tree.

"I would extend your training if I wasn't going on vacation," Cranston said. "But I'm heading off to Hawaii. Aloha. Do you know any of those Hawaiian dances, Mori?"

"I'm Japanese." It wasn't the first time I had shared this information with Cranston, a slow learner. I decided to divert his attention in the way you would distract a small child. "Look at how it lights the sky."

"Must be some fire," he said. "What did dispatch say?"

"A crash involving one car."

After months of training, I was steering our

vehicle toward the real deal. A critical incident, which was rare in Sunrise Lake. Someone needed help, and more assistance than reporting a fender-bender or chasing skateboarders away from the 7-Eleven parking lot.

The radio crackled again. "Fire and rescue on the scene now," the dispatcher reported.

"Ten-four," Cranston barked into the device on his collar, then sat back and scowled. "The real heroes beat us to it. Of course they did. They're the saviors, and we're the scumbags."

"Speak for yourself," I said, though I'd heard this complaint before. Cops groused about how firefighters were held up as heroes, making dashing rescues, while cops were skewered as power-hungry authority figures. Gun crazy and abusive. From my perspective, there were good and bad apples in every barrel. One firefighter in Sunrise Lake was high on my scale of heroism, but rather than poke Cranston with a speech about the goodness of mankind, I kept my mouth shut and my attention on the road.

The crash had happened on a ridge road that circled the small town of Sunrise Lake, and the slight elevation seemed to hold a torch to the night sky. Fortunately, this stretch of road was isolated from the nearby neighborhood. A golf course lined one side of the road. On the other, two soccer fields had been recently constructed on the edge of an orchard, which gave way to the wooded hills of a state park locally known as Stafford Forest. Following the glow in the sky, I clenched my jaw and pressed the accelerator. Cranston whistled through his teeth as we crested over the rise of the last hill and the scene was laid out before us. The road was a battlefield, man against fire. Even through the closed windows of the car, the acrid smoke hit my sinuses hard, stinging.

The fire was a roaring ball of flames, obliterating the car. If there had been license plates on the vehicle, they were unrecognizable in the melting mass of metal. I swallowed against a bitter taste as the flames that engulfed the car licked at the old tree that had splintered but managed to remain upright. The frame of the car door hung open, a black silhouette against the orange fireball.

The open door gave me hope. The firefighters had removed at least one crash victim and were loading a stretcher into the back of the ambulance.

A handful of fire and rescue vehicles straddled the street at odd angles a good distance from the burning car. Spotlights from one of the trucks illuminated the scene like a movie set. A month ago, after the long, dry summer, the firefighters would have been scrambling to contain the fire and keep it from whooshing across dry brush. Now with two weeks of October rain, the fire wasn't a huge threat. A few cars had pulled to the side of the road where the drivers huddled in the haze of smoke.

"Gun it, Mori." Cranston's voice cut through. "Get us on the freakin' scene."

"This is as close as we get." I pulled up behind the firetrucks, choosing caution over dare. "Cars are combustibles on wheels. One spark in the wrong place and everything could go kablam."

With a grunt, Cranston hauled himself out the door as I pushed the gearshift to park. After radioing the dispatcher that we were on the scene, I followed him across the sparkling asphalt toward a cluster of firefighters.

"What've we got here?" Cranston asked as we all stared in wonder at the ball of fire.

"Single-car collision. Hot as Hades." The tall, lanky man who responded was a former classmate from Sunrise High, Skip Werner. With googly, thick eyeglasses and a dopey, ever-present grin, Skip reminded me of Goofy playing with fire trucks. "One witness saw the car spin out of control and hit a tree. We just got the driver out of the vehicle. They're transporting her to Legacy Hospital, but it's kind of a formality. She's DOA."

Something fell inside me as I glanced toward the ambulance, which was crawling away from the scene, no lights or sirens. No rush. The driver was dead.

"Female Jane Doe," Skip went on. "This one's

going to be tough to identify. The head and face are disfigured, severe burns, and we didn't find any ID."

"Any other passengers in the car?" I asked.

"Just the driver, we think. My guys will check the area for anyone that might have been thrown clear of the wreck as soon as we get this fire contained."

"All right, Skip." The sense of purpose seemed to drain from Cranston as he scowled at the burning car. "You do your thing, then we'll do ours."

The fire chief tromped into the street and shouted some orders to his squad. One truck rumbled as it backed closer to the burning fire.

I stared into the roiling flames, a funeral pyre.

"As soon as they get the fire under control, we'll need to tape off the scene," Cranston said.

I nodded, not trusting myself to speak. The swell of emotion balling up in my throat was an embarrassment. Most male officers didn't get misty-eyed at an accident scene. Still, I bet they felt a little sick inside to know that a life had ended abruptly.

Cranston shifted from one foot to another as foam was sprayed onto the wrecked car. "So tell me what needs to be done," he said, drilling me.

"Secure the scene and maintain the integrity of evidence for forensics." It was easier to speak when I was reciting procedure. "Because of the fatality, we need to notify the lieutenant on patrol, as well as Highway." In this case, the Highway Patrol would do much of the forensic work, measuring tread and skid marks to estimate speed and angles of collision. Highway always came to the scene of a wreck that involved a person who was deceased or likely to die. "We need to search the scene and interview witnesses."

"Right. I'll call Highway and Lt. Omak. You take care of the witnesses. Start with the people standing on the other side of that truck."

"Got it." Splitting off from Cranston was always a good thing.

"And, Mori, try to stay clear of the smoke. You never know what kind of toxic shit's in there."

That may have been the kindest thing Cranston had ever said to me. Maybe I was getting through to him. I left Cranston to talk with Goofy Skip and another firefighter, Xavier Moore, who had killed it on our basketball team a few years ago. Tall and quiet, Xavier was another Sunrise graduate who hadn't left the area. "When are you going to get out of the bubble?" my brother Alex frequently asked me, usually over the phone when he called to complain about how hard med school was or how much snow there was in Western Michigan. And I always responded that some of us didn't need to travel thousands of miles to find fulfillment. Recently I had told Alex, "Some of us bloom where we're planted." He groaned, but he hasn't brought up my "provincialism" again.

As I skirted the accident scene, I spotted my neighbor Randy Shapiro among the firefighters heading over to the sputtering wreck with long shovels in hand. After years of admiring him from afar, specifically, from my second-floor bedroom window that overlooked his driveway, I knew the way he moved, that wiry energy, that sense of balance, physically and metaphysically. "Hey, Randy."

"Laura?" He tipped his helmet back so that I could get a better look at his face. He didn't know that I had him memorized. "I didn't recognize you in uniform."

I hoped that meant I looked more authoritative than the goofy kid who used to babble from the driveway while Randy tinkered under the hood of a car. "I'm sure I'll have some questions for you later," I said, focusing on the drivers who watched wearily from the side of the road. "Right now I need to take some statements."

The two witnesses stood apart from each other, but they shared the same haunted, sad look as they watched the twisted carnage now becoming more visible in the dying flames. The middle-aged man and woman listened politely as I introduced myself and told them I had a few questions for them. They both agreed to let me record them on my phone after I explained that it would take less time, not having to take notes.

"She didn't make it, did she?" the woman asked

before I could begin questioning them. Her face was pale and somber beneath her knit cap.

"I'm afraid not," I said, noticing a tear slide down her cheek. "It was good of you to stop. Both of you." Actually, the law dictated that they stop, but I wanted to reward their kind actions. I took their names, realizing I had heard of the woman, Arla Sullivan, a veterinarian in a local practice. "You've cared for my mother's dogs, two Cavalier King Charles named Tigger and Pooh?" Believe me, it was not my idea to name a dog Pooh.

That made her smile through her tears. Just the effect I'd wanted. "Sweet dogs. How are they?"

"Always full of love," I said. If only humans maintained the noble peace of dogs. "I'm so sorry you came across this. I would appreciate knowing what you saw."

"I was behind the car when it went off the road," Dr. Sullivan began. "We were coming downhill, and it was picking up speed like crazy. Can you believe that it was actually headed south? I don't know what happened, but suddenly the car was spinning around. Sparks were flying everywhere. It flew across the intersection and hit that tree, which finally stopped it. Such a horrible boom. You'd think everyone in Sunrise Lake would've heard the noise. Certainly over at the golf course. The rear of the car burst into flames on impact." She pressed a hand to the base of her throat. "It was terrible."

"Were any other cars involved? Anyone coming in the opposite direction?"

"No. Thank God." Dr. Sullivan's eyes opened wide at the realization. "The road was empty, or she would have slammed into another car or . . . or a bicycle or a runner."

"That's true. What happened after the crash?"

"I was the first to stop." Dr. Sullivan seemed eager to talk, and the other witness, a thirtyish man named Austin Sprick, let her speak. "I could see her in the driver's seat, but she didn't answer me at all. I think she was unconscious, but I tried to rouse her, just enough to unlock that door before the fire spread. It all happened so fast. I couldn't get her door open, and the passenger side was smashed against the tree. She was leaning into the steering wheel and . . ." Her voice broke, and she paused to wipe her eyes. "I couldn't get the door open. I tried to smash the window, but by that time it was too hot. A wall of heat and smoke and flames, and the fire grew quickly, but . . . I tried."

"There was no getting her out," said Sprick, a calm counterpart to Dr. Sullivan's anguish. "When I pulled up, the car was completely on fire. Like she said, we had to back off." Sprick was a study in gray as he glanced back at the wreck; the spotlights silvered his blond hair and made his pale skin seem ashen. "I don't know. She might have been gone before the fire."

"Do you think so?" Dr. Sullivan threw the question out. "That would be a blessing, because the fire . . ." She pressed her eyes closed and shook her head, as if to cast away the memory. "I don't know if I'll ever get that image out of my mind. The car wrapped in fire, and knowing a person was trapped inside."

"It's very traumatic to witness an accident," I offered. "Very upsetting. Are you okay to drive yourselves? I can help you call someone. We'll arrange for a ride."

"I'm fine, and my house isn't far from here." Sprick's stoicism was not surprising. "I'm going to head home and try to clear my head. Hug my kids. Watch a meaningless sitcom."

"Take care," I said, watching as he went to his car.

Dr. Sullivan wanted to talk some more after Mr. Sprick left, and she relived her discovery of the crash site a few more times, repeating the same story in different versions scrambled by emotion. It was her therapy, and since there was no helping the dead woman now, I was happy to be useful as an impromptu counselor. I let her talk, listening for any pearl of detail that might prove useful. Nothing jumped out at me, but I'd have a second chance when I transcribed the statements.

The vet's remorse was dwindling to resignation as Cranston approached and summoned me for an aside. I thanked Dr. Sullivan for her help and told her to take care of herself. She gave my arm a hefty squeeze and looked me in the eyes. "Thank you for doing what you do."

One of the big fire trucks rumbled off as I joined Cranston, who was a little peeved that I'd taken so long with the interviews. Cranston wouldn't recognize therapeutic communication if it bit him in the butt. A quick scan of the scene revealed that Randy was still here, poking at the wreckage with a long tool that resembled a hook on a stick.

"FD is almost done," Cranston said in a volume intended for me alone. "They're going to probe for hot spots and check the car's upholstery to keep the fire from rekindling, but we can start setting up our crime scene."

I surveyed Stafford Road. This sloping stretch had been entirely closed since we'd arrived on the scene. Any approaching vehicles had been turned away by the fire department, but on this fairly quiet road, traffic was not an issue at this time of night. "How much of the street do you want to close?" I asked.

"We'll block one lane, from the railed part of the walking path to that hydrant. No visible skid marks. Looks like she didn't use the brakes at all."

"They may not have been working too well.

25

The witness saw her spin and slide across to the opposite lane, and the pavement is completely dry."

Cranston squinted as he scratched the back of his neck. "There's a good chance our Jane Doe was under the influence."

"True." The statistics were still fresh in my mind from the academy. Alcohol was involved in 65 percent of all single-car fatalities. Still, I didn't like to judge the dead, especially without evidence. "We'll need to identify the victim and notify next of kin," I said.

"Right. Soon to be your problem, Mori. Good luck salvaging plates."

"We'll use the VIN. The VIN plate should have survived the fire. Can we search the car yet? I mean, how long does it take to cool down?"

"Talk to the FD guys. I started the report. You're welcome. Lt. Omak is on his way, and I got approximately two hours until end of shift."

"I'm very happy for you, Cranston." Happy to see him go.

"Yeah. Tomorrow at this time, I'll be drinking on the beach. Hey, Rags," he called to one of the firefighters. "Did you hear I'm going to Hawaii?"

Just then a van from one of the Portland TV stations pulled onto the scene, and Cranston hurried over to tell them where they could set up and how far from the wreck they would need to stay.

I set up traffic cones from the trunk of the patrol

car, suspended tape, and set out some fresh flares. The acrid smoke had cleared, and the skeleton of the vehicle, now gray and mucky from fire-retardant foam, sat like a long-dead insect, its innards rotted out of its shell. The car seemed smaller now, like a Mini or a low-slung sports car. That driver's side door still hung open, its frame suspended in the air like an odd gateway to the night sky.

In my months of training, I'd handled a few minor crashes with vehicle damage. In those cases, you clear the road, take a report, and make sure anyone who needs it gets medical assistance. But now that we had a fatality, we would be working with the medical examiner, the Oregon Highway Patrol, and the county forensics lab to determine how and why this happened.

A week ago, the case would have belonged to Cranston. But now that my training was ending and the veteran cop was heading off on vacation, the investigation was mine.

My first real case.

Not the most dynamic investigation—a crash involving one car and one person, who most likely was under the influence of alcohol or drugs. But still worthwhile. I felt an obligation to the dead woman. It was up to me to figure out the circumstances of her death, to identify her and notify the people who loved her.

She deserved that much.

• • •

The flat alley between trees had proved to be the perfect spot. High enough to keep water from collecting and far enough from the boulders to avoid the veins of rock that laced through this part of Oregon, this patch of land was ideal for digging.

Most people didn't understand the physical demands of wielding a shovel. Digging was ranked as a high-intensity physical activity, and if you did it right, the motion involved the shoulders and biceps, the abdominal muscles, and the legs. A complete body-building workout.

Tonight was the first time there'd be no body to fill the hole.

The girl had driven off like a bat out of hell, the engine whirring as the car went a bit too far in first gear, then eased into third. Off into oblivion. Young girls who drove off with failing brakes and a container of gasoline in the back of the car couldn't expect to live a long life. Her body would be someone else's problem.

The shovel was hoisted from the mound of dirt, and the process was begun. It was far easier to fill a grave than to dig one. Still, the transfer of dirt was time-consuming, and the steady movement started to build up heat.

"Doesn't look like she'll be joining you tonight."

There was no answer from the other graves scattered here and there through the alley. Clumps of grass masked the oldest, blending so well with the rest of the clearing that you would never know bodies rested there.

You just never know.

—2—

"I don't know why I was so surprised to see you at a crash scene," Randy told me as we poked at the smoking skeleton of the wreck. I used a stick he had given me, and he swiped away foam with his thickly gloved hands. "Your mom mentioned that you were a cop now."

I could imagine my mother's disapproving remark: *Our Laura, she's trying to do a man's job.* Or on a good day, she might say, *Laura is going to be a police officer until she can get into law or business school.*

"I'm almost finished with my training," I said, staring at the smoking shell that was unrecognizable as a car.

"So how's it going? You liking the cop thing?"

"So far so good." Not the most eloquent answer, but in the glow of a former crush at an accident scene, it's hard to be articulate. "I never see you around anymore." As I stepped closer, my badge, a star in front of a sunrise over a lake, flashed in the lights from the truck. Sometimes I felt like an imposter, a poser. The whole cop thing took some getting used to. "I keep expecting to look outside and see you working on some rust bucket."

"Nah. Those days are over. My folks got too much grief from the neighborhood association."

I missed our talks, though this was the wrong place and time to go out on a limb. I needed to keep a clear head. "Can you tell what kind of car this one was?"

"This was one sweet ride." With a gloved hand, Randy brushed soggy gray foam from the nose of the car, where a round symbol was embedded. "Still hot. See this emblem? It's a Volkswagen badge. This car is a Karmann Ghia."

"Like the opera Carmen?"

"Uh . . . no. Karmann was the designer and Ghia was the company bigwig. Or the other way around. They built the first ones back in the 1950s on the old Beetle floor plan. A sporty two-seater. They stopped production in the seventies, which makes them even more collectable."

"A classic car?" I stood next to Randy, shining the beam of my Maglite over the ravaged vehicle. "An expensive one?"

"Not in the same league as Porsche and Lambo, but still, if it's mint, you might pay fifteen or twenty grand." There was a Zen-like intrigue in Randy's dark eyes as he stared at the car. "Hand welded, air cooled, rear-wheel drive. Yeah. Nice. The trunk is in the front, engine in the back."

"You've got a mind like an auto parts catalogue."

"You know I'm a grease monkey."

There'd been many Sunday afternoons and summer nights as a teen when I'd looked out of my bedroom window to find Randy working under the hood of an old car. Whenever I could, I would hurry downstairs and talk with him and hand him tools. His parents were dismayed and apologetic to have their driveway looking like an auto repair shop, but my eyes always devoured the body leaning into the auto. It sounds much racier than it was, since I could never bring myself to act on my teenage desires. The cultural curse of the Japanese daughter. Instead, I leaned against the garage wall, my legs folded on the cement as I asked him questions about cars and life. What did a carburetor do, anyway? Did he worry about climate change? Did he think there was a heaven?

Unfortunately, I never had the nerve to ask if he'd be my date for prom.

A decade later, we were both twenty-four and I still didn't have the nerve to ask him out.

"Whoever was driving this had some bucks," Randy said.

It wasn't unusual to see a classic car on the streets of Sunrise Lake. On a Sunday afternoon in September, you couldn't avoid seeing spiffy, antique cars on picturesque roads like Lakeridge and Mountain View Lane. While Sunrise Lake considered itself to be a middle-class suburb of Portland, it was actually a haven for the upper-middle class. Workers like schoolteachers, mail carriers, and cops lived in the town, but people in that tax bracket needed some sort of bonus income like an inheritance, a second job, or a lottery win to make ends meet. And the McMansions that boasted stunning views of the lake or mountains were usually occupied by doctors, lawyers, and corporate chiefs.

The good life didn't come cheap, and if you were counting pennies, you would find a better deal in the neighboring towns of Palisades and West Green. People my age who remained in Sunrise Lake often lived with their parents. We lingered in our parents' financial shadows. I was guilty, too, but not for lack of money. My parents refused to let me move from my bedroom until I was married off to a successful Japanese man. Considering current prospects, I was going to die in that room overlooking Randy's driveway.

I shivered at that thought and glanced back at Randy, who was moving around the gnarled doorframe. He was Jewish, not successful by my parents' standards, and not aware that I was still half in love with him, still a little giddy to be this close to him. Why do we want the things we can't have?

"But one of the downsides of classic cars is the

lack of safety features," Randy said as he came closer. "This one didn't have airbags. No antilock brakes. A completely different braking system. But it has—or it *had* a manual transmission."

I loved the passion in Randy's voice when he talked cars. "I need to get the VIN and track down the car's owner." I moved the beam of my light over the passenger side, which had been crushed upon impact with the tree and was now a gnarled mess of shattered glass and contorted metal covered by foam. I moved my light to the driver's side. "The plate should still be intact."

Randy reached in through the empty frame where the windshield once sat and brushed the fingers of his thick glove over the corner of the dash. There was a scraping sound as thick foam and shattered glass were swept aside. He pointed to the corner. "Bring your light in here. Not too close, though. It's still hot. Do you feel that?"

Oh, yes. Undeniable heat.

I moved next to him, so close the sleeves of our jackets were touching, and directed the beam to the corner of the dashboard behind the steering wheel. After he brushed away a few more chunks of glass, the numbers were readable.

"There you go," he said. "You want to write it down?"

"I'll take a picture." I had to shove the flash-light in my pocket while I pulled out my cell phone and snapped a photo. Even in the stark lighting, the digits of the VIN came through perfectly clear.

"Got it." I took a second shot for backup. "Can you hang out a minute while I run this on the computer?"

Randy stepped back, holding out his wet, gloved hands. "Sure."

I walked briskly to the patrol car, fueled by intrigue and importance. This would be our first clue. Well, my first clue. Randy wasn't on the case. Actually, he didn't need to wait by the car wreck, either. It was just that I wanted him to hang out; I wanted to share the progress of the investigation with him.

I slid into the patrol car and closed the door, glad for the warm, quiet privacy while Cranston was off somewhere chilling with his fire-fighter buddies. Tapping at the computer, I set up a VIN search and then put in the numbers from the Karmann Ghia. The results were almost instantaneous, coming back with the owner's name and address: Kent Jameson.

I blinked. *The* Kent Jameson? The famous mystery writer?

I copied the Stafford Road address into my notebook. It was a spectacular house five miles up the road at the hilltop, with views of Mount Hood and the Willamette River as well as wooded acres that backed up into Stafford Forest. I knew the place. Everyone knew that property.

But I had trouble believing that the car belonged to Kent Jameson, the successful novelist who was probably Sunrise Lake's greatest benefactor. It seemed too big to comprehend any tragic thing happening to a celebrity. I ran the number again and came up with the same result. No matter how much you poke it and prod it, the truth keeps staring right back at you.

My mind immediately skipped to the identity of the woman who'd been driving Kent Jameson's car. Was it his wife, Martha, the woman who'd helped Jameson pick up the pieces of his life after his first wife had left him? Or his daughter . . just a teenager? I wasn't sure the daughter was even old enough to have a driver's license. In the last photo I'd seen of her, she'd been a tiny waif, hugging Snow White at Disneyland.

I mulled this over as I headed back to the wreck, where Randy was talking with Cranston and our lieutenant, Charlie Omak. "Did you finish the report?" Cranston asked. Probably eager to end his shift and be on his way to Hawaii.

"I'll finish it later. We have a notification to make." I turned to Lt. Omak. "The car is registered to Kent Jameson."

"The famous writer?" Randy asked, scooping off his helmet.

"No shit." Cranston grinned. "Big shot like that? So who's the dead woman?"

The lieutenant had more skill at containing his

reaction. "We still don't have a confirmed ID on the driver, and let's not go off half-cocked before we do some detective work. I spoke to Hernandez at the morgue, and the body is too far gone for a visual identification."

I wasn't sure where to go with this. "So we talk to Jameson and ask who was driving his car?"

"No." Cranston scowled. "We go to Jameson and make the notification. He'll know who was driving his car."

"That's assuming a lot." I turned to the lieutenant. "We can't make a death notification if we don't have a confirmed ID."

"You're right, Mori. Our first priority is identification. We'll talk to Jameson, but we need to tread lightly."

"I'll bet it was his wife," Cranston said. "I'll tell you, bad things happen to nice people, and she was good people. Picked herself up from nothing, you know? And after she met the author, she didn't let that money go to her head. Always chatting you up and smiling when you see her around town."

"Or his daughter." Randy widened his stance, his bunker coat falling open to reveal a black T-shirt under his suspenders. His T-shirts used to smell like Downy. April Fresh. "My little sister knows Lucy Jameson. They used to be friends."

"Sonia? How old is she now?"

"Eighteen, in her senior year. She hung out with Jameson's daughter back when Lucy went to Sunrise High. Before she switched to home-schooling. Lucy is a good kid."

Usually when someone said this, the implication was that the "good kid" had a few problems that occasionally knocked them off course. I didn't know this for sure about Lucy Jameson, but I'd read that she had left two boarding schools before landing here in Sunrise. Rumor had it that the purchase of the ranch and the addition of alpacas was all done to please little Lucy. It was hard to say whether her "spoiled brat" reputation was deserved.

"We can't spend all night standing here speculating." Omak snapped us back to the task at hand. "Cranston, you stay here with our crime scene until Highway comes. Once they're done, you'll need to inventory the vehicle. Get it towed to the county lot in case we need it for evidence later. Mori, you come with me. The Jameson compound isn't far from here."

I tucked my notebook into the pocket of my coat and gave Randy a nod.

"But, Lou, I've got seniority here," Cranston said, using the casual term "Lou," which was not Omak's first name as I'd once thought but short for "lieutenant." He wanted the case; he wanted the privilege of dealing with the town celebrity.

"You're going on vacation," Omak said.

"Yeah, but . . . we can postpone that."

"Take your vacation." One corner of Omak's mouth lifted in a slight grin. "You're going to Hawaii, man. You'll be sipping out of a coconut while we're knocking on doors."

Cranston mumbled some response, but it was little more than the rumble of an old furnace.

I had to bite my lower lip to keep a straight face as I followed the lieutenant to the supervisor's vehicle. As we approached the Jeep, he tossed the keys to me. "I'll navigate. I've been out to their place, and once you turn off the main road, nothing is marked."

"Yes, sir." For the first mile we drove in silence as I wondered if I should try to make conversation with the lieutenant, who had joined Sunrise Lake fairly recently but had years of experience as a cop in Seattle. Former military and part Native American, Omak was rigid and a little scary because he seemed incredibly perfect.

"This is the part of the job I dread," he said, breaking the ice, "breaking bad news to people."

"It's sad," I agreed. I wondered if it would be even more awkward because Jameson was a famous author. He'd always struck me as a hardworking man who'd run into a stretch of luck and shared the proceeds. Jameson gifts were evident throughout town in facilities like parks and fire stations and programs like after-school tutoring and an endowment for Sunrise Lake's community theater. Trees and sculptures, scholarships and road funds—great things had come to Sunrise Lake through the generosity of Kent Jameson. And from his wife; from the outside, she appeared to be the backbone of his philanthropic campaign.

Dread was a sour taste in the back of my throat as Omak guided me through the dark, telling me when to turn and which fork to take. He seemed to like my slow, cautious driving style. Bon voyage, Cranston.

"So you've been to the compound," I said. "For business or pleasure?"

"Answering a nine-one-one call. The chief wants a supervisor responding to the Jamesons. Apparently it's been the protocol since Jameson started having trouble with the ex-wife a few years back."

"What sort of trouble?"

"Domestic dispute with the ex, Candy, who used to come to town to visit the daughter. This was before my time, but I hear she was the dramatic type. Moved down to LA. Thought she was going to be a Hollywood star, riding on the coattails of her husband's success."

"And that didn't work out?" I wasn't up on my Kent Jameson celebrity trivia.

"She got a few small parts but never landed a big role."

"Is she still living in Los Angeles?"

"She died in LA. Three years ago. Suicide. Didn't you catch that on the news?"

"It sounds familiar." I nodded as if this were normal when, in fact, this was proving to be the most gripping night of my career. "And what were the other calls to the Jameson ranch? Problems with the new wife?"

"The daughter," he said. "Always the daughter. Lucy Jameson, seventeen. The kid's got issues, but that's no surprise. Dead mother and famous father, it's a difficult combination."

"So just to be clear, we're treating this like a possible homicide?"

"Right. Any unexplained death gets investigated until we find out otherwise. Only this one is a little delicate, since we don't have an ID on the body, and we're going to be dealing with the town's biggest benefactor. I've notified the chief, and he said to make this a priority. The coroner's already at the morgue, and we've got forensics coming in for overtime."

Of course I was going to treat my first and only case as a number one priority. As for the special "priority" treatment because Jameson was a celebrity, I wasn't quite sure how I felt about that. For now, I would just be grateful to have total support from everyone in the department.

"And to be fair, I have to tell you that the chief doesn't want you on this case."

"Because I'm a rookie."

"That and the fact that the department has informally assigned two cops to cover the Jameson ranch. Officers Ward Brown and Esme Garcia got that plum assignment a few years back."

"Is that why they don't handle nine-one-one calls?"

"Apparently. If you ask me, it smacks of favoritism. If the Jamesons want armed guards, they need to hire them on their own payroll."

We passed a sign that read, "Slow! Alpacas Ahead," with a silhouette of a four-legged animal with a high gait and tall ears.

"What do you know about alpacas?" I asked. "Aren't they a lot like llamas?"

"They're a slightly different breed. Llamas are bigger and used as pack animals. Alpacas can be worth a lot because of their fleece," Omak said. "Once you get set up, it doesn't take much to raise them. Says my cousin. He's got half a dozen on his land near Bend. He wanted just one, but apparently they're herd animals. They need buddies. The wife made him buy a bunch more."

"So they live as families?" I asked, liking the notion.

"Herds. From what I can tell, they're like glorified goats. Only alpacas grow into fluff balls." We were at least a mile in when the headlights flashed on a carved wooden sign that said, "Jameson Homestead."

"This is the beginning of the ranch," Omak said. "The main house will be up ahead to the left, with a slew of outbuildings off to the right in a horseshoe shape."

We pulled up to a mall of trees that led to a mighty Craftsman-style lodge with a stone façade that intermingled with cedar siding halfway up the two-story building. Limestone and dark wood were subtly lit by those muted LED lights that face down to avoid obscuring the stars in the night sky. The mansion faced a stand of tall fir trees and a half circle of buildings that looked peaceful and inviting, a charming minivillage.

"He's got his office over there." Omak nodded toward the buildings opposite the mansion. "The wife has an office, too. And a bunch of guest houses, a game house, an indoor pool, and a couple garages. He's got a small collection of classic cars."

"Now with one less car," I said as I pulled up to the big house and looked at the clock on the dash. Nearly eleven. Most Oregonians had lights out by this time so that they could be up before dawn, running or power-walking or grabbing a cup at a local coffee shop. "I wonder if they're still up."

"If not, they will be soon."

We spent a few minutes ringing the bell and knocking before a light went on in the wide entryway. There was a flurry of motion in the sidelight, then the Craftsman cedar door swung open to reveal a petite woman wrapped in a glamorous satin robe.

I recognized Jameson's wife, Martha. Her blonde hair was a perfect bob that wrapped behind her ears and curved in at chin level, accenting bold cheekbones and sumptuous lips. With a coif like that and perfect makeup, she had to have been awake before we started knocking. "Officers?" She held the fat bronze doorknob, sniffing the air. "Is there a problem?"

"Sorry to disturb you, Mrs. Jameson"— Lt. Omak could play it cool and compassionate at the same time—"but there's been a crash involving one of the vehicles registered to your husband. A Karmann Ghia."

"Oh, no. Really?" She winced as she gathered the lapels of her robe closer. "Who was driving?"

"We're hoping you can help us identify the driver." The lieutenant tipped his head to the side. "Is your husband home?"

"Kent. Yes. Yes, he's in his office, but I'll get him." She removed a bejeweled cell phone from the robe's pocket and typed in a text message. "I'm sorry but . . . I'm just not thinking straight." She held the phone to her chest and stared at us pensively. "I'm afraid to ask. The driver." She shook her head. "The driver's unconscious?"

"Do you mind if we come in?" Omak asked, distracting Martha Jameson for the moment.

"Of course. Please." The door swung open. "Lieutenant, I know we've met before, but—"

"Lt. Charlie Omak, and this is Officer Laura Mori."

She barely seemed to register our names as we streamed into the wide entryway that led to a great room with a stone fireplace meandering up three stories. It reminded me of the lobby of a western-themed hotel at Disneyland. Pretty spectacular. "It's chilly in here," she said, hugging herself.

She clicked on the fire with a remote, and tall flames began to lick at the gold-and-red-speckled stone. Her phone buzzed in her pocket, and she read the message. "He's on his way."

Omak nodded. "Could I trouble you for some water?"

Martha touched her hair, as if the request was inconvenient. "Of course." She trudged off beyond a sparkly quartz bar to a shadowed room with dark wood cabinets.

"Take a seat." The lieutenant's voice was a low command. "Follow my lead. This is going to be hard on them."

I helped myself to a fat chair in a warm shade of dark pumpkin and let the cushions embrace me. The leather was cool but soft under my palms, which I tucked under my thighs. I was out of my league, in more ways than one. Good thing that the lieutenant had come along instead of Cranston.

The front door clicked open just as Martha Jameson returned with a tumbler of water, her silken robe shimmering in the firelight. The door slammed as quick footsteps approached.

"What the hell?" Kent Jameson strode over to us. Wild-eyed and frantic, he raked his hands back through his already crazy mane of hair. "Talk to me. What's going on?"

"It's about your car." Martha's lower lip contorted, but she clenched them together, handing the glass to Omak. "The Ghia."

"Please, have a seat." The lieutenant introduced us as Kent fell back in the chair across from me and his wife perched on the fat arm, her hand on his shoulder. His words scattered away like dried leaves until he got to the bad news. "There's been an accident involving your car. A single-car crash on Stafford Road. Paramedics tried to revive the driver, but unfortunately, they were unsuccessful. The only occupant of the car was a female driver, but we haven't been able to identify her. We didn't find any ID on her, and she was badly burned. The body is too far gone to make a visual identification."

"Female." Tears shone in Martha's eyes as her chin dropped down toward her husband. "Lucy?"

"Oh, no. No. It can't be. She stormed off to her room. Remember?" Kent pointed toward the dark hallway.

"What time was that?" I asked.

45

Kent shrugged. "Around seven thirty."

"Closer to seven," Martha corrected. "I caught most of *Jeopardy* after she had her little melt-down."

And less than an hour after Lucy stormed out, the crash had been reported just miles away at 19:45. Lucy would have had a few minutes to stew. Or maybe a full-on rage had propelled her to take off in the car.

"Have you seen her since dinner?" Omak asked.

"No, but she's asleep in her room."

I rose. "Do you mind if I check?"

"I'll go. I wouldn't want you to startle her." Jameson was on his feet, striding down the hall.

I hurried behind him, expectant, holding my breath, as Martha and Omak followed. The image of the earlier fireball made me a little nauseous. For Jameson's sake, I hoped his daughter was behind that door.

"Lucy?" Kent knocked on the door and cracked it open. "Honey, are you asleep?" The light flicked on, revealing two twin beds. My gaze shot to the one with the twisted lump in the center. Lucy? No, just a comforter bunched and tousled. The opposite bed was neatly made, the lacey design of its purple, mauve, and white comforter nearly covered by stuffed animals. Teddy bears, turtles, llamas, and puffy dogs. Posters of heart-shaped clouds and flying unicorns reigned over the menagerie. And a seventeen-year-old lived in this young girl's room?

"She's not here," Martha said. "Oh, my God, do you think . . . ?"

"I know it." His voice cracked as he let out a sob. "Who else would take the Ghia? It was her." Head in hands, Kent sank onto the neatly made bed, knocking a lime-green dragon to the shag carpeting. "My baby girl. My Lucy is gone."

Lt. Omak and I stood by as the author cried. Martha sat beside her husband, one arm around his shoulders, a cheek pressed to his head in solidarity. The raw pain of that moment gripped everyone in the room.

There were dozens of questions to ask as well as evidence samples to collect, but Kent Jameson needed a moment to get beyond the initial shock. At last, his wife decided it was best to get him out of "her room," and she led him back to the living room, back to the same fat chair. She stayed close, rubbing his arm and getting him a box of tissues. I sensed that this was the usual tenor of their relationship: the creative, eccentric genius nurtured by a gilded younger wife.

Lt. Omak handed over the water, and I realized why he had asked for it in the first place. Kent took a few sips before handing it back to his wife and patting his hips. "Where's my cell?" He pulled a phone out of the pocket of his jeans and tapped the screen with a sigh. "I should have done this first. Maybe she's just a phone call away, and we're overreacting."

Martha's brows rose in a hopeful expression, and I think we all held our breath as he called her number. A moment later, his lips stretched into a scowl once again. "No answer, and she's got no mailbox set up, as usual." He stared at the cell phone. "Maybe she'll answer my text."

"Please let us know right away if you hear from her," I said.

He glanced up from the phone in his hands. "Maybe it's not her. There's no note in her room, and if I were writing the scene, there'd be a note saying good-bye."

"Don't they usually leave notes?" Martha asked. "Statistically?"

I understood that it was Jameson's job to create mystery scenarios, but it seemed calloused to boil the probability of death down to a plot device. Besides, we had not thoroughly searched Lucy's room for a note. "Every case is different. Is Lucy your only daughter?" I asked, trying to ease into conversation with a question I knew the answer to.

"Yes. An only child. Spoiled more than most, but it wasn't always that way. When she was a baby, her mom and I didn't have two nickels to rub together." Kent raked one hand through his already wild hair. For a man approaching fifty, he still had a full head of thick hair. And the color was wonderful—honey brown with flecks of gold that couldn't be real. He had a large, horsey mouth and skin slightly mottled by teen acne, which kept him from being perfectly handsome.

"Back in your lean days." Martha smoothed down some of the curls on the top of his head like a doting lovebird. I couldn't tell if this was an act for Omak and me or simply a cloying public display of affection, but it made me wonder what their relationship was really like behind closed doors.

"It was a lot harder on Candy." The author tipped his head into one palm. "I've lost both of them now."

"Mr. Jameson," Omak interrupted, "we can't be sure the deceased was your daughter, not until we have a positive match from the lab."

"A DNA test." The author shook his head. "A miserable wait."

Martha Jameson's face creased with a sour expression. "How long will that take?"

"Most genetic tests take twenty-four to seventy-two hours," I said. "I know it's a long time to wait, but you can't be sure your daughter was driving that car until we've made a positive identification. We only need to collect a few things here, maybe her hairbrush or toothbrush, and we'll rush them to the lab."

"And there's always dental records," Kent Jameson said flatly. When Omak squinted, the author added, "I've written my share of mysteries. I know the basics of forensics. Teeth and large bones don't burn to ash. Not even in the cremation process." He heaved a sigh. "I can't believe I'm saying these things about . . . about my own daughter."

"If the DNA testing is inconclusive, we'll consult a forensic odontologist," said Omak.

"In the meantime, is it foolish to hope that it's not her?" Fresh tears filled Kent Jameson's eyes.

"It's possible that the person driving that car was not your daughter," I said.

"Well." Kent sniffed. "That's something."

"It is." Martha squeezed his arm. "We can hope and pray."

"Did you see her leave the house?" I asked.

Martha shook her head, eying me coldly as Kent answered, "I was over in my writing space."

"I'm wondering who else had access to the car," I said. "Does anyone else have a key?"

Martha's mouth puckered in scorn. "A few people have access, but no one on our staff would take one of our cars without asking."

"Sweetheart, wait." Kent touched her knee. "There are other possibilities. Your assistant, Talitha. You let her use your car, and she knows where we keep the keys."

"Once. I let her use the Mercedes once when hers was in the shop."

"And what's Talitha's last name?" I asked. "Is she here now?"

"Talitha Rahimi. She left hours ago." Martha squinted at me. "And I don't appreciate being grilled in my own home after hearing such awful news."

"We're trying to figure out who was driving your car." There was no hint of apology in Omak's voice as he jumped in. "And where do you keep the keys?"

"In the main garage," Kent answered. "There's a key box on the wall by the door, and the keys are tagged by brand."

"I hear you've got a nice collection," the lieutenant said.

"I dabble."

"You don't work on them yourself?" Omak asked.

"Not anymore. When I was a teenager, my brother and I used to drop in engines. We'd change the oil and the belts. You could do that work yourself on old cars. They gave you space to get your hands in the hood. But now, who has the time? I've got a good mechanic."

Omak pointed over his shoulder with his thumb. "How many cars you got out there?"

"Five. Well, five if you include the VW. Some of them are typical rich-man rust buckets, but I've got a Chrysler Turbine car and a '66 Yenko Stinger Corvair. I'll show you some time."

"Some other time," Martha said. "It's late, sweetheart."

"I forget that the rest of the world isn't nocturnal like me." Kent scratched his jaw. "I've always been a night bird. It's my writing time. But I'll be useless tonight. In limbo, with my baby girl. *Limbus infantium.* We try to convince ourselves that we have moved on and evolved, but we don't ever truly escape the unbaptized self."

His words sank in the air, stones in a pond too murky to fathom.

"We've taken enough of your time." Omak rose and stood at attention. He nudged me out of my seat with a glance, like a chastising granny. "We'll collect what we need from your daughter's room and head out."

"Thank you for your time. I'm sorry for your troubles." I bowed to them respectfully before I could catch myself, but it was more like a yoga Namaste. Kent was lost in turmoil, but his wife seemed to be relieved we were wrapping things up. I took advantage of that. "I just have one other question," I said. Actually, I had plenty, but the lieutenant seemed to be in a rush to end the interview now. Maybe Kent Jameson's roller-coastering grief was getting to him. "Who else knows the location of the key box?"

"Our handyman, Carlos Flores, for starters, and our ranch manager, Andy Greenleaf. Andy takes care of the alpacas and Lucy's horses."

"Okay." I wrote the names in my notebook. "How about women? Who, besides Talitha, works or lives here?"

There was a housekeeper named Juana Lopez who did not live on the premises; Martha had seen her leave in her truck earlier that evening.

"No, it wasn't Juana, and probably not Talitha." Jameson's voice cracked with a new wave of emotion. "You can do your tests. I'll hold my breath till you're done, but in my heart, I know it was Lucy. We had a fight earlier, a bang-out shouting match, and she stormed off to her room. She must have waited until I went to my office. With my music up, I wouldn't have heard the car leaving, even if she tore down the driveway in the Ghia." He winced as a fresh wave of emotion reddened his face. "It's my fault. I sent her flying out of here like a bat out of hell."

"Kent, no. Don't say that." Martha gave his arm a gentle shake. "You don't know for sure that she took the car, and if she did, it's certainly not your fault."

"Of course she took the car. She learned to drive a stick in the Ghia. She loved that car." He wiped tears from one cheek and pushed out of the chair. "I need some fresh air." He nodded at Omak. "Walk with me, Lieutenant. Give an old man a few minutes of distraction, and I'll show you those cars and the lay of the land."

I watched them go, hoping for an invitation that didn't come, though Omak did pause at the door just long enough to issue an order: I was to collect DNA samples from Lucy's room.

"Is this your first case?" Martha asked.

"Yes. Is it that obvious?"

"It's just that Officers Garcia and Brown usually come out here when there's police business, and I know most of the cops in town. And they know me because I deliver cookies during the holidays. Besides that, you look so young and eager."

"I'm older than I look. But I don't think youth will hinder my community service."

"With any luck, you'll grow into the job."

Her words echoed the lukewarm support I heard from my mother, but coming from Martha, there was an underpinning of insult. As if I wasn't capable of being a cop.

I smiled, sizing her up.

Clearly she didn't know that I had already tasted the adrenaline rush of a superhero.

In my summers as a teenage counselor at Camp Turning Leaf, I had saved lives in quiet but significant ways. There'd been some drama—plucking three kids from the lake and stopping one kid from overdosing on opioids and another from going into anaphylactic shock. But mostly I had discovered an innate ability to draw people out and stay calm in a crisis. Corny, I know, but I had learned that I had a gift for helping people. The afterglow of these events had left me cloaked in strength, compassion, and commitment and given me the drive and inspiration to make it through the police academy.

I belonged here; I was made to be a cop, and I was not going to be deterred by an imperious prima donna like Martha Jameson. "I need to get started with the evidence," I said politely. "Sorry to bring you this upsetting news."

Martha pushed to her feet wearily. "I'm going to make some tea."

Glad to see her go, I headed outside. The patrol car was stocked with plastic containers, bags, and paper sleeves to collect and inventory evidence. There were special cylinders to collect syringes and paper bags for blood storage, but I didn't think I'd need any of that. I grabbed some inventory bags and a pair of rubber gloves and headed back inside, past Martha in the kitchen, who seemed to have forgotten that I was on the premises. It would be better to work without someone looking over my shoulder.

With its stuffed animals, knickknacks, and posters of wild animals with goofy captions, Lucy's room was cloying. My eighteen-year-old sister, Hannah, would have deemed it "so junior high" and signed Lucy up for the Justin Bieber fan club. There was even a little vinyl pencil case on the desk in the shape of Hello Kitty, my nemesis. "So adorable," my friend Natalie used to say. "And always happy, like you." Was that my demeanor: vapid and cheerful? Really? That was what my friends thought of me? It was like walking down the street and seeing my own reflection for the first time in a shop window. I did tend to smile, but I had a lot more going on intellectually than a vacant feline cartoon.

It took no time at all to bag and inventory the items from Lucy's bathroom—the hairbrush and toothbrush. Closer inspection revealed nail clippings in the trash can under the sink, and I collected them in a bag, hoping that this victory was worth the gross factor. My mother's voice clamored in my mind: *I didn't raise you to pick through strangers' garbage.*

With enough for my DNA test, I looked through a few drawers, wondering if I might find a suicide note or at least some unhappy ramblings about Lucy wanting to end her life. After all, she'd raced out of here after a fight with her father, and there'd been no skid marks on the road, no sign of braking. Suicide was a possibility.

The top drawer of her desk contained her wallet and a junk collection of tangled friend-ship brace-lets, ear buds, earrings, coins, and ChapStick. Her license was in her wallet. The photo showed long brown hair and a smile glittering with braces. Sweet and mousey.

One drawer contained a pile of scattered photos. I recognized the girl with the round dark eyes and sable hair in various lengths. Lucy Jameson's head seemed large for her thin body, and those eyes . . . big eyes, like in those odd paintings. I noticed that she was the only girl in many of the photos, except for one pale-faced girl with wheat-colored hair. Where were Lucy's friends? And why weren't any of these photos framed or pasted up in a giant collage like the one covering my sister's wall? I labeled a bag and sealed the photos inside. One fat drawer contained a French workbook and booklets of assignments for a physics class. Probably from home-schooling. Although they probably wouldn't help, I put them in the box.

The bottom drawer contained a glittery mask, nail polish, and ticket stubs from concerts in Portland and a few notes from her friends—girlfriends with names like Genesis and KT and D-Dawg. These were declarations of friendship, eternal support, and a deep understanding of what it's like to "feel like the world is caving in on you." Again, very junior high. Still, I collected the items in an evidence bag, marking down exactly what drawer I found them in. The academy instructors had hammered that lesson home: voucher everything. Once you left the scene, the integrity of your evidence became weaker.

After I'd combed through the drawers and closets, I picked up the stuffed green dragon Kent Jameson had knocked to the floor. So many stuffed animals. Most were pristine—their fur shiny and smooth, barely a nap on them—except for two worn creatures: a round turtle with a pilly knit shell and a brown bear with a round head and a flat body that looked like someone had literally squeezed the stuffing out of it. Closer inspection revealed that the turtle had a hard bit of shell inside, like a cardboard box. I examined his flippers and found a zipper that ran from head to tail. Ah, yes. I remembered these. Animals that came stuffed with PJs inside.

Except that Mr. Turtle contained a notebook. A diary of sorts, writing in a rough hybrid of printing and script. The penmanship wasn't flowery, but here and there the author made capital letters into stars. A quick scan revealed a few poems and lofty observations of clouds and haunted tree limbs, but it would take me a while to peruse these pages. I added the notebook and the fuzzy turtle to the box of evidence.

Out in the great room, Martha was reclining with her knees to her chest, a Pendleton blanket woven with navy, turquoise, and red wool over her legs. A mug was clasped in her hands, but her eyes were closed.

Deciding to let her sleep, I moved quietly to the door.

"Did you find everything you need?"

Her voice surprised me. "Yes." I turned back to her, lowering my box to the floor and reaching into a bag. "I found these photos in her room. Is this Lucy?" I pointed to the dark-haired waif.

"That's her. Her most recent haircut. She kept going shorter and shorter until that boyish cut. I don't think she's a lesbian, but she seemed to enjoy sporting the look." She squeezed her eyes shut for a moment and pressed a fist to her mouth. "Am I supposed to talk about her in past tense? Dear God, I don't know what to do."

As if a switch had flipped, the snappish Martha Jameson had turned into a genuinely worried parent. Maybe she realized that she'd been blaming the messenger.

"It's difficult," I said softly. "You know, there's something else I want to ask. I know I have a million questions. But I'm wondering, what did they argue about? Lucy and her father?"

"I didn't hear all the details—I left the table to make some tea—but Lucy was wasted and Kent was trying some tough love. He's usually a pushover, but he's begun to see that something has to be done. He's been trying to reel her in and get her to do something with her life. He was expressing concern over her lack of purpose. Her smoking and drinking."

"Sounds like a typical argument between a teenage girl and her parents." I tried to sound conciliatory. "And Lucy is seventeen?"

"Almost eighteen." Martha's lips thinned in disapproval. "But lacking in maturity. She dropped out of high school, supposedly to be homeschooled, though she has zero motivation."

"Who teaches her?"

"She used to have a tutors, but she fired them one by one, insisting she could work independently. Our Lucy is a young rebel without cause. She thinks she knows it all and pretends to reject society, but it's so easy to make that claim when you have it all. Lucy lives in a comfortable little bubble. So do I, for that matter, but at least I admit it, and I'm grateful for the things I have. I held down two jobs for many years, put myself through nursing school, waited in the rain for buses because I couldn't afford a car. So it's hard to see someone so young without an ounce of motivation. Such an annoying spoiled brat."

A brutally honest assessment of the stepchild who had probably died tonight, but then sometimes grief brought good and bad memories simmering to the surface.

"But I can't say those things in front of Kent. He's blind to the realities of his daughter. He was trying, but now . . . it may be too late, and I'm really worried about . . ."

The thud of heavy footsteps on wood halted our conversation as the men returned.

"I'm exhausted," Kent announced. "Too fidgety to stay still, too tired to do my walking." He collapsed on the sofa, and Martha left her chair to tuck her blanket over his lap. "What are we going to do, Martha?"

She took his hand and lifted it to her lips, that nonverbal language of a couple, two people who still adored each other. The lieutenant told them we would return in the morning to interview their staff. "And please, if anything occurs to you, give me a call. Or let us know if Lucy returns. You never know with teenagers, right?" He gave them a card, and we headed out.

The night air seemed colder here on the hill as we made our way out to the lieutenant's Jeep.

"While we're here, let me just walk you around the lane." Omak's voice was a husky rumble in the night. "Chances are, you'll be back tomorrow." The sky had cleared, and scattered stars framed a wedge of moon that cast a silver sheen on the paving stones of the path. The lieutenant pointed out the buildings and cottages as we made a quick circle. I listened carefully and tried to memorize the layout of the little village. The guest houses and pool house here, the garages and clubhouse there. An indoor horse ring beside the path to the barn where they kept horses and alpacas. And, of course, Kent Jameson's writing studio and Martha Jameson's office.

"Her office is as big as his," I observed as we reached the end of our tour.

"I suppose she's got to manage the empire," Omak said. "And she coordinates their charity foundation and donations. They do a lot for the community."

"They built our soccer fields when I was in junior high," I said, immediately realizing it underscored the fact that I was a young rookie. Soccer fields! I sounded like a ten-year-old. As we approached the car, I added, "The Jamesons have always been generous." I pulled out of the clearing and started prioritizing in my head. First get the DNA samples to the lab. While at forensics, check on the body at the morgue. Then, back at the precinct, get the evidence to the property clerk and check to make sure the car had been transported properly.

"While I was off with Jameson, the chief called again," the lieutenant interrupted my mental list. "He's pulling out all the stops on this one, so the pressure's on. I called in the medical examiner and lab tech so we can get things going. But the chief is worried about letting a rookie handle the case."

I swallowed, my throat growing dry at the prospect of watching my first investigation slip through my fingers. In a department the size of Sunrise Lake, we don't have specified detectives. Instead, officers on patrol usually catch any cases that they handle during their shifts. Since all the officers are trained in investigative procedures, we're all qualified to lead a case. "I'd really like to hold onto this case, Lou. I'm not afraid to talk to the Jamesons, and I know the procedure."

"With Kent Jameson's fame, this is going to draw a lot of media attention to Sunrise Lake. Cribben wants to bring in someone more experienced, and the Jamesons are used to dealing with Brown and Garcia, but those two aren't quite right for the case, and frankly, I don't understand why they were handpicked to serve the people in the Stafford Woods community."

I had always wondered why the two laziest cops in the department were rewarded with a plum detail. But when I'd asked Cranston about them, he'd told me it was all about the chief keeping the Jamesons happy.

"Maybe Zion Frazier would be a good fit." Frazier was a thirtyish cop, African American, talkative, and brash. He had fallen out of favor with the big brass before I was hired, and the chief had removed him from patrol and put him into a bogus position as school safety officer. Rumor had it that Frazier had filed a discrimination complaint against the department, ruffling everyone's feathers. Everyone but the imminently fair Omak. "Frazier has a few years on you."

"He does. But that's beside the point." I kept my voice low and steady, my eyes on the road. I wanted this case. I wanted to show what I was made of. "You don't need an experienced cop to conduct an unexplained death investigation. I can handle this."

"That's what I told Chief Cribben. I convinced him to give you a shot for now."

"Thanks, Lou." I bit back a smile, pleased at the lieutenant's show of confidence in my work.

"Don't thank me. Just get it done right. You're the lead investigator, Mori. Don't screw it up."

I nodded. "When you were alone with Jameson, how did he seem?"

"Distraught but hopeful. He's got this mercurial temperament that's hard to pin down."

"Did you gain any insight into his relationship with Lucy?"

"He was genuinely worried about her, but he could suck it up long enough to show me the cars."

"Creative genius?"

"Probably more genius than nutjob. We'll need to interview both Jamesons in depth tomorrow."

As the police vehicle rolled out of the ranch, its lights flickered through the trees, nipping at the observer who stood watching from the forest. Enough of a flash of light to get the heart racing. This was no time to be caught spying, but the woods provided excellent cover for many forms of evil. Here in the underbrush, innocence was lost, promises were broken, and dead things rotted and festered underfoot. A scream could fall away in the forest without making a sound. A violent blow was easily muffled by carpets of moss, the wandering vegetation, the canopy of leaves, and bristly needles.

And so many places to hide. Darkness, underbrush, fat trunks of granddaddy fir trees reaching into the sky, as if trying to escape the dank underworld. Cool, musky pockets of evil at every twist and turn. The police would not find them back here. The cops couldn't hear the cries and whimpers. They could not replay the past or retrace fatal steps. Terrible things had trembled through this forest, but those secrets were buried now.

As the priests said on Ash Wednesday, "Remember, man, that you were dust, and unto dust you shall return."

The earth was made of human dust and dirt, living remains and brittle hair. Every day people stepped on skin flakes and old bones. A person might forget that when walking down an asphalt street or crossing a grassy lawn. But here, with a soft carpet of humus underfoot, the smell and feel of decay never receded.

The woods were full of dead things, but the cops wouldn't see that. Just as they hadn't noticed anything in the glimmer of their headlights tonight.

Funny how people could stare into the darkness and see only what they wanted to see.

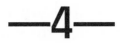

—4—

As we headed back toward town, the lieutenant and I talked through the next steps in the investigation. In a municipality the size of Sunrise Lake, the police department is one of many small-town law enforcement agencies that pool resources. The Oregon State Police process our serious highway accidents. We share some county resources like the morgue and forensics lab. Overnight lodging of offenders—mostly DUIs—takes place at the Clackamas County Sheriff's Office. Police departments across the state of Oregon send their recruits to the Oregon Police Academy outside Salem—a state requirement. And, of course, when you have a federal crime like bank robbery, kidnapping, or serial homicide, the Federal Bureau of Investigation sends a team to work the investigation. I like to think of it as a big family whose members work together and share their diverse skills, though, I admit, that's a bit optimistic.

"We'll go straight to the lab," Omak advised. "I'll wait while you deliver the samples to forensics and check on the autopsy."

I suspected he'd continue fielding calls during the wait. Already he'd been on the phone twice with the police chief and once with the mayor.

Sunrise Lake's leaders were worried about their famous resident.

The building that housed the lab and morgue was a one-story rectangle with small slits for windows. Omak was on a new call when I carried the box inside to drop off the samples. This was easier said than done. Unlike forensic units I'd seen on TV, where you could peer into a laboratory with microscopes and spinners and high-tech gizmos, our lab was a room beyond a concrete wall and a steel door, which was currently locked. Were they closed? It was 23:12. Maybe they were only open during day shifts. I was about to turn back to the front of the building where a sleepy cop sat at the security desk, manning the log, when the steel door opened from inside.

"Oh, you're there. I thought you might be closed. The door was locked."

"Did you knock?" asked the young man with a carved section of blond hair on the front of his head. That hair sculpture looked very stiff, as if it crackled at night when he pressed into his pillow. The bright hair contrasted with his mocha skin, and he wore a necktie that he'd tucked into his shirt under the second button. "You didn't knock. People never do. It's like they're raised in a barn."

"So you're open?"

"We are tonight. Got a special case coming in.

Somebody crashed Kent Jameson's car." He squinted. "Wait. Izzat your case?"

"It is. I'm Laura Mori, the lead investigator." Dang, it felt good to say that. I didn't think any kind of case would land in my lap until I had a few months on patrol, but Cranston had timed his vacation perfectly.

The lab tech, Rex Burns, helped me log in data on Lucy Jameson as well as the possible DNA samples like the hairbrush, toothbrush, and nail collection. Each sample was stickered with a bar code that was easily scanned into the computer for tracking. I explained that we were looking for a match to the corpse being autopsied next door.

"Car crash Jane Doe," he said as he typed. "Amazing how many Janes come through here." His flip demeanor was welcome considering the late hour and my dread of the morgue no more than a few feet from where I stood. "There's no incident report on file yet. You're going to need to input the data on the possible match, this Lucy Jameson. Here. Use this terminal." He set me up and I entered the information. Later on, back at the precinct, I would have to add my incident report of the crash to this case file.

Rex thanked me for giving him overtime, a sarcastic thank-you, then directed me to the morgue.

"I know where the morgue is," I said.

"Then why are you still here? Oh, you

remember the smell. Or the sound of the saw. Greeee!"

"Really?" I cocked my head to one side and gave him a weary look. "Dude, is this your rap?"

"Ha ha! All day, every day." Rex waved at the air. "I'm just funning with you. Breaking the ice. No one can stomach that place."

"Funny. But thanks for your help." I pulled the heavy door open and gave it a knock. "Steel door. Good thinking. Zombies can't break through steel."

"Touché, girl," he called as I headed out.

The door to the medical examiner's office was open, and I stepped into the cold laced with an antiseptic smell. My stomach curled in a mixture of dread and nausea as the memory of my training visit here was suddenly replayed in my mind. The glass wall on my left revealed an office with cubicles and desks. On the right was the refrigerated room where a corpse-sized mound lay covered by a blue sheet on one of the exam tables. I stared. Was that Jane Doe?

"Can I help you?" A short Filipino woman in a scrub suit and rubber apron emerged from the office. Dr. Blanca Viloria was casually braiding her long dark hair behind her. I recognized her from my orientation.

"Dr. Viloria, I'm Laura Mori, investigating the car crash on Stafford Road."

"Okay. I was just getting a look at your corpse.

The face is badly burned. The dermal layer is split, so I'm glad you didn't bring family in to try to ID her. That would have been traumatic."

"I dropped some of her personal items off at the lab next door. Our first priority is to identify her, and, as I guess you've heard, there's sort of a rush on it."

"Sort of a rush?" Her brows drew close in harsh lines. "Not sounding too decisive, Officer."

"Definitely a rush," I corrected.

"Better. That's why I'm here." She finished braiding her hair and tied on a surgical hat. "I don't remember the last time I was called in at night for an autopsy. When I worked in LA, yeah, but never here. We're just about to get started. Anything special you're looking for?"

"ID and cause of death. Single car crash. You'll need to check for alcohol and drugs in the system."

Dr. Viloria was nodding. "We always do."

"And when will we have results?" I asked, knowing the usual postmortem report took weeks.

"My initial exam will take at least four hours, depending on whether we find disease or complications. It takes only a few hours to run her prints, but she may not have fingerprints on file. After that, we look at tissue slides and send out samples for additional tests. Since a corpse can't blow, we'll need to do a blood analysis for alcohol, so we're looking at three days for that."

"Do you think we could have something on her identity by tomorrow?" I asked politely.

"Well, that's why I'm here working a late shift. We'll do our best. Did you input data on the suspected ID of the victim?"

"Yes. Lucy Jameson, seventeen years old."

"The author's daughter? That's tragic. I've always liked his books. He gets the forensic details right. Have you ever read him?"

I told her I hadn't, then thanked her as she turned away.

In the name of manners, I had to restrain myself from running down the hall to escape. The smell in a morgue tells you that death is not a pleasant thing for a human body.

It was well after midnight when I pulled the supervisor's Jeep into the parking lot of the precinct, and I wasn't done yet. I had to get my incident report in before I left, and I was eager to sift through some of the notes and journal entries collected from Lucy Jameson's room. I handed the lieutenant the keys, but he waved me off. "Just put them on the key board behind the desk and sign the vehicle in."

"Yes, sir."

Omak nodded. "Nice work, Mori."

"Thanks." Although I had procedure down pat—I had been at the top of my class at the academy—it had been helpful to have him there, talking me through the process. Lt. Omak's mentoring skills put Cranston to shame. Charlie Omak was a hero. A graduate of West Point, he'd served in Afghanistan as an Army Ranger. After that, he'd served as a cop for eight years with the Tacoma police. He knew police work a thousand times better than Cranston, and he wasn't a dick. That was saying a lot. After working with him tonight, I wasn't so intimidated by him anymore. He might be stiff and brusque, but he was a fair man.

"I'll be in my office," the lieutenant said. "Let me know when you have the incident report."

It dawned on me that he couldn't go anywhere until he signed off on the report. For any other case, the sergeant on duty could okay it, but Omak had to give this one his attention. It was all on me right now. No pressure.

In the evidence room, the moon-faced property clerk, an older man with a box of Hostess CupCakes on his desk, perked up at the mention of the Stafford Road Jane Doe.

"I heard about the crash," Officer Wilkins said. "That's the homicide with the mystery writer's car, right?"

"Right now we're treating it as a possible homicide. It's an unexplained death." Even cops spread rumors. It had only been a few hours and already the narrative of a simple car crash had been embellished and pumped up like the SpongeBob balloon in the Macy's Thanksgiving Day Parade.

I sat down at the computer, accessed our report database, and pulled up the report that Cranston had started. Aside from the time, date, and name of the fire squads on the scene, it was basically garbage. I would have to start from scratch. Plus, I needed to transcribe the witness statements that I had recorded at the crash site. It was overwhelming.

One of my father's pearls of wisdom came to mind. How do you dig yourself out? One shovelful a time.

Charlie Omak scrolled through Mori's incident report on the Stafford Road crash, half-grinning at the simple, linear narrative, the thorough details, the flawless spelling and grammar. The witnesses' statements were clear and concise. Vehicle information was in order. She'd listed all the departments that were following up with reports, including Highway, Forensics, Medical Examiner. She'd included an inventory of vouchered evidence. Her timeline started with the initial call about the crash at 19:45 and ended with delivery of samples to the lab at 23:12 She'd contacted the impound lot and asked for a mechanic to examine the wreck and determine factors contributing to the cause of the crash ASAP.

This was one beautiful report.

Mori had the makings of a fine cop. That rookie eagerness, that sincerity, those were the qualities at the heart of this job. With some experience, she'd gain confidence and solid footing. The moral center was already there. It was a kick in the gut when he thought of some of the good cops that had been hung out to dry by the dirtbags masquerading as cops in this department.

His phone buzzed. A call from the chief of police, Buzz Cribben. Again. Behind closed doors, most cops called him Chief Crappin'. The chief had earned the nickname for two reasons: One, he spent most days reading magazines while sitting on the bowl in the executive office's en suite bathroom. Two, when faced with a crisis, Cribben crapped out, literally and figuratively. The pudgy, pale Irishman could have you in stitches when he was on, but most of the time he was a bundle of nerves, worried more about covering his ass than protecting the men and women on the force.

"Yes, Chief?"

"Yeah, so I was just talking to the mayor, and he's sending flowers over."

"To the Jamesons?"

"No, the Fockers. Of course the Jamesons."

"But, Chief, we don't have a positive ID on the victim yet. It may not be their daughter."

"You know it is. I'm thinking I should send flowers, too."

The level of ass kissing for the Jamesons was about to reach new heights.

"Chief . . . Buzz, no. Please, not yet. Too soon."

"And I'll be the one looking like a dick when the Jamesons get sympathy flowers from everyone but me. You don't understand the political ramifications, Lieutenant."

"Politics elude me, Chief." Omak had no taste for the game. "But I think you want to give the Jamesons some space right now. At least until we know what we're dealing with. Wait a day or two and then send your flowers." Fucking flowers.

Omak checked his watch, wondering if Gina was still up waiting for him with a book in hand and Colbert on the TV. The kids would be asleep, but that was how his nightly inventory went on this shift. Kisses for the girls, curled up under their matching blue princess comforters. And then a quick check on the baby, a furtive rub of his fuzzy dark hair, moving stealthily because Gina would be pissed if he woke their son. Hell, with these four-to-twelves, night stalking was the only way he could be sure of seeing his kids at all during the school week. And now he would be working overtime until this case with the Jamesons' car was resolved.

He wrote his endorsement of Mori's incident report and forwarded it to the chief, then sent a copy to the mayor. Done and done.

Phone to his ear, he rose from his desk and paced the office, walked the hallway, circled the squad room to the water cooler. He was not going to turn into a fat-assed desk cop tucking away donuts. At last he convinced Buzz Cribben to forgo the flowers for now, and they ended the call. Thank God.

He found Mori at her desk, reading over a notebook filled with handwritten scribbles and doodled stars.

"Is that the diary from Lucy's room?" he asked.

"Yes, and there may be something here. She seems to have had a crush on someone. An older man. If the relationship ended badly, suicide could be a possibility."

"Could be. I signed off on your report. Nice work." He would save the report-writing praise for some other time when they were rested and fed. "Time to call it a day."

She smoothed down the page of the notebook. "Good reading. It will be hard to tear myself away."

"It'll be here in the morning, so come in early. You're authorized for overtime to work on this case."

"Okay, then." She closed the book. "Good night, Lou."

"Safe home." Remorse squeezed at his conscience as he turned away. He probably shouldn't have said that. He would never have said it to a male cop, and thus it was a discriminatory workplace remark. He believed Laura Mori could handle herself, but at the same time, there was a vulnerability there that needed protection. A vulnerability that reminded him of his kid sister.

Franny had been a rookie cop once, too.

With a nod to the midnight shift sergeant, he headed into the locker room to call it a day.

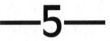

The next morning, I woke with a head full of Lucy Jameson. Her face, her teen memorabilia, her journal entries—she was dancing through my psyche like a Nickelodeon tween star on a sugar high. All things Lucy had fermented during the night, and now they tugged me awake the way our little dog Pooh tugged on her leash. I rolled over in bed, my hands flopping against the white duvet cover until I located my cell phone.

One e-mail from Dr. Viloria:

Preliminary results show the victim had sexual intercourse in the hours before the accident. Appears to be consensual. Immunoassay screen is positive for drugs in the system. We are doing a ten-panel test to determine the type of drug. Look for DNA match results later today.

Propping myself up on my elbow, I forwarded the message to Lt. Omak, although he'd been copied on the coroner's e-mail. Just to be sure.

I fell back against my pillow and held my phone to my chest. So Jane Doe had engaged in intercourse before the accident. Somewhere out there was a man who'd had intimate contact with her in that crucial window of time. Had she been running to or from something?

I opened up the photos on my phone and swiped the pages. Before I'd left the precinct last night, I had snapped a few photos of the Lucy evidence— mostly pages of the journal—so that I could mull them over at home. A good thing, since Lucy's writing was tough to decipher, particularly the capital *A,* which she wrote like half a star.

I am so in love with A! it read. *He's the first guy who's ever really loved me for who I am. I know he's older—he keeps reminding me of that—but it doesn't matter. Yeah, we're gonna get a lot of grief when we go public. But we have a thing. That's the thing people don't get. When you connect with someone on a really deep level, age and experience and past mistakes don't matter. Those things just melt away in the light of love.*

Sweet. Idealistic. Not so practical, though I wasn't vastly experienced in these matters. I'm still crushing on a boy from high school, still living in my girlhood bedroom, still under my parents' jabbing thumbs.

"How much is the age difference?" I asked aloud. When you're seventeen, any guy over twenty could be considered old. And where had A been last night, when Lucy spun out of control alone in her father's car?

I swiped my phone to a different page in the journal. The sex page. *Sex with A is awesome! He makes the other guys I've been with look like stupid little boys. Awesome A. This man has magic hands, and my body knows exactly how to respond. A really loves giving me multiple orgasms. He's so proud of that! And I just lap it up. I wish we could be together, doing it, all the time.*

"Whoo." I let out a breath. Hot stuff. Was she bragging or telling the truth? My sense was that this was the real deal, meant for Lucy's eyes only. In that sense, I felt a little creepy reading the girl's journal, but it was a legitimate part of the investigation, and I felt somehow that it was fortunate that I was on the case instead of someone like Cranston, who would have had juicy excerpts of Lucy's diary posted on Twitter by now.

There'd been no talk of suicide, at least in the last twenty or so days of her journal. The center of Lucy's life had been A, the older man who'd made her laugh and cry and come repeatedly. Who was this guy?

There might have been a quick answer for this. Under different circumstances, I could call and ask Kent and Martha Jameson, and they might respond, "That's Austin Tremaine, guard on the Trailblazers" or "It's Lucy's gentleman friend Alden Fisk, our personal banker." On the other hand, if Lucy hadn't "gone public" yet, her father and stepmother probably knew nothing of this relationship. And what were the chances that A was a man her parents would approve of? Apparently, he had some past transgressions to "melt away in the light of love." That was why people wrote in diaries, right? Because it was a place to spill things other people would have judged you for.

I closed my phone screen, threw back the covers, and stretched. Lt. Omak had authorized overtime, but he'd also sent me home last night. It wasn't yet seven a.m. How early could I come in and get to work? I didn't want to seem overly eager, but I was.

A glance out the window revealed a sea of white. The marine layer of clouds was low today, sealing off a view of the lake but providing a puffy white platform that looked like it would make a great trampoline. An illusion, of course. Ready to start the day, I decided to brave the family and hit the kitchen. Coffee makes everything clearer.

Downstairs, I quickly buttered two slices of toast and brewed a single cup of coffee. My father would be off at the restaurant where he and my mother worked, but Mom didn't go in until later so that she could hover over my sister and me. With the plate stacked on my mug, I thought I might make a clean getaway back to my room when I heard my mother's voice.

"Laura." The ponderous tone of trouble. The click of paws on the wood floor as the dogs trailed her into the kitchen. "What time did you get in last night?"

"It was late." I set the plate aside and took a sip of coffee. "I got overtime."

"I was worried. You didn't call."

"You don't need to worry about me, Mom. Really." Pooh's muzzle pressed to my calf, and I leaned down to stroke the side of her chin. Tigger plopped down in a warm spot near the heating vent, his furry tail fluttering in the jet of air. "The job requires me to be available when people need help, and when that happens, I can't stop and call home."

"Not even for a minute to tell your mother that you'll be late?"

Weary of this familiar back-and-forth, I turned toward the counter and took a bite of toast.

"What kept you so busy that you couldn't lift your phone?"

"We were called to the scene of a car crash, and after that I didn't have a minute to myself."

"A car crash." The refrigerator door thunked shut in disapproval. "A terrible thing. Bad things happen in the world, and as a police officer, those are the things you will be invited to. Always the bad. Never the good." As she spoke, she removed eggs from a carton and cracked them into a bowl.

"I'm good with toast," I said.

"Scrambled eggs are for your sister. She has a long day. Golf team after school and SAT prep class tonight. She's working hard to get into Stanford." The eggs got a vigorous whisking.

"So this week she thinks she's going to Stanford?" I asked.

"Mommy's choice," came the voice of my sister Hannah from behind me. Her name, derived from the Japanese word for "flower," couldn't be further from the truth. Hannah was hard edges, scary brilliance, black hair and white skin, muscle and bone, and bold nerve. On a good day, she made me laugh. On a bad day, her acid eyes and sharp tongue rivaled a mythical beast. "My new first choice school is Columbia." Hannah squeezed in beside me to make coffee, adding under her breath, "It's farther from home."

"I heard that. You want to fly the coop, that's okay. We'll have your sister here in the roost."

"I'm going to get a place of my own soon," I said. Another familiar mantra. "I'm saving for it now."

"You need to stay home until you get married or get a good job."

"I have a good job."

"A lawyer like Koko," Mom went on, referring to my saintly older sister who practiced in the Bay Area, "or a doctor like Alex."

"He's just in med school. Not a doctor yet," Hannah said as she stirred sugar into her coffee.

"He'll be a doctor in a few years. Dr. Mori." The gleam in our mother's eyes was a little eerie.

I shoved in a large triangle of toast and ruminated on my substandard reputation within the Mori family. I used to blame my lack of scholastic überachievement on my poor math skills. I had hated math in high school, when long hours of tutoring and tears had earned me a low B. A failure by family standards. Sure that something was wrong, my parents sent me to an educational specialist for a three-day battery of tests. The results? I was normal. Not a special needs student and not a high flyer. Just normal, with strong verbal skills but weak math skills.

And therefore a failure and a disappointment.

Not that I dwell on it. My Achilles' heel saved me from a boring life of litigation or writing code, but it also prevented me from going into the profession I thought I was best suited for: psychology.

My penchant for listening and guiding people through problems earned me a reputation as the family shrink from an early age. Whenever I worked in the restaurant, my father used to brag about my special gifts. "My daughter, she's a problem solver. You have a problem, you tell Laura and she make it go away, one, two, three! Just like that. She will be a great psychologist, help people with problems."

When I was in junior high, we all believed this, and my father took great pride in my gentle way with customers and employees at the restaurant. Customers adored talking with Koji Mori's middle daughter, who remembered their stories and followed up with each visit. People were always inviting me to sit with them and hear their tales of woe about a toddler who was biting kids in daycare, a college daughter who was flunking her classes, an elderly parent who was a danger on the road but refused to give up driving.

I also had a way with the employees, everyone from the guys who parked cars to the chef, who sometimes went overboard with spices in his rendition of "Asian fusion cuisine." My father would ask me to "talk to the chef about the basil explosion" or "tell Sally no more vacations without notice," and I would handle the situation, making everyone happy with the resolution. On the outside, I'm a peacemaker. But in my heart, I'm drawn to the edge, the chaos, the moment when one choice will change the trajectory of a life. I did not encounter that adrenaline rush in the family restaurant, unless you count the time when I performed the Heimlich maneuver and knocked a piece of flank steak from a diner's throat. When my grades and dismal SAT scores made it clear that I would never become a psychologist, I opted for a more exciting version of the job, helping complete strangers with immediate dangers.

So far, police work seemed to match my skills and interests. Unfortunately, law enforcement was not a profession that ranked on my parents' short list. Doctor, lawyer, or engineer for a dot com. If none of those worked, they preferred that I stick with the family restaurant. My career choice only further disappointed my parents—one of the reasons I tried to avoid my mother at home.

"Mommy, can I have toast, too?" Hannah asked as she took a seat at the table. Pooh nestled at her feet, looking up for love and attention. "Do you have any fruit?"

"Yes, yes. Blueberries. Brain food." My mother fluttered through the kitchen, catering to Hannah's desires while my younger sister sat in a chair cradling her mug, milking her role as baby of the family.

Chewing my toast, I sopped up the tenor of the scene. Even in her most childish role, being doted on by "Mommy," Hannah seemed miles beyond the level of maturity I'd observed in Lucy Jameson's room. If you sifted through Hannah's drawers, you might find some concert ticket stubs, paraphernalia for e-cigs, and maybe worse things—though marijuana use was now legal in Oregon, it was still against the law for seventeen-year-olds, and it would never be permitted in this house. But there would be no trace of glitter or eraser hearts or friendship bracelets.

On the other hand, Lucy's diary revealed a girl who was sexually advanced. Multiple orgasms didn't really match up with unicorn posters and stuffed animals. But then, maybe the room wasn't really a reflection of Lucy. Or maybe she just didn't care that the décor hadn't changed since she was ten years old.

"Actually, can I have some eggs, too?" I asked, thinking of the long day ahead.

"After your sister. She has to get to school. You have all day."

"I'm going in to work this morning. More overtime." I tried to keep the pride out of my voice, knowing they'd pounce on it like a cat on a mouse. "I have my first case."

Our mother didn't lift her glance from the fry pan. "First case of what? Chicken pox?"

Hannah snorted. "First case of chlamydia?"

They laughed together, genuinely amused.

When I was seventeen, I would not have dared to make a crack like that in front of our mother. Although our mother, Keiko, was raised here in the States, she'd spent most of her life in the bubble of a Japanese neighborhood in San Francisco and held fast to Japanese culture. That included a deep and abiding respect for elders. I honored Japanese traditions in my parents' house, but my younger sister, not so much.

"A case of beer?" Hannah could sling them faster than a grill chef at McDonald's, and our mother always seemed to enjoy being in on the joke.

"A case of eggs?" Mom went on, pushing it too far.

"An investigation." I met my sister's dark eyes, hoping to get through. "A woman was killed in a car crash. I'm investigating to see why it happened and who the driver was. She hasn't been identified yet."

"Interesting." Hannah's flat tone made it clear that it was not interesting at all.

"You're working with dead bodies now?" My mother shuddered as she slid the plate in front of Hannah. "That's never good."

"I'm not working with the body, Mom. Would you please watch a detective show and get an idea of what I do at work?" A glamorized portrayal of a police officer might dispel my mother's fears of the bad spirits lurking in the world of law enforcement.

"You work around such terrible people. Let me wash your uniform. Bad dust flies from dead people."

"I have enough clean uniforms for now."

"I need to do the wash." With that, she hurried

out of the kitchen to go off and gather dirty laundry.

"What about my eggs?" I called after her, tipping the empty fry pan.

Hannah popped a berry in her mouth and gave me a bland look. "Sucks to be you."

With a second cup of coffee in hand, I went upstairs and locked my bedroom door behind me, more of a gesture of privacy than an actual guarantee. A copy of the incident report sat on the white princess desk where I'd sweated my way through high school and college, algebra and trig. One more look and then I would shower and get to work. The report was long—five printed pages—and I sifted through it with my refreshed morning eyes. The witness statements from the crash scene seemed solid. That made it a single-car crash. Possible intox. Possible mechanical malfunction. I would start culling information from our forensic experts the minute I got it.

The official timeline on the report began at 19:45 when the emergency dispatcher received a call about the crash from Dr. Sullivan, but now I penciled in the last time Lucy had been seen at home, just after 19:00. Forty-five minutes between the argument and the crash. In that window of time, it was unlikely that Lucy left her parents' house, consumed drugs, and had sex before crashing the car. However, there was no telling what she had done before 19:00. She might have had sex and consumed drugs before she argued with her father. In fact, the argument might have been exacerbated by Lucy's state of sobriety. My fingers rumbled on the desktop as I considered those forty-five minutes. What had transpired during that time?

Looking at the long list of inventory from Lucy's room, I regretted not asking more questions last night. At the time, I didn't want to badger the Jamesons, but I could have asked about the other girls in the photos, maybe gotten a few names, some contact information. I should have asked about Lucy's activities yesterday, her recent trips, her medical history. I would do that today. What time was appropriate to pay a call on a couple in a miserable waiting game? Any time after nine? Would they be angry if I came over with a hundred questions and not a stitch of information on the identity of the driver? If only I could turn the gears of this investigation a little faster.

Leafing through the last pages of the report, I came across the names of people who had access to the Jameson cars. Juana Lopez and Talitha Rahimi. Carlos Flores. Andy Greenleaf.

A is for Andy, the ranch manager.

How old was the guy? I imagined a muscular cowboy spooning petite Lucy on a bareback horse. I would definitely pay attention when I met with

Andy Greenleaf today. My plan was to speak with the Jamesons again and then interview everyone on their staff. In this phase of the investigation, I wanted to gather as much information about Lucy and the other Jamesons as possible.

When I walked into the precinct an hour later, I was a little surprised to find Lt. Omak pacing the aisles between desks, looking crisp and sharp and, once again, a bit intimidating.

"Mori. It's good that you're here. We're arranging for a press conference on the Stafford crash. The chief wants to have it here to divert attention from the Jameson ranch. Give them some peace."

"Sounds like a good idea."

"Yeah. Only we've got those Lost Girls advocates coming through at the same time, and the chief's been dodging them." The Lost Girls were every parent's worst nightmare and every Portland cop's guilty frustration. At last count there were six of them, runaway teens who had vanished from the Portland area. The advocates were going from station to station asking police for help on behalf of families of the missing girls. "Could be a shitshow."

"I'll say." Zion Frazier smirked as he came up the aisle. "Good thing we've got bulletproof vests."

Omak made a sour face. "What's the latest on the Stafford crash?"

"The driver was under the influence of drugs," I reported, "and she had sexual intercourse sometime before the crash. Consensual, it seems."

"Yeah, yeah, I saw the coroner's note." Omak widened his stance. "I was hoping you had something more. I've been fielding calls from the media and the mayor throughout the night. Apparently there are two news vans camped out in the woods just beyond the Jamesons' property, but they know they can't go in there without permission."

"I spent some time going through Lucy Jameson's diary," I offered. When I told him my theory that Andy Greenleaf was Lucy's mystery lover, he nodded.

"Interesting, but you're jumping ahead. Our first priority is to identify the deceased. Second, explain cause of death. With drugs in the system, possibly alcohol, too, it's very likely this is another case of driving under the influence."

"True." I had expected him to be a little more enthusiastic. Deflated, I turned toward my desk, a podgy wood chunk in a room full of scarred workstations. "But I'm thinking maybe it wasn't the argument with her father that set Lucy off. Maybe the cause was a love affair gone bad. It would explain why she went screaming down the road in the sports car."

"Possible." He nodded. "Next steps?"

"I'm going to check the ranch manager for

priors. Actually, I'm going to run background checks on the Jamesons and all their staff. I'll review the police reports from the times we were called up to the ranch. Pull Lucy Jameson's school records. Get DMV history on all the Jamesons; see what kind of driving records they have."

"Good," Omak said. "Do some digging, but be discreet with anything involving the Jamesons."

"Got it." Of course, of course. I logged onto the computer as Omak retreated to his office.

It may sound simple to run a few checks on a list of names, but it was no quick task. There wasn't one master search engine to profile a person. Arrest records, driving records, and warrants all have to be searched separately. And searches worked best with the full name and date of birth or social, and the only person I had a date of birth on was Lucy. I could run searches using a home address, but that didn't always work.

I decided to start with Andy Greenleaf, my choice for "Most Likely to Be Lucy's Lover." I got lucky. Right away, I got a hit—the Stafford Road address brought him up as a registered sex offender.

Sexual assault of a minor.

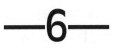

Greenleaf's file included a photo. High cheekbones, dark eyes, smooth skin. Not what you'd
expect. Twenty-eight and, I must reluctantly
admit, an attractive man. Of course, the details of
the case were in another database that I could
only access through the parole division. I sent a
quick e-mail to Greenleaf's probation officer,
Chris Brewer. Then I printed out the criminal
record and brought it to the lieutenant.

"Really?" His mouth curled in a snarl as he
read over the record. "And this guy works for
the Jamesons?"

"For seven years. They hired him not long after
his arrest."

"Interesting."

I thought it was a lot more than interesting.
"With Greenleaf's history of sexual assault of a
minor, it points to him being the older man Lucy
was involved with. Having sex with. Her diary is
explicit. Maybe she wanted to go public, and he
refused, knowing that the violation could send
him to jail this time. The coroner found drugs in
her system. So maybe he drugged her to slow her
down, to make her dopey. Or maybe a date-rape
drug? And when she came home for dinner, her

father got mad at her for being high, they fought, and she roared out of there."

He shrugged. "I'm underwhelmed." He handed back the report. "It's a theory based on one report. We definitely need to talk to Greenleaf, but let's not make assumptions." He glanced toward the door and nodded at two cops coming in for the day tour before lowering his voice. "Keep looking at the Jamesons. We know about that argument before the crash. And from what I recall of the incident reports, Lucy was at the center of other arguments at the ranch. Keep digging. Find out as much as you can before we head over there. When you start interviewing people, you want to have all the available information in your pocket."

"Right." So maybe I had jumped the gun a bit. As more cops for the day tour streamed in, I settled in to cajole information out of the computer. One database for criminal and arrest records, another for outstanding warrants. The Jamesons and the rest of their staff came up clean. The DMV database showed past addresses, and I noted that Kent Jameson had moved here from Idaho twenty years ago, while Martha was home-grown, having gotten her license at the age of sixteen in Tillamook, a coastal town known for its dairy farms and cheese factory. My searches turned up a DUI for the handyman Carlos Flores from three years ago, but nothing popped on

Talitha Rahimi or Juana Lopez. Other than the hit on the registered sex offenders list, nothing else came up on Andy Greenleaf. Martha and Kent were clean as a whistle, but seventeen-year-old Lucy had already had her license suspended ninety days for two moving violations: one for speeding and one for failure to yield at a stop sign. It seemed that Lucy had felt a need for speed. The suspension had ended in June.

The noise of ringing phones and conversations blurred into a dull background as I worked. At one point I noticed the day squad assembling in the meeting room, a space set up like a classroom with one glass wall. Roll call, which I didn't have to attend since I was here on special assignment. The sergeant informed the cops of the deadly crash that had taken place last night involving Kent Jameson's vehicle. The officers were warned to treat this and every critical incident with sensitivity. "Any information you encounter while performing your duty must remain confidential." From where I was sitting, I could hear Sgt. Joel's voice, sour and full of reproach, implying that they were already in deep trouble. I was glad Sherry Joel wasn't my shift supervisor.

"Next item," Sgt. Joel continued, "another mailbox fire on the east side of the lake. This time a security camera caught a suspicious youth leaning into the box before the fire . . ."

Tuning her out, I searched for the police reports

of the incidents at the Jameson residence. Nothing came up.

I switched to the dispatcher's log of 9-1-1 calls. Five hits, all within the past four years, all listed as domestic disputes. Why weren't these incident reports coming up in my other searches? Omak knew of an incident with the ex-wife, Candy, as well as problems between Lucy and Martha. Checking the dispatcher records, I saw that Brown and Garcia had been sent to every job in the past two years. Interesting.

I closed the report on my monitor and went to search the paper archives, which we keep in the precinct only for twelve months or so. A paper copy of the last two reports should have been there, but there was nothing in the archives on the Jamesons' ranch. Such a paper chase. I returned to my desk and sent an e-mail to our records division, requesting all incident reports involving the Jameson residence in the past five years.

To close the gap in my celebrity education, I googled Kent Jameson and his ex-wife, Candy. The author had a website with a smoky background and photos of his book covers. His bio mentioned only his wife and daughter, no names. I clicked on other links and quickly scanned interviews and book reviews. Only once did I find Kent referring to his ex-wife's tragic death and the heartbreak it had brought his daughter, Lucy.

The news articles about Candy Jameson were

brief, her most notable achievement being her past marriage to the famous author. A sad way to memorialize someone. Her death was deemed a suicide, a drug overdose according to the Los Angeles County medical examiner. I found contact info for the LA County Sheriff's Department and e-mailed a request for police and death records.

As my fingers flew over the keyboard, a female voice addressing roll call held a different tenor: soft, beseeching, yet dignified. A fiftyish couple stood at the front of the room next to Sgt. Joel. I moved to the doorway and watched from the back of the room.

"My name is Louise Dupree, and this is my husband, Thomas. As your sergeant mentioned, we're from Baker City. That's eastern Oregon. We're here for our daughter Emma, who's been missing for more than a year now. Emma plays guitar, and she's a wonderful illustrator. And she likes to bake chocolate chip cookies." She held up a flyer with a photo of a teenage girl with wispy blonde hair fluffed in the breeze. Something about her, maybe her innocence or the sleepy look around her eyes, reminded me of a newly hatched chick. "Emma was last seen in Old Town, Portland. Like many runaway teens over the past few years, she came to this area and then disappeared. There hasn't been a single letter posted. She stopped texting and her phone calls ceased. We haven't even been approached to accept a collect . . . a collect call." Louise Dupree choked on the last words, and her husband put a comforting hand on her shoulder.

"We're here to ask for your help." Thomas Dupree spoke in a low, grainy voice. "We're going to every police and sheriff's department in the Portland area because, frankly, we don't know what else to do. We are aware that the Northwest is a corridor for sex trafficking, but the FBI tells us that our daughter's case does not fit the same patterns for a variety of reasons. This led us to compile a database of girls who went missing in Portland. Like our daughter, these girls never appeared in sex ads on Craigslist or Backpage. They simply disappeared." Dupree explained that their database on the Lost Girls included photos, pedigree information, and dental records. "Please," he concluded, "help us find our daughter. Help us bring our Lost Girls home." He pointed toward the hallway, toward the photos of the missing posted on the wall. "Their faces are on the bulletin board out there and in every precinct. We want our girls back."

I bit my bottom lip to keep my mouth from puckering. What had happened to these teen runaways, six girls now, who had managed on the streets and highways until they vanished in Portland? Some had even kept in touch with their families until they disappeared. And each girl's trail ended in Rose City, where a small Missing Persons Division kept searching. Sunrise Lake was too small a department to assign anyone to something so specific, but we'd covered kidnapping and missing persons in the Oregon Police Academy. The good news: most people who were reported missing were found. The bad news: some of them were found dead.

"Mr. and Mrs. Dupree . . ." Sherry Joel stepped forward. Even the ironclad sergeant seemed to be softening. "I can assure you that these officers will do their best to watch for your girl." She turned to the squad. "Do you have any questions for the Duprees?"

As the Q and A began, I returned my attention to my desk and saw that I had an e-mail from forensics: the mechanic's review of the Karmann Ghia was attached. Back to work.

The mechanic's report was choppy, the subject matter a little bit foreign. Axle, frame, and chassis —could be the names of three pop stars. He saw signs that the car had been leaking fluids before the crash:

Most likely the fire started in the engine bay, where most flammable liquids are concentrated. In the Ghia, the engine is in the rear of the vehicle. There's some indication of leaks, possibly in the gas line or brakes or both. Although fuel and brake fluid move along the entire length of the car, the fire would not have spread to the front so rapidly without additional accelerants like leaking gasoline, engine oil, transmission fluid, brake fluid. Once the flames reached the storage compartment in the front, it was fueled by a spare can of gas. A twenty-buck gasoline container.

A gas can. That was bad luck and not wise to be carrying around. And all those leaks. Had the car been poorly maintained? Unlikely. The Jamesons had the money to pay a mechanic. You would expect them to keep the car their daughter liked to drive in good shape.

At the end of the report came the clincher.

Brake lines were severed, not a result of the crash. Point of impact is far from damaged cables. The '69 Ghia did not have dual master cylinder, so the brakes would have lost pressure. Most likely damaged brake lines contributed to crash.

I read those last lines three times. Someone had cut the brakes, though it sounded too contrived. Wasn't that a useless device in bad mystery novels?

The mechanic's name, Bob Balfour, and number were on the bottom of the report. I called him and waited as the call went to voice mail. "Don't slow me down," I groaned. This was the sort of information I needed to have in pocket, as the lieutenant had said, before I confronted the ranch manager.

I tried the mechanic a second time. Again, unavailable.

I happened to know a mechanic with an encyclopedic knowledge of classic cars. My nerves trilled for a moment as I swiped through my phone directory to find Randy's number, which I miraculously still had all these years later. A deep breath, a stilted grin, and I hit call.

When the phone rang the third time, I remembered that it was still fairly early in the morning, probably the reason Bob Balfour hadn't answered. I didn't want to wake Randy, but this was important. He would understand.

"Hello?" His voice was scratchy, hushed. Yup, I'd woken him up. I imagined his dark hair splayed against a white pillow. The scruffy hairs of a day's growth on his jaw.

"Randy, this is Laura." Silence. How many Lauras did he know? "Laura Mori."

"Yeah, Laura. What's up?"

"I'm investigating that car crash. The Karmann Ghia from last night? I've got the mechanic's report back, and I'm wondering about a few things. Car things I thought you could explain."

"From last night? That's pretty fast."

"The police chief put a rush on everything."

"Yeah. So . . . okay." His voice began to warm. "So what'd they say?"

I explained about the mechanic finding evidence of fuel leaks that would have made the fire spread faster.

"Yeah, that makes sense. It's not often that you see a fire sweep through the entire car like that. Generally it stays near the engine."

"That's what Balfour said."

"Bobby Balfour? He's your mechanic?"

"Do you know him?"

"I worked for him one summer. He's good people. You can trust his report. So what else were you wondering about?"

"The brakes. This sounds crazy, but he says someone cut the brake lines and the brakes probably lost power."

"Really? Ha." Randy seemed impressed. "That's not something you hear every day."

"It sounds pretty lame to me. I've read that cutting the brakes is a myth. That you don't just lose power like people think."

"That's true of most cars we drive today. In 1976 there was a new standard requiring that the master brake cylinder be divided into two sections, each with its own pressurized hydraulic circuit. So in cars made after '76, if you cut a line, no big deal. You would lose the brakes on two wheels, but the brakes on the other two would have power. So you hit the brakes, and yeah, it might feel a little mushy, but your car will slow down and stop."

"And, of course, the Karmann Ghia is a '69," I said.

"Exactly. It doesn't have the dual master cylinder, so if someone cut the brake line, you could get into some trouble. Especially going downhill. Which was what the Ghia was doing when it crashed into the tree."

"Right. And we didn't find skid marks at the scene. So if I had an old classic car, someone could cut the brakes and I would careen off the road, just like that. Wow, that's scary."

"Actually, you would have some warning. First, there would be a substantial puddle under the car if it was sitting for a while. Brake fluid. Looks kind of oily."

"She left the Jameson ranch at night," I said.

"You might miss the puddle in the dark."

I wondered where the Karmann Ghia had been parked at the Jameson place. I made a mental note to check for a puddle in that big garage.

"And the brakes wouldn't lose all the pressure right away," Randy went on. "But once you got going down the driveway, you'd realize the brakes weren't working. You'd have to be an idiot not to."

"But she kept going," I said. "There were plenty of places to slow and pull over on the access road to the Jameson estate. Or even along the main road. There were places she could have rolled to a stop before it was too late. Before she was flying downhill."

Swerving across the yellow line and smacking into a tree.

But circumstances had been stacked against Lucy. Dr. Viloria had found evidence of drugs. Maybe alcohol, too. And Lucy had been arguing with her father within an hour of the crash. Fueled by alcohol and anger, she might not have even realized that the brakes weren't working. "She was probably upset," I said, thinking aloud. "Fuming. Her anger amplified by intoxication."

I could see it now: Lucy, wild-eyed and sobbing, so focused on flying out of there that she barely touched the brakes in the first mile or so. And if she'd noticed the problem with the car, she would have been too inexperienced to steer her way to safety once she was headed down that hill. "Plus she was young," I said, "not much experience behind the wheel."

"How old was she?" Randy asked.

"Seventeen. An inexperienced driver who'd already had her license suspended. And at that age, you take risks. You think you can handle anything." I glanced down at a photo of Lucy, her lips curved in a cynical expression that belied the innocence of her doe-like eyes. "You believe you're going to live forever."

I hung up with Randy after nervously making plans to get coffee soon. Shaking off the residual awkwardness, I returned my focus to the case.

Who had reason to kill Lucy Jameson?

The question was foremost in my mind as I checked databases and searched for background information on the family members.

I tried to get in to talk with Omak, but he was tied up on the phone. "It'll probably be a while," advised Zion Frazier, who noticed I was trying to get in. "He's on with Crappin'." Through the glass wall, I could see him pacing methodically as he spoke. I went back to my desk and called the Jamesons.

"Any news?" Martha asked breathlessly.

"Nothing to report, but I wanted to let you know we'll be coming by this morning." I explained that we were gathering information and needed to interview Martha and Kent as well as all the other people who worked in the compound.

A heavy sigh rasped over the phone, a clear signal that Martha was put out. "Is that really necessary? This is a terrible time for us. My husband is on a seesaw of emotion between crippling guilt and hope of finding out that Lucy is alive. At the moment we're organizing a search party to go into Stafford Woods."

With more than three thousand acres to search, the task would be daunting, though I understood the Jamesons' need to try to find their daughter. "Maybe we can help," I said. "I'll talk to my boss to see if we can assign some officers to assist."

"We'd appreciate that. But we've got our hands full with this. Kent is overwrought, and I don't have a single minute to meet with you right now."

"I'm sorry, but time is of the essence in this sort of investigation." I told her I would talk to Omak about the search party and asked her to alert the staff that we would be there within the hour. She signed off with a growl of annoyance.

When I hung up, Omak was no longer in his office. I found him in the community meeting room upstairs, dealing with a malfunctioning audio system that no one seemed to know how to operate. I brought him up to speed and told him about the search being organized by the Jamesons. "We've got Garcia and Brown sitting out there. I'll let them know to join the search."

"Better coming from you than me," I said, well aware that no one wanted to hear a change in orders from a rookie cop. "I was just about to head over to the Jamesons for interviews."

He looked at his watch. "I wanted to go with you, but I can't get away right now."

"I don't mind flying solo."

"Do you feel like you're on solid footing?" he asked. "This is a delicate matter. Do you want to take someone along?"

"I got this," I said, confident in my interviewing skills. "I'm a polite person, and people seem to like talking with me. It'll be fine."

Police officers have little love for the media. Cops portray reporters as vultures, swooping down on innocent prey to steal a juicy story. And maybe the mistrust there is fueled by fear of being portrayed in the media as a bad cop, an abuser of authority.

I know this. But I cannot deny the tingle of excitement I feel when I come across a news van with its antenna and camera unit and lights and famous on-air personality standing by in a crisp Columbia Sportswear jacket. A TV news crew makes you feel that fame is only a few words away, with a ticker-tape parade and presidential award to follow.

Which is miles away from reality. I know this, too. Still, the glittery feeling prevailed as I slowed beside the "Five Alive!" news van on the main road, with its thirty-foot antenna pointed into the glum October sky in the clearing. This was probably the closest spot to the ranch for transmission, as once you turned off the road, tall trees blocked the sky from sight.

I gave the crew a look, not unfriendly. They seemed to hold their breath as I rolled by. In the morning gloom, the woods seemed nearly as dark as night, and I had to pay close attention to make the proper turns. How had the Ghia made it out of here last night, navigating these twists and turns without the ability to slow down? That was assuming that the brakes had been cut before the car left the compound. If Lucy had left soon after the argument with her father, she would have had time to drive off the ranch, where anyone might have had a chance to cut the brake lines before the crash. I still needed to know more about that forty-five minutes.

Just in front of the Jamesons' sign was a van from channel seven, its bright-orange logo boasting "News Twenty-Four on Seven!" A cameraman was taking shots of the Jamesons' wooden sign while a reporter spoke with him. Don Juan. Yep. His real name. Behind the van, a young woman with acorn-brown hair paced along the roadside weeds, her cell phone to her ear. I pulled up alongside her and rolled down the window.

"Nat." I smiled. "How's it going?" My friend Natalie had been given the job of assistant producer as a reward for her two-year internship with channel seven last year.

"I'll call you back," Natalie said into the phone. "The cops are here." She clicked off and leaned into the car to give me a hug. "Oh, my God, you look so smart in that uniform. How *are* you?"

I gave her a squeeze. "Good." I was dying to spill about my first case as well as my two—yes, two!—encounters with Randy Shapiro in the last two days. Natalie would understand how hard it was for me to ask him to meet for coffee sometime. Natalie would also have invaluable insight into the meaning of his answer: "Yeah. I guess we could do that." His lack of enthusiasm had been a concern.

But I was on duty. "I'm fine. I wish I could talk, but I'm on the clock."

"So you're working on this one?"

"Yes. But I can't say a single word."

"I know, I know. But no one is getting anywhere with Kent Jameson. One of our producers used to have a solid connection to the wife, but she's not answering calls. No one on the estate is."

"They must have a loyal staff." In high-profile cases there always seemed to be one employee or friend who was so enamored of the media that they leaked information under the label of an "anonymous source."

Natalie looked down the road behind me. "Are more cops behind you? The big brass?"

"They're back at the precinct, setting up for a press conference." Omak had described the impromptu briefing as "a hot mess" and unnecessary since we hadn't yet identified the victim, and at this early stage, he wasn't going to release any information on the investigation. Still, Chief Cribben wanted to appear in control, and the mayor needed a chance to appear on camera with his signature sad puppy expression of sympathy. The whole thing had burned Omak, who knew his time would have been better spent here at the ranch, interviewing and observing. "I'm surprised you're not there," I told Natalie.

"Another team is covering it." She glanced past the mailbox, toward the ranch. "We're looking for the family's reaction. The personal angle."

Drama, grief, tears, and sorrow that would play on an endless Internet loop or on the evening news as people were sorting through mail or adding butter to the mashed turnips. In some ways, Natalie's job was more difficult than mine.

"Plus we're following up on reports of some indigents living in Stafford Woods," Natalie said. "Some off-grid hippies who've been squatting for months now. Some of the neighbors are concerned. Do you know anything about that?"

"Not on my radar," I admitted. "But I'd better get going." I wished my friend luck and headed up the road again.

Inside the compound, I parked the patrol car beside a tree off to the side of the house and emerged from to car to the silence of the crisp October morning. The door of the mansion was answered by a short Hispanic woman wearing a full green apron. Fiftyish, I guessed, she had soft dark eyes and dark hair streaked with gray, which was pulled back into a braid. Her bold brows were lifted, her movements tense. I felt she was afraid of me.

"Are you Juana?" When she nodded, I added, "I'm Officer Laura Mori."

Her fingers twisted and coiled the string of her apron. "Is there news?"

"No, nothing yet. I'm here to interview you and the rest of the staff."

"Right now? Are you kidding me?" Disappointment shadowed her eyes. "This is not going to be good. I don't think they slept at all last night, and Mr. J, he's giving up. Right now, they're over in the office with an undertaker. I never expected this." She pressed her folded hands to her lips, as if in momentary prayer. "Such a terrible thing. First the mother and then little Lucy. I don't know how Mr. J will bear it."

I glanced through the window at the quiet village across the way. Best to let the meeting run its course and use the time to interview the housekeeper.

"It might be best for us to talk now," I said, nodding toward the great room. "Do you want to sit down for a bit?"

Her frown indicated that she wasn't comfortable with that, but she deferred. "Let's go to the dining room. This way, if they come, they don't look through the window and see me sitting like a queen in their home."

Juana paused to pick up a bag of linens to take with her. She gestured for me to sit as she took a seat at the back of the table with a view of the door.

From my seat, I could see the view that made this hill so valuable—beyond a swath of green, the vista gave way to the river below, valleys, rooftops, and, in the distance, the magnificent white peak of Mt. Hood.

"Are you going to tell Mrs. Martha the things I tell you?" she asked, drawing my attention back to the moment.

"Not if you don't want me to."

"I don't." She worked as she spoke, folding and stacking napkins. "I can't lose my job after all these years. Thirteen years with Mr. J—since he divorced Mrs. Candy. And now I'm too old to go from house to house."

"Do you think Mr. Jameson would fire you after thirteen years?"

"Not Mr.," she said. "Mrs."

"You mentioned the mother dying," I said. "Did you mean Lucy's mother?"

"Yes. Mrs. Candy."

"Did you know her?"

"I met her when she visited Lucy, but I don't know her. I work only for Mr. Jameson, but I know Lucy since she was a little thing." She stopped folding to press a palm to her chest. "My heart, inside, it's breaking."

"I can't imagine. Were you close to Lucy?"

She shrugged one shoulder. "Nobody's close to Lucy. But I take care of her. Like a grandmother."

I reached into the pile of linens. "Mind if I help?"

She seemed skeptical. "Mrs. Martha, she likes them just so. You know?"

"I've worked in my father's restaurant," I said, imitating her moves, folding on the diagonal and then rolling. "I've folded a lot of napkins. Were you here at dinnertime last night when Lucy argued with her father?"

"No. I went home. But I see them fight before. Lucy, she's like the sky through the window. Sometimes bright and sunny, sometimes dark and very stormy."

I continued folding, following Juana's technique. "Was she always that way?"

"She was a sweet little girl. But Lucy and Mrs. Martha . . ." She formed fists and pressed her knuckles together. "They're like this. Very stubborn and very mean to each other."

It wasn't unusual for kids to reject a stepparent, but Juana seemed to think that Martha was just as obnoxious as Lucy. Clearly Juana had no love for the boss's wife.

"In the last few months, do you think Lucy was depressed?"

"Not happy, but not so depressed." She pointed

113

out toward the road. "This accident? It was not suicide, if that's what you're thinking. Lucy, she likes to laugh and be with her friends too much for that." Juana's face grew tense, holding back tears. "I remember when she learned to ride her little pink bike. She loved to pedal her bike round and round the lane. She would be going all day, swimming and riding horses. She was a very happy girl."

"Growing up can change a person's perspective. Especially for teenagers. That's such a roller coaster ride." I thought of my own adolescence, the adrenaline surge of a job well done juxtaposed with a feeling of failure so acute that I could not breathe. The joy of saving someone and the panic because I could not save myself. Even with two supportive parents, I had struggled; it sounded like Lucy wasn't so lucky.

"Did she have friends?"

"Many friends, but one at a time. Mrs. Martha, she don't like them. There was always a girl staying here."

"I was wondering, how did she meet kids if she didn't go to school?"

Juana wasn't sure. With the pride of a grand-mother, she told me that Lucy had many friends in grade school. Her disapproval was obvious when she talked about Lucy leaving school. Juana had two children in college, and she believed education was important in America.

"And now, we are done." She pointed to the empty basket and rose from the table. "You see? Many hands make light work. Thank you."

"You're welcome."

"And you won't tell?"

"My lips are sealed," I said. Martha Jameson did not need to know that the woman serving as her housekeeper viewed her as stubborn and mean-spirited. "And I want to make sure you know that the woman killed in the crash might not be Lucy. We haven't been able to identify the body yet."

"Not Lucy?"

"We don't know yet. The Jamesons seem to be assuming their daughter is dead, but we don't know for sure."

"Mmm." She made the sign of the cross. "Even though it's selfish, I pray it's not her."

I nodded, knowing that one family's good news would be another's tragedy.

Juana saw me to the door and pointed me toward Martha's office. She told me that I would find Mr. and Mrs. there, along with the undertaker and Martha's assistant, Talitha Rahimi. Andy would be over at the barn, and Carlos would be here and there. She gave me his cell phone number in case I couldn't find him on the compound.

When the door closed, I took out my notebook and jotted down details of my interview with

Juana Lopez. I hadn't wanted to distract her by taking notes, and I didn't think I would forget any of the details or nuances of our conversation. Juana was clearly in Kent Jameson's camp and a supporter of Lucy.

Dread weighed me down as I approached the little village. It was a terrible thing to interrupt a family's meeting with their funeral director, and if last night was any indication, I could expect a dramatic reaction from Kent Jameson. High emotion was not something I had much experience with. Although my father poured on the animation for his customers, when bad tidings rolled in, both my parents hid sorrow behind a gentle smile. In Japanese culture, a smile might be expressing happiness or hiding confusion or sorrow. A smile was a thing of mystery.

With my face fixed in a neutral, respectful expression, I knocked on the door of the building containing Martha's office.

The door was opened by a short woman with an emerald-colored scarf covering her face and neck. Her dark eyes grew round at the sight of the police uniform—a reaction I've noticed in many law-abiding citizens who respect police officers and have a flash of worry that they've been caught doing something wrong.

"Officer, can I help you?"

When I explained that I was here to interview the Jamesons and their staff, she stepped back and ushered me in. "Are you Martha's assistant?" I asked as I stepped inside.

She gave a brisk nod. "Talitha Rahimi. They're quite busy, organizing the search. Please wait here and I'll check with her." I stepped into a lovely reception area with twin loveseats and a velvet couch set in a U-shape to face the greenery beyond the windows. The space gave me the impression of elegance and professionalism, and I sensed that this building was where most of the Jamesons' business was transacted, leaving their home to be a home.

A moment later, I was escorted into a posh conference room with walnut paneling, leather chairs, and a long, shiny wood table. The meeting was in progress, but most participants seemed to take a breath, assessing as I entered.

Pale and wild haired, Kent sat in a chair staring up at a large drop-down screen showing a map of Stafford Woods; he seemed so dazed and distraught that I doubted he noticed me at all. Martha stood behind him massaging his shoulders.

The two men who sat opposite the Jamesons were familiar to me. One wore a khaki-colored jacket with a Sunrise Lake emblem on the shoulder that identified him as an employee of the parks department. I recognized the other man, bald with a full white Santa beard, as the owner of Mac's Diner, an offbeat restaurant that was half diner, half Mexican cantina.

"Hi, Mac." I introduced myself, and the man with the parks department identified himself as Chad Hunter.

"Are you going to be helping us with our search?" Mac asked.

"Officers Brown and Garcia should be here soon to work with you." I nodded at the map on the screen, the miles of dark green indicating dense, isolated forest. This was a tangent from my task at hand, but I'd had some training in search and rescue. "Are you planning to go out as one group or split up?"

Chad talked me through the plan to separate into smaller groups that would enter the woods at various trailheads and check the paths for signs of trampled brush or any indication Lucy went off trail. It seemed like a sound approach for the thirty or so volunteers as well as rescue dogs from the mountain recovery team.

"Are these search teams assembling here?" I asked, concerned that they would disturb a potential crime scene at the ranch.

"Martha here has asked for privacy during this difficult time," Mac explained. "The volunteers will meet at a staging area near the barn. We'll start setting up around noon."

That gave me a few hours to check out the barn area before it got trampled by invaders.

"It's important that you contact me or one of the other officers if you find anything." I gave the men my cell number as Talitha came in to announce the arrival of the other officers.

Brown worked the men, shaking hands and making small talk about hunting while Garcia hung back with her usual lemon-sour expression. Something about those two made me feel that we were working on opposing teams.

We exchanged information, and they decided to head over to Mac's Diner to "talk with the volunteers." I suspected Brown saw a free breakfast in the deal, but I was relieved to get them away from the Jameson compound for now.

After they left, I took a seat adjacent to Kent at the head of the conference table, wanting to be on Jameson's level but not opposing him. Sometimes body language was everything.

"It's good that they're searching the woods," I said. "We need to do everything we can right now to find your girl."

Kent's head snapped over to me, as if he'd just noticed my presence. "I fear it's an exercise in futility."

"Forensics hasn't identified the crash victim yet," I pointed out. "Maybe it wasn't Lucy."

"Who else could it be?" Kent's voice was strained, his face flushed with the heat of despair. "It was her car. We argued. She was furious with me." He shook his head. "Royally pissed. But I stood my ground. I should have backed down, given in. I didn't know what a state she was in . . ."

"Kent, no." Martha leaned close, wrapped her arms around him, and whispered something in his ear.

Talitha returned, but she stood in the doorway, as if waiting for her cue.

"I know this is difficult territory," I said, "but let's say for a moment that Lucy wasn't in that car. Who else could it have been?"

Kent sniffed. "It had to be her."

"Sweetheart, there is one other possibility," Martha told him gently, then straightened to face me. "It could have been theft. A girl from that hippie tribe from the woods. They've trespassed on our property a few times."

"Martha, they're homeless."

"All the more reason to be afraid; they have nothing to lose."

"They're harmless," he said.

"Have you met them?" I asked.

Kent waved off the question. "Some of them, a while back. Doesn't matter. I know they're not thieves. Lucy was the driver; she's gone." He raked his hair back and then pounded a fist on the table. "My girl is gone, and I let it happen."

"It's not your fault," Martha said.

"Don't!" Kent held up a hand. "Don't coddle me, Martha."

With a practiced wariness, she stepped back, expressionless as Kent rose and kicked his chair away. As the chair rolled off behind him and bounced against the paneled wall, Martha moved back again, clearing the way for her husband to march out of the conference room and leave the building with a savage slam of the front door.

Martha hurried out after him, leaving me to wonder at this unleashed rage in Kent Jameson. Yes, he had reason to be angry if his daughter was truly dead. But seeing his fury gave me a glimpse of his darker side. This was no cloistered monk on the hill, as Martha tended to portray him to the media. Kent Jameson was strong, potentially acerbic, and capable of violence.

It was hard to imagine a scenario in which a father killed his daughter. Still, as an investigator, I had to go there.

Had he cut the brake lines on his daughter's car and compelled her to flee?

It was my job to find out.

—8—

"Today, you saw a very different Mr. Jameson," said Talitha. "That's not how he is. I've worked here five, almost six years now, and I have never seen him lose his temper before." Dignified and erect, Talitha sat across from me on one of the loveseats in the reception area. While I'd waited to interview her, she had fielded two phone calls and signed for three packages from FedEx.

I glanced from the calm young woman to the woodland view of deep-green ponderosa pines and fir trees punctuated by splashes of yellow and orange leaves from deciduous trees. A serene environment designed to calm negotiations and woo adversaries.

"Did Martha tell you to say that?" In the scurry to jog alongside her boss, Talitha had received some instructions while Martha had pointed her back toward the office.

Talitha's brows rose in surprise. "You heard that?"

So I'd been right; she was trying to "handle" me. "It doesn't matter. I understand why Mr. Jameson is overwrought. Let's talk about your observations during your time here. Did you know Lucy?"

"Of course. She's the daughter of my boss."

"Did you know her friends?"

"Not well. I only know the trouble they caused Mrs. Jameson. She says they're loud and they drink a lot. They are not good girls, these friends."

"When was the last time you saw Lucy?"

She didn't remember. "Maybe a week ago? I am here in this office mostly. I see nothing but trees and people who come in to transact business with Mrs. Jameson."

Her answer seemed evasive. I decided to try a different tack. "That's a very pretty scarf. I love the color."

"It's called a hijab. I like to wear it because it's how I grew up. In Iran."

"The color flatters you. When did you come to the US?"

Softening a bit, she explained that she had come seven years ago with her husband and baby. Talitha had been working as a server at the country club when Martha hired her to work at a dinner party. When Martha discovered the woman had excellent organizational and computer skills, she hired her as a full-time assistant. Around that time, Talitha's husband made a mistake filling out the immigration forms and was deported. It was only because of the help of the Jamesons that she and her daughter had been allowed to stay. They had hired an expensive immigration lawyer who helped them get citizenship. "The lawyer has been working on getting my husband back for two years now. Because we are Iranian, it's difficult. For now, we do FaceTime. But my husband wants my daughter and me to stay. There's more opportunities for her here in the US, and she's a good girl. Just started third grade."

The phone started ringing, and she excused herself to answer. A moment later, she returned, sitting with a sigh. "This was to be a very busy day. Producers coming from Hollywood to talk about making a movie of one of Mr. Jameson's books. I've had to cancel, but they were already on their way. His agent calling and the bookkeeper, and always we get lots of fan letters and messages on his website. Everything must be answered. And now this search in the woods."

"It sounds like Martha is lucky to have you taking care of things."

"I do a good job, but Mrs. Jameson works day and night. People don't understand that. I hear them talking sometimes, saying how lucky she is she struck gold. Things like that. But Mrs. Jameson is the one who keeps the business running. She makes deals that bring in pots of money, a lot of them based on his old books. Not to take away from Mr. Jameson. People love his books. But she works hard, too."

Her opinion of Martha ran counterpoint to Juana's view. Two sides to a coin.

"I'll let you get back to work," I said. "I have a few more people to interview, and then I'll circle back to talk with Mr. and Mrs. Jameson."

"I'll let Mrs. Jameson know," Talitha said as she saw me out the door.

Looking for a few quiet moments to mull over the investigation, I braced myself against the brisk October air and headed out to find the barn. I passed Kent's writing studio, the building dark and cold. My boots sunk into the mushy ground near the round corral when I left the path.

It was one of those open-air arenas, so I could look inside. Nobody in sight.

Back on the path toward the barn—or so the sign said—I breathed in the cool air scented by Douglas firs, the smells of mulch and wet earth. As I walked, I looked for the signs of activity on the edge of the path that I had mentioned to the men leading the search party. This part of the ranch bordered Stafford Woods, and the thick growth of trees darkened the area and made for a feeling of desolation. Without the path, it would be easy to get lost back here.

I was not a horse girl, but everyone in Sunrise Lake knew about the history of the Jameson ranch, formerly a world-class equestrian center. In the 1940s when cowboy film stars traveled to the area, their horses stayed here. Roy Rogers's horse Trigger and Gene Autry's Champion had been boarded here. And Buttermilk, Dale Evans's buckskin quarter horse. My grandmother could not get enough of Dale Evans's movies and songs. I think my grandma wanted to believe that this heroic cowboy world really existed somewhere in America—a place where right prevailed and a horse named Buttermilk could save the day. When the cowboy culture faded from Hollywood in the 1950s, the ranch became a riding academy. It was still some kind of horsey place when Kent Jameson bought it and began to renovate nearly fifteen years ago, building new structures and acquiring alpacas.

How many times had Lucy walked this path, headed out to ride one of her horses? More important, what had been on her mind yesterday when she got into that argument with her father? Had she fled back here, into the woods, harboring resentment toward her stepmother or rebelling toward her father like most seventeen-year-old girls? Having a wealthy father, horses, a classic sports car, and a beautiful home did not preclude Lucy from having problems. Everyone had issues and demons, but I still didn't have a handle on what drove Lucy Jameson.

To that end, I was curious to meet the ranch manager, Andy Greenleaf, wanting to get a gauge on whether he might have been Lucy's secret lover. I still hadn't had a chance to ask the Jamesons if they knew that a registered sex offender was living on their property, sleeping less than two miles from their daughter's bedroom.

The paved path emerged from the woods and curved toward the squat red barn looming ahead. This side of the hill had been cleared of dense timber, allowing a wide view of the pale yellow fields, stone walls, hillocks, and in the distance, the river and Mt. Hood. It was a view of pastoral splendor made comical by the alpacas milling in the fenced-in area beside the barn. The fluffy, arched creatures roaming the area resembled oddly assembled crosses between ostriches and oversized poodles. Some grazed, a few roamed in a pack, and others watched one white oddball roll and twist in a mud puddle.

"Snowbell!" someone called out. "Snowbell! Get out of that mud."

I bit back a smile as Snowbell, the white alpaca, squirmed in delight, staining her coat with brown dirt.

"Come on, now!" A young man called from the side of the corral. Andy Greenleaf was better looking than his mug shot, with chiseled cheekbones and golden hair that was cropped close in the way of an all-American quarterback. The only drawback was the large, square set of teeth that made him resemble the horse grazing nearby.

"That damn alpaca thinks she's a hound dog," Greenleaf muttered to a scruffy cowboy type with a gold tooth, maybe twentyish, who was brushing down a horse the color of caramel corn. The horse didn't seem to care about the alpacas meandering nearby, and the fluffballs on stick legs acted as if the horses were invisible.

"Andy Greenleaf?" I was in uniform, but I showed him my ID, too. It felt so official. "Officer Laura Mori."

"Hey, Officer." He slung me a casual smile. "You got it, Blane?" With a nod, he moved away from the horse groomer and stepped into my personal space. This one didn't seem to fear me at all, but then he didn't seem menacing, either. He moved with a lanky awkwardness, like a boy who hadn't yet adjusted to his man-sized body. Despite his youthful look, he had man hands—calloused and rough from doing manual labor outdoors. "That's tough news about the crash, right? Really sad. Did it turn out to be Lucy?"

His response didn't fit a man who had dated Lucy Jameson. I kept my voice level. "We're not certain yet. Forensics is working on identifying her."

"I feel awful about that. Lucy was a nice kid, and her parents are the best. They are good people and generous employers. I mean, look at this." He gestured to the barn and surrounding hills. "What's not to love here?"

"It's beautiful country," I agreed. "And the alpacas are very cute."

"Yeah. Girls like them until they spit. But they don't do that too often. It's a kind of defense mechanism."

"You live on the property, isn't that right?"

"Sure do." He jabbed a thumb toward the barn. "I got a cabin on the other side of the barn that Mr. and Mrs. J fixed up for me. Just one bedroom, but that's all I need. Got a satellite dish now, so I can watch anything I want. How's that? Not bad for a working guy like me."

"Yes, I saw this address listed in your criminal file. Do the Jamesons know you're a registered sex offender?"

"Hey." He shot a look over his shoulder to see if the other worker had heard, but the young man kept on brushing the horse. "Come on, now." He took a few steps away from the fence, away from listening ears. "I try not to advertise it to everyone. But yeah, they knew from the beginning. I think that's sort of why they hired me. Mr. and Mrs. J, they kind of collect people who need help, and man, I needed saving back then. You know the woods back there? That's where I lived, in a freakin' tent. My probation officer was pissed because I didn't have a real address. If you got nowhere to live, you have to check in with probation every thirty days. It sucked. But my stepfather threw me out, and I couldn't get a job, and you can't get a place to live without a job."

"A vicious circle," I said. He had an easy, winning manner, though a little rough around the edges.

"Yeah. I got lucky with the Jamesons. They could see I was good with animals from the start. Then when Mrs. J saw that I could fix just about anything, mechanical or carpentry or whatever, I got the job here."

So he had mechanical skills, too. I suspected he would know how to disable the brakes in the Karmann Ghia. "So the Jamesons saved you."

"They did. That conviction destroyed me, and it wasn't even my fault. I didn't do anything wrong. Not really."

129

I had not received his case files yet, but I suspected Andy's experience was quite different than the judge's findings. "Why don't you tell me your side of the story," I said.

"I was just a guy in love with a girl whose parents didn't want us to be together."

"A girl," I repeated. "How old?"

"Fifteen, in the beginning. Ginnie Walters. Man, I loved that girl. She was fifteen and I was nineteen. We were in high school together. What do people expect? At that age, you meet someone, you hook up. We were together for two years and it was fine. I mean, her parents didn't like it, but they lived with it."

"And you were protected by the Romeo and Juliet law," I said. In law classes at the academy, we had learned of recent laws designed to protect teenagers who were a few years apart and engaged in willing sexual relationships. "If your relationship was consensual."

"It was. Of course it was! She was my girlfriend." His lips puckered in disapproval. "I wasn't some pervert. But her parents didn't want us together, and some lawyer friend helped them screw me over. When I turned twenty-one, they filed charges against me for sexual assault. Ginnie was seventeen, still a minor, so she didn't have any say in the matter. And according to the law, once I was twenty-one, the Romeo and Juliet thing was out the window."

"Wait. You were prosecuted after two years with this girl?"

"Shit, yeah, if you'll pardon my French. Her parents really stuck it to me, and the county prosecutor, I don't think he had much of a choice."

"And Ginnie?"

"Hell if I know. The Walters sent her away to live with some aunt after the hearing, and one of the terms of my probation was that I had to stay away from her. But that was, like, seven years ago. Yeah, seven. A lot's changed since then. I've got a girlfriend and a good job. So fuck the Walters. You know what they say. Success is the best revenge."

This was not at all the story I'd expected to hear. Perhaps I'd been wrong in thinking that he was A, the older lover mentioned in Lucy's diary. "Your current girlfriend," I said. "What's her name?"

"Heather." He lifted his chin, content as a cat. "Heather Erickson."

"How old is Heather?"

"She's going to be twenty-four next month. And her parents like me. Yeah. I'm not making the same mistake twice."

"What about Lucy Jameson?" I kept my voice level. "Were you ever involved with her?"

"What?" He winced. "Hell, no. That was one of the things Mr. J told me when I was hired.

Keep away from his daughter and out of his business. I respect that. And when you got a sweet job like mine, believe me, you don't want to mess it up. Besides, Lucy was just a rug rat when I got here. That'd be twisted."

"Seven years ago it would have been grossly inappropriate. But now she's seventeen, almost of age." I decided to see if I could call his bluff. "And she wrote about you in her diary . . . that you had a relationship."

"She did?" He blanched, and I couldn't tell if he was shocked or worried. "Well, that's not true. I mean, I run the barn and all, but she barely looks me in the eye when she comes through here. So what did she say about me?"

"She wrote of her sexual experiences with you. Some fairly graphic details."

"What? That never happened," he said indignantly. "The only time I ever talked to her was when she came by to go riding, and even then, I barely said two words. All business. And most of the times she was with a friend."

"So you weren't the sexy, older lover who'd captivated her?" I cocked my head to one side. "Maybe it was all in her imagination."

"Well, she may have been fantasizing about me." He smiled. "I guess a lot of girls do. And Lucy grew up pretty dang nice. She's got a kick-ass body now. But I stayed away."

"Right." It wasn't the most reassuring answer. "I

guess it would have been hard for the two of you to keep the relationship secret from her father."

"Not really. Mr. J keeps to himself. But hold on, now. I'm not admitting to anything." He held up a hand, like a traffic cop stopping a vehicle. "You trying to get me jammed up here?"

"I'm trying to find out who was driving that car and why she blew out of here last night." Those mysterious forty-five minutes. I kept the information about the brake tampering to myself. I didn't want to show my hand. "Did you have an argument with Lucy yesterday?"

"No." He raked his hair back, frowning. "I don't even know if I saw her yesterday."

"Do you want some time to think about it?"

He swatted at the air. "Hell, no." A tawny-colored alpaca seemed to think Andy was flagging it down; the creature trotted right over and parked itself behind him like a loyal pup. There was no question that the animals loved him—nature's endorsement.

"So you don't remember seeing Lucy yesterday. Do you remember where you were last night between six and eight p.m.?"

"Do I have to tell you? Don't I have some rights?"

"Of course you do," I said.

"Just wanted to make sure, 'cause you're getting a little pushy."

I shrugged. "That's my job. A young woman

133

died in that crash, and I'm here to find out why. So. Last night?"

"I was at my girlfriend's house, okay?"

"And Heather will testify that you were with her?"

"Well, sure, but . . ." He let out a breath as he shifted from foot to foot. "Do you have to ask her? It's just gonna get her upset."

"Why would she be upset about clearing your name?" I asked.

"She just would, okay? Nobody wants to talk to the police."

I didn't agree. Plenty of people were happy to be interviewed. But then, most people hadn't faced criminal prosecution for some bad choices they'd made as a teenager.

I would contact this Heather, but also I would keep looking elsewhere for A.

"I gotta get back to work, so we need to be done here."

"Okay. Thanks for your time."

"Like I had a choice," he muttered, moving toward the barn. The alpaca trotted off behind him. This time I noticed that the groomer, Blane, was watching from the open barn doorway.

"I'm just going to have a look around," I called after Andy. Despite the contention between us, there was no reason not to be polite. "Hope you don't mind."

Of course he minded, but he knew better than to

stop me. I ventured inside the barn and blinked as the acrid smell hit my palate. Straw and hay and an earthy mixture of leather and dung. I wondered if that smell ever went away. Tall stacks of hay drew my eye up to the loft, which seemed to be used for storage. I wondered if the alpacas and horses were kept together or if they used the stalls. In one open area, Blane was picking junk from a horse's hoof with a metal hook. It looked painful, but the horse didn't seem to mind.

I introduced myself, but Blane barely gave me a glance. "Do the Jamesons ride often?" I asked.

"Nah. Lucy, sometimes. I never saw him and her out this way."

"So how many alpacas do you have out here?"

"Dozen or so. And three horses."

I asked if he liked his job, if the alpacas ever tried to bite, if the work was hard. His one-word answers allowed no entry to conversation. Although I moseyed around trying to look for something out of place, I had no idea what the ordinary smell and mess of a stable should look like.

A scraping noise came from one of the stalls, where a woman in a beanie, rubber boots, a down vest, and a leather apron shoveled out manure, hay clods, and dirt. With chapped lips and no hair visible, she looked worn down but not unhealthy. I said hello; she barely nodded.

This was not a welcoming crew.

135

I spent a few more minutes there, trying to strike up a conversation with the workers in the barn. They gave short answers and kept to their tasks. My mother would have hired these two worker bees as kitchen help in a heartbeat. In our family restaurant, hard work was not only expected but revered.

By the time I left the barn, I wasn't quite sure what to think about Andy. I didn't want to believe that such a handsome, affable guy would stoop to sexual abuse and murder. Was he the full-fledged boyfriend, the older lover described in Lucy's diary? Someone who had turned her on then turned on her, disabling her car and killing her? It seemed unlikely after his adamant responses to my questioning. Or perhaps he was guilty of one crime but not the other. I needed to speak with the girlfriend, Heather Erickson, as well as the parole officer.

The forest closed in around me as I headed back to the main buildings, and the outside world seemed far, far away. Everywhere I looked, there was lush vegetation. Douglas firs, red cedars, sequoia, and pine trees towered overhead, many of their fat trunks lined in furry moss. Bushes and ferns were so dense on the ground that the path was a dark, chilly tunnel beneath the trees. A rustling sound put my nerves on alert. I stopped, turned, and stared, searching for the source of the sound. A squirrel? A burrowing mole? Thousands of creatures coexisted under the canopy of trees. Was it an animal I was hearing? The throng of life behind my back seemed to be a large creature moving with premeditation and caution. A human.

The thump of my pulse throbbed in my ears as I listened to the distinct rustle of leaves behind me.

Not a critter. Squirrels and deer had never given me that sharp sense of awareness, the sensation that I was being watched.

I turned sharply toward the sound, and it stopped. "Who's there?" I called, giving the watcher a chance to reveal himself. "Andy?" Was it him? I doubted that he could have followed me in a parallel path through the woods, but I figured it might flush him out if I called his name.

There was no answer. My eyes combed the dense brush. Grasses and bushes combined to form a natural screen for the person lingering back there. "I know you're there. I see you."

My bluff produced a rustling sound and then silence again.

Creepy.

My heartbeat began to race and my palms grew moist. The pulse in my dry throat warned me of the panic rising from within.

Deep breaths, in and out. I could calm myself. I could work through this, just as I was going to walk right out of this forest.

"A girl who suffers from panic attacks cannot be a police officer," my mother had told me repeatedly. *"Maybe if you were stronger or one of the calm ones. But law enforcement, it's not for a delicate flower like you."*

She was wrong about that. I was going to prove her wrong.

A deep breath, a cautious look. That scalding sensation that someone was watching me.

"The problem with a panic attack is that it's all in your head," my mother used to say.

Maybe. Or maybe not.

A wise man once said that fear is a gift, an ancient reminder to flee.

Fear had the power to save our lives.

I started running.

Like a naïve tourist, the female cop walked along the path, gawking here and there and peering ahead through the clearing. Too many questions, this pretty Japanese girl. She was crossing the line, asking to be punished. And, oh, he would enjoy punishing her, over and over again. Her innocence was an irresistible aphrodisiac, titillating, seductive.

He shook his head, as if to expel the ridiculous notion. A tumble with her would mean trouble. She was pretty poison.

For now, impulses had to be kept in check, in pocket, zipped shut.

Best to keep a safe distance between himself and the girl cop. If she pushed too hard, then he would push back. He would enjoy pushing her buttons, prodding her body along to a rhapsody of pleasure. Then she would follow the others down the long, dark hole. Falling through the looking glass.

—9—

My clamoring heart slowed as the peaked roof of the riding arena came into view. The safety of civilization. Seeing that the path behind me was empty, I slowed to a brisk walk as my cell phone buzzed.

The caller ID showed "Parole and Probation Dept." My heart was still pounding as I took the call.

Chris Brewer, Andy Greenleaf's probation officer, turned out to have traces of a stutter in his voice. "What can I . . . What can I do for you?"

I explained that I was investigating a possible homicide at the Jameson ranch. "As you know, Andy is a resident there."

"That's right. For quite a few years now. What's the deal? You got probable cause?"

"Still in the early stages of investigating, but I was hoping you could give me some background info on Greenleaf." Walking in an easy stride now, I shifted my cell phone to the other ear. "I just met with him, and he seems like a nice guy."

"Most of them are charmers, but that doesn't mean they won't act out. Our rate of recidivism for child molesters is not good. Not good. You can't trust these guys."

I asked him about the circumstances of Greenleaf's conviction. "Is it true that the girl was his girlfriend? I mean, it seems unfair to split up a couple who've been together for two years just because he turned twenty-one."

"That's the law, and don't believe everything he tells you. The parents seem to think Greenleaf had her brainwashed. She was afraid to leave him."

Of course there were multiple perspectives in every story.

"Andrew has followed the rules for me," Chris went on. "He's checked in once a year and kept his address up to date. But I can't say he's become a saint. For every two perps who clean up their act, I have one that falls back to old habits. If I were you, I wouldn't trust anything he says. With these guys, looks are deceiving."

I knew that the parole officer was right; many child molesters were not the creepy guy that people found revolting. They were physicians and teachers, bankers and cops. Attractive, charming people had a far better chance to win over a young person's trust.

Could I imagine Andy Greenleaf going after Lucy, a young woman he'd known since she was a girl? It was well within the realm of possibility, and he'd commented on her attractiveness. I thanked Brewer and called Omak.

"Mori. What do you have for me?"

"I've interviewed the housekeeper, Martha's personal assistant, and the ranch manager. So far, Andy Greenleaf is a bit suspicious, though Kent Jameson has demonstrated a propensity for violence." I told him about Greenleaf's denials, his charm, his claim that he was with Heather Erickson last night. "I need to check with the girl-friend, but I'm not finished interviewing every-one here."

"Stay at the ranch. I'll send someone to track her down," he said. "I've got to get upstairs to the press conference. Keep me posted."

"Will do." I ended the call as I passed the arena and turned left onto the paving stone path. I planned to take a quick look around the compound and then try to gracefully extract some informa-tion about Lucy from the Jamesons. After that, I would track down Carlos Flores, the caretaker.

The clubhouse door was locked. Inside, I saw that chairs had been stacked on the handful of tables, looking sad and neglected. But the garage next door revealed a sign of life. Two of the roll-up doors over the bays were open in the larger building. Someone was here—that was a relief. I stepped inside to the smell of new rubber tires and motor oil.

With four sleek cars shining like grinning hyenas, the place reminded me of the luxury car dealer on State Street. The five garage doors opened into one large room similar to an airplane hangar. The storage drawers against one wall were modern, as were the lighting and the shiny, speckled epoxy floor.

"Hello?"

Only stillness and four cars gaping at me. One had a fat pinstripe down the center like a birthday present. Another had tailfins that resembled a rocket ship. I recognized the grill of an elegant Jaguar and the Lambo, a sleek, predatory hunter with a wide nose and crystalline headlights to track down its prey. From the way the cars were displayed, parked in scattered diagonals, I couldn't tell where the Karmann Ghia used to be parked. There was no gaping space with a tell-tale puddle of brake fluid.

I wove through the cars, impressed by the tidiness of the place. Like a museum. This was nothing like Randy's garage, with oil stains and wrenches, rags, tools, and cans of mystery sprays and fluids. Did they use the other garage for the dirty work?

On the wall by one pristine workbench was a key box—a glass-enclosed chest with labeled keys. The clear door swung open smoothly—easy access. Anyone walking through here could fire up the Lambo or the Jag.

The second garage was shaped differently. It had two stories, but it was smaller, with only two bays. There were windows upstairs, but they were covered with blinds. No one answered when I knocked, and the door was locked.

As I tried to peer in a window at the edge of the blinds, I heard a whining sound, like a lamb bleating repeatedly. I paused, scanning the panorama for motion. On the other side of the trees, a short, thick man pushed a squealing cart down the path. No, not a cart, but a wheelbarrow, actually. I didn't think he saw me, and he was tuned into earbuds. He rounded some new-growth trees and went off the path. The wheelbarrow bounded over the dirt toward the back of the two-story garage. I followed him around the side of the building to a cemented area bordered by small, trimmed shrubs.

A parking pad, discreetly positioned out of sight. The perfect place for a car that was leaking . . . something. A slick stain, about two or three feet wide, darkened the concrete. The man parked the wheelbarrow beside it and started to sprinkle some sort of sand onto the stain.

"Hey, there!" I stepped in. "Can you hold on a second?" I had my cell phone out, swiping toward the camera function.

"Ah!" He shook his head, grasping his chest

143

with one hand. "Officer, you popped out of nowhere."

"I'm sorry. I didn't mean to startle you, but I wanted to stop you before you got too far." I introduced myself and learned that he was Carlos, the Jamesons' caretaker. His beard was well trimmed, his hair flecked with gray. A belly curved over his belt, but he seemed hardy and strong. "I know this may seem weird, but I'm looking for the spot where the Karmann Ghia was parked yesterday. Is this it?" I snapped photos as I spoke.

He looked down at the stain as if it were an embarrassment. "*Sí*. Yes. The car was here, in this spot." The Hispanic man seemed to have trouble looking me in the eye.

"It was parked here yesterday," I said, thinking of our timeline. "How late in the day did you see it?"

"I check over all the cars before I leave. It's the last thing I do before I sign out at Mrs. Martha's office at six."

"I take it you heard about the crash?"

Still nodding, no eye contact.

"The Jamesons mentioned how much they rely on you," I said. "That you do such a good job running this place."

That brought his gaze up slightly. "I do my best, but it's a big ranch."

"They're very pleased with your work." I

nodded at the puddle. "So the Ghia was leaking."

"Yes, yes. The car was going to the mechanic soon to find out the problem. This is why we parked it outside the garage."

As I circled the puddle, I noticed rings from previous stains. "That's a lot of oil to drain from a car," I said. "We've all been down a quart from time to time, but nothing like that. It's amazing that the car even ran. How long was it leaking?"

"This I don't know." He shrugged. "Cars, I don't know, but the Karmann Ghia, always leaking something. We can't have that in the garage. Mr. Kent, he don't care so much, but Mrs.?" He rolled his eyes. "She can't have all the mess. She's very clean, you know. She likes order."

"So she had you keep the car out here?"

"She wants it out of the garage." He shrugged. "It's because she don't like the mess. But now, so sad. So much sorrow. The car, even a messy car, it's nothing compared to losing a child."

"That's true. Do you know if the car had a gas leak, too?" That might explain the spare container of gasoline in the trunk.

"Gas. Oil. It was always leaking something." He shrugged. "Mrs. Martha called that car a hunk of junk, but Mr. Kent and Lucy, they liked it."

He had a way of dancing around the question, a trait I was well familiar with from my Japanese family. Instead of saying no or disagreeing, there's an artful dodge, a way to veer away from the confrontation and agree on something that was never asked. So if I ask my mother if she likes strawberry, instead of saying no, she would respond that "raspberry is a very good flavor."

"So what's that in the wheelbarrow?"

"This? This is for the cat home. You know. Cat litter. But today, I put it on the stain. I leave it overnight."

I asked him to wait with the kitty litter. "Don't touch anything for two minutes." He seemed confused but agreed, and I sprinted to the police car to find an evidence kit. How important was the dark liquid on the cement? Would the lab be able to match it to the brake fluid in the Karmann Ghia? It was worth a try. The brake lines had been cut; the car crash was more than an unfortunate accident. I wanted to determine whether brake fluid had begun leaking here at the ranch.

My pulse was thumping fast when I returned to find Carlos watchful and concerned. "This is for the investigation," I explained. "Something was wrong with the car."

"Yes. It was always leaking," he repeated.

Was he playing dumb or simply not mechanically inclined? "Did you ever work on the car?" I asked as I leaned down to roll a white swab through the stain.

"Never. Mr. Kent has Mr. Hal come by. Sometimes the cars go off to the shop. Supreme

Auto." He swept a hand toward the horizon. "This ranch, it keeps me busy enough."

"I bet it does." It never hurts to help people feel good about themselves. "There's a lot of property up here. I've been looking around, trying to orient myself, but so far I've only covered the stables." I finished bagging the evidence. "All done."

"Can I put this down now?" He indicated the kitty litter.

"Sure. So that's what you use to blot out stains?"

"It works every time."

"Good to know. So anyway, I saw the classic car collection. Sweet," I said, echoing Randy's lingo. "But the second garage was locked. Do you have a key? My boss says that I should leave no stone unturned. You know how that is."

"We can't go in there." He dispersed generous shovelfuls of sandy product over the stain. "It's only for the mechanic when he comes, and Mr. Kent."

"So that's where the repairs are done?"

"Some. Mrs. Martha wants it locked up. She don't like the mess."

It seemed that Martha Jameson suffered from obsessive-compulsive disorder.

"And I got enough to take care of without cleaning up after those mechanics." There was a hint of a smile on his lips.

"Do they keep gasoline in the messy garage?"

"Gasoline? No. Mr. Hal takes the cars to the service station."

"What about a small gas can?" I asked. "Would that be locked up in the mechanic's garage?"

"Yes, a gas can is there. And I keep a can in the maintenance shed for blowers and mowers. You need some gasoline for your car? I can give you a small bit."

"No, thank you, but I do need to take a look at those gas cans. Maybe take a photo."

"You need to see gasoline?" A hint of a smile graced his face. "This I don't understand."

"Trust me on this. It matters."

He shrugged. "I guess I can show you." As we headed toward the second garage, I pushed a little harder. "I appreciate your help. It's such a huge property; I don't know how you manage," I said.

"One task at a time."

"I haven't made a dent in checking out the entire property." I walked alongside him as he pushed the wheelbarrow out to the front path. "I know you must be terribly busy, but would you have a chance to show me around a bit? I've been out to the barn, but after this, I'm heading over to the pool house and those guest houses."

He paused on the path in front of the garage and lowered the wheelbarrow. "Mr. and Mrs. . . . . do they know?"

As in, did they realize I was snooping around the property collecting evidence on their daughter's possible homicide? As in, did I have a warrant? "Of course," I said. "I checked in with them when I got here."

Carlos rubbed his thick jaw with the backs of his knuckles. "I should talk to the boss first."

"But the Jamesons don't want to be disturbed, and I don't want to get you in trouble with them." I lowered my gaze, respectful and studious. Less Officer Mori, more Japanese student of life. "It's no problem. I can show myself around. Thanks so much for your time."

"You know, Officer, I am heading over that way after I return this to the shed." He picked up the wheelbarrow and gave me a fatherly look. "Some things, I can show you."

I thanked him and tried to soak up the surroundings like a sponge. He showed me the "messy" garage, where we located the gas can. And then, with a minimum of words, Carlos showed me the rest of the grounds. The long, windowed building with a glass ceiling contained a sparkling swimming pool. The balmy air in there smelled of chlorine, and the tiles and cement work were pristine. Aquamarine water and teak lounge chairs with white cushions and fluffy white towels. Resort-like but vacant.

"Will you close the pool for the winter?" I asked.

"It's open all the time."

"I'll bet that hot tub is nice on a cold autumn night."

Carlos shrugged. "I don't think anyone uses it. Lucy and her friends, they used to like it. But not for a long time."

The maintenance shed, tucked out of sight of the other buildings, was tidy and contained the second gas can. *All present and accounted for,* I thought. So where had the can from the Ghia come from?

The clubhouse had a similar air of desertion. The place was well-appointed with a river rock fireplace, a wet bar lined with glimmering copper tiles, game tables, a television that was larger than me, and two rows of pinball and video machines, including *Pac-Man.* The place whispered of laughter and good times, but the machines were turned off and the pool table was masked by a vinyl cover. A haunted resort.

Located at one end of the horseshoe were the guest cottages—five one-bedroom buildings built with Craftsman finishes. Carlos unlocked two of them so that I could walk through the simple but cozy interiors. Each cabin was furnished with a writing desk, an overstuffed loveseat, and a brightly colored Pendleton blanket on each bed. And the cabins were locked up so tight that the air was stale and draining.

"Why do they keep them closed up?" I asked, peering into the window of a third cabin.

"For many years you could go anywhere. Every building was open. Then Mrs. Martha heard about the squatters in the woods. She told me lock everything up."

Natalie had mentioned something like that. "Have the squatters in Stafford Woods been a problem?"

He shrugged. "Mr. doesn't mind. It's Mrs. She worry about safety. This is why the cottages are locked."

Just then a bellowing sound came from the direction of the mansion.

"What's that?"

Carlos pursed his lips. "Mr. Kent."

I darted past a cluster of trees to get a clear view across the road to the parking lot.

Kent Jameson banged on the hood of the patrol car. "Officer Mori! Officer!" The exclamation was as low and loud as the growl of a bear. "Where the hell are the cops when you need them?" He stumbled back from my parked patrol unit, tripping and catching himself. "God help us all! The world has gone to hell!"

His wife emerged from the house and hurried down the stairs, descending like a pink cloud in her brightly colored fleece over cut jeans—that expensive, artfully slashed style. Her voice was inaudible, but her approach seemed conciliatory as she reached for him and said something about coming inside. He was barefoot, his hair standing straight up, as if he had spent the morning raking it up toward the sky.

Kent turned away from her, faced the open horseshoe, and flung his arms wide. "Have you found her?" His voice resounded through the clearing at the community's center. "Have you found my girl? What happened to my daughter? My Lucy."

Holding one arm up to get his attention, I moved toward the dramatic, raw scene. "Mr. Jameson?" My voice didn't carry quite so well. I gave a slight wave.

"Where is she? Did you find my girl?" He darted across the paving stones, running toward me as if I held some divine light. With crossed arms holding her fleece in place, his wife loped behind him.

I walked briskly, trying to meet him halfway. Behind me, Carlos seemed to have disappeared amid the trees and buildings. A wise choice.

"Tell me!" Kent Jameson's voice was inappropriately loud, his tone too fiery, and he wasn't tracking well. I suspected he was either drunk or deranged from grief. "Did the searchers find her?"

"No, sir." We were close enough to speak at normal levels. "The search hasn't begun yet."

"Well, at the very least, tell me she wasn't driving the Ghia."

Misery radiated from his body. I hated to disappoint him. "Not yet. We're still waiting on lab results." I didn't tell them about the disabled brakes.

Jameson seemed to deflate and then puff up again, like a lion roaring before it attacked. "Still waiting?" He tossed his head, his mane oddly golden in the gray light. "Good God, how long does it take you people to put the pieces together?"

"Sir, I can assure you that everyone is working as quickly and efficiently as possible."

"Don't fucking *sir* me."

I was going to apologize but stopped myself, thinking that it might infuriate him all the more. It wouldn't do to poke the bear.

"Where the hell is my girl? My Lucy? *She* should be your first priority." He scraped his fingers through his hair, making it even wilder. "If you haven't found my daughter, what the hell have you been doing all morning?"

At first I thought his gusty list of questions was rhetorical, but he gaped at me, waiting for an answer. "While forensics works on making an ID, I'm investigating yesterday's crash." I kept my voice level, trying to restrain my racing heart from thumping out of my chest and launching another attack on me. "Trying to find out how it happened, what caused it."

"Where's your boss? Where's Chief Cribben? He should be here."

"He's back at the precinct conducting a press conference," I said. "They thought it would be best to divert the media from your compound as much as possible."

"Good luck with that," Kent said smugly. "The media love me. They can't stay away, even on a quiet day. I can be in the bulb section of the hardware store and I hear them in the next aisle, whispering and snapping pictures with their cell phones. Everyone wants a piece of me. I'm Kent-Fucking-Jameson, don't you know who I am?" he roared.

"Everyone in Sunrise Lake knows you, Mr. Jameson." I kept my voice low and measured, despite the trepidation flickering through my chest. Jameson was not a large man, but today he looked fierce, with beady eyes, wild hair, and a beet-red hue to his face. He was fired up with adrenaline and, from the smell, a fifth of whisky. "You're a local hero."

"Damn right I am!" he railed, pointing to the sky as he staggered forward and back.

"Kent. Enough." Martha was observing him carefully, like a doctor mulling over a diagnosis.

He swatted the air in her direction. "I'm trying to find my daughter."

"Kent," Martha said, "you've been drinking. Haven't you? Yes. Oh, my God. After nine years sober? Really, Kent?"

"Yes, broken. I am irretrievably broken," he

said, raising one hand dramatically to the sky like a Shakespearean oracle. "Cast my pieces into the darkness and forget that my heart once beat in tandem with the turning of the earth."

"Kent. That's enough. Please. Do you want some tea?"

Heaving a sigh, he rested his head in his hands. Then, looking sober and dignified, he raised his head and strode down the path. "I need to get back to work."

And just as quickly as the drama had bubbled over, it evaporated.

—10—

"I guess he won't be joining the search," Martha said as we watched Kent turn onto the paving stone approach to his studio. "I hope people don't think ill of him because he's not participating, but he can't appear in public this way."

"I think they'll understand. Will he be okay?"

"Eventually. He'll rant and rave and pace. Some days he'll walk for miles through the woods, working a storyline through, but not today. This is too personal to offer it up to nature. Today he'll rattle around in his studio. He'll scavenge through closets and cupboards for hidden stashes of booze. In between fits of rage, he'll do some writing."

"While he's drunk?" I asked. "Will any of it make sense?"

She stared after him, smoothing down the pink fleece. "He wrote two of his top five bestselling books while he was in the tank. *The Black Rose Inn* and *Dead-End Motel.* Kent was a high-functioning alcoholic when I met him. He was accomplishing great things but was, well, terribly broken, as he said."

I nodded. "I appreciate your honesty."

"It's nothing that hasn't been published in interviews." Martha rubbed her hands together. "It's cold out here."

"And he's barefoot."

"He probably doesn't even notice. When crisis hits, Kent storms off, and I make tea. Come join me. I'll try to answer your questions, and I'd like to go over your time frame so that I can prepare Kent for what's to come."

As I fell into step beside her, I wondered if the task was truly so simple, as if she were helping her husband rehearse a speech or research a Ming vase. Granted, Lucy was not Martha's daughter, but they had lived as a family for many years. Perhaps a dysfunctional family, but no one was perfect. Inside the house, I followed her to the kitchen just beyond the great room, a cross between woodsy cabin and modern chic. The dark cabinets were reflected on the shiny floor and quartz countertops that had pin dots of sparkly stone in them, like embedded jewels. Elegant and icy. The oversized windows looked out over flat garden beds and a greenhouse.

"You have your own gardens."

"We'd like to do farm-to-table, but I don't have a green thumb."

As evidenced by the leggy, brown beds. Even for October, her garden seemed long dead. "Do you enjoy gardening?" I asked.

"I do. So I'll continue moving dirt around and hoping for the best. What kind of tea would you like?" she asked, setting a surprisingly traditional china teapot onto a tray. "I have Genmaicha and Hojicha."

Two popular types of Japanese green tea. Martha Jameson knew her teas. I didn't have the heart to tell her I was a coffee drinker. "How about some Earl Grey?"

"Perfect. I have that new 212 brew from a local tea maker. Have a seat. Juana said you arrived a while ago. Have you had a chance to talk with my staff?"

"I have. When I spoke with Andy Greenleaf, I noticed that there are a few other people working out at the barn. I was wondering why you didn't mention them last night."

"Day laborers." She filled the teapot from an instant-hot water spout. "I don't even know them. Andy hires people in need. It was actually Kent's idea. He wants to help people directly, but he doesn't have the time and he's not a big fan of the limelight. Kent says it's our duty to feed them and offer them work. But the rules are that they never cross over to this side of the estate."

"Where does Andy find them?"

"Here and there. Some of them are passing through. Some come out from the missions in Portland because they want the work and the break from city grime."

"And you're okay with that?" It seemed to contradict what I'd heard from Carlos about her fear of intruders.

"My husband insists on it. Kent and I have a tradition of giving back to the community."

"A very generous one," I added. "You've helped our town in many ways."

"We try." She put a teacup in front of me and poured the steaming liquid through the sifter. "We always hope that people in the community embrace our sense of charity and pay it forward. Everyone can give back in gestures large and small. It's not only about giving away money. It's about believing in people, nurturing people." She poured a cup for herself. "Milk and sugar? Lemon?"

"No, thanks. This is wonderful." The tang of citrus permeated my sinuses.

"The bergamot really shines through. That's so important in an Earl Grey."

I didn't think the nuances of tea mattered

much when the teenage girl who had lived in this house was probably on a slab at the morgue, but I shouldn't judge. Everyone handled grief differently. Perhaps denial was Martha's coping mechanism.

"Where were we?" She took the seat beside me and studied her tea. "Charity. I guess random acts of kindness are important to me because I grew up with nothing. Trailer trash. That's what the kids called me in middle school. Children can be cruel and brutally honest."

"You've seen much success, but you still remember your roots."

"There's a part of me that's still a frightened kid from Medford. That's why I like to surround myself with people I can help. My assistant, Talitha, was just days away from being deported with her son. Her husband had already been sent back to Iran. Kent and I hired a lawyer who knew how to navigate immigration matters. Then there's Carlos, our groundskeeper. A good man, big family. He was dying when we first hired him for some small repairs. His kidneys were failing. The doctors said that only a transplant would save him."

I squinted as I put down the teacup. "And you made that happen?"

Martha smiled. "Kent and I found him one of the country's top nephrologists. Got him onto the transplant list. Within days of the surgery, he was a new man. It's been three years since the surgery, and Carlos takes great care of our place."

But not such good care of his kidney, if the DUI report from two years ago had anything to say about it.

"I don't know what we would do without him."

The Jamesons might have to learn how to do without Carlos if the man kept drinking. In my interview with Carlos, he had seemed sober, and I hoped that DUI was simply an isolated incident. Alcohol use didn't mix well with kidney disease. But I kept mum; Martha was on a roll.

"And then there's Andy. We found him when he was living in a tent in Stafford Woods, out of work and homeless. The courts gave him a tough break with that sex offender status."

"Even so, it's hard to imagine parents with a young girl hiring a convicted sex offender."

"Well, there's where we differ. The first time I laid eyes on him, I saw a lost young man with a special spark inside. He was camped out in the woods and came across one of our fillies that had gotten loose. He brought her in, and right away, I saw that he had a way with horses. He'd spent a few summers on a ranch out in central Oregon. Quite a horseman, and handy, too. I made him promise to follow the rules of his probation, and he has obliged."

"Did he ever seem interested in Lucy?" I asked. "She is seventeen now."

"Not at all. He has a girlfriend, been together a while now. Poor guy. Andy has a youthful look, but he's pushing thirty, and his relationships are still under a microscope for dating a girl from high school. Really, he was just a kid when it happened, and when his parents threw him out and he lost his job, where could he turn? No one wanted to go near a sex offender, no matter what the details of his case were. We gave him a chance, and he has more than proven himself."

"He was fortunate to find someone like you and Mr. Jameson."

"Andy Greenleaf needed help, just like any person in crisis." With a nurturing smile, Martha passed a plate of cookies. "I've always believed that if you love and support someone, they'll go on to do great things. Like the flowers and plants in my garden. If you give them water and sunshine, good soil and a little space, they grow. It's that simple."

Except that Martha Jameson's gardens were dead.

"Has Lucy borne out this theory?"

"Not quite, but then, she's young still. Well"— she winced—"she *was* young. It's beginning to sink in now. She's probably gone, and that's destroying my husband. He's always adored her."

It wasn't hard to believe that Kent Jameson loved his daughter, though it was difficult to imagine Lucy living here on this wooded compound, in luxurious surroundings that for the most part seemed to be sealed tight. That spritelike teenage girl with Goth eyeliner and a pixie haircut would be out of place sleeping in a twin bed across from a dozen stuffed animals. Swimming in that pristine pool. Laughing over a game of Ping-Pong in the stale clubhouse. Where exactly did Lucy fit into all this?

"Did Lucy like living here?" I asked as my cell phone buzzed. I ignored it, determined to give Martha free rein; this one was a talker.

"At times. She was a typical teenage girl in some ways. Some days she loved her home, her dad, her horses. Other times, she hated her father, me, the state of Oregon, the rain, the materialistic culture of the United States. She kept asking us to send her backpacking in Europe, but she would have been such an easy target. Pampered and naïve. It wouldn't have been safe."

After a final sip, I lowered my teacup gently. "Thanks for the tea. This is a nice ritual." Outside the windows, the day had shifted, and the sky beyond the peaks of the tall Douglas firs was pasty gray, the color of pending rain. Another buzz from my pocket. Still, I didn't want to break the mood. "Did Lucy enjoy having tea with you on days like this?" I asked.

"Sometimes. But you know how kids are with their authority figures. Do you have tea with your mother?"

"Not too often," I admitted, thinking of the many ways I tried to avoid my mother's nitpicking. "But back to Lucy. What about friends?"

"There was always some friend or another hanging around."

"Who would you say was her best friend?"

"You need to ask Kent. I learned to stay out of Lucy's business. Whenever I tried to be a surrogate parent, she cut me off at the knees."

"You must remember someone."

"Why would I? Those conniving little brats drove me crazy. They would keep me up all night, blasting music or talking in her room. Useless kittens."

"Why didn't they use the game room or one of the guest cabins?"

"Lucy and her friends couldn't be trusted. The only thing you could count on them for was to make noise and leave a trail of debris wherever they went."

I wasn't surprised by her rancor toward Lucy, though I hadn't expected her to be so open about it when we were investigating Lucy's death. I tried to picture Martha with her blonde bob and perfect eyebrows reaching into the engine of the Karmann Ghia to cut the brake line. The motive was there, though I wondered if Martha would know what she was looking at inside an engine. Then again, there was probably some online tutorial that showed how to cut the brake line in an old car.

"We found some indication that Lucy had a boyfriend," I said, careful not to give away any specifics. "Do you know who he was?"

"Not a clue. Believe me, I would have pushed her into the fella's arms if she'd brought him around."

"You sound quite fed up."

"I am, though I know Kent and I are partly to blame for her failures. She took nothing seriously, and why should she? I'm afraid we've spoiled our Lucy girl. When she stopped going to her tutors and announced that she was dropping her online classes, Kent felt that he couldn't stop her, and I knew not to step in. Believe me, I've had to sit on my hands and keep quiet while Kent gave her whatever she wanted. A little whining and pouting and she got her way. He can't say no to her. So he let her sleep all morning and ride horses in the afternoon. He let her hang with kids who were clearly bad influences. He let her drop out of school and life. And you know what? Lucy was never happy with what we gave her. It was never enough."

I thought of my younger sister, of her secret nights out and her loud group of party girls. Would Hannah slide down like Lucy if our parents weren't always poking and prodding us toward success, achievement, accomplishment?

When my cell phone buzzed for the third time, I knew I'd better answer. "I'm so sorry but I have to take a call," I said, rising from the table and striding toward the great room. I expected to see that the call was from the precinct or my mother.

Instead, it was the medical examiner, Dr. Viloria. I strode toward the wall of glass and answered.

"Mori, I think you and your supervisor need to get over here, ASAP."

I blinked. "Is something wrong?"

"Science is never wrong, but in this case, the truth is going to ruffle a few feathers."

She sounded like a bad fortune-teller. "What, exactly, are you saying?"

"We ID'd the driver, and it was not Lucy Jameson."

That was good news . . . and a little surprising. "Are you sure?"

"That part I'm sure of. You can inform the family that the deceased was not their daughter."

"Wow. Okay." Hardly a brilliant response, but my thoughts were racing ahead. The Jamesons would be so relieved. Their trauma was over.

But it was their car that crashed.

If Lucy wasn't driving, who was?

And where the hell had Lucy been for the last day?

"There's more." Dr. Viloria's voice brought me back to earth. The Jameson house. The sounds of Martha moving behind me, shuffling feet, clinking china, running water. "We're still running tests, but it looks like the crash victim was a young woman named Kyra Miller. One of the Lost Girls."

—11—

The smell of wood smoke hung in the air as Lucy poked at the small fire with a stick. When she first started hanging with the Prince and the urchins, she wondered why they always had fires going, day and night. Now having spent a few solid days camping out with them in Stafford Forest, she understood the cold. Bone-deep and chilling, it settled in and clung to you until you went on a wild running streak or worked up a sweat chopping wood. Which she'd done, like, once in her life when the Prince had dared her to get off her ass.

Across the fire, the Prince looked up from the stone where he was sharpening his knife. Poised there on one knee, a dark jumble of curls falling over one dark eye, he was staring.

She glanced up to see what had caught his attention, but his eyes were on her. "You're so beautiful."

Hiding a smile, she reached up to brush her short, dark hair over her ear. Her pixie cut had been intended to diffuse her beauty, all that feminine energy that scraped at guys' libidos, reducing them to animals. But the Prince had vision; he could see through the mask.

Then again, anyone who lived with a cluster of unbathed urchins would need to have a second sight to see past the odors and the grime. "I just look good to you because I had a shower yesterday," she said.

"Maybe. You smell better than the rest. But don't tell True I said that."

"Why. Is she your girlfriend now?" Lucy couldn't keep the scorn from her voice, and she hoped he didn't realize she was jealous. Sort of. "That's such a stupid thing, girlfriends and boyfriends."

"So . . . what then? What's the alternative?" he asked.

"I don't like labels, and I don't believe in love." It wasn't completely true, but sometimes she felt that way. "People aren't really capable of being that selfless."

"You adorable nihilist," he said.

"Don't be condescending. What do you believe?"

The Prince rose and slid the knife into a sheath on his belt. "I believe in free love," he proclaimed. "Love everyone equally."

"Sounds good to me. Want to give me some of that free love?"

"Sure thing. Come on over here."

He was teasing her—she knew that—and yet, for a second, there was a wash of warmth at the prospect of kissing him, touching him, feeling the rough bristle of his beard against her body, his calloused fingertips on her skin. She wanted to command that sort of attention from him, but not because she loved him. She wanted him because he was the leader, because he was older and mysterious. Because he had power. He had the keys to the truck that held the supplies and food. He had the juju to keep the others in control. She knew she held some sway over him, but he was the one in charge, meting out orders and punishments.

She served the Prince—everyone here did— and already she'd carried out a few of his orders that didn't sit well with her. Things that made her want to cry at the time. Things he called "necessary," though they seemed wrong to her.

But those raw moments lessened with time. Besides, he didn't order her around every day. The Prince gave most of the jobs to True, who did anything he asked because she was totally into him. True tried to hide it, but she was definitely interested. Oh, God, for all Lucy knew, they might have been hooking up whenever Lucy went home, but she didn't think so. You could never tell with the Prince, but clearly, he hadn't chosen his princess yet.

"We could get it going right here and now,"

Lucy said, poking at the fire, "but I don't think you're ready for me."

The Prince lifted his chin and smiled down at her. "No?" He wasn't a tall guy, but he was built, solid and strong. That's what hiking and mountain climbing and survival shit did to a body.

"Not feeling it," she lied.

"Seriously?" He moved closer to the fire and sat down. "Probably all for the best. The girls will be back soon."

"Are they getting food?" Lucy asked. "There's nothing good left and I'm starving."

"The church pantry isn't open today. They're collecting water from the rain catchers."

Lucy wished the girls were off getting food at the local church—one of their regular chores. It was hard for Light to make the walk, five miles there and back, but they liked to bring her along because her skinny frame and pale complexion tore at the nuns' hearts. There'd be peanut butter and canned tuna and thick, salty beef stew when Light went along. Of the four, Light was really the only one who was nice to Lucy. The others—True, Pax, and Light's older sister, Melody—those three resented Lucy's presence at the camp. On the other hand, Lucy knew she had allies in Wolf and Eden, who worked at her father's ranch. Yeah, it was hard work, shoveling up the hill of beans the alpacas produced and grooming and feeding the horses, but they owed her for the setup. They would never cross her.

"And we're going to need more firewood," the Prince added.

"Just chop a tree down."

"Lucky Lucy. You can run home to the safe lap of luxury while the rest of us forage for food and firewood. Have you made a convert out of Blossom yet? Is she going to play the game and get your old man to send her off to some trade school? Step into the money pond the way Genesis and Clarity did?" Genesis and Clarity were the Prince's names for two urchins who had traveled with the Prince's clan for a while. The Prince had names for everyone; it was one of his things.

"Those mercenary bitches," he went on. "Be nice to the big author and he'll set you up for life."

"Don't give me your anticapitalist bullshit," she said. "You take stuff from him, too."

"Yeah, but I don't suck up for it. I don't suck up to anyone."

They were interrupted by a bird call—Guardian's signal—from beyond the ridge. Guardian was standing watch. Always standing watch. Lucy suspected that the tall, dark-skinned dude just liked being alone. One of those hermit types.

"Someone's coming." The Prince was on his feet. "Not the girls. Wolf?" He nodded at the young man coming over the rise. "You're back early. Did you get fired?"

Wolf looked spooked, his eyes wild, his mouth

170

strained. "I asked for time off to find Lucy, and Andy just told me to go. It's bad. The cops are at the ranch, and they're closing in on Andy. Only you can save him, Lucy. You gotta get back there and show them you're alive."

Lucy squinted at him. "What the hell are you talking about?"

"The cops think Andy killed you. There was a car crash last night, a really bad one, and the driver died. This lady cop was talking about how you and Andy had a fight and you took off in the car. They think Andy is responsible for the crash. It was one of your father's cars. That little one."

"And they think I'm dead? Wait, wait! They think Andy killed me?" Lucy let out a squeal. "Oh, my God, that's hysterical." She laughed again.

"Not so funny for Andy." Wolf wasn't laughing. "He's going to jail if you don't get over there. He's real upset. Might get fired. And if he goes, I'm out of a job. Eden will be fired, too."

"Daddy won't fire Andy or anyone else." Lucy brushed off his concerns; Wolf could be such a fatalist. "Just chill while this blows over."

"Yeah, let's think about this," the Prince said. "We know that Lucy is still in the realm of the living. So that leaves the question of the driver. Who died in the crash?"

Lucy clapped her hands together in prayer position. "Please, God, let it be Martha."

Wolf shook his head. "No. Martha's fine. We know who was driving. There was only one other woman who was at the ranch last night. You old us she wanted to stay when you tore out of there."

The realization stabbed at her chest. "It can't be. Blossom?"

Wolf nodded somberly.

"No. You're wrong," Lucy protested.

"I sneaked over to the house to look for her." He shook his head. "She's gone. She was in that car. Maybe stealing it? I don't know. She's gone. I just know—I can feel it in my gut."

In that moment, Lucy knew Wolf was right. No need to steal the car; Blossom had been handed the keys plenty of times, sometimes by Lucy herself. A whimper escaped her throat at the unfairness of it all. Another lost friend. She curled up, hugging her knees, watching as the Prince strode over to the stump, lifted the ax, and hacked away at a log. Chips flew as he grunted and pounded repeatedly.

In the stillness that followed, Lucy's mind churned. If the cops thought Lucy was dead, did her father believe that, too? If Blossom had crashed the car, then why were they blaming Andy? Had they caught him perving around with her? If the cops searched the ranch, would they find their way out here to the camp?

"I can't believe she's gone." The Prince tipped

his head forward so that dark curls masked his eyes. "I never thought I'd see Blossom again. She was free to leave. But I didn't think she'd get herself killed."

"Same," Wolf said in a dull voice.

"If the cops are coming around, we need to be careful." The Prince rubbed his chin. "You need to go back, Lucy. Let everyone know you're alive. That will smooth things over, at least for your father. And Andy."

"Andy's a big dork," Lucy said. "Did you know he raped a girl?"

"That's not what really happened," Wolf said. "I talked to him, and it was his girlfriend, only she was—"

"That's his side of the story." Lucy sat up and poked the fire once again. "Maybe he hooked up with Blossom. You never know."

"But he didn't kill you," the Prince said. "Go back and make that clear."

"But I don't want to go back." The last thing she needed was to walk into a media circus—more hype for the brilliant writer and his charming wife, while she would get dumped on. "Not yet."

"Come on. We could use some more of Juana's cooking," Prince said. "When the food is good, everyone's happier around here."

"Nope." Lucy stood her ground. "Not doing it."

"Then at least clear Andy's name." Wolf had a way of holding onto an argument like a dog with a bone. Right now it was pissing Lucy off. "Talk to someone in the media. There's this chick from one of the news stations who wants to meet you. Natalie Amichi from KATY News. She's real nice."

"There you go," the Prince said. "You can talk to her. Save Andy's ass and get your face on TV. Be a celebrity. Go home, Lucy."

"I don't want to answer a bunch of questions for some reporter," Lucy snapped. "Why don't you do it?"

"Maybe I will. The real question is when are you going home?"

"Not now, so get it out of your head." Lucy wasn't convinced this was the right time to go home. She wasn't going to face the mess there just to score some food and money for this pathetic group. "I like the idea of my father and Martha stewing for a while." They could suffer through the attention. Let them suffer.

—12—

I ended the call with Dr. Viloria and took a breath as I turned toward Martha Jameson. "Good news," I said. "I'll need to speak with your husband about this, too."

Her brows lifted as she placed a small wrought-iron teapot on the granite counter. "About Lucy?"

When I nodded, she gave a gentle sigh of relief and texted her husband. I don't know what she wrote, but it brought him running toward the house a minute later. His hair was still wild, but the coloring in his face had returned to normal and there was a mellow look of compassion in his eyes. Maybe he'd passed out and finally gotten some rest.

"Mr. Jameson . . ." I pressed my hands to my heart. "I'm happy to tell you that Lucy wasn't driving that car. Early results are in at the lab, and the woman who died in the crash was not your daughter."

He spread his arms wide and opened his mouth, staring at me with tears in his eyes. "Thank you. Oh, thank God." He stepped closer and put his hands on my shoulders. "Thank you so much for taking care of us. When I snapped before, it was . . ."

"I understand," I said.

He squeezed my right shoulder and then turned to his wife. "Martha, our girl is okay."

She nodded and then flew into his arms like a young bride. "I'm so relieved," she said, resting her head on his shoulder.

I looked away from their sweet embrace, a bit tentative about their complete relief. Just because Lucy hadn't been driving the Karmann Ghia didn't mean that she had made it through the night unscathed. She was still missing from the ranch.

And yet, they seemed to assume she was fine.

"I understand your relief," I said, "but there's still some concern for Lucy's welfare. She disappeared around the time of the crash, and no one has seen her since. I want to issue an AMBER Alert."

Martha patted her husband's shoulder and eased out of his embrace. "I know it sounds bad, but it's not unusual for Lucy to disappear for a day or two. Whenever things go wrong, Lucy takes off. Escape is her coping mechanism, I guess."

I kept my teeth set to keep the obvious retort from flying out: *You could have told me that last night.*

"Yes," Kent agreed with a sigh, "our Lucy is quite the escape artist."

"As you used to be," Martha said, looking up at her husband.

"Until I met you."

"But where does she go?" I asked, trying to bring these two back to reality.

"Lucy has . . . *friends,* for lack of a better word." Kent shrugged. "I can't say that I approve of them, and there's really no way to contact them, but it is what it is. Worry no more! Our girl will return home soon."

"She'll turn up when she's ready," Martha said, dismissing any concerns. "I'm just utterly relieved to know that she wasn't in the car."

To me it felt like a hollow victory, but the Jamesons seemed to be satisfied. "So the search of Stafford Woods will go on as planned?" I asked, thrown off by their utter confidence that Lucy was okay.

"Of course," Kent said. "We'd love to have our girl back."

I nodded, waiting for the inevitable question: if Lucy wasn't driving the car, then who was?

But it never came.

The Jamesons shared a few hugs, and then Martha went to the kitchen to brew a celebratory pot of tea while Kent called his agent in New York.

"Skeeter has known Lucy since she was a little girl," Kent explained to me as he tapped his cell phone. "He's been waiting this out with me, hour by hour. He's going to be so relieved."

"Ask him if he's heard from Twilight House," Martha said.

"I will." A glimmer of pride was in his eyes. "Martha has a book proposal in at Twilight. Isn't that fabulous? Looks like we'll have two authors in the house soon."

I nodded and smiled.

"Sweetheart, that's only if they buy it," Martha called from the kitchen.

"Of course they will." He turned away as his connection went through. "Yes . . . Skeeter, it wasn't her! Lucy wasn't driving the car. She's okay!"

How do you know that? I wondered. But even if the Jamesons asked, I couldn't reveal the identity of the driver until the next of kin had been notified.

Declining Martha's offer of tea, I let myself out of the lodge-like building to make the drive to the morgue.

—13—

I walked into the morgue with a sense of purpose. The smells faded to the background, and the creepy feeling fell away in my eagerness to scoop up new information from Dr. Viloria. I found her inside the lab, speaking with Omak.

"Right off the bat, when I compared the hair from our Jane Doe to a sample from the brush you brought in, it was clear that the dead girl was not Lucy Jameson. The corpse had Afro-textured hair. Under the microscope, the pigment granules are larger, and the pigment is denser than Caucasian hair." Dr. Viloria stepped back, allowing Lt. Omak and me a look through the microscopes set up on the counter.

"That first one is Kyra Miller, who is of mixed race. Her father is Greek and her mother is African American. The other sample is from Lucy, we think. It was also on the hairbrush."

"You *think?*" I asked.

"Well, it turns out that hairs from two different people were on the brush. They must have shared it. Anyway, I was confused by the hair samples at first, but then one seemed to be a match with our corpse. So I went to dental records." She moved over to a computer monitor and clicked open a file. White chips of teeth lined up in a semicircle against a field of black. "I'm not a forensic odonatologist, but it's easy to differentiate our corpse from Lucy. Lucy Jameson had braces in junior high, fairly good teeth. No major work." Dr. V switched to another screen. "Kyra broke two teeth in a fall down icy steps, so she had crowns on the upper right. Same spot as our Jane Doe. We're bringing in an expert for final analysis, and we'll run the DNA match, which will take a while, but at this point, that's a formality. Our Jane Doe is Kyra Miller."

"One of the Lost Girls." The image of Emma's tearful parents turned over in my mind as I turned to Dr. V. "I understand how you ruled Lucy out, but how did you connect Jane Doe to Kyra if there was no fingerprint match?"

"I went scrolling through the missing persons database and something sparked my memory about those Lost Girls. I found out no prints existed for Kyra, but they have dental records for all the girls. When I saw those crowns on the upper right, I started looking for more. They seem to match."

"I'm impressed, Blanca." Lt. Omak nodded. A gush of approval for him.

"We need to notify Kyra's next of kin."

"Right. Family first, and then the media." Omak turned to me. "You didn't mention Kyra's ID to the Jamesons?"

"No. I held back, and actually, they didn't ask. Isn't that strange? I understand their relief that the dead girl wasn't Lucy. They kept hugging each other and thanking me. But they never asked who might have been driving the sports car, and they didn't seem worried that their daughter is still missing."

"It will be interesting to note their reaction when they learn that Kyra Miller was driving their car. I'd say they've been withholding information," Omak said. "They had to know Kyra Miller for her to have access to the car."

"With her hairs entwined on Lucy's brush?" Dr. Viloria squinted. "I'd say the parents saw this girl around the house. Probably served her pancakes on Sunday morning."

"But they didn't mention her. Didn't suggest her as a possible driver of the car." Omak tapped his fists together. "So they were holding back. Or distracted by relief."

Looking back, I wondered if Kent Jameson's tears were true trauma or drama.

"So let's look at what we have," Omak said. "Frame it up, Mori."

"We know that the brake lines on the car were cut. That the victim had drugs in her system." I turned to Dr. V. "Do we know what she took?"

"We'll have a detailed drug analysis in a few days." She pointed a thumb toward the door. "I need to get back to work, so I'm giving you two the boot."

Omak gave half a smile. "I've been thrown out of worse places."

"I'll bet," Viloria said, holding the door for us.

I continued as we walked down the hall. "We know that Kyra Miller had sex with someone— consensual, we think. Though her records indicate she was only fifteen, not of consenting age. For some reason, Kyra Miller was compelled to get in that car. Trying to find someone? Stealing the car? Trying to escape? But there were drugs in her system, and the brakes were giving out. She lost control and died."

"Anything interesting crop up at the Jameson compound?"

"I found a parking pad with puddles of viscous fluid near the garage at the Jameson compound, and the groundskeeper told me he'd seen the car parked there yesterday. I just dropped off some samples at the lab to see if it might be hydraulic fluid."

That got Omak's attention. "So it appears that the brakes were cut at the Jameson compound."

I nodded. "We still don't know when, and we

don't know what compelled Kyra Miller to drive off in that sports car last night."

"What was your take on the registered sex offender?"

"Andy Greenleaf seemed earnest but a little creepy. Kind of stuck on himself. He denied having a relationship with Lucy, but of course, I didn't ask about Kyra."

"I sent Frazier out to check Greenleaf's alibi—the girlfriend," Omak replied. "I've asked Frazier to work with you on the case. Right now there are too many leads for one person to track down."

I nodded, wondering how that would play out, working with Frazier. He had more experience—a good five years—which might make him tend toward bossy. He was also being avoided by a lot of cops who considered him to be a whistle-blower. I had nothing against the guy, but I wasn't crazy about the idea of sharing my case.

After leaving the morgue, we picked up soups and salads, though Omak made me promise I wouldn't tell anyone he frequented a "stinking granola joint." He stuffed his salad into a brown paper bag, and we went back to the precinct so that Omak could work on something with the mayor and I could pick at the scab of the case a little more.

I settled into my desk, grateful for some alone time to reboot and rethink everything. Tuning out the phone chimes and voices of the squad room, I sipped carrot ginger soup and made a list of people who might have been present at the compound the night that Kyra left in that car.

Who had set her up for disaster?

Maybe it was Carlos the handyman, upset because she'd caught him drinking again?

Or Andy, who could have taken on a girlfriend as a cover while he continued to pursue teenage girls. Or the mysterious Lucy, who had disappeared around the time of the crash. And finally Kent or Martha for reasons currently unknown.

Professor Plum. In the parlor. With a wrench.

It was ludicrous to guess without more information. A trip back to the Jameson ranch was definitely in my future. Omak wanted to bring out a couple of units and do a wide sweep of the area, talk to neighbors, and step up the investigation at the compound.

I went to the Lost Girls database for a profile of Kyra Miller. Fifteen years old, from foster care in Salem. Dad was out of the picture, and Mom was an alcoholic who had lost custody of both daughters. At thirteen Kyra began leaving her foster home to try to find her mother. A little over a year ago, when Latitia Miller died of a drug overdose, Kyra landed in Portland, panhandling in Pioneer Courthouse Square. In her photos, there was a shy grace, that teen self-consciousness as she looked away from the camera, her lips curved in a hopeful smile. In some photos, her hair was in cornrows; in others, it was straightened and short. Her tan skin was not dark enough to cover the smattering of freckles across her nose. Cute kid. Still a kid.

"How do we notify your next of kin?" I asked softly.

I called Brook Eastern, the Salem caseworker listed in the file. She seemed surprised to be hearing from me. "Really? You found Kyra?" When I told her how, the spirit drained from her voice. "Poor Kyra. Poor baby. Well, she's with her mother now. That was what she . . ." Her voice broke. "What she always wanted."

Brook would make the necessary notifications to state agencies. "But honestly," she said. "I don't think there's any next of kin to notify for Kyra. That was a big part of her problem. Her mom, Latitia, was unable to care for her, so the kid spent most of the last decade in foster care, and she was fed up. She headed to Portland, as so many of them do, and that was the last we heard from her. When the Duprees contacted me about including her information in the Lost Girls database, I was glad to see someone dusting off the case. But I'd hoped for a much happier ending for Kyra."

I thanked Brook for her help and invited her to call if she learned anything of Kyra's whereabouts the past few months of her life. As we hung up, I imagined Kyra's case dropping from the system, like a pushpin being plucked from a crowded map of pushpins. One down, a few thousand to go.

"Kyra Miller," I muttered under my breath, "tell me who you were." I clicked through Kyra's files on the database. The Duprees had wisely posted every shred of material they could get their hands on. There was even a file that showed pictures she'd drawn as a kid and letters to her mother. Heart-rending letters. When I clicked on the most recent note, I was stopped short.

The handwriting, so childlike, almost printing, with the capital K in her name containing a loop in the center and each capital A shaped like a star. So familiar.

I'd been an idiot.

I went to the pages from Lucy's diary that had been scanned into the computer. Wrong. Not Lucy's diary, but Kyra's.

Each big, starry capital A jumped off the page now. The unsophisticated print, the tendency to turn letters into stars. It was a match.

Which put a new light on Andy Greenleaf. He hadn't been lying when he said he had no involvement with Lucy Jameson. He had left the boss's daughter alone.

But I had never asked him about Kyra Miller.

—14—

"If Andy Greenleaf is A, he's probably going to see jail time just for his involvement with Kyra Miller. That's not even assuming that he caused her death tampering with the brakes and drugging her." Omak scrolled through the samples of handwriting from the journal that I had posted side by side with documents from Kyra Miller's file. "Big A. Kyra Miller was smitten with him."

"But it's still not conclusive," I said. "And even if Kyra was having a relationship with Andy, that doesn't mean he drugged her and cut the brake lines."

"Well, with this diary pointing to A, along with Andy Greenleaf's history as a registered sex offender, I'd say we have probable cause."

"Did Andy have the means, motive, and opportunity to kill Kyra?" I posed the question. "Means and opportunity, yes. But motive?"

"If he was having relations with an underage girl and things went bad, he would have wanted to shut her up so she couldn't turn him in to the authorities. But let's wait and see if he's got an alibi for last night. Frazier texted me that he's talking with the girlfriend and her parents." Omak rose and paced behind me. "If Greenleaf doesn't have an alibi, we'll bring him in. The DA may want to charge him."

The case was moving swiftly, faster than I had expected, and I felt a thrill at the prospect that it could be all wrapped up within twenty-four hours of the crime.

The lieutenant checked his watch. "If the DA thinks the charges will stick, I hope she makes a move before the dinner-hour press conference. People are always reassured to hear that we've got someone in custody."

"Wait . . . another press conference?"

"The mayor wants transparency, and it's not a bad idea." Omak lowered his voice, looking around as he spoke. "This department has been a cloak-and-dagger organization for too long. But the worst of it was before your time, Mori. Lucky you."

"What exactly was going on behind the scenes?" I asked. "Are we talking failure to follow procedure or actual corruption?"

"We don't have the time to get into it now."

"Wait." I checked the squad room—no one seemed to be paying attention to us. "And it's still going on?"

"Some other time," Omak said firmly. "Right now I want to be sure we've got everything covered on the Miller case. I dispatched our available patrol officers to canvas the Stafford Woods area, find out what the neighbors knew about Kyra Miller or if they'd heard anything unusual going on at the Jameson compound over the past few days."

I nodded. It was standard procedure, except that our crime scene for Kyra Miller's death was beginning to spread out through Stafford Woods.

"And I want to know if the neighbors have had any run-ins with the homeless campers in the area. It's hard to believe that sort of thing might have been going on for months and no one has filed a complaint."

"The state park is on a big parcel of land. Anyone camping back there could easily keep out of sight of the neighbors."

Omak squinted, skeptical. "For months?"

"Stealthy squatters," I suggested.

We were interrupted when my cell rang. "It's Frazier." Probably with information about Heather Erickson. "I'd better take this."

It turned out that Frazier was having trouble getting Heather to talk. "She says she was with Andy, but that's all she's saying. Her parents keep pushing her, but whenever I ask her a question, she just bursts into tears. Am I that scary?"

"You big bully," I teased. "Do you want me to talk with her? The female thing might work to my advantage, and I can be warm and fuzzy."

"Good point. Let me make the offer and I'll see what she says. Call you back."

While Omak took a different call, I opened up the database for the Lost Girls and called the number listed there. Maybe it was wrong to call before the information was released to the general public, but the strained voices and worried faces of Thomas and Louise Dupree had left a lasting impression. They deserved to know that one of the Lost Girls had been found.

"This is Officer Laura Mori calling from the Sunrise River Police Department," I said, trying to roll as much out before I lost my nerve. "We thought you would want to know that we've recovered the body of one the Lost Girls listed on your database."

"Is it . . . ? Not Emma."

"No, it was Kyra Miller," I said.

There was an awkward pause as Louise's voice gave a whimper and then quickly recovered to ask me what had happened. I gave her some of the details and asked that she not share the information until after it was announced at our press conference tonight. "This is an open investigation," I said.

"Of course. Thomas and I won't say a thing until it becomes public information."

"But I wanted you to be one of the first to know. Your database is so conclusive; it's been very helpful to us in this case." I wanted to add that I admired her courage, but I was afraid that would sound trite in light of the campaign she and her husband were waging to recover their daughter.

"Officer Mori, should we come back to Sunrise Lake? My husband and I could meet with you to discuss Emma's case."

My eyes swept over the busy squad room, a slight panic surging up as I imagined the Duprees landing at my desk. "I'd be happy to meet with you," I said, worried that I had stepped into the muck, "but I'm not in the Missing Persons Squad. I'm just saying, I can't make any promises."

"I understand completely." She thanked me for calling and told me she would set up a meeting the next time she and her husband were in the Portland area.

With a heavy heart, I hung up and delved into Greenleaf's file from the parole division. I made a few calls, trying to track down people from his past. I spoke with a former minister who remembered Andy as a good kid who'd fallen through the cracks of the system. I tried to reach his parents, but the phone line had been disconnected. Most of all I wanted to talk with Ginnie, Andy's high school girlfriend and the alleged victim of statutory rape, to get her side of the story. Since she was a minor at the time of the incident, there was no contact information for her. I left a message for her parents at the number in the old case file. I was searching Ginnie, Ginny, and Virginia Walters on Facebook when Zion Frazier came in and perched on the empty desk next to me.

"You were right," he said casually. "Heather Erickson said she'll talk to a woman."

"Look at that. I have a gender advantage on the force."

"Probably won't be the last time," he said. "But that's not PC for me to say."

I gave a little smile. At least he was honest. "I can head over there now."

"No need. I got Heather and her parents coming in for an interview."

"No way."

"Coming right in. Heather was reluctant, but that's one of the down sides of living in your parents' basement. When they found out why I was there, they insisted she do the right thing. The parents are all religious. They're like, 'Lying is a sin, Daughter.' So I think Heather's going to be pretty square if you can get her to talk."

"That's great." I was impressed.

Frazier nodded. "That's them." He waved to two blonde women and a bald man and ushered them into the interview room. I went over to them and introduced myself. The Ericksons seemed stern, while their daughter dabbed at her eyes with a wad of tissues, still crying.

I patted Heather's arm and led the way to the interview room, grabbing a fresh box of tissues for the table.

"We want to come in, too," the mother said. I

told them they would have their chance after I spoke with Heather.

The girl was as wobbly as Jell-O. She jumped a bit when I closed the door behind me. She was a big girl squeezed into tight jeans and a blouse that gaped at her bra line. With gold hair down to her waist and smooth, pale skin, she could have been Andy's sister.

"You poor thing," I said. "I know this is hard, but I just have a few questions for you and then you can go."

"I know but . . . I don't want to say the wrong thing."

"You don't have anything to be nervous about if you tell the truth."

"I know, but . . ." That brought a fresh wave of tears. "I don't want to get Andy in trouble."

I decided to back off a bit. "Did you know Kyra Miller? From the Jameson ranch."

"I may have met her once or twice. I never paid much attention to the ranch workers. Andy says they're a royal pain. They're the reason he comes to my house. Andy doesn't like me at the ranch. It makes him nervous."

"Really? When your boyfriend has his own house in the country—a place that rivals any luxury rental cabin in the northwest? It seems like the perfect getaway for a young couple like you two."

"I was there a few times. I got to meet the

author and his wife and all. But Andy says it's not safe for a girl like me with those hobos wandering around in the woods."

The word *hobo* was comical, and I had to bite my lower lip to keep from smiling.

"So instead, Andy comes and hangs out in your parents' basement," I said.

"It's my room, and Andy likes it. He says it feels like home. We'll get our own place when I finish school, but for now, he hangs out at my house."

"Does he stay overnight?" I asked.

Her cheeks flushed pink. "Sometimes. He'll stay a few days, but my parents don't know. He comes in and out the basement door." She glanced toward the door to the squad room. "You don't have to tell them, do you?"

"I don't have to tell them. You're twenty-three years old."

And still afraid of your parents, I thought. I got that. Heather and I were in the same boat, except that she was getting steady sex in the basement, and I was still barely pursuing my high school crush.

Now that Heather was more relaxed, I pushed a little more. "Did you see Andy last night?"

"Yes. He was with me." She looked down at the table and started picking the cuticle of one thumb. "He got there around six and stayed overnight."

"What time did he leave?"

"Early this morning, around six thirty. He likes to get back early to shower in the cottage. Less evidence for my mom to find at my place."

"And you're sure he got there around six?"

She shrugged, looking toward the side wall. "I guess."

"What were you doing when he got there? Maybe watching TV? That might help us pinpoint the time."

Her face flushed pink and her eyes filled with tears again. "I don't know," she sobbed.

"Think about it, because this part is very important." I stayed calm, knowing the tears meant something. "Take your time."

"I don't know. I . . ."

I waited, the clock on the wall ticking off the seconds.

Heather sobbed again. "I don't remember, okay?"

It was not okay.

"So," I started, "there are two men standing on a hill when a cloud moves and the sun shines down on them. One man sees his shadow and shrieks in fear, thinking that all the bad choices he made in the past are catching up with him. He runs and runs, but he can't get away from his shadow."

Heather blotted her eyes and squinted at me. She was skeptical, but I had her attention.

"The other man sees his shadow and smiles in

delight. He thinks his shadow is an angel who has collected all the good things he has done in his life. He jumps for joy, and the shadow jumps with him. He jumps so high, he quickly reaches the top of the hill."

She sniffed. "Is that some Chinese proverb?"

"I'm Japanese, and it's just a story my father used to tell me. But sometimes, when I have choices to make, I ask myself, will I smile back at my shadow? Or will this choice send me running down the hill?"

Heather straightened and took a deep breath. "I wasn't home when he got there, okay? But after I got home, he was there with me all night long. And I know he didn't hurt that girl. He wouldn't."

"What time did you get home, Heather?"

"Around eight fifteen or eight twenty, I guess. I was at school—a chem class. I'm going for my med tech certification at the CC. Class ends at eight."

"And Andy was there when you got home?"

"Asleep on the couch. He does that all the time, comes over after work. He says he got to my place around six, let himself in. He's got a key. He fell asleep watching the news, and the next thing he knew, I was walking in the door."

"So you don't really know what time Andy arrived there."

She shook her head, dabbing at her eyes with a fresh tissue.

"Why did you lie to us?"

"When Andy called, he was so upset. I promised him I'd fudge the time for him. I don't want to get him in trouble."

Right now that was beyond her control. "Do you know if your parents saw him come in?"

She shrugged. "Probably not. There's a separate entrance to the basement around the side of the house."

After I'd finished talking with Heather, her parents wanted to be heard, too. Like two puffed-up birds, they sat, stern-faced, while Frazier and I went over the timeline from last evening with them. Heather was correct: they hadn't heard or seen Andy at all.

"Have you ever had any issues with Andy while he was dating your daughter?" I asked.

"We've trusted Andy Greenleaf," Liam Erickson said, his bold brows high on his forehead. "We have enjoyed his company and shared our home with him. Now we're apprised of his previous difficulties with the law, for which he's begged forgiveness. But if he's going down the wrong road, our faith will not allow us to keep company with him."

Frazier held up one hand, interrupting the lecture. "Just what are you saying, sir?"

"I'm on the church council, and my wife sings in the choir. We're steady, law-abiding citizens." The bald man's face was set in a stoic expression.

"We will not have our daughter dating a criminal."

"Dad, he didn't do anything wrong," Heather insisted. "Didn't you hear the detective? They're collecting evidence to clear him. It's a routine investigation."

"Is that true?" Liam asked.

"As of this moment, we have no charges against Andy Greenleaf," Frazier said.

I leaned back in my chair and glanced down under the table to see Frazier's left hand on his thigh. He was crossing his fingers.

With the cell pressed to his ear, Charlie Omak paced behind the closed door of his office, hating the airless, confined space. If he thought about it too much, he could feel his throat closing up, the light in his head exploding to superwhite as the IED rocked the armored vehicle, sucking the air out, sucking the life from the other soldiers. White to black, light to darkness.

You got lucky, everyone told him. Yeah. So lucky.

The others had gone home in body bags, but he had walked away with a scar, thirteen more months of deployment in Iraq, and an expanded vocabulary of terms. Improvised explosive device. Green Zone. Route Irish. Posttraumatic stress. Traumatic brain injury.

You got lucky.

Years of therapy had helped him see that it

was true. He was lucky to be alive, lucky to have a good life, a woman who loved him, a family, a job.

But still . . . the closed spaces could bring him back to that dusty road, the heat and grit and pain that could snap him back in an instant. The noise and smell, the alarm and fury. He had no choice but to breathe slowly, sweat it out, and keep pacing.

"Are you there?" asked the mayor.

"Yes, Ron. Sorry. My mind's scattered in a few different directions."

"Understandable. I know the situation up on the Jameson ranch is cracking open even as we speak."

"Yes, it is." Omak would rather have met with the mayor—a face-to-face was always better—but this investigation had to be kept confidential; Omak couldn't simply stroll into the mayor's office on Liberty Square, and it would cause a stir if the mayor walked into the precinct, let alone took a closed-door meeting in Omak's office. No, one-on-one was possible only during late hours, through back doors, in vacant parking lots. Hence the closed door, the stuffy office, the pacing.

"Do you have an update for me on the Jameson crash?" Ron asked.

"You know the driver was identified as a runaway girl, fifteen. We're checking on a possible suspect. I'll have more on that soon.

Right now, I need to know how much latitude I have with the Op-C investigation." The internal investigation—called Op-C for Operation: Corruption—had been Mayor Ron Redmond's brainchild, a way to sluice out bad cops from the inside. The secret nature of the operation appealed to the mayor because he wouldn't have to share details of police corruption with the media until the culprits were satisfactorily rooted out. It appealed to Omar because he saw it as his chance to delve into the mystery of his sister's death while on duty. "How far do you want this investigation to go?"

"Not sure I like the sound of that question," Redmond said. "Sounds like the wound is deep."

"Seems like."

The shorthand between them was more a matter of trust than camaraderie. Both men were former military, and though Omak didn't know Ron Redmond well, he'd served in Iraq with Redmond's son, Jacob.

"Are we talking highest level?" Redmond asked.

"Could be. I don't have time to go into detail, but it appears that Cribben is aware of at least some of this. Lazy cops. Cops on the take. Cops turning against each other. Cops who set up the whistleblower."

"And the chief of police. Are you telling me it goes that high?"

"It's pointing in that direction. We've got cops with special assignments to cover the Jamesons' neighborhood and squash complaints against them. The same cops always get assigned to respond when a resident dies alone." Omak had seen that bit of thievery back in Seattle; while waiting for the coroner, the cops stave off the family and pilfer the home, stealing any cash under the mattress or untraceable coins in the closet. "When I talked to the dispatcher, she said she has a standing order from the chief to put Brown and his partner on those cases."

Redmond let out a low growl, like an awakening bear, and Omak imagined his gray eyes, steely and magnified behind his glasses. He had the look of fruit drying on the vine, but there was spunk and gristle in that wiry old man. An inveterate runner, Redmond always placed when he ran half-marathons in the area. Yeah, he was a local treasure. Omak knew he wouldn't be serving on the Sunrise Lake Police Department if Redmond hadn't invited him to come investigate and, in the process, given him the opportunity to find out the truth behind his sister's death three years ago.

The official story was that Officer Franny Omak Landon had been shot and killed walking into the scene of a bank robbery. The notorious Twilight Bandit had been hitting locations around town, and Omak understood his sister's eagerness to stop the thief. Some said she was overzealous and careless. Others pointed out that the dispatcher had told her backup was on the scene, when in fact, two other units were a block away. Other discrepancies in the case had suggested that Franny had been set up by her fellow cops sworn to protect and serve.

When all this was coming to light during the preliminary investigation, the cover-up began. The dispatchers' recordings went missing. Officers' personal logbooks were reportedly stolen from their lockers. The roll call from that shift was still intact; there was a record of every cop on duty. But all records of the squad cars' assignments and locations had vanished. The weasels had covered their tracks.

His sister had been hung out to dry, and the dirty cops thought they were free and clear. But Omak would never forget. He'd been trying to get information about his sister's death and stewing over the suspicious details when Ron Redmond had reached out to him. Redmond sensed corruption in Sunrise Lake's police department, but the guilty had eluded detection, and the cover-up was fueled by camaraderie that ran deep in the department.

"Why don't you come on board here," the mayor had suggested. "Work in the department. Try to shake the vermin loose from the inside?"

Omak couldn't say no. He'd moved his family

to Sunrise Lake and dug in for the long haul. He was determined to find the cops who'd abandoned his sister, determined to make them pay.

"These cops on special assignment," Redmond said, jarring Omak back to the present. "Are these the same players you've been watching? These cops were on the job with Franny?"

"The same crew. Five- and six-year veterans. But culpability is pointing to administrators now."

Redmond gave a low groan. "It's going to get ugly, but we can't put blinders on. When you've got a cancer, you have to cut the diseased tissue out. All of it. Only a half-assed surgeon would leave a few tumors behind."

"Okay, then." Omak opened his office door, grateful for the curl of fresh air. "I'll go where the trail leads."

"That's right," the mayor said. "Take it all the way to the top."

—15—

As we headed along the wooded road to the Jameson ranch, I felt myself sagging in the seat. Double shifts made for a long day, and the lulls between adrenaline rushes made me crave coffee. What I wouldn't give for a shot of espresso with a lemon peel! I contented myself knowing I could have one tonight, after our family dinner at the restaurant. I needed to take a few hours off at the end of the tour, but Omak didn't mind as long as I was caught up.

I slowed and Omak lowered his window as we pulled up to a cameraman and reporter who stood poised under a giant umbrella. "How you holding up?" he asked.

"It's been a long day, but we're happy to talk to you, Lieutenant." The reporter smiled, greasing the pan. He was a middle-aged Asian man with a gorgeous smile. How did he get his teeth so white? "Do you have a minute for an on-camera interview?"

"Sorry. We need to roll."

The reporter gripped the windowsill, unwilling to let go. "Do you have an identity of the driver of Kent Jameson's car?"

"No comment," Omak said, "but check with the police information officer. I think we've got a press conference coming up this evening."

The reporter thanked him and backed away as I drove the Jeep off. I was about to execute my first search warrant, and I wanted to get going. Since the Ericksons had left the precinct, I had done a little more digging on Andy. First, I'd finally managed to locate his former girlfriend Ginnie Walters, who now went by Ginnie Walters Blue on Facebook. When I sent her a message to call me, she had gotten back to me within half an hour, driven by curiosity, I think. She had spoken fondly of Andy, though she had come to believe that their relationship was a mistake. Now married to Tyler Blue, with two kids and living in Utah, she had more questions than answers for me. How was Andy doing? Was he married? Had he stayed in the area? Any kids?

I answered what I could and told her I was interested in her version of what had happened seven years ago. "Andy remembers you fondly," I said.

"Aw. I still feel bad about that. Andy was a good guy. He didn't deserve what happened to him, but my parents, they were trying to protect me. I understand that now, but Andy was the one who got hurt from it."

Her statement made Andy seem like less of a creep, although he had still broken the law.

Another theory had cropped up when I discussed Heather with Frazier. "She was so overwrought. What if there's more behind this than lying about an alibi?"

"Like what?" he asked. "You think she's trying to cover something up?"

"Well, if Andy really is the A mentioned in Kyra's journals, if he was having an affair with Kyra, Heather would have been upset to find out about it. What if she didn't go to chemistry class? What if she found out about Kyra or accidentally walked in on her with Andy?"

Frazier held up his hands. "Now you're thinking like a detective."

Figuring that it was worth checking out, we decided the easiest way to check the theory was to see if Heather had attended a class that night. On the community college website, there was a chemistry class scheduled Mondays from six to eight p.m., but when I called the school to confirm Heather's attendance, the dean told us that they could not release that information without Heather's permission or a warrant.

"Damn privacy laws," Frazier said.

"That's because I was just an anonymous voice on the phone," I said. "It could have been anyone calling. But in person, in uniform . . ." I knew we could get an answer.

And we did. Frazier and I drove over to the campus and tracked down the professor, a Dr. Rawlings. Thirtyish and dynamic, with sparkling blue eyes, he seemed interested in contributing to our investigation.

"This has something to do with the Jameson crash?" Rawlings's face was lit with interest. "I've always enjoyed his books. Did you read the one about the chemistry professor who dies when someone switches the labels in his lab?"

"A classic," I said, though I hadn't read the book. Dr. Rawlings remembered seeing Heather Erickson at class, but he checked his roll book just to be sure. "Yes, she was here. A good thing for her. These students get dropped from the class if they miss more than one session."

And so that little tangent had reached a dead end.

"No shame in that," Omak had told me. "Not every theory is going to pan out. You investigate and eliminate."

Although I understood deductive reasoning, I had to acknowledge that all clues did not lead to Andy Greenleaf as a suspect. If he had been involved with Kyra, wouldn't there have been some indications? The people who lived and worked at the ranch must have known about it. I wanted to ask around, but Omak wanted to do a search before anyone tipped Andy off.

And so we headed to the Jameson ranch with a warrant to search the cottage and barn for evidence that he was involved with Kyra Miller's death. We bypassed the main entrance to the Jamesons' compound and took the access road that swung along the ranch perimeter and ended at the barn. Decked in a green rain slicker, jeans, and work boots, Andy Greenleaf sliced open the netting on a hay bale in the pen. Two of the animals seemed interested in his work; the others were scattered toward the back, following a rust-colored alpaca in a zigzagging line. When he peered out from under his hood and saw it was us, he put the wire cutter back in his pocket and stomped over to the fence.

"Aw, come off it! Why don't you leave me alone?"

"Wow. I get the feeling you're really not happy to see me," I said, trying to keep things light as my boots squished through a patch of wet earth. It had stopped raining, but a mist hung in the air, a fine rain that couldn't decide which way to fall. "This is Lt. Omak. He wanted to meet with you and the people on your staff."

"Staff?" He pulled a face. "Like it's all official."

"Are they in the barn?"

"They're all gone now. Cleared out of here once you came through. You cops have a habit of clearing places out, especially when you go and blame things on innocent people."

His animosity surprised me a little, but then he was on the defensive end.

Omak let the comment roll off him. "So tell me about the people who work here. Where do they live?"

"They all flock in from out there." Andy flung an arm toward the wooded hills beyond the barn. "They come out of the woods when they need food money or a place to warm up. Mr. K says it's our moral obligation."

"Your girlfriend mentioned the homeless people in the woods," I said. "She said you were wary of them."

"They don't scare me. I been there, sleeping in the woods myself." Defiance glimmered in

Andy's eyes. "But I gotta look out for Heather, and those panhandlers can be really sketch. Not for nothing, but they already ruined Portland, and now they're infesting the woods. I don't want my girlfriend anywhere near that."

"If they make you uneasy, why do you hire them?" I asked.

"That's what Mr. K. wants. And some of them do a good job. Blane is pretty steady, and Eden, that girl you met this morning, she's quiet but a good worker. By the way, she *is* eighteen. Case you were wondering. They come and go."

"How many young girls come and go, Andy?" the lieutenant probed. "Do you employ under-age youth? Doesn't that violate the terms of your probation?"

"Whoa—whoa! Those charges were seven years ago, and I've been on the straight and narrow since then. But if my job has me hiring street urchins for the day, there's nothing wrong with that, Officer. Yeah, I got saddled with trumped-up charges, but I'm an American citizen, and I've got every right to life, liberty, and the pursuit o' happiness in the good ol' US of A."

"Listen, son," Omak said, "I'm going to level with you. We've identified the driver of the vehicle as being an underage youth. That's one dead girl whom we believe had close proximity with you. And we're still concerned about the whereabouts of Lucy Jameson, whom you knew

208

well." Omak shook his head. "None of this looks good for you, Andy."

"I told her before, I didn't *do* anything!"

The desperate look he gave me tugged at my sense of fairness. If Andy was telling the truth, he hadn't really done anything wrong. Yes, it was a violation for him to be around underage girls, but to feed them and help them? On a human level, that was an act of kindness.

"Come on, Andy," Omak pressed him. "Pretty girls, young and on the run. Hungry and cold. I'll bet they fall hard for a guy like you."

"If girls like me, it's because I'm a nice guy. I am. But I don't play around. I've got a girlfriend, and she's over twenty-one. And *that* is all you need to know about me."

"Don't be that way, Andy." My tone was soft now. "We've got some other bad news for you. The girl who died in the Karmann Ghia last night? It was Kyra Miller."

He shook his head. "That name means nothing to me."

"Really?" I opened a photo of Kyra on my cell phone and expanded it to full size. "You can honestly say you've never met this girl?" I asked, holding up the screen.

His eyes flickered in reaction. "Her?" His head began to retreat into the collar of his plaid shirt. "Her name's Blossom."

"Blossom?" I asked.

Andy shrugged. "A lot of the kids take street names."

"So you did know her," said Omak.

When Andy didn't respond, I answered for him. "Yes, he knew her." The lurid details from Kyra's diary swirled in my mind. She'd been so in love with Andy, the older guy with "magic hands." "According to her journals, you were intimately involved, right, Andy?"

"No!" He winced. "No way. I only knew her because she worked here a few months. She was one of the workers who came in from the woods."

"And you liked her. Tell us about Blossom, Andy," I coaxed him.

"She was a good kid," he said, his voice raw with emotion. "Blossom loved the animals. She was a big help around here until . . ." He looked away.

"Until you got involved with her?" I asked. "Relationships tend to muddy the waters. They can really mess things up."

"That wasn't it. Things changed when she moved in with Lucy. She stopped coming around here."

Kyra had lived with the Jamesons? "When did that happen?" I asked.

"She moved in with them in the summer. August, I guess. And I was sorry to lose her because she was good with the animals. That girl would get in the corral and try to think like an alpaca. She used to talk to the alpacas like they were her babies. Singing them songs and telling them stories. Like fairy tales and stuff. I had to tell her to go at the end of the day. She used to say she'd been an alpaca in a previous life. She was a really good kid."

"How long did she work here?" Omak asked.

"I don't know. A few months."

"Did you know she was underage?"

"I never saw a job application, if that's what you mean. Mr. K wanted her to be on the payroll, so I gave her work. That's all up to the Jamesons. For all I know, they might have kept her on the payroll when she moved into the house even if she didn't have time to work. Apparently it's a full-time job being Lucy's pet." He poked a fingernail at a knot in the wood fence. "I can't believe she was the one in the car—that's just so wrong." He frowned. "I feel awful about . . . about everything."

I believed that he felt bad, but that didn't vindi-=cate him from involvement with Kyra's death.

"Can you tell us how Blossom ended up in that car yesterday evening?" I asked.

He shifted from one foot to another, his eyes flicking from me to the lieutenant. "I didn't even see Blossom yesterday, I swear! I was at Heather's house all night."

"But your alibi doesn't hold up, Andy. Heather didn't get home until around eight fifteen, and

211

her parents didn't see you arrive at their house. No one can account for your whereabouts at the time when an underage teen was seduced, drugged, and killed in a car crash so that she cannot tell us her story." I reached into my jacket for the envelope containing the search warrant. "We have a warrant to search the premises, Andy. We're not trying to set you up; we just need to know what happened to Blossom. Can you help us out, Andy?"

His face grew tight, his eyes bulging in a panic. "I got nothing to say to you."

"That's too bad." Omak turned to me. "Call in Frazier and Rivers." They were checking on the parking areas of Stafford Woods, waiting to join the search. I was already sending a text to Frazier to come on in.

"I'll talk to Andy while you three conduct the search," Omak said, his eyes on Andy.

"I'm not talking to anyone." Andy turned away, goading two alpacas away before unlatching the gate. "I got work to do, and I don't need to be poked with any more questions. We're done." He stomped into the corral, slamming the gate behind him. He remained in plain sight as he crossed the field, talking to a group of alpacas and heading toward a lean-to where bales of hay were stacked.

Omak and I observed in silence. If only the alpacas could talk.

"Do you believe him?" Omak asked under his breath.

"I feel sorry for him. But I think he's hiding something."

"Agreed."

After retrieving an evidence kit and gloves from the Jeep, I started on the cottage. The door opened to a cozy space with rustic wood floors, braided rugs, and a woodstove. The main floor was a U-shaped plan with a living room that opened up to a dining area, which led to a kitchen.

With gloved hands, I looked in closets and drawers, searched under cushions, and felt under tables and counters. The rooms were fairly tidy, though closets and drawers had a lot of papers and junk jammed inside. I found birthday and anniversary cards from Heather, but no correspondence from Kyra. Not even short notes with her star-shaped *A* and looped *K*. I realized Andy might have known not to hold on to something like that, especially if his girlfriend came here, snooping around, although the drawers of grocery receipts, matchbooks, and junk mail indicated that he was not quick to toss anything out.

I sorted through a crate of DVDs that included all the Star Wars and Indiana Jones movies. On the bookshelves, I found two binders of a baseball card collection along with a fairly complete set of Kent Jameson's novels. As the spines of the books didn't seem to be cracked, I suspected Andy wasn't a fan and that these had been stocked by the Jamesons. I was about to head up the narrow stairs when Frazier and Rivers arrived.

"I'm just finishing on this floor," I told them. "Do you want to head out to the barn and I'll join you when I finish up here?"

"I'll do it," Frazier said, snapping at a latex glove, "but I'm staying away from those horses. Those giant teeth could do some real damage."

"They're more likely to kick you," I said. "Don't get behind them. And they should be out in the pasture right now."

"I hope so," he called over his shoulder.

The upstairs contained a tiny room with a desk and two file cabinets. Half of the cabinets were empty, and the other one was stacked with monthly financial reports for the ranch. I remembered Talitha telling me that all the ranch operations were handled through Martha's office, so I assumed these were just copies to keep Andy up to date. The bedroom was tidy, the bed made with a black-and-gray-striped comforter. On the nightstand sat two books about the Vietnam War, one bookmarked in the middle.

"Nothing here," I said, standing at the top of the stairs and looking over the place one more time. The walls were barren in a buttery shade of yellow, and the ceiling was textured white, except for a square cutout by the bedroom door. A hatch to the attic.

Hardly easy access, but I had to take a look. The chair from the desk allowed me to reach the dangling cord. I pulled it down, and a ladder unfolded with a creaking noise. I didn't want to go up there. In movies, nothing good ever happened in dark attics filled with cobwebs and vermin. But this was my job.

My pulse began to quicken as I turned on my flashlight and climbed the bottom rungs.

Don't panic, not now.

Panic attacks came at the worst times, usually unexpected. But often they weren't linked to conscious fear. I hoped that my thudding heartbeat and sweaty palms were just symptoms of genuine fright.

The ladder creaked under my weight as I climbed up, testing each rung with a boot before I trusted it. My first glimpse of the attic revealed rafters stuffed with insulation and dusty plywood flooring. Plenty of dust and some cobwebs, but no crawling insects or bats in sight. No skeletons.

In fact, the attic space was fairly empty but for some furniture: a brass headboard, wire box springs, and some metal folding chairs. I swept the beam of my flashlight across the space.

Nothing to see here.

My pulse began to even out as I climbed onto the planking. This would only take a minute. Just then the light caught a gold, rectangular object on the floor about a foot from the hatch.

What was that? I reached for it: a slim envelope, oddly placed and isolated, as if someone had dropped it without noticing.

I took a photo of the envelope's position with my cell phone before I opened the prongs and looked inside.

There were a few pages of photographs—and my first impression was that the subject was naked and provocative. In the first shot the young woman stood with arms lifted overhead to rake her hair back, her breasts high and glossy.

In the second shot, I recognized her face.

Fifteen-year-old Kyra Miller.

Omak's jaw clenched as he glanced quickly through the photos.

"They're a poor quality," I said. "Probably taken with a cell phone and printed on a personal computer."

"You combed the house, and this is it?" he asked.

I nodded. "No notes, though we know Kyra was a writer. I didn't see a laptop, but I'm sure he has a cell phone."

"Which we can confiscate if he's arrested."

Omak seemed to be considering this as he stared out at the corral. "We might find more pictures on his phone."

"It seemed a little odd to me that they were sitting there, just above the hatch," I said. "Also, the attic was dusty, but the envelope is fairly clean. Like it was placed there recently."

"He might have shoved it up there when he knew we were investigating him," Omak said. "Get it out of plain sight."

"Or someone else might have left it there." I couldn't ignore this possibility. "Someone could be trying to set Andy up."

Omak winced. "It's possible, but right now we don't have much choice, do we? With his arrest record, no real alibi, and now these, we need to bring him in."

When we approached Andy with the envelope, he reacted with disinterest.

"Do you want to tell us about these photos?" Omak asked.

Andy protested that he didn't know anything about the envelope or the photos inside. "What's in the pictures?" he asked.

When I explained, he let out a curse and slipped into a funk.

"But I didn't have anything to do with those photos. This is so unfair."

But we have motive, means, and opportunity, I wanted to say, but this was no time to argue, especially since he hadn't confessed to being involved with Kyra Miller. Feeling not entirely secure in my role, I read him his rights and cuffed his hands behind his back. As we were guiding Andy into the back seat of the car, Omak got a call he had to take. I made sure that Andy was as comfortable as possible before I closed the door.

The call was brief, but the lieutenant was scowling when he ended it. "That was the police chief giving me an earful." We were a few feet away from the car, out of hearing range. "Apparently Martha Jameson called and asked that we 'kindly withdraw' our officers from Stafford Woods now that the case is solved. Solved."

"Does she think we won't investigate because the dead girl was homeless?"

"How would she even know that?" he asked. "We haven't revealed the driver's identity yet."

"The Jamesons have to know that Kyra was driving the car. The girl was living with them. They've been holding out on us. I'm not sure why, but I don't appreciate it."

"Such a nice way to say that the Jamesons are liars."

"Manners matter," I said, hearing my mother's voice once again. I'd better watch that.

"I need to swing over there and do some damage control. It shouldn't take long. I'll probably have to set up a time to bring Chief

Cribben over, since the Jamesons demand special attention. I have no patience for this political shit."

Inside the car, talk of the Jamesons ceased, and we drove in silence toward the woods that loomed, still and eerie, beneath a pearly sky. Somewhere in there was a flock of hippie campers. I braced myself, warding off a bad memory of those woods that I had tried to forget.

As we pulled into the parking lot, two women were heading toward the main house from the semicircle of buildings. One was Martha Jameson with her neat blonde bob. The other wore a dark dress and a hijab in a deep shade of royal blue: Talitha Rahimi.

"Lieutenant?" Martha Jameson called. "I thought that was you. What's going on?"

"Who's the short one?" Omak asked under his breath as we waited for the women to draw closer.

"Martha's assistant, Talitha."

"I'd like a word with you, Martha," Omak said.

"Of course." Martha turned to the younger woman. "Talitha, go inside. Start the tea." Her assistant nodded and strode into the house.

"I understand you've requested that our officers back off."

"Yes, that would be lovely since the crisis has subsided. Thank you so much."

"The case is still open." Omak's tone was gentle but firm, as if he were chastising a young child. "We're investigating a possible homicide."

"I didn't realize . . ." She thumped a fist to her chest. "How awful. I assumed it was a matter of suicide and auto theft, and, well, of course we wouldn't press charges."

"It's not that simple, Martha. Our investigation is in the early stages, and while I'm sorry for the inconvenience, we need to press ahead."

"Of course you do." Martha's iron stare had latched onto the Jeep behind us. "Is that Andy in the back seat?"

"We're taking him in to the station," Omak said.

"Taking him into custody?" Martha moved out of Andy's sightline, grabbing hold of Omak's upper arm for support. "Oh, my goodness. Are you arresting him?"

"In the process," Omak said.

"I should have known." Martha clasped one hand to her mouth, then said, "Kent is going to be devastated. We've always trusted him. And when I spoke with Andy just an hour ago, he insisted he was innocent of any wrongdoing." She closed her fleece jacket around her neck and folded her arms. "We were too trusting. What are the charges?"

"We suspect that Greenleaf contributed to the death of the driver, Kyra Miller," Omak explained.

"You probably knew her as Blossom?" I added, monitoring her face as the complacent mask slipped away, the jaw clenched, the eyes grew shiny with tears.

"Lucy's friend." Her body seemed to sag with the news. "Kent and I suspected Blossom was the one who had taken the car, but . . . we didn't want to tell you. We were hoping it wasn't true, and it seemed to open a Pandora's box about Lucy's relationships that . . . You see, some matters are best left unexplored."

"You should have told us," Omak said. "You hindered our investigation."

"I'm so sorry, but we had to look out for the girls. For years Lucy has had a reputation for being—I don't know. Odd, I guess. It's hard for her to keep friends. And Blossom, that girl had such a sad upbringing. It's no wonder she chose to end her life."

"We're not sure it was suicide," I said, glancing at Omak. I didn't want to reveal too much about the investigation—the drugs, the evidence of intercourse, the damaged brakes, the journals and photos—but I couldn't let Martha off the hook. "And you're correct about Kyra's difficult childhood. It surprises me that you would take in a young girl without notifying her parents or guardian. Please don't think that I'm judging you, but whenever I wanted to host a sleepover, my parents made sure that they acquainted themselves with my friends' parents. Just a simple phone call was all it took."

Martha's gemlike blue eyes glazed over with contempt. "Blossom told us she was an orphan, on the run from abusive foster parents. A *simple* phone call would have sent her right back to that abusive environment."

"Or maybe it would have saved her life," Omak said. "I'd like to think that there are people in the child welfare system who will protect a kid like Kyra once the abuse has been reported. You and Kent were harboring a runaway child."

"Please, spare me the lecture. Kent's daughter has a penchant for bringing in shifty young people and dumping them on Kent and me when she's through with them. It's terrible the way she trifles with these girls, but Kent can't control Lucy and I'm just the stepmother, so you can imagine what Lucy thinks of my advice. In the end, it's up to me to pick up the pieces for these kids. I can't tell you how many teenage girls I've fixed up with cash and a bus ticket or job leads in Portland."

"Have you ever considered calling the Department of Social Services?" I asked. "They could help these girls."

"They have no resources," Martha snapped. "And how would that look, the fat-cat author calls social services to get rid of his daughter's friends? It's my job to protect Kent's public image."

"In the case of Kyra Miller, I wish you had

called us." Omak kept his voice steady, though I sensed the bristle of annoyance in his eyes. "She was entered into a database of missing teenage girls from the Portland area. She was one of the Lost Girls."

Martha squinted, as if it were difficult to decipher Omak's words. "People were looking for Blossom? No, I had no idea." She glanced back at the house with a sigh. "I'm sorry I didn't call. I feel terrible about all this. Poor Blossom. I didn't think a fifteen-year-old girl would be swayed by an older man like Andy. And you think he killed her? I mean, I thought it was a car accident."

"The accident is under investigation." Omak stood tall, his voice low but commanding. "Mr. Greenleaf is coming to the precinct with us now. Most likely he'll be lodged in the jail, at least overnight, maybe indefinitely, so you'll want to get someone over to the barn to tend to the animals. He asked that we remind you to get the alpacas in the barn before dark. I guess the coyotes are their predators?"

"Yes, yes, I'll let Carlos know." She pressed two fingertips to her temple. "What a mess this thing has become. My husband is distraught. His daughter is still missing, and now you're taking our ranch manager away." Her creamy blonde hair stayed in place as she tilted her head and pressed fingertips to her temple again. "I'm sure that sounds incredibly selfish, considering a life was lost, but people I love are imploding all around me, and I feel helpless to stop it."

I felt a flicker of compassion, but Martha Jameson had a skill for weaving all the events into a bundle of pity with herself at the center.

"This is bound to be a difficult time," Omak said.

"It's been really hard on Kent, but I've lived through worse. It's the things beyond your control that break your heart. The betrayals. Realizing how Andy must have pulled Blossom in. God knows, he might have made a few moves on Lucy, too. Maybe that's why she's gone now. The shame and disappointment, it hits us all in different ways."

"Did you have any indication Kyra—Blossom —was involved with Andy?" I asked.

She shook her head. "I had no idea what was going on over there. When you give someone a fresh start, you count on them to maintain trust. I thought Lucy and her friends were riding horses and helping Andy care for the alpacas. Yes, he was a young man with a criminal strike against him, but it was long ago and truly unfounded. He seemed like a good kid and he's always treated me with respect, but I guess you never know what another person is capable of. If it was murder, I'm not sure that even Kent will be able to forgive him. Even a liberal, generous man like my husband has his limits." Martha sighed.

"It's getting cold. Please, Officers, come in for some tea."

Martha nodded toward me. "Officer Mori knows how much I enjoy tea time."

A hot cup of tea would ward off the gathering cold, but it would do nothing to thaw the uneasiness taking hold of me. I felt as if I'd been tricked by the Jamesons, and now my mind was paddling fast to process this new information.

"I'm afraid we need to get Mr. Greenleaf to the precinct," Omak said. "Some other time?"

"Of course." With a shiver, she glanced toward the car. "You can't let your prisoner get away while you're off chatting with me."

"That would be embarrassing," I agreed. "But I have one other question, if you don't mind. About Kyra Miller. How did Lucy meet her?"

"She was one of Lucy's friends from the woods. Ragamuffins, Kent calls them." She glanced toward the semicircle of buildings containing her husband's office. "Those homeless kids in the woods. Kent made some kind of deal with them to leave us alone, but I know Lucy goes off with them sometimes. Their leader, the one who calls himself the Prince, that one's a piece of work, and she seems to be crazy about him."

I had not heard of this "Prince" before. "What is the Prince's real name?"

Martha rolled her eyes. "God only knows."

"Is the Prince Lucy's boyfriend?" I asked.

"I'm not sure, but that young man has far too much influence over her—over all of them. It's cultish."

And it might be the key to finding Lucy and more of the Lost Girls. "You mentioned that your husband made an informal deal with the Prince and his group. Does Mr. Jameson know how to get in touch with them?"

"No one knows. Whenever their location is spotted by an outsider, they move on. Blossom came from that group, but she wasn't so anti-everything. Lucy brought her home, made her a pet. Best friends forever. That's how the cycle goes. Lucy befriends them, adores them, and obsesses over them until she squeezes the life out of them. It always ends badly, with the poor friend having to call her parents or find employment elsewhere because Lucy couldn't stand to be around them one more second. With Lucy, it always goes sour."

"Was Lucy's relationship with Kyra unraveling?"

My question seemed to alarm Martha. "I think the girls were still going strong, but what do I know? Lucy didn't confide in me."

Omak was quiet, stoic, soaking it all in.

I was beginning to get a clearer picture of Lucy Jameson, a portrait that fit with the girlish bedroom. "So when Kyra was friends with Lucy, she stayed here?"

"Yes. In Lucy's room."

My mind seized on the image of that single bed laden with childish stuffed animals. Had Kyra Miller squeezed in among the unicorns and teddy bears, her freckled cheek snuggled against a pillow as she sought a sense of safety and belonging? Had she believed that Lucy's friendship was real? That the generosity of the Jamesons was genuine?

"Sorry. I know you have to go, and here I am playing the bitter stepmother. Every family has its issues, I guess."

"And believe me, we've seen it all," Omak assured her. He spoke with her as he walked her back to the porch of the giant house and then returned.

I went back to the car to check on Andy, who seemed forlorn, leaning against the car window. A cooperative suspect. As I looked ahead to the process of booking Andy Greenleaf—inputting pedigree information, fingerprints, mugshots, notifications, safe lodging protocol—I wished I could hand off the arrest and join the others searching those sodden woods. After getting an earful from Martha, it was becoming more and more clear that Lucy Jameson might be a menace to others and to herself and that something very strange was happening in the forest. When I mentioned this to Omak, he didn't seem concerned.

"You need to learn to delegate," Omak assured me. "And right now, finding Lucy

Jameson is not as important as following through on this arrest. You need to work with the prosecutor's office to make sure we arm them with all the ev idence they need. Besides, the chief will want you at the press conference, near the podium, and they'll probably bring out a handful of officers to make it look like there's a strong police presence in Sunrise Lake. Any warm bodies that look decent in uniform. All that pomp and circumstance horseshit."

"I don't need to be part of the show."

"The press conference is all part of the game. And a good investigator knows how to delegate and work with the team."

"Yes, sir."

"If you have any questions or follow-up for the prosecutor, work with Frazier. He's a good cop. You'll see."

"He did a great job bringing in Heather Erickson and her parents," I admitted.

"That's right. You'll learn a lot working with him."

I wasn't looking forward to "sharing my toys" with Zion Frazier, but I wasn't going to be a crab about it. If he did his job, then we'd both be working toward the same goal.

We were received at the precinct with a few high fives and lauded words of praise.

"You got him!" barked the desk officer, Sgt. Stanford. "Good for you."

A human trophy is an odd phenomenon. Somehow I didn't feel like dancing on my desk. Calmly, quietly, I cuffed Andy to a chair and began the process of booking him. If Omak wanted me to get through the paperwork and notifications in time for the press conference, it was going to be tight.

As I filled out the captioned forms, my thoughts wandered back to the campers in Stafford Woods —"ragamuffins," the Jamesons called them—all led by a young man they called the Prince. This reclusive group provided much more fertile fodder for speculation than Andy Greenleaf, who didn't seem to be bright enough to have pulled off having an affair with a young girl while in a steady relationship with a grounded girl like Heather. Who was this Prince? My Internet search led only to the rock star, and I didn't want to take too much time when there was an arrest to process. Martha Jameson claimed to know nothing about the Prince, although her step-daughter had close ties to the campers.

My eyes lit on Andy, who sat with his head tipped back against the wall. He had told us that he hired most of his staff from the campers in the woods. Even if he had never met the Prince, Andy would know a way to find him.

"Andy," I called gently. "Tell me about the Prince."

He brought his chin down, his mouth puckered. "The dude in the woods?" He shrugged. "I never met him."

"But you must have heard about him. You hired people from his camp." I swiveled my chair around to face him. "Where's he from? What's his real name? What prompted him to live off the grid?"

Andy lifted his free hand to scratch his chin. "If I tell you, what's in it for me?"

I smiled. "I'll treat you with dignity and respect."

He tipped his head to one side. "Yeah. You probably would anyway. You're nice for a cop."

"Thanks. I can let the prosecutor know that you were cooperative," I said, thinking ahead. "And if the information you give me leads to another arrest, you might be getting yourself off the hook."

"So you're telling me to save myself by solving the crime?" Andy looped his fingertips inside the collar of his shirt and scratched his neck. "Good one."

"Don't be that way. Help me help you. What's the story with the Prince?"

He sighed. "He's actually a poser, homeless by choice. He's got a house and a place to live, but from what I hear, he can't stand to be walled in. Something happened when he was a kid, he got stuck in the woods or something, and I guess he learned how to live like a wild animal. He's into all that survival shit."

The Prince was not the first kid to play at homelessness. "Is his real name Prince?"

"Nah. It's something dorky like Clive Vanderpoop or Vandyke or something like that. When you hear his name, you'll know why he makes people call him the Prince."

"How can I find him?" I asked. "I know it's a big secret, but you must know . . ."

"Nope." He shook his head. "Much as Lucy talked about him, I never got under his spell. Why would I suck up to some crazy guy in the woods when I have a nice house and a good job? And why do you care so much? He's not the one who killed Blossom. She left the woods months ago, and as far as I know, the Prince never comes out."

"If I find him, I think I can find Lucy," I said.

"Maybe. But Lucy's lived on the edge of those woods most of her life. If she wants to disappear, she knows how to do it."

"Still, I need to try."

"And I need to get a break from the prosecutor." He pointed to my computer. "I hope you're adding all this to your notes about how cooperative I'm being."

"Just like I promised." I clicked the mouse, returning to the forms to process his arrest. But already my mind was elsewhere, pursuing another track. Lucy had been at the estate the night Kyra was killed. Maybe Lucy had done something to send an intoxicated Kyra driving off in a vehicle with no brakes. Lucy had been on the compound; she had argued with her father and then disappeared around the same time as Kyra. Was she hiding to escape culpability?

The clock told me I had better get moving if I was going to make it to the press conference. I completed the arrest report, adding in comments on Andy's cooperation. Then I called the prosecutor's office and spoke with one of the prosecutors, a woman named Claudia Deming. In a deep, calming voice, she promised to review the report I'd filed and meet with me tomorrow.

Handcuffs removed, Andy stood somberly at the table to have his prints done. "Did they use the Live Scan when they fingerprinted you last time?" I asked him. It was one of the procedures I had aced in the police academy. "I think you'll like it better. No messy ink." I tapped his hand to help him relax.

"Ouch. Police brutality," he said, then shrugged a shoulder. "Kidding."

Someone had the news on his computer monitor, and as I rolled out Andy's prints, the mention of Sunrise Lake caught my attention.

"An odd twist of events, a case of mistaken identity, and an apology from the police." The reporter relished the intro. This was national news coverage, with sophisticated graphics and lighting and widespread impact. "Sounds like a lead in to the latest mystery novel from best-selling author Kent Jameson, but in fact this is the strange sequence of events that has been playing out over the past twenty-four hours in the author's home at Sunrise Lake, Oregon. Last night the police came to the author's doorstep to notify him that his daughter had been killed in a car crash. Today it was found that the driver of the fateful car was not, in fact, Lucy Jameson, and the police had to backstep and apologize for their error."

"We did not," I said aloud, scowling at the exuberant reporter. Where had he gotten his facts?

"The question becomes," the reporter continued, "who was driving the car and why did the driver crash on a deserted road in perfect weather conditions?"

At least that part was true.

"One reporter from our Portland affiliate suggests that the answers lie in the miles of forest surrounding the Jameson property, an area known as Stafford Woods."

In a blink Natalie was on the screen—my best friend Natalie—standing before a dense copse of fir trees, all silvery green needles and strong brown vertical lines.

Nat was freakin' adorable on camera. It concerned me that she was covering my case, but there was no denying my excitement for her, getting national exposure.

"Many people in the Portland area have fond

memories of Stafford Woods, the local forest named after Oregon's poet laureate William Stafford." Natalie's jacket was open at the top, her hood casually flopped toward one shoulder. She made it look easy. "We may recall field| trips or hikes, kayaking on the Willamette or attending the holiday concert at the Grove. But lately the woods have wielded a twofold menace: a threat for local residents who express concern about a band of roving indigents. And the mysterious death of a young woman in a fiery car crash that is still under investigation."

The report was intriguing and a bit poetic. When I looked over at Andy, I noticed that he was watching, too.

"See that?" Sgt. Stanford said. "This is already big news, and she doesn't even know that the driver of the car was one of the Lost Girls." He turned to Andy. "No one in the media knows that we have you in custody, but they will soon. Everybody's going to know your name."

"You'll give them my name?" he asked, his eyes bleary and pink now. "So everyone's going to find out about this? My parole officer, too?"

"An arrest is public record," I said.

"That's right, son," the sergeant said, taunting Andy. "You're going to be on TV and in the papers. They'll have access to your mugshot. You're a notorious outlaw now."

A loud breath hissed out of Andy as he doubled over as far as the handcuff would allow.

"You'll have a chance to make your case," I said, wishing the sergeant wasn't riding him so much. "You can prove that you weren't involved with Kyra. Explain why you had photos of a naked fifteen-year-old in the attic."

"I told you, I never saw those photos before. I don't know who put them there."

"Just make sure you tell your lawyer that." I went back to typing up my report.

"Do I at least get to call Heather?"

"One phone call."

Andy groaned and dropped his head to his chest. "Well, eff me."

—17—

"As you know, it's rare for me as the mayor to be making this sort of announcement in a community like Sunrise Lake." Mayor Ron Redmond paused to scan the crowd, his owlish eyes stern behind his reading glasses before continuing. Our mayor had always struck me as a crabby, dried-out prune of a man, popular because he did not upset the status quo. Today I saw the appeal in a staunch father figure, someone who could reassure people that justice would forge on despite tragic events.

I had never been quite so close to Mayor Redmond, and I didn't like feeling that eyes and cameras were focused on me. From where I stood on the stage, lined up with half a dozen cops, I didn't want to eyeball the audience of reporters and community leaders, so the mayor was the most likely focal point.

"To hold two press conferences in one day is probably unprecedented in our peace-loving community," Redmond said with a note of sadness, "but here we are. Chief Cribben has information on the identity of the victim of the Stafford Road car crash, so I'm going to turn the podium over to him." The mayor stepped back and motioned to the police chief at front of the line of cops.

I watched blandly as Buzz Cribben swaggered forward, the medals on his dress uniform glimmering like a Christmas tree. Frazier once mentioned that there used to be a time when you could write yourself up for a medal for helping an old lady cross a street. Cribben had obviously been on the beat during that time.

Even the goofballs like Brown and Rivers stood at attention as the chief walked by on his way to the mike. Not so much out of respect but out of awareness that all four major news networks from Portland had cameras rolling.

From Brown's face, I couldn't tell if he had

gotten dressed down by the lieutenant yet. When we had gone over the results of the canvassing in Stafford Woods, Brown and Garcia had been conspicuously absent. Rumor was they'd left the woods early because people weren't answering their doors. But the story from Rivers and Frazier was altogether different.

"Everyone we ran into was eager to talk," Rivers said. "But not to Garcia and Brown. They've been assigned up on the hill a long time but got nothing to show for it."

"Yeah, the residents feel like Garcia and Brown have been shit-canning their complaints, running interference for the Jamesons," Frazier explained. "All these people, the neighbors, they're very respectful of the Jamesons. Everyone says the Jamesons are great neighbors, quiet and all. You can tell no one wants to say anything against them. No problems with the Jamesons, but they're pretty angry about those hobo kids in Stafford Woods."

"We talked to a lady, Marge Bloom, who's seen bands of homeless cut across her property. Gypsies, she calls them," Rivers said, reading from his notebook. "Says they have an old covered truck they use, but she's caught them taking apples and pears from her tree. Not that she minds so much, but she doesn't like them trespassing. You know, a woman living alone. She's locking her doors now."

"She should," Omak said. "Why didn't she call us? I would have sent a car out."

"She says she called twice in the past year." Frazier's lip curled in annoyance. "Garcia and Brown came out and talked to her, but nothing ever changed."

"They never filed a report, Lou," Rivers added. "I checked."

From the hard set of Omak's jaw, we could all see that this was a problem. But Brown stood onstage, badge gleaming in the lights, and Garcia had supposedly taken sick time for a dentist appointment. *Right,* I thought. *Spontaneous root canal.*

I got a whiff of a citrusy cologne as Cribben walked by. Was the perfume compensation for his nickname? I stifled a smile and forced myself to focus on the moment. With a square jaw and salt-and-pepper hair, the chief was one of those men who had probably gotten better looking as he got older. Those bright teeth made me want to reach for my sunglasses.

"As the mayor said, these are highly unusual circumstances for Sunrise Lake. My team of investigators has identified the victim of yesterday's car crash as Kyra Miller, a fifteen-year-old girl from Salem. Her name may sound familiar because she is included in the group of so-called Lost Girls, the young women who have gone missing from the Portland area."

Although I knew for a fact that Omak had

written the script, the police chief and mayor did all the talking. Funny that they called it a press conference when there would be no conferring going on. Cribben had once told a reporter that the last thing he wanted to do was answer a bunch of stupid questions.

"At this time we are ruling the crash that took the life of Kyra Miller as a suspicious death, and as such it is being investigated by our very capable police force. We do not know how Ms. Miller obtained access to Kent Jameson's vehicle, and we are investigating Ms. Miller's connection to the Jameson family."

I clamped my teeth together at the bullshit of that statement.

We knew that Kyra Miller got access to the car with a key from the garage. She had been living with the Jamesons.

Why didn't the chief include this information? Probably because he wanted to protect the Jamesons' reputation.

"Kyra Miller was an orphan," Cribben continued. "She was in the care of the state of Oregon's foster system for nearly a decade. We believe she arrived in Portland during the past year . . ."

We had been told not to eyeball the audience, but I couldn't help but scan the faces of the two dozen or so people in the sterile meeting room. Natalie had to be here; with her story hitting the five o'clock news, she would definitely be hot on the trail of developments.

Azula Parks, a petite female reporter from channel six, sat in the first row, nodding attentively. Among the clusters of camera crews was a heavyset bearded man who wrote a column for the *Oregonian* as well as Sunrise Lake's colorful veteran reporter Marigold Chase, decked out in a turquoise hat that matched the collar of her blazer.

At last I found Natalie standing at the back of the pack, still zipped into her jacket and cradling a paper coffee cup. Had she just come in from the cold? Knowing Nat, she'd returned to those wild Stafford acres to search for her story. I wished I'd been able to traipse through the woods with Nat. I'll bet she hadn't turned back at the first sign of rain and scratchy brambles, like most of the officers Omak had sent out to canvas the woods.

"It was pouring out there," Garcia had said. "I couldn't see a foot in front of my face, and then we started running out of trail. Brown wanted to head back, and I didn't argue with that."

With nearly twenty years on the job, Brown had seniority, and he never let us forget it. Along with his police skills, he had finely honed the ability to do as little work as possible.

Now the chief was finally acknowledging the rumor that had drawn the media here. "We do have a suspect in custody in relation to Kyra Miller's death. Andrew Greenleaf has been arrested for parole violation." Cribben lifted his eyes from the paper and gave the crowd a mournful look. "No further comments. Thank you for your time."

"Chief!" a handful of reporters called in unison. "Just one question!"

"Is the suspect being charged with homicide?"

"How did the victim die? Cause of death?"

The corners of Cribben's mouth curled slightly as he held up a manicured hand to stop the questions. He was enjoying this. "That's all, folks."

"Nat!" I descended the stage and waved her over. There would be no hugging in the precinct, but we could chat. "You made the national news. I was doing paperwork so I saw the whole thing. Very impressive."

"Thanks. It's kind of a fluke that the network picked it up, but what a story. I'm psyched."

I lowered my voice. "By the way, you looked amazing. Perfect hair." Natalie had a thing about her hair, which she complained was too thin and flat. She'd taken to back-combing it underneath so that it puffed up on top, sort of like that mound atop Malibu Barbie's head. I found that it had a warping effect, but it was supposed to elongate the face.

"Did I?" She grinned. "Thanks. It was thrilling

to have the network pick up our coverage, but it's sort of a nonstory unless I can get an interview with one of the campers. I gotta tell you, I am fascinated by those hippie campers."

"Same! I'm dying to talk to their leader, but I understand they move whenever someone gets too close. Some people think they've been eluding society for more than a year. Have you found them yet?"

"I'm getting close, working some connections. I met a kid who knows the Prince," Natalie said with raised eyebrows. "If I could snag them, I'd have the juiciest interview Sunrise Lake has seen in twenty years. My source tells me he knew Kyra Miller."

He did, I thought as goose bumps rose on my arms. Natalie was closer to a big story than she realized.

"But even if that doesn't pan out, the story of young hippies living off the land in a prosperous suburb will appeal to weird Portland. It's all I can think about. And you know I can be a stubborn bitch when I want to."

"Uh-huh." We both laughed, and I gave her a prod with my elbow. "You're a Taurus. The stampeding bull."

"And I'm not backing down until I get a face-to-face with the woods people."

"Yeah, good luck with that," Frazier interrupted. "Chasing down people who don't want to be found. That never works. And if you do manage to corral one of those stinkbugs and get an interview, people here don't want to sit in their living room and watch some toothless girl talk about the hermit in critter hollow. Portland may be weird, but most people around here fancy themselves way beyond enjoying a hillbilly moment."

"Wow." Natalie folded her arms, checking Frazier out. "I'm feeling the burn. I'm Natalie Amichi, and you are one hostile media critic."

"This is Zion Frazier," I said, then introduced Natalie.

"I've heard your name, Officer Frazier." Natalie extended a hand. "I followed your case with the department. I didn't know it was resolved."

Suddenly icing over, Frazier gave her hand a reluctant shake. "No comment on that." It was the first time anyone had acknowledged Frazier's lawsuit against the department. I'd never heard a cop go near it, and Frazier never brought it up. "And don't call me Frazier. That's that affected white shrink on TV who gives bad advice. I go by Zion or Z. Your choice."

"Okay, Z. Tell me what you know about the band of campers in the woods," Natalie said.

"All I'm saying is, if you're thinking about trying to meet up with those homeless kids, just watch your back. Some of them are mentally ill and some of them are tweakers. They don't play by the rules."

"I'll be careful," she said.

"You'd be better off not going after those runts."

"It's her job," I said. "She's going to meet with them if she has the chance."

"Yeah, yeah. Everybody wants adventure until it all starts going south. That's when you call us to save your skin."

Zion didn't seem to realize that Natalie wasn't a damsel-in-distress type. "Well, I'd like to talk with those campers, too. I'd go with you, Nat, but I know having a cop along would kill the deal on something like this."

" 'Fraid so."

"Do you have any background on the Prince?" I asked Nat. "You've got to wonder what drives a guy to go survivalist. And to have followers, he must be charismatic. But what's his real name?"

"I've heard him called Prince Aragon, but when you Google that, you get these medieval cartoons."

"His last name begins with a *V*, something that sounds Dutch," I said. "That's all I have so far."

Natalie's eyes sparked. "That's a start. I heard he comes from a wealthy family up in the Seattle area. My contact said he was in a plane crash as a kid, and he's never been the same since."

"Seriously?" Intrigue sizzled through my body like an electrical current. Fascinating info. I wanted to run to my desk in the squad room and dig deeper. "I wonder if that's the reason he's rebelled from society."

"He's just a spoiled brat." Zion Frazier shook his head in disdain. "All those campers, they're squatting on state lands. The governor should go in and chase them out, the whole pack of them."

"But they're not hurting anyone by living there," Natalie pointed out.

"And it's not easy to find a dozen or so people hiding in four miles of forest. It's the proverbial needle in a haystack."

"There are plenty of ways to do it," Frazier insisted. "Smoke them out. Starve them out. You cut off their clean water and then wait them out."

"But they're people, Frazier," I said. "Don't forget that."

He sighed. "Political correctness is ruining this job. And listen, if you're going to partner up with me, you need to call me Z."

As Z continued verbally sparring with Natalie, I had a vision of finding those campers in the woods. If one Lost Girl had emerged from the woods, who was to say there wasn't an entire subculture hiding there, living off the land?

When I excused myself to return to work, neither Natalie nor Z seemed to notice. Interesting.

Back at my beat-up desk, I immediately pushed my copy of Andy's arrest report aside and started plugging in terms to find more on Prince Aragon. Natalie was right about those cartoons. I switched away from the Prince moniker and started searching for "Seattle survivalist" and "Seattle prince"—also a no go.

I searched for the top ten wealthiest families in Washington. Well, hello, Bill Gates. Three people on the list were from Microsoft, and then Amazon, Starbucks, and a few other familiar brands. None of the people in the top ten began with *V,* but then I suspected that the Prince came from more of a low-profile family. Maybe older money but not exceptional.

So what was exceptional about the Prince's past?

In the search bar I typed "Seattle youth in plane crash."

Yes!

Two hits took me to articles about a Seattle boy who had been the only survivor of a flight that had crashed in the mountains on a private Cessna to Canada. When I saw the name Emory Vandenbos, I knew this had to be the one Andy had mentioned. An heir to the Boss Shoes dynasty, Emory had been twelve when the plane crashed, killing the boy's aunt and uncle and the plane's pilot. Stranded in the woods, Emory had managed to survive by building small shelters at night and eating wild berries. After almost two weeks, he came to a road, where he waved down a trucker for assistance.

"Emory Vandenbos," I whispered, clicking on two black-and-white photos of a boy with serious eyes and thick, brown hair. He'd been twelve when the crash occurred sixteen years ago. That made him twenty-eight now.

Kind of old to be camping in the woods with a bunch of teenage girls. I wondered if the hippie campers were older than people realized. Or maybe Vandenbos had a fondness for younger girls.

—18—

After a bit more digging on Vandenbos, including a few failed attempts to reach his parents, I put that line of inquiry aside to go over the details of the case. I wanted to be prepared for the meeting with the prosecutor in the morning, and there were still a few loose ends.

In my e-mail inbox was a message from Andy's lawyer, Harrison Baylor, indicating that Andy was considering our request. I rolled my eyes. We had collected Andy's cell phone as evidence, but we needed the passcode to access his data. A clean cell phone would help vindicate him. That had been my proposal. Now that he was stalling, I wondered if the phone contained some incriminating text messages or photos. It was up to Andy now.

I spoke with the Jamesons' mechanic, Hal Burke, who agreed with the assessment of the Ghia that our mechanic had made. He was surprised by the gas can, saying that it was not typical for any of the Jamesons' cars to carry gasoline. "I can't imagine Martha allowing that—fuel sloshing around in the trunk. She's such a neat freak, she won't even let me keep gas in the main garage. There's just the one in the maintenance garage."

I thanked Hal and ended the call, thinking about that gas can. If the Jamesons' fuel cans were accounted for, where had the gas container in the car come from? As I hung up, I realized that some local gas station attendant might remember filling a gas can, as it didn't happen that often. I pulled up a map of gas stations near the Jameson estate and started calling. The first person I spoke with told me he wouldn't recognize the Jamesons or their staff if they came in with a gas can. The second place I called told me they respected their customers' privacy and wouldn't give out that information. Confidentiality at the pump? I realized that this was another job that had to be done in person, and I was short on time tonight.

I texted Randy, deciding to reel in that coffee date sooner rather than later, using my investigation as an excuse. He had mentioned that his sister Sonia was once friends with Lucy Jameson. By asking them both to coffee, I could multitask. Coffee, investigation, and Randy. Tomorrow would be the perfect morning.

Next I fielded a call from the Los Angeles County Sheriff's Department regarding the death of Candy Jameson. Detective Chase Dupont verified that Candy Jameson had died three years ago of a drug overdose, which was ruled a suicide. He agreed to send me a copy of the report. In my e-mails I found a correspondence from our records department with an electronic attachment from the archives. It was the police report from the domestic dispute four years ago when Candy had paid her ex a visit. News accounts from that time had mentioned an argument between Candy and Kent, but the officer at the scene reported that a confrontation with some physical violence—a tossed teapot, a brandished knife—had ensued between Candy and Martha.

Interesting. Why was the public version switched? To protect Martha's reputation? The report had been filled out by Officer Esme Garcia.

Z came in from a meeting on another case, and I told him about the missing reports from the 9-1-1 calls to the Jameson estate. "There were at least two calls there in the last two years, but there's nothing on file."

"No paper copy?"

"Nothing. What do you make of that?"

"Some funny business." He checked over his shoulder to see who was in the squad room, then added, "Another example of fine police work by Brown and Garcia."

249

"How do you know they were the cops who responded?"

"It's their gig now. I'm kind of surprised they're letting you step through the hallowed gates."

"Who's stopping us? Are we kowtowing because Kent Jameson is a celebrity? That doesn't mean he can get away with murder."

Z leaned in close and lowered his voice. "Just let it go right now, okay? I'm in enough trouble. So . . ." He straightened, looking down at my desk. "What else have you got?"

I updated him on my call with the mechanic and my discovery of the Prince's identity.

"No kidding. Another spoiled rich guy who thinks he's Peter Pan. Just what this town needs."

Biting back a smile, I looked at the time and sighed. "I'm supposed to be cutting out of here, but I haven't resolved this gas can issue." I started to explain, but he held up a hand.

"Yeah, yeah, I saw the report. A full can of gas contributed to the fire in the sports car. So we need to check local service stations and see if they remember filling a gas can for any of our friendly suspects."

"I tried calling around, but the people I talked to gave me the brush-off."

"Yeah, this calls for some face time." He checked his watch. "I'll go. Most stations are open till nine or ten."

"Thanks." As I rose to head out, part of me

wanted to bow out of the family dinner and stay. But that would have been the easy choice.

In the women's locker room, I quickly changed into a print pencil skirt and a black sweater. I was slipping on my leather jacket when Garcia emerged from the restroom.

"Cutting out early?" she sniped as she opened her locker.

I wasn't sure if it was my own guilt at leaving or if she had meant to make it sound like I was a loser.

"We missed you at the press conference," I said sweetly. "Which surprised me, since I know the Jameson estate is your special detail."

"I had an appointment."

"Actually, I was just looking at a report you wrote from the Jameson place. One from four years ago. It's the only reference I have, since there are no reports on file from other calls to the Jameson compound."

She stopped moving but stood staring into her locker. "Really."

"Did you forget to file those reports?" I asked. "Or did something happen to them?"

"I do my job, Mori. Those reports were done. I filed them myself."

"Well, they're gone." I hung my uniform shirt in my locker. "Do you remember what the nine-one-one calls were about?"

"The daughter. The pompous wife. Those two fight like cats and dogs."

"What did they fight about?"

"I'm no psychologist," Garcia said. "I gotta get back." She closed her locker but didn't slam it.

A good sign, I thought. The words of a failed psychologist.

After a stop at home to pick up my mother and Hannah, we headed, as if on autopilot, to the restaurant where I'd spent so many hours of my life. As I drove, I told my mother and sister the story of Emory Vandenbos's plane crash and survival. "He's the leader of that hippie group living in Stafford Woods," I said. "And now we're thinking that some of the campers living there might be the Lost Girls, those missing runaways."

"Bad girls," my mother said, clucking her tongue. "Leaving their parents like that."

"Mom, some of them don't have parents. They're orphans. Foster kids."

"I like the story about the kid surviving in the woods after the plane crash," Hannah said. "So he's really rich now?"

"Apparently."

"Is he cute?"

I sighed. My family never really listened to my stories.

The family dinner was a ritual started by my mother when I was in junior high. My father had been working long days and nights, getting the family restaurant on its feet, and my mother realized that we might never see him if we didn't come in to dine at the restaurant once a week. My father still works long hours, but as his children grew to have various commitments, the dinners dwindled down to once a month.

In the restaurant, we paused beside the gold leaf screen hand-painted with a sakura blossom to hug the hostess, Yoshino, who is like an auntie to me and my siblings. I believe my father's enterprise has singlehandedly subsidized the Japanese American community in Portland.

"Such a beautiful coat, Keiko!" she told my mother. "And here's our lady cop, Laura!" she said, hugging me. "And the famous scholar, sure to be valedictorian!" she told Hannah.

We all hugged her back, basking in her lilac perfume and telling her how good it was to see her.

Inside, my father was sitting at a table of five, giving lessons on Japanese customs. He is a slight man, only five feet ten inches tall, but when he smiles, his joy fills the entire room. "So in Japan, when someone makes a toast, you raise your glass. Look them in the eye and say, 'Kanpai!' That means empty cup or bottoms up. And you take sip. Even a small sip is good. Let's all try." He lifted a glass of water and said, "Kanpai!"

The others at the table lifted a glass and toasted.

"Very good! And don't forget, very polite to look the person toasting in the eye. Don't forget, now," he said, smiling at the two boys wearing soccer jerseys.

"We won't," one of the kids said.

Dad looked up and, noticing us standing by the table, scrambled to his feet. "Oh, look at that! This is my family!" He patted Hannah's shoulder. "Somehow, they found me. I can't believe it!" I sagged a little as he introduced my mother, the love of his life; my sister, the brightest scholar; and then me, "our resident psychologist."

The slip brought me back to Dad's litany when I had worked at the restaurant:

My daughter Laura, she going to be a famous psychologist. She got the right stuff. Her brother, he's studying to be a doctor, and I got a lawyer already—the oldest. When everyone done with school, we open up one big business. You come here to fix your head and heart and get legal advice and a full belly, all at the same time.

My father used to repeat this little ditty as if it were the funniest joke in the world. Customers loved it. I laughed along, enjoying it. That lasted for many years until, toward the end of high school, it became clear that psychology would not be my destiny.

"So very nice to meet you," my mother told the diners. "We'll leave you to your dinners now." And she led the way to our table.

Dad followed her, and I hurried to catch up and take his arm. "Dad, I'm a police officer now."

"Yes, yes, I know. But when you want to come back here, you can be our resident psychologist again. Everyone misses you! There wasn't a problem you couldn't fix."

It was hard to be annoyed with his enthusiasm.

We didn't need the menus my father passed out before hurrying off to attend to something. As usual, we would share a plate of salmon teriyaki, miso soup, and salad. But ten minutes later, Dad still hadn't joined us.

"Where is your father?" Keiko asked, her dark eyes skimming the restaurant.

"I see him over in the sun-room," Hannah said. "I think he's delivering a dissertation on the history of the rice bowl."

"Stop that. Your father works hard."

"We know, Mom." I rose from the table. "I'll go put our order in." I knew my way around the place, and it felt good to step into the kitchen, past the staff bulletin board where people posted photos of themselves and notes. Dad had posted a note in his lovely script: *Who will work Halloween? Everyone wearing costumes!* And on a table beneath that was a prank candy bowl with a green monster hand that would grab you when you reached for candy.

I planned to give our order to the chef personally so that he could add a nice little touch for Dad. Radish roses or a side of cauliflower tempura. It was always fun to surprise someone who delighted in the details. From here, I could see that the chef had stepped off the line and was talking with Yoshino. It would be rude to interrupt.

As I waited, I sneaked a hand around the side of the bowl and grabbed a peppermint patty. Yes! But that was too easy. I tried again, daring to go closer to the green hand.

"Hahaha!" the voice cackled as the hand snapped over mine and I jumped back in glee. In some ways, I was my father's daughter.

Peeking around the wall, I saw that they were still talking.

"Tell Koji I want to come out and say hello," said Michael. He had been our chef since I was in high school.

"I will, but after the meal, of course. I'm telling you, it's so good to see them, but sad, too. I don't know about Laura. When she became a police officer, it broke Koji's heart."

Pain sliced my heart, immobilizing me.

"She's a good kid," Michael said.

"Yes, but a disappointment," Yoshino said. "What can we do? He's still smiling, so we must do the same."

Michael said something, but my ears had gone deaf from the thickness in my throat and the thrum of my racing heart. My legs seemed frozen in place, but I commanded them to move, and they did, quivering as I staggered out the door. Head down, I held myself together long enough to pause at a computer terminal, tap in my ID code indelibly lodged in my brain, and place our order.

Then it took all my might to force myself to keep breathing, even tiny breaths, as I hurried to the ladies' room. My heart was racing so fast, I felt sure it would burst. Inside the stall, I fought the tight, choking fist of panic as the hand dryer roared and voices echoed out in the hall.

Deep breaths, just take deep breaths, I reminded myself.

Our resident psychologist, my father said so proudly. *She can fix anything.*

Sometimes you can't fix things. Sometimes the broken pieces simply don't fit together anymore.

That night, Hannah came into my room with Tigger in her arms. "I can't believe you missed most of dinner," she said, standing over my bed. Imperious Hannah.

"I just had the worst cramps," I lied.

"Feeling better?"

"Much."

She sat on the bed and put the dog down between us. Tigger stretched out and rested his chin on his paws. Hannah and I cooed and stroked his silky fur as he stared up at us with bulgy eyes. Overkill.

"I used to love going to the restaurant," Hannah said, "but now it feels a little strained, like we have to perform."

"I guess the novelty has worn off."

"Or Mom and Dad don't see us for who we really are."

I looked at my younger sister, as if seeing her through a new pair of lenses. "You are exactly right. And that doesn't make it easy."

"I know." She stood up and yawned. "That's why I brought you Tigger. He'll sleep with you tonight. You know, Cavaliers make great therapy dogs."

"They do. Thanks."

Hannah left, quietly closing the door. I placed my head beside the sleeping dog, and my eyes filled with tears of thanks. My sister was becoming a human being.

I woke up the next morning feeling recharged and ready to kick some investigative butt. It was Wednesday—my day off, except for an appointment with the county prosecutor that I would be paid overtime for. Since my meeting with Randy and his sister wasn't really police business, I wore jeans, a white sweater, and my favorite black boots.

"Get anything you want," I told Sonia. "I'm buying."

"I love their caramel macchiatos. I would drink one every morning if it wasn't a helluva lot of calories." She ordered one with a triple shot but declined any food.

258

I ordered a latte and splurged on an almond croissant. While I hadn't been able to run the past few days, I also hadn't been eating much. I deserved a treat.

"I'm good with water," Randy said.

"Seriously? Did you give up caffeine?"

"I don't need a fancy drink."

"How about a regular coffee?" *Just a coffee, not a commitment,* I thought, noticing his uneasiness. He seemed ready to bolt out the door.

He got a small coffee, and we settled into a table under a red pendant that looked like an artist's rendition of a bomb.

"I have to be at school by nine twenty," Sonia said. "I don't have a first-period class this year. Finally."

"So you're a senior?" I said, tearing off the corner of the flaky croissant. "How's the college search going?" As she talked of universities she'd visited, I realized that Randy's little sister was growing up, just like the rest of us. The dark hair that used to resemble a wild garden was now tamed into long ringlets, the fierce brows plucked to reveal the same smoky eyes her brother possessed. As a member of the dance team, her direction at school varied from my sister's quest for the Ivy League, but both approaches held a generous measure of obsessiveness.

"Anyway, that's that. Randy said you had something to ask me. Like, real police business."

She sipped from the straw, staring at me with narrowed eyes. "You don't really look like a cop, Laura. Do you wear a uniform?"

"I do. With a shiny badge and a real gun."

"Have you ever shot anyone?"

I laughed. "No. But I haven't even been on the streets for two months."

"I can't even." She shook her head. "That is freakin' amazing."

Her admiration pumped me up a bit until I looked over to Randy, whose sour expression drained my enthusiasm. Whatever. I would deal with him later.

"I wanted to talk to you because I'm trying to track down Lucy Jameson," I said, explaining that she had been missing since the car crash.

Her curls bobbed as she nodded. "Oh, my God, yeah. I heard about the crash. Only I haven't seen Lucy for years. I don't know where she is."

"I'm more interested in how she was back when you knew her. Was that your freshman year of high school?"

"That was when it ended. We hung out in junior high, all through eighth grade. It was super fun when she went to school. We had a couple of classes together, and she always sat near me and sent me funny texts until the teacher started taking our cell phones at the beginning of class. Then she started passing notes. She was a sweet girl. I used to love going over to her house. I remember her room was like a fairy-tale kingdom with tons of stuffed animals. We would stay up late listening to music and talking."

"So you met her father and stepmother?"

"Yeah. They were cool."

"Did you guys travel in a group of friends?"

"No. That was the weird thing. It was always just the two of us, and when I invited Lucy to play on my soccer team or come to the movies, she cut out. When I wanted to go to the spring dance, she got kind of mad at me. I sort of shook it off. I had some other friends. It was cool."

"So what happened in freshman year?"

She shrugged. "High school was different. There were a lot of new people at school, and I wanted to spread my wings. Lucy didn't like it. I think she was overwhelmed. One day she just stopped coming to school. I called her, and she said she was homeschooling and that she didn't want to hear about any of our friends. The next thing I knew, she was hanging out with some girl who didn't even go to our school. Katie something. She was older, like sixteen and driving. When I suggested that we hang out one weekend, Lucy blew me off and said it was over. Just like that. She stopped answering my text messages and everything."

"Wow. That's harsh."

"It wasn't a huge deal," Sonia insisted. She poked at the fading mound of whipped cream at the top of her drink. "I had other friends, and I was meeting new people every day. It was just . . . abrupt."

"And that was when she started home-schooling?"

Sonia nodded. "She disappeared from Sunrise High. I figured she went back to one of those boarding schools, but someone said she was getting her diploma online."

"Isn't that ironic?" Randy said. "One of the few kids in town whose parents could pay her way to any college in the world, and she's probably settling for a GED."

"If she even got that far," I added, recalling the workbooks I had come across, many of which were only partially completed. Of course, Lucy would probably never need to work a day in her life, but that didn't mean she could sit around eating Twix bars. Everyone needed a purpose.

"So that's all I really know about Lucy." Sonia's mouth opened wide, and she blinked rapidly. "Oh, my God. You don't think Lucy is dead, do you? I mean, since she disappeared?"

"I don't think so. Kent and Martha don't seem too worried. Apparently she's disappeared from the compound before. More than once."

"Well, she dumped her friends more than once, too. I heard that girl Katie was out of the picture in six months, and the new girl was Darla or Darcy or something. Disposable friends. That's how Lucy was." She checked her cell phone and rose. "I have to go. So are you dropping me off, Randy, or should I use your car?" she asked, obviously hoping for the latter.

"I'll take you."

Cups in hand, the three of us left the table and headed out. Juggling her cup and phone, Sonia was texting as she pushed through the door.

"Thanks for bringing Sonia," I told Randy as the door gently dropped closed behind her. "Maybe the two of us can have coffee some other time and talk about what's bothering you."

"Me? I'm fine."

"Then why have you been scowling at the floor since we came in here? Do you hate the tiles that much?"

"It's nothing."

Something dark squeezed my chest at the realization that the easy banter I'd enjoyed with Randy at the scene of the car wreck was a thing of the past.

"Okay." I lifted my chin, acting as if I didn't care. "Then never mind." I started to yank open the door but he stopped me.

"The thing is, it's not you. I don't want to piss anyone off here. I might be seeing someone else." His brows shot up. "I mean, are we talking about coffee or more?"

"Today was just coffee," I said, reminding myself to keep breathing. There were many fish in the sea, plenty of guys in my place of work. But only one Randy Shapiro, my guy next door. "If you're sort of, maybe seeing someone else, let's leave it there."

He smiled, turning my heart to butter. "See? You're good at handling this stuff."

As I headed out into a gust of wind, I was glad that the light of my life was about as observan as the leaves swirling around in the parking lot. He waved good-bye, looking straight through me. I was invisible to him. Too bad that didn't make me care for him any less.

—19—

When I arrived at the precinct, a few of the cops did a double take as I walked into the squad room. I discreetly checked my fly and looked back at the heel of my boots for a streamer of toilet paper. I was clear. I suspected they liked my street clothes, which was salt in the wound after coffee with Randy, who hadn't seemed to notice what I was wearing.

I was logging onto my computer as Z came sweeping in. "Hey, hey, now. Look what I got."

He held up a black cell phone, and it took me a minute to piece things together.

"Andy Greenleaf's cell phone?"

He grinned. "His lawyer called this morning,

gave us the go-ahead and the pass code. I spent the last two hours going through his text messages for the past two weeks, and there's nothing from Kyra Miller."

"She could have used another name."

"No, believe me, there is nothing interesting here. Mostly messages to the girlfriend saying, 'What time you coming over?' and 'I'm so lonely without you.' Junior high shit."

How I would have loved to text a boy messages like that in junior high. "Have you looked at the photos? May I see it?"

"No time for that. Omak and Deming are waiting for us in the conference room."

"All right." I grabbed my paper file with notes and followed him down the hall. "Can I just see his phone for a second?"

"Patience, Mori. We got bigger fish to fry now."

"You are such a tease."

Inside the conference room, Omak was seated next to a white woman dressed in an ill-fitting suit that made her resemble the Mad Hatter.

"Hello. I'm Claudia Deming from the county prosecutor's office. Thank you for coming in on your day off. Have a seat and we'll lay out the evidence that we have against Andy Greenleaf." She wasn't the person I was expecting from the creamy, rich voice on the phone. She was older than I had imagined and not nearly as soft and fuzzy as her voice. She wore navy slacks and a man-tailored striped shirt with billowing sleeves under a baggy vest. With electric blue glasses stuck in her straight silvering hair and piercing blue eyes, Claudia Deming meant business. "Please, bear with me as I'm having trouble wrapping my brain around this one." She looked down over her glasses as she tapped a pale fingernail on her electronic tablet. "Oh! By the way, Officer Mori, those samples you scraped up from the Jameson driveway? That viscous substance? It was a match to the brake fluid in the Karmann Ghia that was involved in the crash."

"So the car's brake lines were severed at the Jameson place," I said, feeling a small surge of victory as one puzzle piece fell into place.

"Where was it parked?" Omak turned to me.

"Just outside the garage. The groundskeeper, Carlos Flores, saw it there when he left Monday at eighteen hundred."

"And the crash was reported at nineteen forty-five. So we can argue that the brakes were cut at the Jameson residence." Claudia turned to me. "Which reminds me, locating the stain to determine where the car's brake lines were cut— that was a nice bit of detective work, Officer Mori."

"Please, call me Laura."

She pointed her blue glasses at me. "Okay, Laura. I'm wondering what sort of shape those brakes were in, considering it was an old car. A classic, yes, but not necessarily in mint condition."

"I spoke with the Jamesons' mechanic, Hal Burke, last night," I said. "Sorry I didn't get the notes into the case file yet. He said that the Karmann Ghia was serviced recently and the brakes were in good condition. Kent Jameson loved his cars, babied them all. Hal works on their cars exclusively two times a week, maybe three."

"Could the brakes have failed without tampering?" Z asked. "It was an old car."

"It's highly unlikely on a car that is regularly serviced," I said. "Hal is vehement about the safety of the cars he works on. Both Hal and our mechanic agree that someone tampered with those brakes. Someone who knows cars."

"Because you can't easily disable the brakes in a more recent car, which isn't common knowledge," Claudia said. "Am I correct?"

I nodded. "Cars made after 1976 have a different braking system to prevent the loss of pressure. And if you add in the gas can in the trunk of the car—more fuel for the fire after crashing—the evidence points to premeditation. Someone meant for Kyra to crash."

"We could certainly argue the point," Claudia said. "Have you tracked down the source of the gas can? The fact that there was one in the car suggests foul play."

Breathless panic seeped through my chest as I looked at Z. Oh, please, have an answer.

"We checked around at the local service stations," Z said.

He'd done it . . . and he said "we" to share the credit. What a great partner.

"No one recalls selling gas to Andy Greenleaf, but we found a kid, J. J. Metz at the Shell on Oak, who remembers that Lucy Jameson came in with two gas cans to fill."

"Lucy Jameson?" Claudia squinted. "The daughter? Really?"

I was almost as surprised as Claudia. Almost. After talking with Sonia this morning, it was clear that Lucy had a tenuous grip on stability. But what had happened to the second gas can?

"Lucy came in last week. Put it on a credit card, so there's a record. He advised her against it—told her it was too dangerous—but she acted like she knew what she was doing."

"Well, that's an interesting turn." Claudia turned to Omak. "Have you met this Lucy, Lieutenant?"

"None of us have. She's still missing," he said.

"Of course she is." Claudia smiled. "That little twist reminds me of a Kent Jameson novel, only I'm afraid we're not going to be able to wrap it all up with the same panache."

"We'll give it our best, Claudia." A rare joke from Omak.

"Now for our man in custody." Claudia tilted her head to one side and squinted at some distant spot. "I agree we have probable cause against Mr. Greenleaf. And he has a criminal record. One charge. Seven years ago. And there are the naked photos. Not a good thing for a former sex offender. But there's something missing here. I had a brief conversation with Andy Greenleaf before he lawyered up, and I'm not convinced he's our guy. Andy Greenleaf is no rocket scientist, but he does have enough smarts to know that his movements were being watched by the Jamesons, their staff, his own girlfriend. To engage with Kyra Miller? Unlikely. And you got his cell phone this morning. Did you find anything?"

Z shrugged. "Nothing so far."

"People put idiotic things on their cell phones, but if you haven't found it yet, you won't." Claudia shook her head. "Something doesn't feel right to me. Andy claims he never saw those photos of Kyra, doesn't know how they got there. In fact, his prints are not on the photos or the envelope. And as Officer Mori noted, the envelope hadn't been up in that attic long. It was placed there recently."

"So you think someone else planted the photos there," I said.

"It's quite possible. I don't know *who* put them there. That's for you guys to figure out." She leafed through the file. "What was Andy's relationship with Kyra?"

269

"He talked to me about Kyra," I offered. "Granted, he may have been putting a spin on things, but he sounded like he was talking about a younger sister." I told them about Andy's accounts of how Kyra had related to the alpacas, how she had seemed to genuinely love the animals.

"See that?" Claudia's tone was not critical; she seemed utterly intrigued. "We have some contradictory evidence here and very little physical evidence. I'm waiting on a court order to take a blood sample. Then we can check if his DNA matches the semen found in Kyra Miller's body. A match would prove they had intercourse but not that he murdered her. And, as we all know, the real test procedures aren't as quick as the process you see on TV. It takes about a month to get a DNA match back. Obviously, we can't hold Andy that long without more substantial evidence. Let's talk tomorrow, Lieutenant. In the meantime, I'm intrigued by Lucy Jameson. Quite intrigued."

As was I.

At home I pulled off my boots and considered watching a movie. The wind had blown in inky gray clouds and rain that pelted the street so hard drops bounced on the pavement. It was that turning point in October when any vestiges of summer seemed gone forever. The driving rain was miserable enough to make me glad that I could hole up inside for the day.

But I wouldn't be able to focus on TV when my mind was conjuring images of Lucy and the Prince, sparking fires and spearing wild animals like half-barbaric winners of *Survivor* in Stafford Woods. I collapsed on the soft corduroy sofa and pulled my computer onto my lap. My mother must have taken the dogs somewhere, and the luxury of having the house to myself almost made up for the rotten feeling of getting rejected by Randy and then realizing that we had most definitely arrested the wrong person.

Before I'd left the precinct, I'd suggested to Omak that we release Andy. I'd given him a crash course on what I'd learned about loony Lucy and the Prince, rich kid-turned-survivalist. He stuck with the wait-and-see attitude Claudia had recommended. Which bothered me, because the instinct to correct a mistake shrieked in my head.

My father liked to spin off Japanese proverbs (or at least he said they were ancient words of wisdom) to his family, customers, and staff at the restaurant. Right now, he would tell me that "Many failures lead to success." Which might sound positive, but I didn't want any failures to begin with.

I needed to get my ego out of this and go with the developing facts of the case, wherever they led. That meant working with Z and letting go

271

of the desire to be a hero. Another Japanese proverb: "If you understand everything, you must be misinformed." I had to stop expecting to have everything figured out as smoothly folded as an origami crane.

The next step in the investigation seemed to be in finding Lucy and the Prince. Kyra had lived with the Prince in Stafford Woods and then with Lucy at the estate. These two would have answers and insights if I could just get to them.

The prospect of hiking into the woods to find them was equally tempting and frightening. I remembered a trek into those woods with my friends that had gone awry. Natalie, Rebecca, and I had decided to hike to the Cliffs, a crazy-steep ridge that cut through the woods. It was fourteen miles round trip, but we were junior high kids without a sense of distance or consequences.

I brought up a map of Stafford Woods, three thousand acres of mostly wooded area with the scar of a huge gorge running through the center. The Cliffs were attractive to naturalists because there was no access road to the site. I had thought the wilderness aspect cool, until the woods had turned on me and there was no fast escape.

The walk to the Cliffs took us so long that we had snacked on our sandwiches and depleted our water in the first five miles. Then on the way back, the weather had changed. Darkness fell over us and the sky began to pour, swift and cold. We huddled together under tall fir trees for the worst of it, with our jackets over our heads for cover. But after that we all had to pee, and when we separated for privacy, I lost my friends.

A thread of that panic in the woods still comes back to me whenever I get sticky pine sap on my hands or scrape against the rough bark of a tree. The smell of damp soil and the sight of raindrops glimmering like diamonds in the fine needles of fir trees can jar me to that time. Something about those woods beckoned me to go deeper, something compelling and thrilling and frightening. Acres where someone could grab you and no one would hear you scream. Nooks and hidey holes that neighbors or campers or creeps could watch from.

I had sensed the danger there, and I couldn't get away fast enough. But instead I froze, panicked, choked up, chest swollen in fear as my heart raced.

I shuddered against the sofa cushions. The irony of my relationship with the woods was that our family name, Mori, meant "forest" in Japanese. So I was torn: drawn to the beauty of nature but frightened by the possibility of losing myself in the mossy, damp darkness.

Thank God Camp Turning Leaf was east of the Cascades on flatter, high desert terrain. If it had been a camp in the woods, I probably wouldn't have lasted long as a counselor.

Zooming in on the map, I imagined combing the woods for Lucy and the Prince. A total fantasy. Even if I had the nerve to try, the search would be futile.

I left another message for Hans and Christine Vandenbos. I was reading a lengthy article about how young Emory survived the plane crash when the whir of the electronic garage door opener warned me that someone was home. A moment later, I heard the tap-tap of paws on wood as the dogs came in. When they saw me, their tails began to wag as they darted around the bookcase and came straight over. I patted the sofa, and they both jumped up and snuggled in beside me, looking for affection. Never underestimate the power of a King Charles spaniel to lift your mood.

My mother took a moment longer, probably unzipping her boots in the garage. When she emerged, she looked elegant in a black trench coat, her gleaming black hair styled in a cloud around her face. Don't ask me how she kept it dry. My mother seemed to be immune to weather.

"Oh, it's you. What are you doing sitting around like a hobo in the middle of the day?"

"It's my day off. But I just got home from errands."

"Me, too. I dropped off food from the restaurant to the church mission." My father had worked out a deal in which he could donate leftovers to the church so those not-so-crisp green beans or rice that had been steamed the previous day could feed the poor. But Dad couldn't spare an employee, so Keiko usually drove into Portland and loaded up her Acura for transport to St. Benedict's on the outskirts of Sunrise Lake. "What kind of day off is a Wednesday?" she asked. "Everybody's working on Wednesday."

"Mom, I told you." I had explained this a million times. "Cops have to work weird hours because someone has to be available to help the public twenty-four-seven. And as a newbie, I'm not going to get weekends off. Not for a while."

"So maybe I shouldn't tell you on your day off, but Sister Mary Grace said you should call her."

I stifled a groan. "Please tell me you didn't volunteer me to teach Sunday school."

"No, but that's a good idea. You should be doing something for your church. Sister wants to talk to you about the Lost Girls."

"Really." I perked up. "Does she have a tip?"

"She's not sure, but three girls who come in for the food pantry, they're not from around here, and they don't seem to be old enough to be on their own. Maybe they're the Lost Girls you're looking for?"

"Does she recognize them from the Lost Girls photos? Has she seen the posters?" I was already scrolling through my phone directory for St. Benedict's number. "I'm calling her right now."

"You can't reach her now. I just told you, she's running the food pantry. If you want to talk to her, you need to go over there."

"Have the girls been there today?" I stepped into a boot. "What time does the food pantry close?"

"Ask Sister. She didn't tell me everything. You see? I do pay attention to you. It just doesn't look like I'm listening."

"That's for sure."

"I told Sister you were with the police now, looking for the Lost Girls, and it made her ask about these three little vagabond girls. You see? God makes good things happen when you go to church."

If that were true, the churches would be packed. I pulled out a green rain slicker, too rushed to argue with her twisted logic. "I'm heading over there now. Thanks, Mom."

"Yes, Laura. I'm glad you're here." Sister Mary Grace still had that Boston accent and the authoritative voice I remembered from Sunday school. "You know, these girls have been coming to our pantry twice a week, every Monday and Wednesday, and I'm getting concerned about their welfare."

"Have they been here yet today?"

"Not yet, but they usually come in the last hour."

"What do they look like?" I asked, taking out my phone. "Do you remember their skin color, eyes, and hair?"

"It's hard to tell. All three seem to be white, but their skin is dirty, and they wear beanies that cover their hair. Otherwise, they're in down outerwear, gunnysack skirt, or army fatigues. It would be hard to tell them apart if one wasn't so thin and frail. The tallest one, her name is True, she claims that she's eighteen, but she might just be saying that so they qualify for free groceries."

I handed over my cell phone to show her the photos on the Lost Girls database. "Do you recognize any of these girls?"

Sister narrowed her eyes to take a careful look. On the second photo, she let out a sigh of satisfaction. "Oh, yes, indeed. This is one of them. That's the one who goes by True. Those electric blue eyes are unforgettable. Real stunners."

I glanced at the photo she'd chosen. "Nicki Welsh." I was glad to be on the right track.

The nun nodded. "She seems to be in charge of the other girls. Maybe the oldest."

"Where do they live?"

"You know we don't require addresses. Some of these folks are living in campers in someone's driveway or in a van, moving from place to place. They say they're in a small house about a mile from here, but I know this area well. I suspect they really belong to the group of campers in the woods. Which means conditions are only going to get worse for them over the winter months. These girls worry me. The small one seems to be sick, or maybe just malnourished. So I'm glad you're here. I've tried to engage them in conversation, but I don't want to scare them away. Maybe they'll talk to you."

"I'll wait for them."

Two frail-looking women had just come in, dripping wet from the rain. A volunteer led them over to the table to register.

"If you're going to be here, I'll put you to work."

Sister had the janitor roll out a mop so that I could wipe up the water people were tracking in. Lingering by the door, mop in hand, was not the way I envisioned ensnaring the Lost Girls. But I mopped and smiled at the people, most of whom were apologetic. "You can't stop the rain," I told them.

Around ten minutes before closing, the three girls came in. Two of them wore blue plastic ponchos and one of them was completely soaked from her knit beanie to her olive-green army fatigues. Beautiful girls in rags. My senses jumped to high alert.

"Hello, True. You made it through this terrible rain." Sister Mary Grace met them at the door. "Have you met Laura?"

Three suspicious sets of eyes turned to me, and I nodded, trying to appear casual. "How's it going?"

"We need our food, please, Sister," True said, ignoring me.

Although she refused to meet my eyes, it was easy to identify her. Those cerulean eyes, her high cheekbones, the shape of her chin. This was Nicki Welsh, one of the Lost Girls who had escaped the foster care system in Roseburg.

"Of course, True," the nun said. "Just put your name on the registration list."

One of the girls squeezed out of the dripping poncho and held it by the door. "Can I leave this here? It's totally soaked."

I nodded, and the other girl removed hers, too. She was the little one Sister Mary Grace had mentioned. Thin as a rail and uncomfortable. These two poncho girls didn't seem to fit the profile of any of the Lost Girls, but I couldn't take my eyes off the one who called herself True. She was signing the register now, gesturing for the other girls to follow. I strained to hear as she spoke with the volunteer, a middle-age woman with long, silver hair and solemn eyes. Something about trying to put some meat on the bones of the frail girl named Light, who was truly a girl, more junior high age than high school. Light had a persistent cough and a sunny smile—a female Tiny Tim ambassador of goodwill. With her back to me, True was saying that she could fill her backpack and carry a box and that Melody could carry two bags.

True, Light, and Melody. They sounded like escapees from a '60s hippy commune.

As the volunteers were handing out cans and boxes for the girls, I approached True. "Hey, there."

"Hey." She did not look up from loading cans into her backpack.

"You look familiar. Did you go to school around here?"

"I'm not from here."

I turned to Light, who was more friendly. "Are you from around here?"

"My sister and I are from Wyoming, the loneliest state in America, and we're never going back," Light said.

"Don't talk to strangers, Light," True snapped.

Light started to respond, but she lost herself to a round of coughing.

"You're just bitchy from the rain," Melody muttered to True.

"Besides," Light said, "everyone here is a stranger."

"And this is a church, a safe haven," I said. "People here want to help others. Sister mentioned that the three of you have been coming on a regular basis. That you seem to be on your own. Maybe there's more we can do for you than just providing groceries."

True's eyes flashed in suspicion. "Are you from social services?"

"No, I'm not, but I want to help you."

"Really? Like I haven't heard that before."

She moved away from me, but I edged along with her. "Look, I can take you to a place where we can talk. Someplace warm and dry. I have a few questions for you."

True stepped toward me, squaring off, and I could see the exhaustion in her face, the grime on one cheek. "I have some questions, too. Like, what's your deal? Taking us to some gentleman's club where we can give full body massages for minimum wage?"

"I would never . . ." I turned back to see if Sister Mary and her volunteers had caught that comment, but Sister was talking with a family that had just arrived, a Hispanic woman with three kids who were hugging the nun.

"Come on, Light. We need to get out of here before this one drugs us and sends us up to Seattle to work as sex slaves. Or maybe ships us off to Asia? We're not stupid; we know how that works. No one gives you anything without wanting something in exchange."

"I want to help you . . ." I said, trailing them to the door. "All three of you. I can get you food and clothes and a safe place to live."

"Don't bother. We're fine just the way we are." True waited at the door while the other two shook out their ponchos. "Just grab them. You can put them on outside," she said, ushering them out the door.

"They say it stopped raining outside." Sister Mary smiled up at True and me.

"This one is leaning on me, sister," True said, cocking her chin toward me as she shifted the strap of her backpack. "If she's here next time, we won't be back."

"Sometimes we have to trust others, True. I don't know what your story is, but I promise you, Officer Mori is here to help you."

"Officer! You're a cop?" Her blue eyes turned icy as she scowled at me and plunged into the lobby. "It's the cops," she shouted backward. "Go! Run!"

I scrambled out behind them, right on True's heels, but even with her heavy backpack and a box in her arms, she moved at a good clip. "Give me a chance to help!" I yelled at her as she dodged behind a car.

As she got farther away from me, I stopped running and projected my voice. "I know you're Nicki Welsh, and people are looking for you. People want to help you."

She slowed at the edge of the parking lot, looking around for the others.

"I'm not trying to arrest you. Please, let's talk. And then if you still want to go, I won't stop you."

Panic seized her as her gaze swept the parking lot. Where had the other two girls gone? I couldn't imagine that Light could run very fast, considering her strained movements and pale skin.

"Please, just thirty minutes."

Sneering, she dropped the box of groceries and gave it a kick toward me. It didn't travel far, but the message was clear. "Leave us the fuck alone."

"Nicki . . . wait." I started to run after her as she quickly cut between two boxwoods and plunged into the yard next door. I paused at the break in the hedge, calculating as she ducked behind the neighbor's shed and disappeared. She knew the lay of the land better than I did; she would slip away from me, if she hadn't already. Besides, the other two couldn't have gotten too far.

I turned back and walked the perimeter of St. Benedict's parking lot. I'd handled that one poorly, but I'd thought the girls would want to confide in me. Rounding a cement staircase that led to the church office, I heard a high-pitched noise. A squeaky hinge? No, a crying girl, collapsed against the foundation of the building. A bag of groceries was spilled on the ground beside Light, who was coughing and cradling one hand. And her face was ghostly pale.

"I scraped my knuckles," she whimpered with a

gasp, and I realized that she was not sobbing but gasping for breath. "I fell and scraped my knuckles, and I told her to go without me."

"Your sister?"

"I told her to go." A series of coughs overcame her. "She has to get away. Please, don't go after her. Don't arrest her."

"I'm not arresting anyone right now." I kneeled beside her. "You're sick, aren't you?"

Her face puckered in pain as a series of coughs shook her body. "I used to have leukemia. I think maybe it's back."

"When was the last time you saw a doctor?"

"I don't remember." She gasped, panting now.

I touched her forehead; she was burning up. "I'm no doctor, Light, but I think you need to see one." I took out my cell phone and dialed 9-1-1.

—20—

Omak wanted to get out of the chair and pace or stand or lean against a wall. Anything was preferable to staring at Chief Cribben's handsome square face and barrel-chested physique with the open door to his infamous "Crappin'" room looming beyond him. But the chief seemed to feel threatened whenever Omak left his seat, and since he'd managed to weasel his way out of the majority of Cribben's proposed weekly meetings, it was probably best to take a deep breath, utilize the coping skills he'd learned at the VA hospital, and stay seated. Besides, they had gone through every item on Cribben's written list.

"Looks like we're done here." Omak shifted forward in the chair. "Anything else before I get back to work?"

"There is one thing." The chief tossed the agenda aside and leaned back in his chair. "I understand you were reprimanding Garcia and Brown."

Omak had sensed that they were the chief's favorites, but he didn't see why. Charmless and lazy, those two cops were a liability to the department.

"That's right. In the past year, they failed to file more than a dozen complaints that were made by residents near Stafford Woods." Omak shrugged. "They needed to be taken to task for it. All the residents up there deserve to be heard. The Jamesons aren't the only ones on that hill."

"So you took Garcia and Brown off the detail?"

"I didn't think the patrol of a wealthy, famous citizen warranted its own detail. If the Jamesons want personal guards, they can hire them. So the answer is yes. I spoke with Sgt. Joel, and we terminated the detail and reassigned Garcia and Brown to regular patrol duty. From now on, any nine-one-one calls from the Stafford Woods area will be answered by officers on duty."

"No good." Cribben leaned forward and flashed an amicable smile. "Listen, Charlie, I'm sorry to step on your toes, but we need Garcia and Brown back on that detail."

Omak lifted his splayed hands. "What's the point?"

"The Jamesons are more comfortable having them around."

"We're not here to make anyone comfortable, and we don't have the manpower to spare, even if Kent Jameson did put a few million into the city coffers over the past few years. A man with that kind of money can afford to hire his own security force."

"You're missing the beauty of this. We have a situation here that has worked for the last year. Dare I say, an accord that transcends both you and me." When Omak frowned, the chief nodded. "That's right, this one comes from a higher authority."

"You must be talking about God in heaven." Because Omak knew the mayor was out.

Cribben smiled. "That's right. The Father, Son, and Holy Spirit."

It was total bullshit. Omak knew that the mayor would never approve a deal that smacked of nepotism and cronyism. But he needed to give Cribben a long enough line to sink his own ship. "It's hard to justify a detail when there's no objective we can put in writing."

"Just do it," the chief said with a flick of his hand. "And while you're at it, pull the black cop and the Asian girl off the Jameson compound."

"I'm going to pretend I didn't hear you refer to Officers Frazier and Mori that way."

"Take the PC stick out of your ass, Omak. You know how this works. The Jamesons deserve to have seasoned cops working on their behalf."

"Last time I checked, I thought we were working for the victim here—a murdered fifteen-year-old girl."

"A girl who was inebriated and, shall we say, fucking around."

Omak struggled to contain the fury that burned inside him, fueled by the chief's words. A handsome, thick turd like Cribben was used to getting away with snarky jokes behind closed doors. Omak couldn't afford to show disrespect, but he didn't have to pretend he liked the locker room scuttlebutt.

"I have two daughters, Chief. And I would hope that if they're ever in a difficult situation, someone in law enforcement will have their backs."

"Ah, see that? You're taking things the wrong way."

"Am I?"

"Sometimes my jokes go too far, but you can't blame a guy for trying to keep things light. Just put Garcia and Brown back in Stafford Woods. Better yet, put them on the Kyra Miller case."

Was this what the chief had been pushing for all along? "To hand over an ongoing investigation at this point would compromise the integrity of the case," Omak said, watching Cribben for reaction. "I brought Frazier in to work with Mori because he's an experienced cop. She's green, but she's determined, and she has a way with people. They're a good team, and they will continue to work under my supervision." He was not backing down on this.

"Fine." The chief had heard enough. "Just get Garcia and Brown back on the hill, okay?"

"Yes, sir." It was the lesser of two evils.

"How you doing there, girly girl?" asked the paramedic. "You breathing better?" When Light nodded, the woman patted her hand and checked something on the monitors. "Yeah, your heart rate is looking more like a normal person's again. It was moving like a jackrabbit before."

After the EMTs had loaded Light in the ambulance, I was surprised when she had asked for me to come along. I was a stranger, but a familiar stranger at this point, and it meant something that she trusted me. Maybe I hadn't totally botched things by approaching the three runaways.

It was a relief to see Light in the paramedics' capable hands as they monitored her vital signs, gave her fluids through an IV line, and put her on oxygen. As we drove at a steady clip toward Evergreen County Hospital, I tried to remain cheerful and stay out of the paramedics' way.

Once we reached the hospital, Light was seen right away—triaged to determine the level of the emergency—and then moved to a bed that was cordoned off from other patients by a curtain.

"I'm so glad they let you stay with me," she told me, her brown eyes looking huge in her pale, narrow face.

"Me, too." The nurse in charge had ordered me to the waiting room until I had flashed my police ID and mentioned Light's involvement in a case I was investigating. "Sometimes, you just got to flash them your EZ Pass," Cranston had told me during training. Today, it had worked.

I had kept out of the screening process as the clerk had asked Light's real name and address. "No address," she had told the man, admitting that she was homeless. She told him she had lived in Montana, Idaho, California, and Wyoming. The first ten years had been in Sheridan, Wyoming, "but they were the worst years," she said emphatically. She had no health insurance. "And my parents aren't going to pay for me, unless they won the lottery while I've been gone." And she was only thirteen years old.

"So I heard you talking to the nurse who was checking you in. You told her your name was Ellie Watson. Is that true?"

She nodded. "I'm Ellie and my sister's real name is Morgan. We used a few different names since we left home almost two years ago, but we took on Light and Melody when we came here. The Prince names everyone when they come around. He says it's because we're creating a whole new world; people should have new names, positive names."

The Prince.

"So you're part of the group camping in Stafford Woods?"

"We've been there for a few months now. Since the spring. The summer was really nice in the woods, but now it's getting cold at night, it rains all the time, and everyone's getting cranky. Except for the Prince. He never complains about the rain or the cold, and I know he must be hungry sometimes."

"I like a clean bed at night," I said.

She smiled. "Me, too. Do you think my sister is okay? She's never left me before, but I made her go. I can't let her get in trouble over me."

"Why do you think she'll get in trouble?"

"Kidnapping. Our mother said that if we ever turned up, Morgan would go to jail for kidnapping me."

"That doesn't sound right to me. First, your sister is still too young to be tried as an adult. And I've never heard of a case of sibling kidnapping. Are you sure that's what your mother said? Maybe she was trying to scare you into coming back."

"No." Her jaw clenched as she probed at the clip on her fingertip. "The last thing she wants is us coming back. But I don't want to talk about her. Makes me even sicker."

"Then tell me how you met the Prince. How did you find the group in the woods?"

"The Prince found us in Portland. Morgan and I were with our friend Maya."

Maya Williams? The African American beauty from the list of Lost Girls. I wanted to pounce on this with a million questions, but I didn't want to freak Ellie out.

"Was Maya her real name?"

She nodded. "The Prince called her Genesis."

The name rang a bell from something I had seen recently, but I couldn't place it. "The Prince chose a name from the Bible?"

"He said it just meant the beginning. Maya was African American. He said she was one of the original people on Earth because she had dark skin."

"Interesting." This had to be the Maya I was looking for. "What's Maya's last name?"

"I don't know. We met her in California and came to Portland with her."

"Where were you living in Portland?"

"When the Prince found us, we were sleeping in doorways and stuff. One of us would be the lookout while the others slept. Before that we slept in the back of this hair salon. Maya had a key to clean it at night, so we helped her clean, and then we slept on the floor. That was nice, 'cause we had a bathroom and we could do each other's hair and that shampoo they use smells so sweet, like strawberries. But then the owner came in late one night and caught us. That was a bad night."

The three girls had earned some money by picking fruit down in California, though they'd had to sneak around because Ellie was noticeably underage. Morgan had gotten a fake ID, but people were suspicious of the threesome. Before that Ellie and her sister had traveled through Montana, Idaho, and Nevada. Occasionally they found odd jobs. Sometimes they shoplifted or stole from trucks, gardens, clotheslines, stores. I was trying to press on for more information about Maya when the doctor appeared.

"What's this gabbing going on?" a bald man in green scrubs called from the other side of the curtain. "You two sound like you're having way too much fun in here." He offered his hand to Ellie, then to me. "I'm Chris Riggs, the doctor at the moment here in the ER. And you"—he pointed to Ellie—"seem to be a very sick young lady. Let's take a look."

I stepped back as he examined her and asked her questions about her medical history. She told him she had been diagnosed with leukemia when she was eight. She had one round of chemo-therapy but left Wyoming before the second round.

Dr. Riggs examined the glands in her neck with his fingertips. "Sounds like you picked a bad time to skip town."

"Not really. My parents couldn't afford the first treatment, but people in the town pitched in to help. They were pretty mad when they found out their money went to a hot tub and a camper."

Dr. Riggs brows lifted. "That's quite a story."

"It's true. That's why I can never go back."

"Well. It's not your fault the money was squandered."

She shrugged. "That's how people see it, and I'm okay with that. I'm never going back to Wyoming. It's a very lonely state."

"And you're a people person," he said with a hint of a smile. "Good for you."

Dr. Riggs ordered some blood tests and told Ellie that she would probably be admitted to the hospital. "At least for the night, until we can get a better gauge of what's going on with you. Right now you're dehydrated and you've got a fever, and our preliminary test shows that your white blood cell count is high. You need to hang out and rest. I'll see if we can move you to a room sooner than later so that you're not in the middle of this circus down here."

After the doctor left, Ellie turned her pleading

gaze toward me. "Can you stay with me? Please? I hate hospitals, and I'm so worried about my sister. Maybe I shouldn't stay. Morgan isn't safe."

"I'll stay with you," I said. "But you need to relax, like the doctor said. Morgan will be okay back at the camp."

"Maybe not." Ellie's lower lip trembled. "What do you think will happen to her?"

"The woods are a dark, scary place. It wasn't so bad for us because we had each other, but the other girls . . . Maya and Blossom. I'm just so scared for her."

"She'll be fine," I said.

"You don't know that." Suddenly she tossed the sheet aside and swung her legs over the side of the hospital bed. "I have to get back to her. Can you get this needle out for me?"

"Don't mess with that, Ellie."

Ellie stared down at the IV line inserted into the back of her hand. "I bet I can do it."

"No, you can't. Don't. The tip could break in your vein. Don't touch it."

"But I have to go." Her voice was louder and high-pitched now, her panic heightened. She seemed to be spiraling out of control, delirious.

I stepped to the other side of the curtain and waved at a young woman in bright elephant-print scrubs. "Need some help here."

"Morgan needs me. Something's going to happen if I'm not there. I know it." Ellie peeled back the edge of the surgical tape. "I have to get back to the woods to save her. I need to save my sister. Please, Laura, take me back to my sister." She gave the tape a yank as the nurse came rushing in.

In Stafford Woods, a handful of people grunted and strained as they packed the truck under dripping trees.

Like ants digging in a colony, mindless and obedient, Lucy thought. Breaking camp in the aftermath of a pounding storm was a disgusting, cold process. Lucy had her silver Titanium jacket zipped up to her chin, her hood over her head, but still, the cold seeped into her bones. Everything she touched was either damp or soaking wet, and the dirt gathering under her nails made her long for a hot bath and a salon mani-pedi.

Maybe she should go back, dodge this whole scene. It was a lot of work to move the entire camp, and half the people weren't helping. Wolf and Eden were off working at the ranch. Light was gone now, not that she was much help, being sick and weak all the time, and Melody was sobbing about missing her sister. Pax moved around like a zombie, and True kept calling to Melody that Light would be fine, telling her to get her ass over there and help pack up.

Guardian and the Prince did most of the heavy lifting. The truck was nearly loaded with tents, bedrolls, sleeping bags, and supplies. No room for anyone to ride, but Lucy didn't mind the walking. She'd walked these woods for years, long before the Prince came along, and though she wasn't the outdoorsy, survivalist kind of chick like True, that bossy bitch, Lucy had come to learn that the woods held a hell of a lot more peace than any camp or house or purebred boarding school.

"We can't just leave without her," Melody said, back on her sister again. "She's coming back. The police got no reason to arrest her. She never did anything wrong. And nobody can say no to Light. She'll be back, and we need to be here or she'll . . . Oh, God, can she find her way back? There's, like, miles of forest out here."

"Four and a half square miles," Lucy said. "But it's getting smaller every time we have to pack up and find some new, pristine space." Actually, many of the acres of the enormous state park were uninhabitable marsh areas along the river; woodlands too dense to walk in; and hills, cliffs, and gullies that were too steep to negotiate unless you were a deer.

"We'll find a place." The Prince lifted a bag of tent poles over one shoulder as if it were a sack of feathers. He was so calm, so undisturbed, while everyone else was stressed. That was the thing about the Prince—he liked moving on.

"What about when Wolf and Eden get back?"

Pax asked, looking from True to the Prince for an answer. "They're going to wonder where we went. And they'll never find us in Stafford Woods."

"But we know how to find them," the Prince said. "Lucy will drop in on them at the ranch and tell them our new location. She's going back soon."

"I don't think so," Lucy muttered.

"You know you will," he teased at her. "Everyone here has a job, and yours is peace-making and gathering. Thanks to you, the cops stay away."

Well, thanks to my father. But she would never say that aloud. She couldn't give the other girls ammunition to use against her.

"I don't want to go," Melody sobbed for the hundredth time. "I'm going back to get Light. I'll find out what hospital they took her to, and I'll bring her home. Or I'll bring her to the new location. Who's going to help me?"

"Let it go!" Lucy barked. This girl was wearing her patience. "Can't you see what an idiotic idea that is? You'll get arrested for sure. They'll ship you back to bumfuck Wyoming and you'll never see your sister again."

Everyone stopped working as they turned their gazes on Lucy in the awkward stillness.

"Just shut your pie hole and think about the facts, Melody. Your sister was sick, very sick. Probably going to die out here. Now she'll get help from the doctors. They'll probably save her life. So stop crying and be grateful that your sister is going to live a good life. And when you're ready to leave here, then you can go hunt her down."

"You don't understand," Melody said in an accusing tone. "Light needs me."

Lucy narrowed her eyes and stared at Melody as if she were speaking gibberish. "Then go to her. Nobody's stopping you. But don't expect this whole group to go running into the police precinct because you miss your sister."

"That's pretty harsh," True sneered.

"Lucy's right." The Prince stepped into the center of the group, looking from one to another. "Sometimes you have to sacrifice one to save the rest."

"But not my sister," Melody begged in a timid voice. "Not my sister."

—21—

For a wisp of a girl, Ellie could certainly put up a fight. It took the strength of two of us and a stern scolding from the nurse to keep the girl from ripping out her IV and walking out of the hospital. But the outburst was a glimpse into her fragile state of mind. The years of poor health and transient living had taken their toll on the girl, not to mention whatever home situation had driven her and her sister away years ago.

While Ellie was being moved from the ER to a room, I called the precinct and got Z on the phone. "You are never going to believe this," I started.

"Oh, my God! Like, it's amazing," Z said in a poor imitation of a vapid teenage girl.

"I met three runaway girls from the Prince's group of campers," I continued. "I think one of them is a Lost Girl. The other two must be on the national registry of missing children. And get this: she's friends with another African American girl named Maya. I think it has to be Maya Williams."

"What? How did you . . . Shit, Mori. This is your day off."

"I followed up on a tip that couldn't wait." I explained about my mother's information about the girls visiting the food pantry, my close brush with Nicki Welsh, and my trip to the hospital with Ellie. "I'm thinking that once Ellie is released, maybe she can lead us to the camp. She wants to reunite with her sister. And it sounds like Nicki and Maya are there. Maybe some of the others."

"When are they going to release her?"

"Probably not until tomorrow. But while I'm here, maybe you can do a search for me. I'm wondering if you can do a check on the girl and her sister. She says their real names are Ellie

and Morgan Watson, from Sheridan, Wyoming."
I had driven through parts of Wyoming years ago when our family visited Yellowstone Park. There was a desolate beauty to the yawning red rock canyons, the green-and-gold meadows, the broad mountains rising to the skies. I understood Ellie's comment about loneliness. It strikes from within.

I got coffee and a hot pretzel from the hospital cafeteria while Z did the search. My cell phone jingled before I'd finished the pretzel, but it wasn't Z. The call came from the Evergreen County Lab. It was Rex Burns with some test results.

"We've been able to isolate two different drugs in Kyra Miller's system at the time of the crash. There was a small dose of diazepam, commonly known as Valium, and a toxic dose of GHB. That's the common name for one of the big three date-rape drugs."

"So maybe the sex wasn't consensual?"

"That's a possibility. But let me emphasize the amount of GHB in her blood system was certainly enough to kill her."

"What does GHB do?"

"It's used to treat narcolepsy, but often it's made on the streets. It's a dangerous drug, known to cause seizures, blackouts, breathing problems, and a slowed heart rate. Usually in liquid form, it kicks in fast—in fifteen minutes—and the effects last three to four hours. If you wake up. It's easy to overdose on GHB."

"Sounds absolutely horrible."

Rex was sending a copy of his report to Omak and me. I asked him to copy Z, realizing that it felt good to know someone else was trying to think through this case.

I was polishing off a container of frozen yogurt with walnuts when Z called me back.

"The girl wasn't lying to you. Morgan and Ellie Watson, reported missing fourteen months ago. From the online profile, it looks like four other children were removed from that home around the time the girls were reported missing. I've got a call in to Sheridan's local law enforcement and a social worker for more background."

I thanked him and told him to look for Rex's report. "Call me if you need anything else. Everyone's in a foul mood here over . . . well . . . things. I'll tell you when I see you. I wish I was out in the field, too."

Ellie's new room in the pediatric ward was quiet and clean, with gleaming tile floors and colorful walls stenciled with bamboo trees and pandas. While I'd been waiting, she'd been given a more thorough exam and blood had been drawn. She'd showered and changed into a hospital gown and robe that hung like a sheet on her sparse frame. Her clean hair, long and straight, was the color of sand, and it seemed far too thick for a tiny girl. She sat picking at a food tray with a turkey and mashed potato dinner.

"Look at you, propped up in bed with a hot meal." I smiled. "You're getting the princess treatment."

"I feel bad. I won't be able to finish. Do you want some? You can have the bread."

"I ate downstairs, and I brought us apples. You can save yours for later."

"Good idea." She put her apple on the nightstand. "I learned not to waste anything."

"Do you guys get most of your food from the church pantry?"

"A lot of it comes from there." She stabbed a few string beans with her fork. "The Prince and Guardian do some hunting, and we gather fruit from the neighbors' trees and wild blackberries in the summer. Right now we have two people working on the Jameson ranch, so they get money and sometimes food. And then Lucy brings stuff. Food and sometimes money. She steals from her father, but it sounds like he doesn't care." She looked up from her tray of food. "Do you know who I'm talking about? Lucy Jameson?"

"I've heard of her."

"I thought so, since you're a cop and everything." That pensive look had returned; her mouth was a slash of tension. Her fork dropped to the tray, and she pushed it away. "There's something wrong with Lucy."

"What do you mean?"

302

"Morgan says she's just a mean, spoiled brat, but it's worse than that. I think she's evil. The girls who go live at the ranch with her? Lucy acts like she's doing them a favor. But they never come back. None of them."

"And you think . . ."

"Lucy has been killing them, and her rich parents probably pay someone to cover it up."

I took in air, surprised to hear her spell it out so clearly.

"That's what happened with Blossom," Ellie went on. "You know, the girl in the car crash? The girl who died?"

"Yes . . ." I waited.

"Did Lucy kill her?" she asked.

Her question threw me. Here was a girl who knew nothing of the investigation—the compromised brakes, the two cans of gas Lucy had purchased, the drugs in Blossom's system—and yet she thought Lucy was the killer?

When I didn't answer, she went on. "I know that Andy was arrested, but that's wrong. Wolf and Eden say he's a good person. I think Lucy caused her death. Lucy gets rid of anyone who gets in her way, and Blossom was starting to do that with the Prince."

"What do you mean?"

"There's something between Lucy and the Prince. Sometimes he calls her his queen, and sometimes she acts like she likes him. She's really jealous of any girl the Prince looks at, and I think he had his eyes on Blossom."

I perched on the edge of the heater by the window, wondering if Ellie was a bit psychotic or extremely insightful. "But people get jealous all the time without killing someone."

"But Blossom liked him, too. A lot. She was in love. She would whisper about him when we were off fetching water from the rain catchers or when we were gathering kindling."

"Blossom was in love with the Prince?" I squinted. "He's more than ten years older than she was."

"But she really loved him."

"Did you ever see them together?"

"No, but she had to keep it a secret because he was still with another girl. And she never talked about him around Lucy. That was what made me guess it was the Prince. Blossom called him A, like it was her secret code. A was going to break up with the other girl and marry Blossom."

"A." I nodded. "Are you sure she wasn't in love with Andy Greenleaf?"

"Andy?" She laughed. "He's got a girlfriend. Blossom was in love with the Prince. A stands for Aragon, you know?"

I had considered that possibility, but it didn't seem likely when, for the past few months, he'd been in the woods, and she'd been living at the Jamesons'.

"I bet Lucy knew what was going on," Ellie continued. "That's why Lucy wanted Blossom to leave the camp. She took her away and got rid of her, I just know it."

"That's a strong accusation, Ellie. How do you know for sure?"

"It wasn't the first time Lucy killed someone." Ellie was fading, her tone growing soft. "Last spring, she left with Maya, and Maya never came back."

"Ellie, that doesn't mean the girl is dead."

"But she is." Ellie's eyes filled with tears. "She went to the big house to stay for a few days and never came back. She never came back for her stuff. Her sleeping bag and her necklaces. She loved those necklaces. She would never have gone off without them. And she left without saying good-bye to Morgan and me, and Maya would never do that. We had a deal that we would always come back for each other. We were the Three Musketeers; Maya wouldn't have left us behind. She went off with Lucy, and now she's dead. Just like Blossom. Two girls gone and two girls dead." Tears glistened in Ellie's eyes. "You don't have to believe me, but I know it's true. Lucy killed them."

"Lucy Jameson is a killer?" Omak winced, probably at the thought of all the feathers that would be flying if we investigated the daughter of the celebrity author. "Where'd you get that tip?"

"Ellie is convinced that she killed Maya Williams and Kyra Miller, two of the Lost Girls." I had hurried over from the hospital to break the news to Z and the boss. Although the notion of Lucy as a killer had seemed crazy at first, I saw how the threads of evidence were weaving together, and I felt more determined than ever to find Lucy Jameson. "Here's what I'm thinking . . ." As I detailed the scenario of Lucy as Blossom's killer, I wrote her name on the white board. Under that I wrote,

Gas cans
Access to car
Experience with Karmann Ghia
Jealousy over Prince
Emotionally unstable
History of broken friendships

"It's a theory," Omak agreed, staring at the white board. "How about the GHB? How did Lucy or the Prince get their hands on the date-rape drug?"

"That wouldn't be hard," I said. "More often than not it's a street drug. They could have scored it anywhere in Portland."

"We know it wasn't prescribed," Z said as he studied the white board. "Martha Jameson told us that no one on the ranch has easy access to GHB or Valium. Well, she did make it clear that she couldn't vouch for Andy Greenleaf."

"Trying to point the blame on Andy still?" Omak said.

"Probably," I said. "She and Kent have withheld information all along. Now I suspect they're desperate to save Lucy's skin. Kent out of love for his kid, Martha because she worries about her husband's sales slipping."

Z pointed at the notes on the board. "So it was your basic love triangle. Kyra had sex with the Prince. Lucy found out and killed Kyra."

"That's what I'm thinking," I said. "The anger had to be simmering for a while. That gave her a chance to plan the murder, fill the gas cans, and get the drugs. The brake lines were probably cut on the same day."

Omak frowned at the notes on the board. "I wish we could interview this young lady."

"That's our next task. We've got to find Lucy Jameson and get some answers. The Jamesons don't seem concerned, but she's seventeen and she's been missing for forty-eight hours."

Omak wrote "AMBER Alert?" on the white board. "We could try it."

"I would do it if I thought it would help us find her. But chances are she's holed up in the woods with the campers."

"And if that list of names Ellie gave you is correct, Lucy can lead us to the Lost Girls in Stafford Woods."

"That would be an added bonus." Ellie had

given me the names of the campers—three males and six females, including Ellie. There were two known Lost Girls in the group: True, whom I'd recognized as Nicki Welsh, and Pax, whom we believed to be Emma Dupree. Lucy Jameson came and went, as did Eden, the older girl I'd met in the stables. And then there was Ellie and her sister Morgan. Blane, the groomer at the barn, went by Wolf at the camp. And the group was led by the Prince with the help of Guardian, a tall black boy whom Ellie described as "quiet as death."

The pleas of the Duprees from the other day were still fresh in my mind: *"Please help us find our daughter. Help us bring our Lost Girls home."* And now we were so close to bringing their daughter back home.

"I wish I knew how to reach out to those kids in the woods," I said.

"It's not going to be easy with a survivalist like Vandenbos at the helm." Omak capped the marker and tucked it on the ledge. "He's avoided cops and park police for months. Although he's off the grid, he seems to have access to news."

"He's got more than four square miles of forest to hide in," said Z. "And those woods are treacherous."

I was glad that Z had said it. I had no desire to beat the bushes in those wooded acres of shadow and desolation. "Conducting a foot search would take at least a week, and it would require more manpower than we can spare."

Z snapped his fingers. "We can go in through the air. How about we fly over in helicopters with infrared devices?"

Omak considered this. "You know, Portland owns two Cessnas with infrared FLIR cameras. It's tempting."

"That would be awesome. We would find them in no time."

Z's enthusiasm made Omak cautious. "I can hear the accusations of paramilitaristic policing already. And a lot of these campers seem to be minors. We know Lucy Jameson is only seventeen. We have to proceed with caution."

"I'm telling you, it would work, Lou. I'd be down with the infrared thing."

"I'll think about it. Much as I want to bring those kids in, I can't sanction an operation in which someone might get hurt. And I'd rather use psychology than force."

"I was thinking the same thing," I said. "It would be a lot more effective to draw the campers out of the woods than to stage a widespread search."

"How you gonna do that?" Z frowned. "Dangle some carrots at the edge of the woods?"

"Psychological force. Looking at the Prince's well-to-do background, I'm thinking he might be concerned about his reputation. If we can get the word out about him and the group of girls, reveal what we know about him, he might be tried in the court of public opinion."

"Not a bad idea." Omak rubbed his jaw. "Another press conference?"

"It would pack more of a punch if it didn't come from us," I said. "I was thinking of contacting—"

Z snapped his fingers. "Your reporter friend. Natalie."

"Natalie Amichi," I said, noting that Z had remembered her. "She's a producer for channel seven news. She's already working on a story about the campers. I'll pass on the information about Emory Vandenbos. If I call her now, we have a chance of getting it on the eleven o'clock news."

"It's worth a try," Omak said.

"We can also try other connections to Lucy. Martha didn't pan out, but Kent Jameson might give us some insight into her habits, ways to reach her." I checked my watch. "It's almost nine, but Kent Jameson suffers from insomnia. He'll be up. Let's give it a shot, Z."

Z grinned as Omak rose from the table. "All right then. Keep me updated."

Z gave me a curious look.

"What is it?" I asked.

"Isn't this your day off?"

—22—

"Just saying, if it was *my* day off, I'd be home making a dent on the couch," Z grumbled as I showed him where to turn onto Fir Ridge Road en route to the Jameson ranch.

"Omak told me I can put in for overtime. And time is of the essence here."

"Yeah, but at nine o'clock at night? Didn't your mother teach you basic manners? You leave people alone between nine and nine."

I smiled. "That does sound like my mother. But this is different. We're cops."

"And this couldn't wait until morning?"

"I'm sorry if you had something to do tonight. The last thing I'd want to do is put a crimp in your social life to solve a murder investigation." I was half joking, half probing. I had no idea what Z's social life was like.

"Bullshit. You're into this stuff, Mori. Lucky for you there's no football on Wednesday night."

No mention of a girlfriend, and I knew he wasn't married. Interesting. I was curious to know what really happened when he'd been investigated by the department, but it was too soon to ask. "Lucky for me," I said.

"Let's just hope we don't get in a shootout with Garcia and Brown. Asshats."

I laughed, though there was a grain of truth in his concern. While I'd been away, a little scandal had broken at the precinct, leaving almost everyone disgruntled. Chief Crappin' had intervened in Omak's order to put Garcia and Brown back on patrol, and they'd been returned to the supreme detail of being armed security for the Stafford Woods area. "Everyone knows they're up there to protect Kent Jameson, Mr. Richie Rich Moneybags," Z said, talking with the side of his mouth clenched.

"Why is the chief micromanaging? Omak knows what he's doing."

"Money talks."

"So now those two are just spending their shifts parked in Stafford Woods?"

"Apparently. Not much different from what they've been doing the past year. Which is nothing."

"Where do you think they're hiding? Or do they work day shifts?" I stared into the woods, a dark, foreboding blur. "I've never seen them at the Jameson compound."

"Rumor has it that the Jamesons tell them where to stand guard. Like the fucking king and queen of England. But I wouldn't be surprised to find Brown and Garcia having a pancake pig-out at Mac's Diner."

I pointed the way to the main compound and described the horseshoe configuration of buildings as Z parked the patrol car by the main house.

Since I'd already spoken with Martha a few times, I thought it best to avoid her. "She tends to make excuses for Kent—that he's busy or distraught or overworked—so let's go straight to his studio."

It was perfect October weather—clear and crisp—and the three-quarter moon in the indigo sky cast a silvery glow over the paving stones, grasses, and plants.

The author opened the door soon after we knocked, his broad shoulders cutting a massive silhouette against the warm light inside. I didn't know what to expect from this volatile man, but tonight he welcomed us in.

"Don't mind the mess. I always say a creative mess is better than organized boredom, but Martha doesn't quite agree."

The studio was welcoming with walls in warm shades of mocha, cinnamon, and paprika. How long had it been since I'd eaten? I was starting to see things in the color of food. A corduroy couch and two leather chairs sat before a gas fireplace. A very basic table with a laptop and mounds and stacks of scattered notes, open books, clippings, napkins, eyeglasses, calendars, and so on faced the back window. Two walls were covered in books. One wall was shiny windows and a sliding glass door that led out to the inky black forest. The other held a kitchenette that boasted a full fridge, stove, and microwave. Otherwise, there was plenty of space to pace.

Z introduced himself, and Kent offered us something to drink. "Help yourself. There's tea and a Keurig. Hot drinks are my daily vice."

In true Martha form, I went over to the tea basket in the kitchen and made three cups of Darjeeling from the hot water spout. Sometimes people felt bonded when you shared food or drink.

"We don't mean to alarm you, sir, but we wanted to talk to you about Lucy." I kept my voice level as I dunked the tea bags. "We're concerned that no one has seen her for forty-eight hours now. Before we alert Missing Persons, we thought we'd gather any pertinent information that might be helpful."

"Missing Persons?" He seemed shocked.

I brought over two cups and handed them out. Kent nodded in thanks, but Z looked as if I'd handed him a cup of motor oil. "That would be the next logical step."

Kent straightened to his full height, puffing up impressively. "That's not necessary. She knows how to handle herself."

"She's only seventeen. A girl close to her in age just died in suspicious circumstances. It's reasonable to assume Lucy could be in some danger. We could put out an AMBER Alert for her." Somehow I knew Jameson wouldn't go for that—too much publicity.

"Let's not go overboard," he said. "I hate to

waste town and federal resources when I know where my daughter is." When he realized Z and I were waiting, he said, "Stafford Woods, I think. She hangs out with that group, the Prince and his loyal subjects. I'm not thrilled about it, but it's an improvement over her earlier escapes to Portland. She would spend the night in shop doorways or dark corners of Pioneer Courthouse Square. That kept me up at night."

"I can imagine what goes through your head. It can't be easy." From observing my sister at home, I had witnessed the difficulties of a teen breaking away from her parents. "I have to be honest—I'm worried about Lucy. Do you have any tips on how we might find her in the woods?"

His eyes twinkled as he looked up from his tea. "If I had them, I would have used them long ago. If there's one thing I've learned in life, it's that not all lost souls want to be found."

"A sad thing to say." Especially from a man who was seemingly at the top of his craft, on top of the world.

"Sad but true. But don't get me wrong. Although I allow Lucy a long tether, I do love my daughter. I may not be an überdad, but I am an involved parent. Lucy and I are a team— I'm the only family she's got—and she knows I'm committed to her well-being. If I cut corners here and there and spoil her . . . Well, there are worse things a father can do."

It struck me that Kent Jameson, although surrounded by a full-time staff and an adoring community, lived a life of isolation.

"I haven't met Lucy," I said, "so right now, she's a total enigma to me."

Kent took a sip of tea, nodding. "It's no wonder. She's a complicated creature."

"Were you close?"

"We were and we are." He lowered the mug and lifted his chin. "Two people don't need to see each other all the time to maintain a strong connection. Honestly, I miss her when she disappears like this, but a child needs to spread her wings."

"I can't help but worry about her right now. Alone and grieving the death of her friend. It sounds like she and Blossom were close."

"Ah, Blossom! She was a sweet girl, like a sister to Lucy. Everyone here became quite attached to her. It breaks my heart when I think of what Andy did to her." He drew in a raspy breath.

So . . . he believed Andy was guilty? Was he simply misinformed, or was he placing blame on Andy to cover for Lucy?

"I can't let my mind go there or I'll lose a day or two in a funk. When the heart is broken, the brain shuts down."

"We don't want to throw you off, sir," I said, "but we'd appreciate any observations that might help us solve this case. As a writer of suspense stories, I'm sure you know how that goes. Building a case, collecting evidence."

"Ah, yes, profiling the killer. I know that Martha suspects Andy, and perhaps she's correct. But I've always found him to be polite and hardworking. He had that incident when he was younger, but I've not seen any lingering hints of pedophilia."

"Then you don't see him as a murderer?" I asked, gripping the warm mug with both hands. I'd added a generous amount of honey to my tea—a sweet boost.

"As an employer and a friend, no. But as a writer, I have to say, there's that scintilla of doubt. A registered sex offender. A man approaching thirty—that's a transition time for men, though Andy seems stuck in perennial boyhood. A Peter Pan. I don't want to believe he's a killer, but let's say I could imagine it. I could write him as a villain."

"That's very insightful," I said. *And incredibly indecisive.*

"Yes, well, I dream up character profiles for a living."

"I like that game, too. Trying to figure people out." I took a sip of the tea. "At one time I wanted to be a criminal profiler."

"And why didn't you become one?" asked Kent.

"It required too much school. I wanted to finish with college and start living." I also didn't have the grades to go on to a master of forensic science, but Kent and Z didn't need to know that.

As we were leaving, I asked about the alpacas, and he told us that all the animals were purchased to indulge Lucy. "She quickly lost interest, but that's kids for you. The alpacas can be a lucrative business, and Martha is a brilliant manager." He told us that his wife had hired someone to fill in for Andy, at least for the time being. When I asked who, he shrugged, saying he stayed out of the day-to-day business of the ranch.

Back in the car, Z gave his observations. "He loves himself and he's full of bullshit. Lost souls don't want to be found. Hell yeah they do. Wait till your soul is lost, Mr. Author, and see if you'll be wanting any help."

I smiled. Partnering with Z was more amusing than I'd expected. "He's also a liar."

"That's a given. The man makes things up for a living."

"I'm talking about his comment about staying out of the ranch business. Andy said that Kent was always pressuring him to hire young people from the woods. That's why they hired Kyra Miller." I thought about my visit to the ranch. "And other people from the woods. The guy with the gold tooth, the girl with the chapped lips."

"Say what?"

I pointed to the turnoff for the barn. "Let's take a detour to the barn and the caretaker's house.

I have a feeling I've already met the new hires."

The silver moon lit the sky in the clearing, illuminating smoke rising from the chimney of the cottage. Sure enough, there were lights on in the windows of the ranch manager's cottage. Someone moved past the windows. "Looks like they heard us pull up," I said. "At least we know they're still up. You can park over there."

"What for?"

"We're going in."

"Mori, I'm going home. We interviewed Jameson. I'm done."

"You're going to like this. If my hunch is right, the people in there are part of the group in the woods."

The outdoor light went on as we approached. Z's hand went to his gun, reminding me to stay on alert. Sometimes people didn't welcome a visit from the police.

A face filled the window, and the door opened a second later.

"Hey. I thought that was you." Blane, the cowboy type, stood at the door in flannel shirt, jeans, and socks. His longish hair was damp, as if he'd recently showered. "You're the lady cop who came by the barn and got Andy."

"Right. I'm Laura Mori, and this is Officer Frazier. Mind if we ask you a few questions?"

He looked behind him, hesitating. "Are we in trouble?"

"Not by us. We're trying to find out who killed Blossom."

"Yeah. Okay." He opened the door wide, and we stepped into the cozy living room Z and I had searched yesterday, except that tonight the woodstove glowed with warmth. At first I didn't recognize the girl on the sofa. Dressed in black leggings and an oversized sweatshirt, she was combing out long, dark hair. Something flashed in her eyes, and I recognized the girl with the chapped lips, only she didn't seem as worn and raggedy. The grime had been rinsed away, her lips conditioned.

"That there's Eden and I'm Blane. Mrs. J asked us to stay on to take care of the animals while Andy is gone. She offered us the use of the cottage, and we said yeah. We've known Andy a while. He won't mind. We're just here till he gets out."

"He is getting out, right?" Eden asked.

"Maybe," I said, moving closer to the stove. Z moved into an alcove inside the door so that his back was against a wall: a defensive strategy. I found a spot on the opposite side of the room. "That fire feels nice. It's good that you could jump in for Andy."

Blane shrugged. "We know the routine, but even with us, the animals sense that something's gone. They miss him."

"Really?" I said. "I didn't know alpacas were that sensitive."

"They are," Eden offered. "Did you ever see them follow Andy around in a line? It's like he's the Pied Piper. The animals love him."

"Is he a good manager?"

"Maybe not with the books and numbers," Blane said. "School was never Andy's thing. He may not be the sharpest pencil in the box, but he's a nice person."

"A kind person," Eden said. "He would never kill anybody. Especially not Blossom. If anything, he tried to look out for her. Tried to keep her from moving over to the big house. Like he knew something bad would happen to her there."

"Don't say that," Blane told her under his breath. "That's what you think, but Andy never said that."

" 'Cause he doesn't want to lose his job, but you know he was getting freaked out about this place. About those girls and the way Lucy . . . devoured them. Like an earwig." She made a tiny biting motion with her fingers. "She whispers in their ears, and her evil crawls inside and eats their brain and kills them."

This was the second time today that someone had implied that Lucy was a killer.

Z winced. "I'm pretty sure the earwig thing is an urban legend, but you make it sound convincing."

Giving my right earlobe a tug for good measure, I turned to Eden. "To be honest, we're here about the earwig. We're trying to find Lucy."

"Good one." When she grinned, dimples formed in her cheeks. "Well, we're not her keepers. I know that's her father over in the big house, but honestly, the longer she stays away, the better."

"She's just spoiled," Blane said. "Makes her hard to live with."

"How long did you live with her and the other campers?"

Eden and Blane exchanged a nervous look.

"Yeah, we've been living in the woods," she said. "But we're not really followers of the Prince. Blane's worked here for a year, and he's cool with Andy. We're both done with taking orders from the Prince. And I'm older than those girls. I'm eighteen now, so I don't have to hide out in the woods to escape parents and social workers."

"Are you still in touch with the group?"

"No real way to stay in touch. We've been living with them off and on, but we're done with that," he said.

"If you can call that living." Eden put the comb down and snuggled into the sofa. "Their camp is kind of disorganized, and no matter what the rich girl brings from home, it's still a camp."

Looking at her now, with her shiny hair and clean face, I wasn't sure she was really eighteen, though she was probably close. A sudden pang of guilt hit me; I'd been so intent on finding Kyra's killer that I'd overlooked this girl who'd been scavenging for some time. "Eden, whether or not you're eighteen, if you need help, I can hook you up with social services."

"Another foster home or halfway house?" Eden rolled her eyes. "No, thanks. I'm doing okay now. If this job doesn't last, I'll move down toward Eugene. Lots of sheep farms down that way, and now I got experience."

"Just saying, Officer Mori's right," Z said earnestly. "If you need help, we can get it for you. You, too, man," he told Blane.

Blane shook his head. "We're cool, man."

"I know that," Frazier said. "You cool enough to show us where the group is?"

Blane winced. "No."

"None of those kids out there want your help." Eden tugged on a lock of her hair and rolled her eyes, clearly annoyed with us. "They're done with social services. And the Prince, you probably just want to arrest him, right?"

"It's not that simple, Eden. Blossom was murdered, and we don't want any harm to come to those campers. And there's also the matter of finding the killer."

"I get it," Eden said. "Yeah, it's complicated."

"Could you take a message to them?" I asked.

"Not any time soon. Whenever there's an incident, they move. They pack up camp and relocate. You running into the girls at the food pantry—yeah, we heard—that sent the group packing."

"Where will they go?"

"They'll stay in Stafford Woods. Just move a few miles. We'll hook up with them sooner or later."

"Or not." Eden gathered her hair and brought it around to her face to take a whiff. "Sweet. It's nice having a shower. All that freedom shit is overrated. They're about as free as a squirrel running from a coyote out there. Lugging water and eating out of cold cans. I'm glad to be inside, warm and comfortable. We don't need to keep the fire stoked in here all night. I don't know about you, but I'm gonna sleep like a baby."

Just then a noise at the front of the house caught our attention. There was the scratch of footsteps on the front steps before the door was flung open.

"Oh, my God, can't you guys hold it together without me? I'm gone two days and Andy gets arrested and you two are playing house in his cottage?"

I stepped out from the nook by the woodstove and stood face to face with a slender teen with a short pixie haircut.

My wish had been granted.

"Hello, Lucy."

Dressed in skinny jeans and a silver jacket, Lucy was skittish when she caught a look at Z and me.

"Cops? Shit!" She wheeled and socked Blane in the chest. "You're working with the cops? I should have known."

"We were just talking," I said, "and they haven't told us anything we don't know. But we need to talk, Lucy."

She scowled at me. "Stick it up your ass." Just as quickly as she had burst in, Lucy flew out the front door.

"Come on!" I called to Z as I followed her out. Down the stairs, across the gravel lot. I was getting my share of running in today. When I saw that she was headed toward the woods, I fumbled to release the flashlight on my belt without breaking stride. I didn't want to lose her or stumble in the dark.

Behind me, I heard Z mutter, "Shit, Mori."

Just ahead of me, Lucy sprinted onto a path into the forest, and I braced myself for a plunge into the darkness.

At least there was a path.

My flashlight's beam bounced through the darkness ahead, flickering over Lucy's silver jacket, which was not much in the way of camouflage. I usually run three miles a day, but the adrenaline kick of the chase gave me unprecedented speed. I closed in on Lucy and kept up with her until I was able to grab her by the arm and slow her down.

"Leave me alone." She twisted out of my grip and rubbed her arm, but at least she wasn't running anymore. "Oh, my God. I thought you were going to yank my arm out of its socket."

I had barely tugged at all, but I appreciated her flare for drama. "That's what happens when you run from the cops," I said. "A lot of people have been concerned about you, Lucy. I want to make sure you get home tonight."

"Then just leave me alone. That's where I'm headed, and I can make it back just fine without you."

"What's going on?" Z came running up behind me. "You okay, Mori?"

"I'm fine. I was just telling Lucy that she needs to come with us and that we'll drive her home."

"I can walk home. I'm almost halfway there."

"A young woman like yourself shouldn't be walking through the woods alone," Z said. "It's not safe. Come on, now. You can ride in the patrol car."

"Thanks but no thanks. If I have to go home, I'm doing it my way." Lucy started walking, demonstrating the stubbornness the Jamesons had mentioned.

I suggested that Z meet us at the house in the cruiser while Lucy and I walked back together. I didn't mind going on foot, and it would give me a few minutes alone with Lucy.

Skeptical, Z shined his flashlight on the path, its beam catching stones protruding in the path, brambles, and low-hanging branches. So many obstacles. "I'd feel better if the three of us drove it."

"I've been on this path before," I told him. "It comes out between Kent's studio and the riding ring. We'll meet you there in ten minutes."

When I turned back, Lucy was a ways down the path, and I had to hustle to catch up. "I'm glad to see you in one piece," I said. "Your father and Martha are really worried about you."

"Did they tell you to say that? Or are you making it up to make me feel better? Because they really don't care whether I stay or go as long as my father can get his work done and rake in the big bucks."

"Things have changed in the last few days. Your friend was killed in a car crash. Kyra Miller?" I put it out there, testing her reaction.

"You mean Blossom, right? Yeah, she was my friend. I heard all about it. It's too bad, but, you know, life goes on."

"Wow. Not to judge you, but it seems a little

cold to dismiss a best friend so easily. Someone who lived with you for months, like a sister. Your stepmother said you two were close."

"Martha doesn't know shit, okay? And why are you trying to get into my personal stuff? You need to back off."

"I need to learn everything I can about Kyra Miller's death."

"You won't get anything about her from me. I was out in the woods when that happened."

"Actually, you were arguing with your father around that time."

"Is that what he told you?" She gave a snort. "The world-famous storyteller."

"Is that not the way you remember it? Monday, around seven . . . seven thirty?"

"How am I supposed to know? I've had plenty of fights with my dad and plenty of friends who took off. Blossom just happened to kill herself on the way. Too bad, so sad. No big newsflash. She was taking my car." She paused on the path and pointed her index finger at me. "And you guys think Andy killed her, right? That's hysterical. Really."

"You think we're wrong to suspect Andy?"

"Hell, yeah. He's just a big teddy bear." Like the pristine stuffed animals on Lucy's bed. There was something haunting about that collection. "So if Andy didn't kill Kyra Miller, why don't you tell me who did?"

Lucy laughed. "What? Like I'm supposed to know?"

"I think you do."

When our eyes met, I sensed a definite shift. I thought her next words would be a confession. I was wrong.

"Wow. Just wow. I've got nothing else to say to you. Just leave me alone, okay? Or I'll get my father to sue you for police brutality or something."

Ahead of us lights glimmered through the trees. We were getting close to the compound, and I was running out of time to win Lucy over. "Look, we got off to a bad start. Is there somewhere we can go and talk after you check in with your father? There are lots of holes in our investigation, questions about Blossom, and you might be the only person who can answer them." I hoped the friendship angle might appeal to her.

In the moonlight her face seemed to have harsh angles and dark shadows. Whether it was anger or fear, I wasn't sure. "Not tonight," she said. "Maybe not ever."

"Look, my name is Laura, and this is my first case." Maybe finding some common ground would open her up. "You know how it is when you do something the first time. It takes a few tries to get it right."

"Yeah. Sucks for you," she said.

"Sure does."

"Watch this," she said, jogging ahead on the path. "I love sneaking up on my father. It scares the crap out of him."

I jogged along behind her, more aware of the weight of my patrol belt on this run. She veered off the path to the right, bounding up behind Kent Jameson's studio.

"He's there. He's working." She did a little victory dance. "This is going to be great."

Warm golden light glowed in the wall of windows where Kent walked the length of the studio, turned, then walked again. Slow, methodical, like the changing of a guard.

"Are you sure you want to scare him?" I asked.

"It'll be hysterical. He loves it." Staying in the shadows, she crept around the perimeter of the lot behind the studio, then cut over to the house. She motioned for me to watch, then sprang onto the back patio of the house with an ear-blistering shriek.

Kent's arms flew out as he twisted around toward the noise, nearly slipping off his feet. By the time he opened the slider to Lucy, he had regained his composure. "My exotic daughter of the night!"

"Daddy!" Lucy ran up to her father and hugged him. She seemed to have forgotten that I was behind her, and she didn't notice Z dash around the side of the house in response to the scream.

I emerged from the shadows, motioning Z over.

330

"Everyone's fine. Lucy's idea of a joke to scare her father."

"What the hell?" Z scowled, holding his hands out. "She runs off, no accountability, and Daddy welcomes her home? Not to mention there's a good chance she may have killed off a few girls."

"He doesn't know she's a suspect," I said, catching bits and pieces of the cheerful exchange on the patio of Jameson's writing studio. As I watched father and daughter, something occurred to me. "Or does he? If Lucy's been killing off some of her friends, don't you think Martha and Kent would suspect something?"

"I don't have kids, but I'd like to think I'd notice if they started murdering their friends." Z folded his arms. "Should we take her in for questioning? Arrest her?"

"I don't think we have probable cause. We'd be arresting her based on circumstantial evidence. On top of that, she's only seventeen. Omak warned us to tread lightly."

"What you're not saying is that she's a Jameson. In this town, that's like having a nonstick coating. No charges are gonna stick."

"She's advantaged," I said. "But just to be straight, you and I are not like that. If we had probable cause, we would take her in."

"True dat."

"We might as well go."

"Did you get anything out of Lucy?"

"No, but I'll try again tomorrow."

"What? Giving up so soon? That's not like you, Mori."

"Don't tease me. If you want, we could wait here all night."

"Let's go," he muttered.

I smiled as we headed back to the car. Z and I had developed a rapport in a short time. Maybe Cranston would decide to stay in Hawaii.

With so many loose ends in the case the night before, I expected to toss and turn in bed mulling everything over. The prospect of Andy being falsely accused. The image of Lucy as an entitled spoiled brat who danced with mental illness. The cloud of mystery that surrounded the potentially dangerous man in the woods who called himself the Prince. But exhaustion overcame my concerns, and I sank onto the mattress like a stone and slept for a solid eight hours.

I awoke Thursday morning to a string of text messages from Natalie. The first one was a link with the message "Aired on eleven o'clock news." Rolling over in bed, I clicked on the link to the studio segment with the anchor Don Juan at the news desk. Behind him a map of Stafford Woods was projected with the caption "Forest Prince Wanted for Questioning."

"Sunrise Lake Police announced today that the head of the cult of runaways living in Stafford

Woods is wanted for questioning regarding the murder of fifteen-year-old Kyra Miller." Don's voice hinted at intrigue. "You might remember, Miller was the victim of a crash earlier this week on Fir Ridge Road. Anyone with information on the whereabouts of the Prince, also known as Emory Vandenbos, is asked to contact the Sunrise Lake Police Department."

"Yes." I responded with "Perfect!"

Her second text said that she was going to push hard for an interview with the Prince, telling him it would be an opportunity to clear his name. I thanked her and rolled out of bed.

At the precinct, Z and I updated Omak on our interviews the night before.

"I've spoken with Claudia, and we're going to release Andy Greenleaf. That leaves us investigating Lucy Jameson, the Prince, and the Jamesons, who have been obstructing our investigation and hiding their daughter's connection to a murder. By the way, good job getting the word out on Emory Vandenbos. We've gotten three calls this morning. No leads, but people are concerned."

"Natalie is trying to follow up with an interview with the Prince. If anyone can crack that reclusive weirdo, it's Natalie."

"It may be easier getting to the Prince than to Lucy. Kent Jameson called Chief Cribben this morning and asked that we give his daughter some time to readjust to being home again."

"We need to talk to her now," I said. "There's nothing to stop her from running off or returning to the woods."

"The chief was adamant about it. We need to stay away until I can get this straightened out."

"I've never seen Cribben so eager to get his finger in the pie," sneered Z.

"I'm working on the chief." Omak looked around to be sure no one was paying attention. "I hate to go above his head, but I will if I have to. In the meantime, stay away from the Jameson ranch for now."

"You might as well handcuff us," Z complained. "This is no way to handle an investigation."

"You're preaching to the choir, Frazier."

Z was steaming mad.

"I'm sure Omak will work it out," I said. "In the meantime, let's do some more digging. See what else we can find on the Prince. Or on the Jamesons. Was Martha really a nurse? Has Lucy been in therapy? Maybe she's on heavy medication."

"Lot of that information is confidential."

"Since when has that stopped you?" I said.

"It's the same old story with Crappin'. One step up and two steps back."

"Are you talking about the suit you filed against him?"

His dark eyes slanted over toward me, though he didn't lift his head. "I don't want to talk about that."

"Just saying, if you ever . . ."

"I won't. But thanks, Dr. Oz." Z logged onto his computer. "All right. I'll start with the Prince, you do the Jamesons."

"I'll get on it as soon as I get back."

"Where the hell you going?"

"The hospital. I need to check up on Ellie Watson and meet the social worker who's taking her case. Smooth things over for the girl."

Z thumped his chest with a fist. "I feel for the girl, but isn't that what the social workers are for?"

"Ellie is thirteen, separated from her sister for the first time ever with a leukemia diagnosis. I think the kid could use a little support."

"You'll never last around here, Mori. You're way too nice."

I smiled as I slid my arms into the sleeves of my patrol jacket. "Thanks, Z."

I spent the rest of the morning trying to advocate for Ellie Watson.

"In cases like this, we usually send the child back to her state of origin," said Alma Hernandez, the social worker assigned to the case. The Latina woman with long, dark hair had a no-nonsense manner and a cheerful lilt to her

335

voice. I suspected she was in her forties, but she seemed younger, maybe due to the row of half a dozen diamond studs lining the shell of one ear. They sparkled when she moved. "We're supposed to send Ellie back to Wyoming and let the social workers there sort out her situation."

"But that would devastate her right now," I said. "It would destroy her spirit to leave her sister behind." We sat in brightly upholstered chairs in the waiting room of the pediatric ward. "Her health is already compromised. We can't do that to her."

"I'm not planning to do that, okay, honey? I'm just telling you what the procedure is. We're going to fight it, but it won't be easy. Mostly because of her medical costs. The state of Oregon doesn't want to take something like that on. No state would. We've got to get this girl on Medicaid, but she needs an address and a placement before we can start all that. Right now this little girl is in no-man's-land. But we really have no choice. We don't know where her father is, and the mother is in jail for selling drugs. I was told that four other children were removed from the home when the mother and her husband went to jail. Some hers, some his. No other family members came forward to care for them. I don't know; maybe there's no family. All I know is, this girl has nothing good waiting for her back in Wyoming."

"But she does have a sister here," I said. "Morgan Watson."

"And maybe we can save two girls with one generous foster family." Alma had pulled Morgan's records and learned that she was seventeen. "The sister may be her only family member who isn't incarcerated. I'm hoping that we can find this girl, and maybe the two sisters could be placed together. Down the road, once the older girl turns eighteen or nineteen, maybe she'll get a job and a way to support her younger sister. Or we might find a family to support the girl while she goes to college. That would be our goal."

Alma left me with a promise to work things out for Ellie. I was on my way down the hall to Ellie's room when Z called.

"We got an invitation to the Jameson ranch," he said.

"Omak convinced the chief?"

"No, but Martha Jameson called here and asked for you by name. She has something private she wants to discuss. I told her we'd be there at one."

"I wonder if her husband knows she invited us over."

"Who cares? We got a foot in the door."

Now that Z and I had permission to be on the Jamesons' estate—sort of—we decided to go over early and scope out the trails into the woods. Lucy seemed to be coming and going easily between the camp and the house; was the camp closer than we thought, right under our noses?

"I have to take another look, this time with the camp in mind," I told Z. I was glad when he insisted on going with me, since I did not do well with solitude in the forest.

As Z turned off Fir Ridge Road, I noticed a van headed our way up ahead. "Hey, isn't that the channel seven van?" I asked. "It is. There's Natalie." She waved from the passenger seat and motioned to the side of the road. "Pull over a second."

"What? Girl talk?" Z teased as he pulled onto the shoulder.

"Business. I showed you the piece she got on the news last night. She's been trying to interview the Prince."

I was about to get out of the car but she came around to the shoulder and leaned in my window.

"Oh, my God, I was going to call you. You'll never believe." Her blue eyes sparkled and her face was flushed with excitement. "Hi, Z." She leaned in farther, smiling flirtatiously.

"Wassup, girl."

The spark between them was unmistakable. "Did you reach him?" I asked Nat.

"I got to meet him! This morning one of the ranch workers led us into the camp, and my cameraman and I met the Prince in person. He talked with us for a while and actually let us film the camp. We got video of their setup and the girls."

"Really?" I turned to Z. "Maybe we can identify some of the runaways from the footage. We need to call Emma Dupree's parents. They'll want to watch."

"Part one airs tomorrow night. I was trying to look out for the Lost Girls, and I think I saw one, but none of them interacted with me. And there's one lost guy—this tall, scary-quiet dude who stands guard. Interesting. Thank you, thank you *so* much. This story is big. Huge. There's talk of promoting me to special projects editor."

"Who took you into the camp?" Z asked. "Was it a guy with a gold tooth named Blane?"

Natalie leaned farther into the car, a bit surprised. "That's right. How did you know?"

"Just a hunch. What's your take on the Prince?" I asked. "Be honest. A weirdo?"

"Actually, he's kind of interesting. Not creepy as I expected. Kind of good looking and he seems noble, though self-absorbed. Living through the plane crash really changed him. He was only a kid, but he survived in the wilderness and walked to a logging camp. He said he never really returned to civilization after that. He's become a true survivalist. And ironically, he could live anywhere he wanted. His family is loaded. They're the—"

"I know. Boss Shoes."

"Right! But he's not into money. My sense was that the whole runaway cult thing is wearing a little thin for him. He talked about being a guide for nature tours in Alaska. He's also thinking about trying to get on *Survivor.* His self-confidence knows no bounds. He gave me enough for a three-part story that will begin airing on the late news tomorrow. Supertight deadlines. I need to get back and do some editing. And then I'm working on a print story for the *Oregonian* that's supposed to run tomorrow. I'm telling you, Laur, this story is a gold mine."

"You did it, girl!" I said. "You found the Prince!"

"Not my prince, but it's an awesome story." She lifted her buzzing phone and winced. "I gotta take this. Thanks so much! Love you lots!"

"Love you back!" I said, letting all professionalism drop for the moment.

"Bye, Natalie," Z called.

"Call me, big guy!" Nat tinkled her fingers at Z as she hurried back to the van.

Z seemed to be smiling as he put the car into gear. "O-M-G. Can we go now, girlfriend?"

"Shut up and drive. Take the turn off to the barn. We'll park back there to avoid being seen before our appointment."

We decided to take the shortcut from the Jameson ranch to the Cliffs, as the trail on this side of the great divide rarely saw hikers. "If they set up camp here, it's very unlikely anyone from the Stafford Woods parking lot would wander by." Z had the GPS open on his phone and navigated the way.

"There's a trail that leads to the Cliffs," he said. "But there are a few forks with smaller trails. A few of them lead back to the Jameson property. One goes to their neighbor, Marge Bloom, and one trail zigzags down to the park."

"I vaguely remember this, though it's been a long time. See those three trees? Those are giant sequoias. They're hundreds of years old. You know, you can tell they're sequoias because they're shaped like a pencil." We paused to stare up at the towering trees. "I learned that in school."

"We didn't have botany in my school."

"Didn't you go to outdoor school? No summer camp?"

"Poor black kids don't do summer camp, unless

you go with one of those government programs, and they always freaked my mama out."

"So did you ever—?"

"Enough with the pity, Mori. And the only camp I'm interested in right now is the one where the Prince is holding court."

"Right." My curiosity about Z had gotten the better of me. Honestly, he was the first black person I'd hung out with, having attended a school with only a handful of African American students. The Portland area had a notorious history of discrimination, and consequently Sunrise Lake was barely 6 percent African American. The Asian population wasn't much larger, which might have been one of the reasons I felt comfortable with Z. We were fish out of water, both in our jobs and in our hometowns.

"Keep your eyes open," he said.

Z continued to navigate until the cell phone service cut out. "Shit. I didn't think about that."

"We can follow the trail markers, but I think I remember the rest of the way." We walked another ten or fifteen minutes without seeing any signs of human life. Then we came upon the ridge overlooking the Willamette River in the foreground and the white slanted peak of Mt. Hood in the distance.

"Wow." I breathed in the magnificent panorama. I'm not a nature freak, but whenever I catch sight of that mountain—which is not every day with our overcast skies—I want to do a happy dance. "I love it when it's clear enough to see Mt. Hood."

"Awesome," he agreed. "So we're at the top of the Cliffs now?"

"Right. You get this great view up here, but we're a few hundred feet above the ground below, and some of the cliffside has no barrier. In fog or snow, this area is treacherous."

We moved closer to the edge, but I stopped a few yards short. "That's close enough for me. This is where my knees turn to jelly."

"Got a fear of heights, Mori?"

"A healthy fear. Especially when there's no safety net." I went to the side where a waist-high fence marked off the steep drop.

Scary.

Even with the barrier holding me back, a sick feeling made me want to double over.

I could see the small houses built along the ridge. "See those two blue rooftops? That's the park section. They've got ball fields, picnic shelters, and tables. There's a fishing area on the river as well as a boat ramp and dock."

"Nice. But I bet it's a bitch getting down there."

"There's a trail, kind of steep, but most people just drive into the park." I held onto the metal pipe top of the fence, trying to fend off the feeling of being tugged forward over the cliffside.

Sometimes I have nightmares, anxiety dreams, that I'm at the top of a mountain or a steep building and I don't have the courage or skills to make it down safely. And I just hang on, clinging to life. My friend Becca had gotten a book on dream interpretation and diagnosed my problem. "You have high goals and standards for yourself," she told me, "but you worry that you'll fail to fulfill other people's expectations of you." The word "failure" was enough to inspire a new round of nightmares. Maybe I chose to be a cop because my successes and failures on the job could not be measured as easily as my siblings' careers in law and medicine. Maybe. Still, I wanted to succeed. And right now, that meant solving this case.

"We should head over to the compound," Z said. "Don't want to keep Martha waiting."

"Right." It was easier to breathe after I backed away.

Z seemed to sense my discomfort. "Good to know the lay of the land," he said. "And I'll remember to stay away from the Cliffs."

"Yeah. Sometimes a great view is overrated."

Juana answered the door and ushered us into the great room. I would have liked to ask Juana what she knew about Lucy's current whereabouts, but Martha was there, staring out the window. Watching her reflection in the glass, I saw her brace herself before she turned toward us.

"Officers, please have a seat. Would you like

some tea?" she offered without the usual insistence.

We declined, and Martha waved Juana off as she perched on the seat opposite us. Z sat on the edge of the sofa, bolt upright and ready to spring into action. I could tell he would have preferred to stand.

"This has been heavy on my mind since last night." She lowered her voice. "I haven't mentioned it to Kent. Mostly because I know he would have tried to stop me." She pressed fingertips to her temples, composing herself before going on. "First, I have a confession to make. Officer Frazier, when you called to ask if anyone in our family has access to GHB, well, I wasn't completely honest. I told a little white lie. I worried about the information getting out to the media. It would look bad that Kent has access to a drug that some people consider controversial. I know it's been used for date rapes, but Kent has a prescription for it. Honestly, it's the only thing that addresses his narcolepsy. Without it, he paces day and night."

"So his doctor has prescribed GHB," I said, trying to keep my mind from flying ahead with assumptions. Kent Jameson possessed a date-rape drug. Had he used it on Kyra Miller?

"Yes. He's used it for a while now. Not every night, but when he hits a bad patch, it helps him break the cycle of insomnia. Well, last week he misplaced it. Couldn't find it anywhere. So I called the doctor's office to get a refill for him." She shook her head. "It's nearly impossible to get the doctor to sign off on an early refill for a controlled substance. So many questions. Anyway. The doctor finally came through for us. We worked it out. It's just that . . ."

She pressed her mouth shut, blinking back tears.

"Mrs. Jameson. Martha? Are you okay?"

She shook her head. "I'm afraid things won't be right around here ever again. You see, last night, I was helping Lucy move the stuffed animals so she could use the bed, and I felt something hard in the Velcro belly of one of the animals. The unicorn. I slipped it out when Lucy wasn't looking. This was inside." She unzipped the pocket of her raspberry fleece and handed me a vial. It was GHB, a labeled prescription for Kent Jameson. "Use as directed for insomnia."

Had I missed this in my examination of the articles in Lucy's room? Embarrassment heated my cheeks as I considered that very real possibility. Still, I pushed on. "Did you ask Lucy about it?"

Martha nodded. "She acted like she'd never seen it before. When I pressed her, she became angry and started cursing. I tucked it into my pocket and just let it go. I don't know what to think," said Martha.

"I think you do," Z pushed. "You're an intelligent woman. You know that GHB was found in Kyra Miller's body. A large dose of it, actually."

I held up the vial. "It appears that Lucy played a role in drugging Kyra."

"But I don't want to believe it." Martha's eyes were shiny with tears, and she quickly looked away. "You know, I'm not her mother, but I've tried to fill the gap. I've tried to lead by example, show her how to be not only a strong woman but a good person." She reached up to dash away a tear on her cheek. "I've failed her."

Again, that toxic *f* word.

"You tried," I said. "Kids reach a certain age and you can't control them. Young people make their own choices."

"The wrong choices." She sobbed, covering her face with her hands.

We gave her a moment to work through it and compose herself. As she sniffed and dried her eyes, I wondered at the sense of loss in knowing someone you loved had taken a life. It was hard to know what would be greater: disappointment in the killer or disappointment in yourself for not seeing her deadly potential.

"You did the right thing by telling us," Z said.

"I know that Mr. Jameson wanted us to keep our distance from Lucy, but this changes things. Do you think we could talk to her now?"

She rose, as if she had to do this quickly or risk losing her resolve. "She's in her room. Kent's in his studio. He spent the night there. Come with me."

And just like that, the door that had been slammed in our faces that morning opened right back up.

Lucy sat on the floor of her room, surrounded by a circle of stuffed animals that were lined up and facing her. I could have sworn I heard her talking to them softly as Martha knocked on the door. Dressed in pink-and-purple geometric leggings, fringed boots, and an oversized white hoody, she was hugging a floppy white stuffed dog. "What's up?" she said, as if we always dropped in on her.

I introduced myself and Z.

"I know who you are from last night," Lucy said. "I'm not crazy, you know."

"Is it okay if we ask you a few questions?"

"Sure. Do you want to come into the circle?"

I did, sitting on the floor beside her. Martha sat on the edge of the empty bed, while Z stood against one wall, watching.

"First, I think we should look at some photos. These are your pictures. I collected them the night of the crash, when we thought you were driving the Ghia. But I don't recognize a lot of the people. Maybe you can help me identify them." As I spoke, I went online on my phone and brought up the case file photographs that had been scanned by the property clerk. I went to the oldest photo first, a pale-skinned girl with wheat-colored hair. I'd been unable to identify the girl from Missing Persons or the Lost Girls database. "Do you recognize her?" I asked, tilting the phone screen toward her.

"That's my friend Alice," she said. "And she was a lot prettier than she looks in that picture. But she was a wreck. A hot mess. She came from a family of addicts; she was always looking to drink or smoke or get some pills."

"Did you do drugs with her?"

"Me? Never. But she dragged me into Portland, which was not my scene. It was too boring hanging out downtown, and those homeless people smelled really rank. But there was one good thing about Portland. While I was hanging out at Pioneer Courthouse Square, I met the Prince and some of his people. And eventually, he ended up moving out to Stafford Woods."

"Are you still friends with Alice?"

"No, she left a long time ago. But she wasn't a very good friend. Dad said it was because of her addictions. I try to forget Alice. But let me show you what a real friend looks like." Lucy rose to her knees and started going through the drawers of her desk. "Where are all my photos?"

"We took them in as evidence when we thought you were missing," I said. "But this is the only other girl you had pictures of."

"That's not true. I had a lot more . . . all my friends." Her head snapped around toward her stepmother. "Martha, what happened to my pictures?"

The older woman shrugged. "Just as she said, Lucy. They took them into the police station."

"But the photos of my friends. Where are my friends? Did you steal them?"

Martha stared down at her hands, trying to compose herself. "No, I did not. Lucy, please try to calm yourself."

"I hate this place." Lucy put the stuffed dog down and snatched up a blue bear. "I have a lot more friends."

"Tell me about them," I said. "Who are your friends?"

"Well, I had friends in school. People liked me for me, and that was before my father was famous and throwing money at everyone. But I lost all my friends when I switched to home-schooling. Well. Until I met Katie."

"Katie Cohen?" Lucy nodded. She was the first girl reported missing on the list of Lost Girls. And hadn't Sonia mentioned that Lucy was friends with a girl named Katie? I should have put that together.

"When was that?" I asked. "A few years ago?"

Lucy nodded. "She was babysitting for a neighbor when we met. Katie was sixteen, and I was like thirteen or something, but we hit it off. She turned out to be a good friend. We were meant to be together. She moved in with us, slept in that bed right across from me. It was like having a sister. Dad taught her to drive, and she would take me anywhere I wanted to go . . . to Sonic or the movies or for frozen yogurt or just riding around. Those were good times."

"Are you still friends with Katie?"

"No. Because she ran away. She was living here, but then she left for no reason." Lucy hugged the bear and crumpled forward. "Oh, God. That was really hard for me. People act like I'm a brick, that things don't hurt me and eat away at me inside. That pisses me off. They're so clueless."

"It hurts to lose a friend," I said.

"Yeah. And I wasn't the only one who was upset. Katie's friend Darcy was kind of mad when she came by looking for her. They had plans. Once they turned eighteen, they were going to Hawaii together to volunteer on organic farms. Darcy and I were both upset. We talked a lot about Katie one day and ended up making grilled cheese and playing some Ping-Pong in the game room. And that's how Darcy and I became friends."

"Darcy Bernowski?" I asked, another from the Lost Girls registry.

"That's her. There must be some pictures of Darcy around here." She stood up and started rifling through the dresser. "What happened to my stuff?"

"Sorry about that," I said, though I knew we

351

had no photos of Katie or Darcy in the precinct. "We'll return the things that we brought in. So tell me more about Darcy. Did she move in here, too?"

"Of course. She loved working in Martha's garden, right?"

Martha nodded solemnly.

"And Darcy was an artist. She showed me how to make sculptures out of salt and flour. We became best friends. Dad called us two peas in a pod."

"Are you still friends?"

"No. I told you, friends always leave." She slammed the dresser drawer, scooped up a bunch of stuffed animals, and fell onto the empty bed with them. "People are so mean. Picking on me because I can't hold onto my friends. But I'm not the pathetic one. They're all screwed up."

"It's hard to lose people," I said. "I know this is difficult to talk about, but I have to ask you about Maya Williams. I understand she was your friend, too."

"Yeah, the Prince named her Genesis. I'm kind of friends with everyone at the camp, but Genesis really liked me. She wanted to be a model, and she wasn't really into the whole camping scene. She wanted to work her way out of it, so Daddy gave her a job shoveling out stalls in the barn. And before long, we were good friends and she was living with me. We were like sisters. She got me into music, and we went to some concerts together."

In my mind, I saw Ellie crying in her hospital bed over Maya's departure; she'd lost her friend to Lucy, then lost her to some unknown fate. Did Lucy not see the big picture? She was the last person to see these girls alive; it seemed likely she was involved in their deaths.

"And your next friend, after Maya left." I pressed her. "Was it Kyra Miller, the girl people called Blossom?"

"Well, yeah. She was more like a little sister. But she—"

"And after Blossom? Is there someone in line to be your next unfortunate friend?"

Her bottom lip jutted out in a pout. "Why are you being mean to me?"

"Aren't you a bit concerned that all your friends have disappeared? Some of those girls are listed as missing. Doesn't that seem unusual to you?"

"I don't know why they leave me."

"Maybe they don't leave at all. Someone who knows you well is convinced that you killed Kyra Miller and Maya Williams. Maybe you got sick of them; maybe they did something to piss you off."

"No. No!"

"In the case of Kyra Miller, we have two strong connections to you. Kyra had toxic levels of the date-rape drug GHB in her system when she died, and your father's prescription drug was found here in your room."

"What? That's insane."

"Did you take the drug from your father's studio?"

"No. No way. I hate drugs. Haven't you heard? That's my problem. All the shrinks want to dumb me down with drugs so I won't get moody and depressed. But I don't like them. I don't take them anymore."

"You don't take them yourself," said Z, "but maybe you would give them to someone else. Have you ever dosed someone to get back at them for something? For being mean to you or stealing your boyfriend?"

Her face soured. "Why would I do that? That's a horrible thing to do."

"Lucy, we need you to be honest. Did you put drugs in Blossom's drink? Did you dose her?"

"No!" she snapped. Then something struck her, a spark of fury. "Blossom was my friend. I didn't make her sick with drugs."

"Maybe you didn't realize what would happen when she crashed with a gas can in the car," Z said. "But you did buy the gasoline. You were seen purchasing two cans."

Her eyes flared with anger. "So? That's not illegal."

"It is if you put a gas can in the Karmann Ghia to intensify the explosion at the crash scene. The investigators found remnants of a full gas can in the trunk of the car."

"I bought the gas for the Prince's truck."

"And you left it in the Karmann Ghia for what reason?" Z asked.

She shrugged. "I didn't. I carried one can out to the woods, and it was freakin' heavy, too. I left the other can in the garage." She pulled a large purple gorilla to cover her face. "Why are you being so mean to me?"

Just then the door flew open and a wild-haired, beet-red Kent Jameson burst into the room. "Stop this," he said indignantly. "You will stop this now. Stop torturing my daughter."

—25—

Looking up from my spot on the floor, I saw that Kent was flanked by Garcia and Brown, looking very much like a couple of uniformed thugs. I ignored them. "Mr. Jameson, Martha thought it would be a good idea for us to talk with Lucy."

"So Andy's out and Lucy is in?" Kent protested. "This is a travesty. The only crime my daughter is guilty of is that she was a friend to some confused, fucked-up runaways."

Garcia stepped forward making a calming motion with her hands. "Let's everyone take a deep breath and recognize our purpose.

We're here to protect the family, not arrest them."

"But, Esme," I said, surprising her. I think she expected me to blend into the background like one of the stuffed animals. "We're officers of the law, not security guards."

"Lucy's not under arrest at this time, but we need to question her," Z said.

"Martha, call Armand Winchell," Kent barked. "You shouldn't have let them question her without my lawyer present."

"But with or without a lawyer, the truth is going to come out." Martha's chin was lifted, a noble bearing, despite the sallow look of her face. Unlike the smooth, calm celebrity wife who had answered the door a few nights ago, this was a woman who had suffered in the past few days.

"We'll discuss this later," Kent insisted.

"They know about Lucy, Kent." Martha rose and faced her husband, eye to eye. "Anyone can see that she's disturbed. You can't protect her for the harm that she's done. A girl died in a crash out there because of Lucy. Don't tell me that girl's life matters less than your daughter's."

"Hello? I'm right here." Lucy pushed away the stuffed animals. "I hate when you talk about me like I'm not here." She tossed a donkey at her father and stormed out of the room.

I followed, mostly to keep tabs on her, though everyone spilled out of the room behind us.

"I hate them. I hate them!" she chanted as she

marched out to the great room and wheeled around to look back. "She always tells him I'm crazy, and he believes her!"

Kent strode down the hall, pausing to tell me, "It's an impossible situation to be in: the two women I love at odds with each other."

I wanted to tell him it was far worse than that. His wife was calling his daughter a murderer, and the evidence was in her favor.

As the others exited the room, Z told Brown that he ought to be ashamed for obstructing a murder investigation, Garcia assured Martha that Lucy would not be arrested at this point, and Martha cried, "Oh, but she should be!"

Watching all this, Lucy shrank back against a river rock pillar and motioned me closer. "I can't go to jail," she said in a small voice. "Are you going to send me to jail?"

Her naiveté was touching. "You wouldn't go straight to jail," I explained, more in the tone of a tour guide than a cop. "First we would arrest you, and then you would have a chance to defend yourself in court."

"I can't! I would lose. Everyone thinks I'm crazy!"

Sad but unfortunately true.

I gave Lucy my card with my cell phone number. "I'd like to talk more. Call me when you have a chance."

She frowned at the card but shoved it into

the pocket of her hoody. Although Lucy had accused me of being mean to her, perhaps the straightforward communication we had was preferable to this circus. I hoped she would call.

Garcia came over to me, her face an angry shade of red as she gestured toward Z and Brown. "Your partner's a loose cannon," she snarled. "Get him out of here before we all lose our jobs."

I had been too distracted by Lucy to notice that Z and Brown were toe to toe, snarling and growling like two angry bears. Brown had a few inches on Z, but Z was right up in his grill, pointing at him and talking fast and furious. I couldn't understand what he was saying. Brown answered back, his face contorted with eye-bulging fury that made him look monstrous.

"I called Omak," Garcia told me, "but you guys better get out. Before we all get written up."

"That was a train wreck," I said, keeping my eyes on the road as I drove Omak, Z, and me back to the precinct. I avoided looking in the rearview mirror, where I knew I'd catch the fire of Omak's glare. The lieutenant had come to the Jameson ranch to try to soothe the Jamesons and extricate us from the fray. He had left Sgt. Joel behind to keep an eye on Garcia and Brown and further pacify the Jamesons.

"I don't like surprises," Omak said, sounding like an annoyed parent. "Explain to me how you two managed to get into the Jameson estate when you were told it was off limits."

"We were invited, Lou," Z insisted.

"Martha called the precinct and asked us to come," I said. "It started out promising, with Martha's admission that she had covered up some facts of the case." I explained about the drugs found in Lucy's room and Martha's willingness to let us talk with Lucy, who admitted to being friends with a string of girls, most of whom had disappeared. "It makes me grateful that my friend's sister Sonia escaped Lucy's influence unscathed before the pattern of death developed." As we talked my cell phone buzzed, but I ignored it.

"That Lucy is a wild card," Omak went on.

"She takes after the old man," Z said. "A real nutjob."

"And we know she grew up in an unstable environment," I said.

"Well, after that fiasco, it's going to be harder than ever to get to Lucy," Omak said.

"Although we may have an ally in Martha," I pointed out. "After all the subterfuge, she now seems determined to bring out the truth about Lucy. Kent was furious with her. He told me he's torn between the two of them."

Omak leaned forward, filling my rearview mirror with his stern face. "Be careful with that. Martha Jameson strikes me as being out for Martha Jameson."

"She's totally mercenary," I agreed. "But I think that now she sees Lucy is going down, and she knows the importance of getting in front of a story. Communications 101. She needs to break the bad news so that she can shape the story. I don't relish the idea of allying with a backstabber; however, if my only access to Lucy is through Martha, I would make the most of it."

"Don't go back to the Jamesons' before I do some damage control," Omak ordered.

"Lou, we're investigating a homicide," Z pointed out.

"And we know Martha and Kent have been lying to us," I added. "We could use far more extreme measures than interviewing. I don't think they'd like it if we got a search warrant for the entire compound."

Omak groaned. "Calm down, you two."

As Omak warned us about keeping the investigation within legal parameters, my cell phone buzzed again. Annoyed, I pulled it out of my pocket while waiting at a light. I had a series of calls from . . . my family's church. Just then it buzzed again, and I answered.

"This is Laura Mori."

"Why don't you answer your phone?"

"Who is this?"

"The Prince." There was a pause. "Do you know who I am?"

"The Prince of Stafford Woods, right?" Was this a prank call? Prince Albert in a can?

Omak gave me a curious look.

"Hold on, Prince. I'm putting you on speaker." I switched over the phone and pulled over to the side of the road. "So you're Emory Vandenbos?"

"Please. The Prince. I got this number from the journalist Natalie Amichi."

"And you're calling from St. Benedict's?"

"They let me use the phone here."

It took a few seconds for my mind to catch up. "Prince, I'd really like to talk with you in person."

"Maybe. I just wanted to give you a message for the legal beagles. Tell them to back off, and we'll all come in. We're coming in from the woods."

We fumbled to pull everything in place for the arrival of the runaways. It seemed that Natalie had persuaded the Prince that it was time to disband the camp, and all the girls were willing to come out of the woods and get help.

"I don't get it," Omak said. "What did the Prince mean when he asked you to stop calling his mother?" During our phone call, the Prince had seemed rattled by my attempts to communicate with his parents. "Did you really speak with his parents?"

"I called and left messages, but they didn't call me back."

"Really?" Z grinned. "You told his mommy?"

"Who else can reel in a survivalist gone rogue in the woods?"

"I wonder if Vandenbos is coming in to avoid facing charges," Omak speculated. "You heard him on the phone. He claims that he was a Good Samaritan, just helping the girls survive and escape worse fates on their own in the city."

"From my conversations with Ellie, I think that's a reasonable representation."

"Well, right now, there's no way we can promise the Prince immunity. But if the girls are all right, he won't be charged with kidnapping. We have every reason to believe the girls are in that camp of their own volition."

My first call was to Alma Hernandez at the hospital to ask for her help and advice. "The Stafford Woods campers are coming in this afternoon, and I'm not really sure what to expect."

"No worries, honey. We'll take care of them. How many do you think?"

"Four or five girls, and some boys, too." The thought of these kids coming in filled me with hope. "I know they need to be taken in and processed, but we don't want to scare them away again."

"Okay. We'll have a few social workers on hand. I'll get some nice ones. And there's a private facility—it's called the Children's Fort— that will take them in right away." She explained

362

that the Children's Fort was staffed with medical doctors, nurses, social workers, and psychiatrists so that children who suffered trauma or abuse could be treated in a single facility. "At this facility, they videotape interviews with the kids so they don't have to repeat their stories over and over again for social workers and police and whatnot."

We discussed the need for our department to be copied on all interviews. "And I might need to talk with some of the kids to get more information on Kyra Miller or Emory Vandenbos," I said.

I told her there would be a small police presence and an ambulance, just in case. "I would like to invite the Duprees as there's a possibility that Emma is in the group. And I would like to have Ellie there. I think that would make the other girls more comfortable."

"I agree. And little Ellie is going to be so happy to see her sister."

"And it all needs to happen tomorrow morning at ten on the Jameson ranch. They'll be coming in near the alpaca barn."

Thursday morning, Z and I parked out by the Jamesons' barn. Out in the corral, Blane was hammering away at a latch on the fence, and Eden was walking a bridled horse when we approached.

"Hey! Did you hear Andy got out?" Eden called to us.

"I know," I said. "That's good." But maybe not

so good for these two. Would they have to hit the road now?

"But he's not coming back." Eden didn't have to shout now as she came closer. "I think he's mad at the Jamesons. I'm not sure why. He said he's going to stay with his girlfriend till they save up enough to get their own place. As far as he's concerned, we can have his job."

So it was very good news for them. "Do you want to stay here?" I asked.

"Hell, yeah!" said Blane. "This is a great place, and I don't mind the hard work."

"We were ready for a change," Eden agreed. "But we're not sure what the Jamesons are going to do. They haven't offered us the job yet."

"You might want to let them know you're interested," I suggested. "Remind them that you've been working here for a while. Negotiate a salary. Actually, speak with Martha's assistant Talitha first. She might handle decisions like this, especially while the Jamesons are wrapped up in other matters." Like the possible murder charge against Kent's daughter.

Blane dropped the mallet and put a hand on the fence. "You don't think they'd get mad about us asking?"

"I think they'd be relieved to have a smooth transition. But that's just my opinion. Give it a try."

"We should go together," Eden said, reaching

up to stroke the horse. "Tell her we're like a package deal."

"Yeah, we could do that." Blane didn't seem as enthusiastic as Eden—typical reluctant guy.

I couldn't help thinking of Randy grudgingly agreeing to a coffee date and wriggling out of seeing me again. I had to push it to the back of my mind, but it still hurt to think that I wasn't his first choice. Silly, but when were emotions ever rational?

Omak and a lawyer for Emory Vandenbos pulled up just before 10:00. Z and I stood with the other professionals lined up at the fence overlooking the alpaca corral. Alma was there with two other social workers, both young, both tattooed. Louise and Thomas Dupree spoke with Alma, trying to appear calm in a cloud of hope. Ellie Watson, delighted to see Eden and Blane, who she called Wolf, had joined them in the corral to get hands-on experience with the alpacas.

"They are so ugly, they make you feel sorry for them," Ellie said, tentatively touching the flank of an ivory creature. "I love the way they follow each other to the poop pile."

The tension at the fence was broken by some chuckles.

Omak hung back by the patrol car, keeping an eye on Elliot Steiner, attorney at law, who waited in the Mercedes. He'd given Omak his card and announced that he was there to represent his client, Emory Vandenbos. Omak was less than happy about it.

They appeared in a group, moving together in grungy clothes and beanies. They were so similar, I found it hard to distinguish one from another.

Then individuals emerged.

Morgan dropped her pack and came running to embrace her sister.

Guardian, tall, strong, and solemn, strode up to Alma and told her that his name was Shawn Wilkins, he was from Chicago, and he didn't want to return there. When she asked his age, he said he was fifteen years old.

Louise Dupree let out a cry, and her husband's hands quivered as he reached out to embrace his daughter. "Emma," Louise cried, "oh, our dear Emma. We've missed you so much."

"I know. I'm sorry," she responded, her face crumpling in tears. "I'm sorry, but I needed a change. Maybe it was stupid, but I had to go, and sometimes there's no turning back."

"You're always welcome in your home," her mother said, hugging the stiff girl. "Always."

Thomas shook his head, but Louise kept hugging her daughter. I suspected their family would heal, though not overnight.

True went over to the social workers and talked with them. I couldn't hear what they were saying, but they were engaged.

I looked toward the trail; it was empty.

"Where's the Prince?" I asked.

True turned back to me, a look of concern in her eyes. "He left early this morning. Said he was going home. I promised him that I'd corral the others out of the woods. Some of us didn't want to come in, but the Prince was worried that we wouldn't survive the winter in the woods without him."

Omak turned to the lawyer, who now stood outside his Mercedes. "Where's your client, Steiner?"

"My client has no reason to come forward. He has acted as a benefactor to these young people, supporting them through their difficult times. They're now safely delivered to you. My client is seeking opportunity elsewhere."

"Meaning he's flown the coop," Omak said.

"Whoa, whoa, whoa." Z held up a hand. "Technically, your client is a suspect in this case."

"There are no charges against him, and he's broken no laws." Steiner smiled. "*Technically,* he's a free man."

I turned to Omak. "What should we do?"

"Not much we can do," he muttered, then turned to the attorney. "We'll be in touch if we need to depose him. In the meantime, tell him I don't ever want to hear that he's living in Stafford Woods again."

"It's been a pleasure." Steiner got into the car and drove off.

Alma assured us that everything was under

control. "We'll take good care of these kids . . . All these girls and a lost boy, too." She winked.

I tried to feel a sense of relief as they boarded two vans. Some of the Lost Girls had been found. Some families reunited. Some would begin new lives. But for all the girls that had been found, other kids were still missing . . .

"Good on you," Omak told us with a look of pride.

I tried, but I couldn't force a smile. My job wasn't even half done.

Z and I stayed at the ranch until after all the others left and then headed back to the precinct. Later in the day, there would be recorded interviews with the runaways to review, but for now we needed to leave Alma and her team to debrief the young people while we got back to work. Z contacted the Missing Persons Division and other organizations to update their records on the kids who'd come in today while I went through Lucy's school records—bad grades but glowing reviews from teachers—and the report that had just arrived from the LA County Medical Examiner. The written report wasn't surprising, but when I saw the list of toxins in Candy Jameson's system, I took note. A lethal dose of GHB or Rohypnol had been found in her blood. They believed it had slowed her heart and lungs, causing death.

Had Lucy poisoned her own mother?

Just then my phone buzzed and I saw a text from an unknown number.

This is Lucy. Can we meet?

My heartbeat quickened as I told her yes and saved her number in my directory. Then I called her.

"How soon can you be here?" she asked.

I wasn't supposed to be visiting the Jameson estate; the event at the ranch had been an exception to the rule. "I thought we could talk on the phone."

"I didn't kill Blossom or anyone else. But I know things. Dark, scary things."

"Tell me. I'm listening."

"Not on the phone. I'll show you. But only you. No one else."

It sounded like I was being set up, but it didn't feel that way. With a look toward Lt. Omak's office, I made an executive decision. "We can't meet at your house. After yesterday, your father and Martha don't want us trespassing."

"Meet me in the woods. Park at the ranch and walk on the trail back toward the house. Halfway there, there's a fork in the path near two grand ponderosas." My palms were already sweating at the prospect of a solo venture into the woods again. Being a Mori meant I should have felt at peace with the forest—all serene and tranquil and Kumbaya. Instead, the prospect made my hands tremble. "I'll be there in twenty minutes."

—26—

Considering what we knew about Lucy, neither Z nor I were happy at the prospect of me taking the trip alone. "But it's the only way," I said, and he made me promise to call in within the hour.

Twenty-some minutes later, I found Lucy waiting at the designated spot, hands on her slim hips, head cocked as if she were about to rumble with a rival gang. In her short fringed boots, silver jacket, and tights, with her slim shape and pixie haircut, she could have been Peter Pan beckoning me to Neverland. Hardly intimidating. But then again, some notorious killers banked on charm. She could be the female, teenage version of H. H. Holmes or Ted Bundy.

"Where would we be going?"

"Out in the woods. We have to walk, but it's not far. Like, twenty minutes to get there."

One-on-one it seemed safe, but there were other factors in the woods. Cold surprises. Solitude. And a dark, deep forest of fear.

"Promise me, no surprises."

"Oh, you'll be surprised," she said, glancing nervously over her shoulder. "But I won't hurt you. I'm not the person who does the hurting around here. That's the part you guys have got wrong. I'm the one who's always getting hurt."

The flicker of pain in her eyes grabbed me, and I empathized with this loner of a girl caught in a dysfunctional family triangle—the famous, brilliant father who treated her like a pet and the stepmother who pretended to hold the family and fortune together but actually seemed determined to kick Lucy out of the mix. Did this impossible situation mold a girl already dancing with mental illness? Yes. Did it mean she was a killer? Not necessarily.

"Okay," I told her. "Show me the way."

Lucy's throat was tight as she walked alongside the female cop. Laura Mori looked too young to be a police officer. If Lucy had met her under other circumstances, they might have been friends. The other day when Laura had come into Lucy's bedroom, seeing Laura sitting among her stuffed animals, Lucy imagined the pretty Japanese girl there just hanging out, listening to music, painting their nails, and talking. Lucy liked the way Laura actually listened to what she said. The way she seemed to have a patient smile in her eyes. And how she didn't yell when she got upset.

They could have been friends, but that probably wouldn't have ended well for Laura. Most girls who were friends with Lucy ended up buried in the dirt.

Not that Lucy was sure about any of it. It was just a theory, a wild scenario that occurred to her over time as it became clear that someone had been digging in the clearing. Some people said that she'd inherited her father's wild imagination. But from the way those cops had been talking and the way the bitch had pointed all the blame, it looked like they were going to arrest Lucy. Arrest her! Lucy hadn't hurt anyone, but she wasn't stupid, either. She saw the patterns of her friendships, the abrupt endings, the girls who, every last one, had dropped off the face of the earth. Why did all her friends leave—and where had they gone? Suspicious? Hell, yeah.

Lucy knew this was the only way to save herself.

"So I don't know if this is nothing or something really huge, but it's scared me for a long time, and then it sort of grew on me, and now—I don't know. It's not like I hang out with the dead. But then everything around us is dying or dead. But . . ." She grunted, annoyed with herself. "It's all coming out like vomit. I hate when I don't make sense!"

Laura was squinting as if there were some important speck in the panorama of tall fir and cedar, moss and fern surrounding them. "Maybe start at the beginning. Make it a story."

Storytelling was nothing new to Lucy; keeping it real was the problem. Sometimes she confused reality with daydreams.

"Okay. Whatever. The first time I noticed the little patch of dug-up dirt, I was hiking with Darcy, looking for wildflowers or a place to smoke weed. I don't really remember. But then we found this little nook that had a carpet of soft grass and little purple flowers. It seemed like a haven, a fairy cove. In summer it's bordered by lilac bushes that smell supersweet. And there's an opening in the trees overhead so sunlight breaks through. We thought it was a good place to chill, so Darcy spread out the blanket and we hung out.

"We were there awhile when Darcy noticed the loose dirt . . ."

Lucy could see Darcy, sitting there on a weather-smoothed boulder. Her curly, dark hair was pulled back in a ponytail, but little springs of curl popped out. The girls had to spend hours smoothing that hair with the iron to get it straight, and most times Darcy just let it curl up.

"Look at that patch of dirt. Someone's been digging," Darcy said.

"A little garden bed." Lucy looked around nervously. "This part is state land, I think. Do you think there's some creepy mountain troll watching us, ready to swoop down and protect his cabbage patch?"

"Right. Or maybe it's an animal. You know how squirrels dig?"

"In an oval shape like that?"

"Why not?" Darcy paced along the patch of loose soil, surveying.

"Or maybe it's a grave. Somebody probably buried their dog there."

"A grave?" Darcy reached out in mock horror and grabbed Lucy's arm. "Oh, God! Maybe it's a body!"

Loving the hysteria, Lucy grabbed the blanket and the girls fled, screaming. Their shrieks must have swept from the wind-tortured hilltop to the park down by the river. Darcy vowed never to return to that spot. And she never did.

At least, not alive.

A month or so after Darcy had gone, Lucy was tearing through the forest in a snit. Talking to herself out loud. Crying off and on. The doctors told her to take the medication to keep from getting depressed, but sometimes a good cry helped. Besides, after a few months on that icky medication, it took not just the tears but the fun times and joy, too. She and Darcy had joked about the place being a secret burial ground, and Lucy felt connected to Darcy through the memory. She went off the path and trudged over to the grassy clearing to calm down.

The fresh patch of overturned soil stood out like a charred wound in the earth.

"Now there are two graves," Lucy said to no one, though the meaning wasn't lost in the silence. Two friends gone, two graves. Maybe a coincidence. Maybe her friends were fine, off having better lives somewhere.

When Alice left, things were different. At that point, the Prince and some of the others had moved to the woods from Portland, giving Lucy a new social life just beyond her back door. Besides, she'd been kind of relieved to have Alice out of her room and out of her life. That girl was lost in so many ways. Cool when she was stable, but most times she was strung out on drugs or all knotted up in desperation to find more. Lucy didn't care so much about pathetic, druggy Alice.

Until she made it out to the clearing and saw the third grave.

Three patches of dirt. The soil on the newest area was darker than the others, newly turned. Weeds and leaves had begun to mask the older areas of soil, but the lines of demarcation were still clear.

Three graves. Three girls.

The clearing became a touchstone of terror—nightmares, scary movies, and ugly memories of Mom at her worst. Lucy saw the specters of her friends rising from the graves. Lovely silken images drifted up from the ground and begged her to come closer, to help them, to give strength to their dead whispers.

"No! Get away!" she yelled at them as she stumbled back and quickly fled.

Lucy avoided the clearing after that. She told herself that she had just imagined things, that soil shifted on its own, that some large animal was digging for wild onions. In some ways it was easy to forget because of her increasing involvement with the Prince and the urchins in Stafford Woods. When Maya became her friend, Lucy thought about the little nook in the woods with the three holes, but she was convinced that she'd made too much of a simple coincidence.

"You're always twisting things to suit your needs," Martha told her time and again. Maybe the bitch was right.

But the curse was not broken. Within a few months of their friendship, Maya left, leaving behind some of her personal things at the camp and breaking Light's heart. Even Lucy could see that the frail girl was hurting. And when Lucy hiked up to check the clearing, the fourth grave stretched out before her, a gaping wound in the earth.

Lucy was convinced that evil was following her like a dark shadow. Was it a real killer or just a bubble from her imagination? Dark thoughts soaked her soul, dragging her down.

Then one morning as she'd been tromping through the woods, she had a change of heart. While passing between two trees, her foot had landed on something squishy and soft. The odd sensation underfoot had set her off balance and made her shudder.

An animal?

A dead shrew. Very dead, though she could still make out its pointy little nose and tiny paws with needle nails. Actually, it was cute. It would have fit with the other stuffed animals on her bed.

But the shrew was a rotting corpse. Probably smelly, though you didn't notice in the earthy smell of the woods where everything on the ground was molding and decomposing . . .

Like a diver coming up for air, Lucy emerged from her storytelling and sucked in a deep breath of earthen scents: pine and wood smoke and molding leaves. Laura the cop walked alongside her, taking in every word. The listener.

"Everything is dying and decaying," Lucy said. "Everything and everyone."

"Yes, but if there's a secret graveyard hidden in the state park, chances are that the bodies buried there did not die of natural causes."

"If there actually are bodies buried there. I mean, I never dug anything up. That would be so gross. But to me, it looks like a graveyard."

"Okay. Let's go see this secret cemetery."

"Five graves?" Lucy's eyes searched the clearing yet again, as if her first two counts were incorrect. "How can there be five now? No one else died." She seemed genuinely surprised.

"No one else that we know of," I said, trying

to ignore the sick feeling in my stomach that some-thing had happened to one of the girls in the woods while we were off interviewing the wrong people.

"That one." Lucy pointed to a low mound of darker soil carved out of the ground—a wobbly oval that touched another grave at the top, creating the impression of insect wings. "That one is new." She stared but made no attempt to go near the newly turned earth.

Although Lucy had explained her suspicions on the way here, I felt unprepared to process what this hidden graveyard might contain. Walking in measured steps across the clearing, I moved with a reverence appropriate in a final resting place. In the cemeteries I'd visited—Arlington Cemetery in Virginia, the Pioneer Cemetery in Sunrise Lake, and a marble mausoleum that contained the ashes of my grandfather in the suburbs of the Bay Area—the sober, quiet atmosphere had been palpable. Respect the dead. Walk with knowledge that someday your path will lead to the same destination.

I felt the same vibrations here in the clearing.

Of course, we would not know for sure until a team of forensic scientists was able to delicately excavate these covered holes, but I sensed that Lucy was correct in assuming there were bodies buried in this clearing. Lost souls who had disappeared without answers or closure for their loved ones.

A few feet away, Lucy made a sour face and hugged herself. She had shown me this grave site in an attempt to avoid arrest, and I was convinced that she believed her friends were buried here. "You're leaving something out," I said. "You told me how you came upon this place and how you watched it change over the past few years. But someone dug these holes. He or she probably buried bodies here. Who do you think did all this?"

Her eyes grew wide and froze in panic. "I can't tell you that. And the truth is, I don't know."

"But you have an idea. A theory." I tilted my head to one side, softening toward her. "Who do you think did this?"

Of course, "this" was a broad reference, but she knew what I meant.

"I think . . . I shouldn't say anything. It's just a feeling, and for a long time, I've tried to put it out of my mind. Ahh! I don't want to believe it, but I can't help it. I think my father killed them all."

—27—

"We have equipment that can give us an idea if there are human remains buried here without disturbing anything. A device that uses ground-penetrating radar." Rex Burns looked more like a

British rocker than a forensic scientist strutting through the clearing in his leather jacket and boots, his sculpted gold hair gleaming in the autumn sunshine. "I already put in the call. God, I hope the rest of the team can get the radar equipment up here this afternoon. The sooner, the better. With this weather, if we find bodies, we could begin excavation immediately." He seemed giddy at the possibility.

"If we have bodies, as in plural, we're going to need to notify the FBI," Omak said soberly. He and I were trailing along behind Rex while Z strung crime scene tape across trees at the edge of the alley of graves. "And five bodies? Five homicides would be a record breaker for Sunrise Lake."

"And in poshy posh Stafford Woods. There goes the neighborhood," Burns quipped cavalierly.

"Mr. Burns, you of all people should show some respect for the dead—and for the town we are trying to protect." Omak's voice rang with reproach. "Let me assure you that death brings pain to people in all socioeconomic backgrounds, rich and poor."

"I'm sorry. You're right." The forensic scientist winced. "It's such a surprise. The last thing I expected when I accepted a job in Evergreen County was the possibility that I'd work on an excavation site in Sunrise Lake. And this is my specialty. I spent nearly every summer in college on archeological digs, brushing and blowing granules of sand away from any small protrusion in the earth. Those were good times."

"But you were digging up relics," I pointed out. "This is different. Well, it will be different if there are bodies buried here. This isn't an ancient dig site."

"I stand corrected." Rex took out a tape measure and handed me one end. "Let's get a measurement of the plot. That will dictate how much equipment we'll need."

Following Rex's instructions, I carried the end of the tape to the back of the clearing.

"Who do we think is buried here?" Rex asked. "Do you have any idea? It's always most expedient if we have a hypothesis that we're trying to verify."

"The bodies of teenage girls. I'll give you a list of four of them," I said, thinking of Lucy's missing friends. "Two of them are in the Lost Girls database, so we have some dental information and medical records."

"E-mail your list to me as soon as possible." Rex and Omak discussed the logistics of bringing equipment in. Omak would try to get permission to access the park trail from the Jamesons' property to save the forensic team from walking the three miles from the park's trailhead.

I went over to help Z finish up with the crime scene tape. "Did you hear Burns talking like an event planner?" he said under his breath. "Shit. We're talking about dead bodies here."

"A little overenthusiastic," I agreed.

"Not that it isn't a huge find. How'd you get Lucy to bring you here?"

"I think she acted out of self-preservation. She thought we were going to arrest her for Kyra Miller's murder."

"Right. So to prove she's innocent, she takes you to five more bodies? The girl's not the sharpest pencil in the box."

"She's scared," I said, realizing that I was defending Lucy, but the girl clearly needed someone to look out for her. I had sensed her composure unraveling while we were walking back to the compound. I told her to call me if she ever felt threatened. "I'll be fine," she had said in that immortal manner of teens. "I'm a survivor."

Right now I hoped she wasn't overestimating her skills.

Although Z and I wanted to stay at the grave site, Omak sent us away. "Go. Work your cases, which you've been doing a splendid job with. You're not welcome at the Jameson place right now, and the forensic team has enough workers. You can come back and check in later when we have more information. This whole thing could be a dud, anyway. If there's a God in heaven, let these holes be empty. I'd be happy with a ruse."

• • •

The lieutenant's prayers were not answered.

I had just returned to the precinct from visiting Ellie and her sister, Morgan, at a youth facility, having left Z to file the paperwork on the gruesome discovery. What I had learned from the sisters was burning a hole in my mind, but my phone rang as I got to my desk. Omak was calling to let Z and me know they had confirmation. "We have bodies."

The surprise was that the most recent mound of dirt showed no human mass beneath the surface. "There are four bodies," Omak said. "The forensic team is already staging for an excavation. We're hoping to have lights and equipment in place so that they can dig through the night."

I ended the call with Omak and turned to Z. "Bodies. This is a serial killer who doesn't mess around. I'm really scared for Lucy Jameson. What if that fifth hole was meant for her?"

"Not likely if she was diggin' the holes."

"I don't think she was."

"Mori, look, there are bodies up there, and she knew exactly where to find them. If she killed these girls, she's going to jail."

"But I'm not sure she killed anyone. I know, I was hot on her trail a few hours ago, but hearing her talk about her friends, these runaways that she embraced, I don't see her turning on them so completely. Especially since she sees the pattern of them leaving her as a series of rejections. She believes that her former friends ended up in those graves, and I'm afraid she's right. And unless she's a terrific storyteller, someone else killed those girls."

"She's the daughter of a bestselling storyteller," Z pointed out.

"And what if his storytelling skills have helped him get away with murder all these years?"

Z considered this. "Possible, but where's our evidence? And what's the motive?"

"Sexual abuse," I said.

"Reasonable, but we can't speak to his victims to verify it."

"I just did." I showed him a copy of a report I had taken from Morgan Watson at the hospital. "You know I've been working with the psychologists at the Children's Fort to cull information from the runaways. It turns out Morgan and her little sister visited the Jameson mansion one weekend as Lucy's prospective 'friends.' Morgan says that Jameson came into Lucy's room at night and lured her to his studio to supposedly come up with a surprise for her sister. Morgan said she became ill in Kent's workspace. When she awoke before dawn, she felt sick and sore, and her underwear was gone. The girls grabbed their stuff and made their way back to camp. Lucy was there all night, but she appeared to sleep through the incident."

Z's eyes were dark with rue. "And Martha? She slept through all this, too?"

"She was out of town. Apparently on location for one of Kent's novels being made into a movie."

"Shit." Z scowled.

"When I asked Morgan if she had had anything to drink, she said Kent gave her a Pepsi. She loves soda."

"Okay, you got me." He reached for his jacket. "I think it's time to visit the lieutenant"—he made air quotes—" 'on location.' "

Dusk approached as we drove up the ridge toward Stafford Hill, turning the wispy clouds in the sky punch bowl shades of orange, cherry, and grape. Autumn skies in Oregon always held a heaviness, as if bracing for winter. As Z drove, I couldn't help but think of those four girls who would never glimpse the sky again.

In the gathering darkness, the grave site cast a ghostly light so bright it could be seen from a mile away. From up close, the white glare of construction-site lights that turned night into a stark facsimile of day cast an eerie pallor over everything. It would have been creepy even without knowing bodies were buried there.

Omak was on the phone, but Rex Burns noticed our arrival and seemed eager to explain the process. They had reached the eggplant-dark rotting skin of the first corpse—a foot with lime-green toenail polish—and the sight seemed more tragic than gruesome. Z took one look and walked away, but I stayed and listened as Rex described how every bit of soil was sifted through, how they brushed the soil away from the remains grain by grain, how they photographed every stage. Burns was a true forensic aficionado.

Decaying flesh and bone seemed at odds with the girls in the profiles that I'd been reading about on the Lost Girls database. Not Maya, the tall, star basketball player and aspiring model. Or Darcy, who loved digging in the dirt and wanted to work on a farm in Hawaii. I would probably cry over these girls once they were identified, but for now, these earthen shapes seemed more geologic than human.

And then Omak was there beside me, frowning. "I thought I told you two not to come."

"We were finishing out the shift and had a few things to discuss," Z said.

"You could have called." Omak gestured for us to move away from the open grave. "This is nightmare material. Remember those girls the way they appear in photos. Happy. Smiling. Whole."

"It's all part of the process." I told the lieutenant about Morgan's statement. "All signs point to Kent Jameson being behind these killings."

Omak nodded. "I've been wondering when

we'd get to him. After the daughter brought you up here and showed you these bodies, I figured it couldn't be her. Even raving lunatics don't usually give themselves up that way."

"Tomorrow I'm going to dig back further into Jameson's background, see what I can find." I looked around the site. The forensic team was working slowly but steadily. "Do you want me to stay here, Lou? The site needs to be secured."

"You've got bigger fish to fry tomorrow. You're coming with me to break the news to the Jamesons. We've got Rivers assigned to guard the site through the night, and the forensic team is going to work twenty-four-seven until these graves are uncovered. Go home. Sleep."

"I don't think I'll be able to sleep." Although I was tired. Exhausted and discouraged.

"Got insomnia now? Is Jameson's condition contagious?"

"He is so stinking guilty. And a pervert. I can't believe I didn't see it before this."

"That's your gut instinct, and it may be right. But for now, we need to make it look like we're backing off the Jamesons. Sometimes when you give a suspect a little rope, he hangs himself."

"He's too narcissistic for that."

"Just keep your cool. When we meet with the Jamesons in the morning, I'll conduct the interview, and you can listen and observe. I'm afraid that if you engage with Kent, your disapproval might burn through. We don't want to tip our hand just yet," Omak pointed out.

"I'm fine with that," I said. "But now, knowing what we know about Kent, I worry about Lucy spending the night in that house. He presumably has never targeted her before, but I would feel better if I knew that she was safe. She's not answering my texts, and we know her support system in Stafford Woods is gone."

Omak frowned. "Do you think her father would hurt her?"

"I don't, but what if I'm wrong?"

"I think you're right. And legally, we can hardly go down to the ranch and demand that Kent Jameson produce his seventeen-year-old daughter because of a bad feeling."

Logic could be difficult to digest. I would sit on my hands and keep my lips sealed shut. Anything to get this killer behind bars.

—28—

Two porcelain pots of tea sat on a table in the living room when we arrived for our meeting Friday morning. "We have Darjeeling and Oolong," Martha said, refusing to meet my gaze as she gathered cups for us. "What's your preference, Lt. Omak?"

I chose Darjeeling with honey and was grateful

for something to keep my hands and mouth busy. Better to sip tea than verbally attack Kent Jameson, whose wild hair and hooded eyes made it clear that he was not a morning person, nor did he welcome us being back in his home.

Omak drank his tea quickly and then started the meeting by thanking the Jamesons for the use of their property to access the trails to the dig site.

"You can always count on us to cooperate," Kent said. "How is that going, by the way? Have you found anything?"

"We have." Omak put his teacup down. "There'll be a media conference later today at the precinct, but because of your proximity, we wanted you to know first. The scanners revealed four bodies buried there."

"No. Right up here in our park?" Kent looked at his wife. "And Lucy has been wandering around back there for years. I thought it was relatively safe."

Right, I thought. *Safe without perverts like you.*

"How awful." Martha lowered her teacup. "When we built up here, people left their doors open. There was no crime. But now, four bodies . . . The world is changing."

"It gets worse. We believe that the bodies buried in the Stafford Woods will be identified as Lucy's former friends. We'll know more in the next few days, but you've met these girls:

Maya Williams, Alice Weiler, Darcy Bernowski, and Katie Cohen. All of them runaways."

Kent let out a sigh of pain, and Martha reached over and squeezed his hand. "We knew them," she said.

"I wanted to talk to you about your practice of hosting runaway girls at various times over the past few years," Omak said.

Martha and Kent exchanged a stern look.

"Lucy's friends." Kent gave a contrite sigh. "It's true. Yes, it's true, but—"

"Don't you think your boss should be in on this discussion?" Martha interrupted the question aimed at Omak. "Buzz has been aware of the situation from day one, when we worried about Lucy's attachment to Katie. Katie Cohen was the first. She was a sweet girl, but when we learned that she was only sixteen and a runaway, we were concerned."

"I reached out to Chief Cribben, and he assured me that no one would fault us for feeding and housing a homeless teen." Kent fluffed the hair over his eyes and shrugged. "We figured that was that. If the police didn't find fault with what we were doing, we were happy to continue taking care of Lucy's friends."

"I see. It sounds like you had the best of intentions," Omak said.

Reading between the lines, I saw the subtext: harboring teen runaways was still illegal, no matter what Buzz Cribben said. But Omak's professionalism wouldn't allow him to criticize the police chief behind his back. While I respected the lieutenant for his restraint, sometimes I longed to see him curse the big boss out.

Tears filled Kent's eyes. "They were good kids. They didn't deserve to die."

Then why did you kill them? I wanted to ask him.

"Well, it's good that we had this conversation," Omak said. "The chief didn't tell me you'd been in touch with concerns about the runaways, and we have no record of a police report."

"I'm glad that part is cleared up," Martha agreed, "but what about the real crime here? I know you think Lucy killed those girls, but you must know that she didn't act alone. What are you doing to get the real killer, that Prince what's-his-name?"

"Emory Vandenbos," Kent said quietly.

"That manipulator. I saw the interview this evening. If a reporter can get to that deluded Emory Vandenbos, why can't you cops get him? That young man has four bodies to account for! Five if you include Blossom. I think he forced Lucy to participate. I always knew he was no good, but I never dreamed he was a serial killer. Pure evil and manipulative. He has those girls under his spell, and Lucy is one of them.

Whatever role she had in . . . in any of this, you can be sure it was a result of pressure from that punk Robin Hood."

"Martha . . ." Kent patted the air with his hand, trying to shush her.

But she would not be dismissed. "What a fraud. A dropout from a wealthy Seattle family? And he acts like he lives a life of simple poverty. With a brood of young girls half his age? There's the real crime. He's the culprit. Our Lucy is just another victim here."

An interesting change of pace from trying to get Lucy arrested for Blossom's murder last night, I thought.

"We're doing everything we can to find this killer," Omak said patiently. "I wish I had access to Emory Vandenbos. I wish we could move faster, but sometimes investigations take time."

They chatted for a little longer, and then Omak excused us, saying that we had to get back to work. As Martha was walking out the door, I thanked her for the tea and asked about Lucy. "How's she doing?"

"I wouldn't know." Martha folded her arms. "You people scared the wits out of her. She took off when that heavy equipment started rolling in yesterday, and we haven't seen her since."

"How did the meeting go?" Z asked when I met him at the grave site.

I shook my head. "I'll be glad when they're both locked up and unable to do further harm. They don't seem to care that Lucy's been gone since last night."

"Here's the bright side of that situation. We know Lucy's a survivor, so she's probably better off miles away from those two nut balls."

It was a good point, but it didn't alleviate my concern.

Fortunately, I didn't have to worry about Lucy for long. As Z and I met with Rex Burns at the grave site, I got a text from her.

Panic attack. Don't know who else to talk to. Meet me at the clubhouse? Please?

Relief washed over me as I texted her back. This time, I would try to talk her into some sort of safe house for her own protection. For once, my experience with panic attacks might come in handy. I told Z that Lucy was back, and I was running down to the house to talk with her. He would catch a ride back to the precinct with Omak.

The clubhouse looked as deserted as usual with chairs stacked on top of tables, though today the tracks of a vacuum cleaner curved around and under the furniture. The door was unlocked, and the bells and clicks of a pinball game alerted me when I crossed the threshold.

"Lucy?"

She didn't answer, presumably lost in her game.

I moved around the mirrored bar setup to the games in the back. "I'm glad that your panic attack has eased enough to—"

The sight of Kent Jameson standing at the *Elvira and the Party Monsters* pinball machine made me freeze in midstep.

"Where's Lucy?"

"In the restroom." He turned to me and smiled, the sorrow of last night gone from his eyes. He cut a lean figure in a black T-shirt, denim shirt, and faded jeans. His hair was sculpted to a refined wildness, and the scent of lavender filled the space near him.

He was an attractive man. I suspected he'd had no problem charming girls into his trap. After that it would have been easy to slip them the drug so that they didn't have the power or strength to stop him.

The pinball machine clicked away as the ball dropped and it calculated his score. "I don't know how many times I play these things and still never quite master them," he said. "We were just shooting some billiards." He nodded toward the pool table in the alcove where a game seemed to be in progress, balls spread on the green felt and two sticks propped against the wall. "Do you want to take her turn?"

"No, thanks. I'll just wait." I folded my arms and leaned against the paneled wall.

"We were hoping you could join us for a ride." He leaned over the table with a pool stick, practicing a shot. "Did you know I got a new car? A Shelby Mustang. It's a beauty. Do you know how to drive a car with a manual transmission?"

"I do." I glanced toward the hallway. Was Lucy okay in there? Maybe she was freaking out. "My boyfriend Randy taught me." A harmless half lie in the presence of a pedophile who was almost certainly also a serial killer. Randy really had taught me during spring break of sophomore year when I'd missed out on a Hawaii trip with Becca's family because my parents made me take a special session at Japanese school. I'd been so angry at them. Now, in retrospect, I realized they were my champions. A little strict, but good and kind people. "But I can't go for a ride right now. Do you think I should check on Lucy?"

"She's fine. Sometimes people need a little space."

That was rich, coming from the man who invaded the personal space of young girls.

"I'm glad you came." He took a shot, sinking a striped ball. "The last few times we met, I could tell there was something going on here."

"Excuse me?"

"You and I, we're so much alike." He rubbed a cube of chalk over the tip of the pool cue. "Strong minded. Secretly passionate. Goddamned sexy. And we share a love for little Lucy." He pulled the tip of the stick within an inch of his lips and blew on it gently. "We would be dynamite together."

This was ludicrous. "You're creeping me out. I'm done here." I headed down the hall and flung open the door to the women's restroom. The lights were off, the two stalls empty.

I checked the men's room for good measure, then stomped back to the billiards area. "You fucking bastard. Where is she? What did you do to her?"

"You know Lucy well enough to know that she can hold her own, and I would never hurt the only person on this planet who really and truly needs me." He leaned over the table and took another shot. "Lucy is fine."

"Where is she?"

"Hell if I know. She ran off again in one of her usual mad furies. But this time, she left her phone behind. I took the liberty of texting you." He winked, his eyes sparkling. "And you came running."

"I came for Lucy."

A low murmur of contentment trilled in his throat. "And someday soon, you'll come for me."

"You're disgusting."

"Am I pushing too hard? I'm sorry. I forget that the dance is sometimes the best part." He cradled the pool cue in his arms. "Those first experiences together. You know that I taught them to drive? The Karmann Ghia was a good car because, really, if you are going to operate a vehicle, you need to know how to drive a stick. To feel the momentum and shift gears at the right moment. It's a fine dance, easing off the clutch and easing into gear, the power and impetus of motion. Moving forward. Speed!"

He smiled down at the pool stick. "I love it! The poetry of motion."

I turned and checked the distance to the front door. Of course, I had a gun and I knew self-defense. I had tools. But flight was my best choice.

"Where was I? Oh, yes, driving lessons, an intimate instruction, physical, intellectual, and spiritual, if you do it correctly. I taught the girls how to make the engine purr. When to give it the gas and when to ease off. How to grip the gear shift, firm and steady. Nothing to be afraid of."

The sexual innuendo was disgustingly obvious, and if I had any doubts, watching him caress the pool stick negated them. "That's it, Mr. Jameson. I've heard enough."

"Call me A. That's what the girls always call me."

Of course. The very sexual older man seducing his daughter's friends. *Awesome A.* And poor Kyra had actually believed he was going to throw Martha over and hook up with her for good.

"Kent is such a pompous name," he was saying, "and Mr. Jameson is my father. One of the girls started calling me A because I'm a big-shot author with a capital *A*. The name sort of stuck."

Awesome A. I wanted to smack him, but not yet. Not until he admitted everything.

"Tell me about your relationships with Lucy's friends."

"I loved them all. Spiritual love, of course. I would never lay a finger on an underage girl. That, my dear Officer Mori, is a crime against the law and our society's moral code. Sordid and illegal."

"You're lying."

"I've made a living out of creative lies." He smiled. "But you're of age, Laura. You're old enough to consent, although you look like a teenage girl on the brink of womanhood. And from what I can tell, you've got a stunning figure." His gaze combed my body like a tiger on the attack. Could he smell my fear? "You want to show me? I can make it worth your while."

"That's never going to happen."

"Oh, I think you'll reconsider when you think about what I can do for you. A promotion in the department and more money than you'll ever see from your career in law enforcement. What do you like, Laura? Clothes? Cars? Jewelry?" He put the stick aside and opened his arms to me. "Little girl, you've just won the lottery."

"Did you kill them, too?" I felt my way to the

398

wall behind me. "Or would you like to call that spiritual murder?"

"I didn't kill them. No one, not even my own family, believes me, but I didn't kill anyone. I'm a lover, not a fighter."

His breath was raspy as he looked me up and down, making my skin crawl. "Did you say you had a boyfriend?"

"Yes," I lied again. "A great guy. We're really into each other."

"I'll bet he's young and inexperienced," he breathed. "He doesn't know how to manipulate a woman's body in the throes of passion. He doesn't understand the way pain and pleasure are interwoven. I can show you." He moved around the table, closing the distance between us. "Let me show you."

"No! Stay away." I reached for my gun as I backed away, breaking the holster lock.

"Ah, you've got a gun." He paused beside the table. "You can have your way with me. Have you ever used a gun in your love play?"

I stepped back, maintaining distance between us as a pulse thudded in my throat. "Stay back. I'm not messing around, you bastard!"

"A feisty one. You know, Maya was a fighter, too. She was a tall girl, very athletic and into sports. But that's okay. I can handle you, little girl. It makes it that much more satisfying when you come around."

I'd heard enough. "I'm not one of your victims." I lifted the gun and aimed at him, centering my body mass as I backed toward the door.

He put his hands up. "Honey, I have no victims. Only lovers."

"Bullshit."

"You'll be back. You little girls always come back."

"Not this time."

"I never hurt anyone," he called as I unlatched the door behind me. "My girls always came to me. You'll be back. You'll always come back."

—29—

As I bolted from the clubhouse, I started crying, sobbing like a baby. Yes, yes, I had a gun and I knew self-defense. I could have stopped Kent Jameson before he went too far. But I had to let him go long enough to know his game. As Omak had said, I had to give him enough rope to hang himself. In the process, I had glimpsed the belly of the beast, the ugly manipulations he had used on Maya, Kyra, Alice, Darcy, and Katie before he had tired of them and killed them.

The horseshoe-shaped path was empty as I ran along the paving stones and headed straight for authority, straight for the one person who could reel Kent Jameson in tighter than anyone. His wife, Martha.

She needed to know. She needed to protect herself and Lucy. Ah, Lucy! Where was she? I hoped she was all right.

Martha seemed to sense the urgency the minute she opened the door. "Oh, my goodness. What's wrong?"

"It's Kent. He tried to . . ." I stammered in a ragged voice. "He's a sexual predator and a killer. You have to get out of here. You and Lucy have to get out. Is Lucy here now?"

"No, but . . . Oh, dear Lord! You poor thing." Martha threw her arms around me. "Come inside, please."

Juana stopped dusting the huge mantel to stare as I followed Martha into the living room and let out a sob.

"I'm sorry, I'm such a mess." My entire body was trembling.

"It's understandable. Juana, start some tea for Officer Mori." Martha placed a hand on my shoulder, and the gentle touch made me want to cry even more. "Poor girl. You look like you could use a moment alone. The powder room is right down the hall there. Take all the time you need. I'm not going anywhere."

I nodded, longing for one safe moment alone to pull myself together. I slipped inside the cheerful room with frosted glass-cube windows and bright-turquoise walls. Locking the door behind me, I doubled over and let out another sob.

I told myself I wasn't crying for myself but for the other girls, but that wasn't entirely true. Seeing the balance of power shift in Kent's favor, even for a minute, had rattled me. But I couldn't give in to fear. Where was my mettle, my backbone, my strength?

Deep breaths, deep breaths. I had looked him in the eye. I had survived. And dammit, I was going to take him down. He would spend the rest of his life in jail.

But first, I had to make sure the people closest to him were safe.

I fumbled with my cell phone, trying to text Omak. The shaking in my hands made it difficult, but I managed to get a message out.

Kent J is sex predator/killer. Warning Martha now.

I splashed cold water on my eyes and buried my face in a fluffy towel. It took a few minutes to compose myself, breathing slowly and washing him from my mind. When I emerged from the powder room, there was silence. Juana must have gone upstairs, but Martha was waiting for me in the kitchen.

"I made you tea. A spicy chocolate chai that I mix with steamed milk. It's divine." She brought the small cast-iron teapot to the dining room table, and we each took a seat.

"Feeling better?" She poured tea into a delicate china cup with green ivy climbing the side.

"Much better. Thank you." I lifted the cup and took a small sip. The tea was sweet and chocolatey and comforting. I took another sip, trying to get my bearings. "Do you know where Lucy is? I'm concerned. Kent has her cell phone."

"Oh, she left that here when she took off yesterday. I wouldn't worry. She always lands on her feet."

"I am worried for her—and for you. Your husband is a killer. So far he's killed and sexually abused four young women, and there are no guarantees he won't go off the deep end."

"Did he confess to you?" she asked, her eyes shadowed with concern.

The room seemed suddenly warm, and I swiped away beads of sweat on my upper lip. "Not . . . not exactly. But he joked about his abuse of those girls. He made it clear that . . ." I took another sip of tea to gather my thoughts. "He's a dangerous man. I didn't get a full confession, and we may not have enough to arrest him today, but no one is safe around him. You can't stay here, Martha. You and Lucy need to go to a safe place until we can get him locked up."

"I won't leave my husband," she said flatly. "Don't you see? I love him, flaws and affairs and flirtations included. That's what real love is. You have to take the sad times with the good times, the bitter with the sweet."

"But your life might be in danger." A wave of weariness came over me, but that was to be expected. After the adrenaline burst of an escape like that, the letdown made energy levels sag. "Did you know there were five graves dug up there in that little clearing? There was a fresh grave, but it was empty." I took a deep breath, feeling my heart rate calm. "I wonder who that grave was for. Maybe for Lucy. Maybe for you. The fifth grave . . ." My thoughts wandered and an image of the open grave floated into my thoughts. A girl's foot, decaying and blackened, but the toenails were green. A bright, popping shade of green. Green that exploded like a sweet tart in my mouth, a field of clover in the sun, a green octopus grabbing at my throat and pulling me down . . .

"I'm so. Sah. Tired." It was becoming difficult to get the words in my head to pass through my lips. "Sorry." The weight of my head had brought it down to the table, and from this angle, I saw Martha's hands, her fingertips meticulously picking at the cuticles of her fingers, tugging at any wisp of loose skin.

"I can assure you that the fifth grave is not for me. I know, because I dug every one of those graves with these two hands and a shovel. And people think I lead a pampered life."

She left the table and went to the sink. I heard the sound of running water—the instant-hot spout. She returned to the table with a steaming cup, dipping a tea bag.

She had not imbibed the chocolate chai. That pot was drugged just for me.

I tried to lift my head, but it only created a whimpering sound in my throat.

"You've failed to see what's right before your eyes. My husband loved those girls, each and every one. Repeatedly, I suspect." She made a snorting sound. "If anything, he loved them too much. But he didn't kill them.

"Oh, no. Mr. Sweetheart couldn't bear to kill them. He just wanted to throw money at them. Put them up in a cottage here and make babies to throw more money down the drain because he couldn't keep it in his pants. His tragic flaw. He couldn't clean up his own messes. So I did."

Martha's face swam before me.

"Someone had to stop them from blabbing and destroying Kent's brilliant career. I let him have his dalliances, but in the end, they had to disappear. I felt sorry for them, but really, most of those girls weren't going anywhere good. Welfare mamas in the making. Trailer trash."

Those hands placed a turquoise-inlaid tea canister on the table and removed a brown medicine bottle. She leaned toward me and dangled it before my eyes. "My little stash of

GHB. It only takes a few drops, and it works so fast. Takes effect in less than fifteen minutes, and it's not the worst thing in the world. You probably feel drowsy and weak. Maybe nauseous. Your heart rate is slowing, and you just want to close your eyes and go to sleep." I felt something on the top of my head, a gentle pressure. She was stroking my hair. "Relax."

The woman who had poisoned me was patting my head, trying to keep me calm. Not a heinous person, just a heinous killer.

"But the grave . . ." My tongue and lips struggled to form the words, forcing myself to focus on each syllable. "No grave for me."

"You're right. I can't use that graveyard anymore now that Lucy ruined it for me. But you, my dear, will have a much more dramatic ending. Over the Cliffs you'll go. One quick toss and it will all be over. Your body would be shattered . . . decimated. Some poor nature lover walking with his dog will find your body crushed thirty feet down. The police will think you took a wrong turn, a misstep in the dark, lost in the forest while in the midst of your dogged investigating."

Forest . . . Mori . . . it was my name. My destiny. My place to die.

"Graves . . ." I was thinking that someone in the woods would see Martha trying to dump my body. Or did it matter? I would be dead. Drugged. Dead . . .

But Martha couldn't bury me in the fifth grave. Then why had she dug five graves? It was a moot point now, and yet my mind was on that track, working, and I knew the minute my mind stopped making connections, I would be good as dead. "The fifth grave," I said, my voice a raspy whisper. "Why five?"

"That fifth grave was meant for Kyra Miller, and you know, maybe I should have stuck with that plan. But when I came home and found them in my bedroom. *My room.* And the girl was so insistent that he was going to leave me for her. That little street whore. I knew it was time to make a statement with Kyra Miller, something that would let Kent know that he was walking on thin ice with these girls. That Awesome A business had to stop. So I cut the brake lines and offered up Kent's beloved Karmann Ghia as a parting gift for Blossom. And she took it. Kent had already given her a soda doctored with GHB. His way of greasing the pan. So slutty little Blossom got in that car and smashed it into oblivion.

"And that was the end of our problems. At least until you came along. You pushy girl."

I could no longer keep my eyes open, but I tried to cling to her words as they washed over me.

"It seemed like a happy circumstance when you started looking into Andy. Over the years I'd asked him to vacate the caretaker's cottage when I was getting ready to send one of Kent's girls off. I would take them there, cook them a delicious meal. Promise them bus fare or a job with a friend of mine in Portland. They drank the Kool-Aid, so to speak, and went off to their happy endings from Andy's place. And that fool boy was none the wiser. So Andy was the perfect fall guy. I dropped off those disgusting photos of Kyra at his place when I went over to sympathize with him over the police harassment. I thought that would seal his fate, and God knows Kent never missed the photos. He's got plenty of homemade smut on his computer.

"But no, you kept pushing. Always pushing . . ."

I wanted to keep pushing, I did, but the darkness tugged at me, pulling me away from her words and the kitchen and the beautiful Craftsman house on Stafford Hill.

"No one appreciates the work I do around here," Martha muttered as she leaned close to the cop and pulled the automatic weapon from her holster. "Probably loaded." She put the gun in the pocket of her fleece and zipped it closed. Martha didn't know much about guns, but she would have to wipe this one down and send it over the Cliffs with Mori when she got there. One more thing to do. Martha needed to finish this task and get back here to start dinner. She had promised Kent shrimp scampi, and she'd been just about to pull the shrimp from the deep freeze when Mori barged in.

She opened the French doors to the garden and lifted the folded blue tarp from the porch. Damned heavy tarp, but Martha sucked in her abs and lifted with her knees—always lift with the knees. She'd learned how to do body lifts in nursing school, and she wasn't afraid of the hard work. Oh, no. Hard work was underrated, a mystery to these lazy girls who thought money was going to fall from the sky.

Dried mud and dirt spilled out when she placed the tarp on the kitchen floor. "Will my work never end?" She had sent Juana off to finish her day cleaning the office, which meant Martha would have to vacuum up this mess herself.

The Japanese cop wouldn't be heavy, but maneuvering an unconscious body was always awkward. "You just wait right there," she teased. "Back in a flash." She stepped outside, closing the French door behind her, and headed to fetch the wheelbarrow from the small, shingled shed at the back of the garden.

Normally she wouldn't attempt transporting a body in daylight, but the police had closed the park because of the dig, and the cops had been warned to stay away from the Stafford property beyond the trailhead. No one would dare wander this separate trail leading to the Cliffs.

In the shed, Martha found the wheelbarrow

tipped against the left-hand wall, as always. Everything in its place. She pulled on her rubber-coated garden gloves and thought of the beating her hands had taken these last few years, digging graves and transporting bodies through the forest. Blisters and broken nails. It was embarrassing to get a manicure.

She'd thought Kyra Miller, little Ms. Blossom Sex Machine, would be the last grave to dig, but that had all been a waste of time. Kent had agreed she would be the last. But Laura Mori had pushed them to their limits. This one just pushed too hard. This one just did not know when to give up. She pushed and pushed and pushed. Relentless girl. When Martha had first met her, she'd thought the curious, polite young thing was going to be easy to manipulate. She'd underestimated her.

And, of course, brilliant, sensual Kent perceived her inquisition to be a sexual come-on, processing her questions with his cock instead of his brain. It was his tragic flaw—a costly one in the past few years—but Martha was determined to move beyond this difficult period and rein her husband in. Every marriage went through rough patches now and again.

As she maneuvered the wheelbarrow to the back porch, her eyes swept the yard and beyond. No one lurking about. Good. Those cops had been warned to stay away. It was a gift that they'd been allowed to take a shortcut through the Jameson property.

Back on the porch, Martha parked the wheel-barrow by the open French door and took a deep breath. One more time. For her darling, brilliant husband and their happy future together, she would do it one more time.

She stepped inside and paused a moment, waiting for her eyes to adjust to the darkness. The air in the kitchen seemed a bit off—foreign and sour. Had Mori expired already—faster than Martha had planned?

I was pressed against the wall by the door, staring at two Marthas as my eyes strained to focus in the painful light. Any second now she was going to notice that my chair at the table was empty, that I had scattered and smashed cups and saucers and spoons in a desperate attempt to thrust my sluggish body from the table. She was going to notice the sheen of sweat on my body and smell the desperation that lodged in my throat, keeping me from breathing properly.

Quiet breaths. Sips of air. I couldn't afford to make a sound.

I had heard her say she'd be back, and I knew my deadened reflexes would not let me escape in time. No escape. No phone call—if I could even find my phone. Attack was my only choice.

Getting out of that chair and moving across this

room had taken a few years off my life and an ocean of energy. And when I'd reached for my gun and felt only the empty holster . . .

As if caught in a volatile dream cloud, I was off-balance and nauseous. It was impossible to focus my vision, impossible to stop the spinning. I'd had to feel my way along the granite countertop to stumble to the double French doors emitting light that made my eyes ache.

Now trying to focus my blurred vision, I saw a bulge in her jacket pocket. A tumor in her belly. No . . . my gun.

That bitch had stolen my revolver. My fingers closed over the handle of the cast-iron teapot, which I'd had the sense to lug with me across the kitchen, probably sloshing tea along the way.

I figured I had one chance.

One shot.

Failure was not an option.

In that split second, she noticed the table, the mess. She started to turn, to look right and left.

Bracing against the dizzy lethargy, I summoned all my might, hoisted the cast-iron piece in the air, and brought it down hard on her head. As she turned toward me, the teapot hit her skull with a satisfying crack. Stone on bone. With a whimper, she crumpled to the ground.

Neutralized.

The last thing I remembered was yanking my gun from the pocket of her fleece.

—30—

A cold ache thrummed in my head, and my throat was scraped raw and dry as I heard words swirling around me. Smells and sounds, the tang of antiseptic, the softness of a cotton blanket under my palms. A pinch on my finger and tubes running along my arm. I was safe in a hospital.

I forced my gluey eyes open. Z, Omak, and Garcia were talking. I asked for water, and Z held a cup with a straw for me. I loved him madly in that moment.

I let their words flow for a while as my mind rose to the surface and I sucked in air. At last, I croaked out, "What happened?"

"Garcia found you and Martha unconscious in the Jamesons' kitchen," Z said. "Martha's got a welt on her head, probably a concussion. You just looked like you were taking a nap, except you had your gun pointed at her."

"She drugged me," I said through the pain. "GHB. Her husband's medication."

"We found the vile in the kitchen," Garcia said. "The paramedics were able to give you something to counteract the effects."

"I thought she gave me a lethal dose, but I guess

413

not. She probably didn't want . . . the coroner. You know. Too much drugs when they found my body at the bottom of the Cliffs."

"The Cliffs?" Z asked. "Shit. She was gonna toss you over?"

"She thought everyone would think I wandered too close to the edge and fell."

"We came as soon as Omak got your text about Kent," Z said. "Well, actually, we went to Kent first and eventually found you. Good thing you got that text off."

"He's not the killer," I said.

"That's what he kept insisting," Z said.

"It's her, Martha Jameson. She killed Lucy's friends to shut them up after Kent Jameson sexually abused them."

"They were working together?" asked Omak.

"I don't think so. I'm not sure that Kent knows what Martha's been doing, at least not on a conscious level. But the bodies in the graves, they're the girls Lucy befriended. Kent seduced them and . . . and . . ."

"We get that part," Z said. "Martha couldn't have the girls sticking around or demanding money or blabbing, so she offed them. And here I thought Kent did it all himself. I knew he was no good, but getting his old lady to run cleanup for him, that's low."

"He's the predator, she's the killer. And Lucy . . ." The thought of the girl made my heart ache along with the rest of my body. "Is Lucy okay?"

"No one has seen her. They're still searching the Jameson place, but the Stafford Woods . . ."

"I know. The forest." I closed my eyes. Dark. Deep. Mysterious. But not my undoing.

I wanted to keep my eyes closed, but that caused the bed to spin too fast, so I opened them and fixed my gaze on the most stationary thing in sight—Garcia. She hadn't said much of anything, but she was definitely in the group, in the con-versation. Like a friend. I felt incredibly grateful that she'd saved me, and a little surprised, too. I had thought she hated me.

The Tilt-a-Whirl spin sped up, and I fixed my gaze on Garcia's shield to get a grip. That sparkling sun rising over a lake. A beautiful badge for a beautiful place. A badge I had earned. I kept staring at that star, hoping for normalcy and balance. And an end to this dizziness and nausea.

"I think I'm going to throw up," I said.

"Nurse?" Z called. "Officer Mori needs an antinausea shot." He left the room, and Garcia stepped closer.

"The doctor says you're going to be okay," Garcia said. She smiled. "I'm glad for that. GHB usually wears off in three to four hours."

"Where's Brown?" I asked.

"We don't do everything together."

I chuckled but instantly regretted it. "That hurt."

"Listen, Mori," Omak said in a quiet voice, "I can't go into detail, but I want you to know that Garcia is a damned good cop. If she seems lousy, it's because she's working for me. An undercover operation. I can't really talk about it since it's ongoing."

This seemed really unimportant compared to the pain hugging my skull, but I tried to indulge him. "Is it about your sister Franny?" My compromised state allowed brutal honesty.

"Maybe."

Z popped back into the room. "The nurse is coming. Hold on, Mori."

I didn't have much choice. "Z, you need to find out what Martha Jameson was doing three years ago in the month of November. Find out if she traveled to Los Angeles. Ask Talitha for her calendar."

"What's that about?"

"Candy Jameson. I think Martha drugged her, too."

"I thought that was a suicide," Z said.

"Just . . . check it out."

A male in scrubs appeared in my line of vision. "I understand you want some medication for nausea?" He was tall and blond, a little washed out, but for now he could be my hero.

"And headache," I said.

"I can give you something, but it will make you drowsy."

"You're a prince," I said, suddenly realizing how hysterically funny that was.

I fell asleep with a smile on my face.

The next time I awoke, my father was sitting beside the bed. It was such a strange sight to see Koji Mori in stillness that I thought I was dreaming.

"You're awake! Your mother was so worried. She ran off to get you coffee from the cafeteria. She thought the smell of coffee would wake you right up."

"It couldn't hurt," I said, struggling with a dry throat. I pointed to a cup of water, which he handed to me. I sipped from the straw, realizing that it had been years since I had seen my father in any location other than home or the restaurant.

As my eyes focused, I noticed the tears in his eyes.

"Dad." I reached out and touched his hand. "I'm going to be okay."

"Your mother was worried. I worry, too. The doctor said you'll be fine, but this job. It's dangerous, Laura."

My usual instinct to argue was tempered by the truth in his words. "Law enforcement can be dangerous," I agreed. "But so can life. I don't want to be like the man running from his shadow, missing out on life because he's afraid to live."

Recognition was a glimmer in his dark eyes.

"I want to be happy with the shadow behind me," I went on. "Proud of the things I've done. Being a cop, I can leave a good shadow, Dad. I can be proud of my work."

He sighed, shaking his head. "Being a cop, then, with your good shadow . . ." He lifted his eyes to meet mine. "Will you jump for joy?"

"In my heart."

He squeezed my hand. "Then this is good."

It took a few days to really kick the effect of the drug, but when I returned to work, Z, Omak, and Claudia Deming had already been hard at work building separate cases against Martha and Kent Jameson. Martha shut down and spoke to no one, but once she was in jail, her staff members came forward with anecdotal evidence of her crimes. Proof that someone always does see something.

Kent talked to everyone and anyone, playing the victim of childhood abuse by his uncle and begging for mercy and a shot at rehabilitation. But as the forensic team identified the girls in the graves and their photos and stories filled the media, the public turned against the famous author. Claudia thought he would take a plea bargain and serve the state-mandated three hundred months in prison. That was twenty-five years.

After Martha and Kent were arrested, the compound was scoured in search of evidence. I'd been scared that Lucy had been locked up there—or worse—but there was no sign of her beyond her room and her cell phone. The continued news coverage of the case asked viewers to be on the lookout for the missing girl.

The day I was released from the hospital, Omak called to tell me that Lucy was accounted for. "I got a call from the Seattle PD saying Lucy Jameson is safe. Went into a precinct so that people would stop looking for her."

"When can we interview her?" I asked.

"That's the thing. The address she gave them doesn't check out, but it's definitely her. She just doesn't want to be found."

Despite the news, I still worried about Lucy.

"It's so hard when you start to care about these kids," Alma Hernandez told me during one of our meetings. "You just need to say a little prayer that God is watching over her. That's all you can do, honey."

I'm not big on prayer, but when I went for my run each day, I thought of Lucy and imagined her in a safe, loving place.

About two weeks after the arrests, my cell phone rang with a call from Washington State. It was Lucy.

"Where are you?" I asked.

"Just chillin' up north with my homey the

Prince." She laughed. "You know he's from Seattle. But did you know he owns an island? It's pretty cool."

"Are you okay?" I asked. "Are you happy?"

"Some of the time. But if this goes bad, I know I've got options. There are plenty of places I can go, and maybe I'll do that. New York and Paris and London. Maybe the Prince will go with me. If he's lucky."

"He's still making you call him the Prince?"

"What would you do if your name was Emory?"

"That's true. Lucy, it's good to hear your voice." She sounded so . . . normal. Maybe even happy. "Are you going to come back to testify?"

"I don't want to, but my lawyer says I'm compelled, whatever that means, and my therapist thinks it's a good idea."

"I'm glad you're getting help."

"Yeah. It's all good. Well, mostly. I wanted to thank you for looking out for me. No one ever did that before."

"Then it was about time."

"Thanks. I gotta go. I'm learning how to sail a boat. Don't laugh. I'm actually pretty good at it."

I told her to call me anytime, but I knew she wouldn't. With her eighteenth birthday, her trust fund had kicked in, and her world had shifted. She was fiscally free. In time, I hoped she would find emotional freedom, too.

As for me, I tried to be nicer to my mother. I

started making an effort to visit my father at he restaurant more often. And I started looking for an apartment to share with Natalie. Time to leave the nest and get away from my room with a view of Randy's driveway.

Z and I received commendations and medals for our work on the Kyra Miller homicide and the Lost Girls recovery. I have never seen Z so serious as when he stood behind the podium to receive the medal and handshake from Lt. Omak. The achievement meant a lot to him because under that cynical façade, I think he really cares for people. In the aftermath of the investigation, Cranston was transferred to another rookie cop, and Z and I were officially made partners. I'm honored to have him as a partner, but I could never say that to his face.

Natalie was in the audience at the commendation, not as a reporter but as Z's invited guest. I'd been right about that chemistry. Nat beamed us smiles from her seat beside my parents, who sat motionless as stones during the brief ceremony. When it ended, my father led the applause, clapping like a maniac. My mother smiled as if I'd just discovered the cure for cancer. My parents really knew how to get to me.

So I guess that, in a weird way, the Jamesons did me a few favors. Well, sort of. I won't be sending them a thank-you card anytime soon.

—Acknowledgments—

Many thanks to everyone who helped me bring Laura Mori and the town of Sunrise Lake to life.

First to my agent, Robin Rue, who is always tossing out seeds to sow. You're the best.

The editorial team at Crooked Lane really dig a good mystery, and their enthusiasm is contagious. They generously shared their treasure chest of tips, tools, and magic to make this book sparkle and sing. Their knowledge of the mystery paradigm and their faith in these characters made this novel a joy for me. Thanks to Matt Martz, Sarah Poppe, Heather Boak, and the mysterious Maddie.

I am lucky to have a proofreader who understands Oregon and catches my blunders. Thank you, Victoria Groshong!

And how lucky am I to be married to a former cop from one of the finest police departments in the country? Thank you, Sig, for your patience, your inside information, and your wealth of knowledge, procedural and otherwise.

Center Point Large Print
600 Brooks Road / PO Box 1
Thorndike, ME 04986-0001 USA

(207) 568-3717

US & Canada:
1 800 929-9108
www.centerpointlargeprint.com